OF WIND

AND

WOLVES

J. M. ELLIOTT

OF
WIND
AND
WOLVES

The Steppe Saga

BOOK ONE

———◆———

WARDEN TREE PRESS

RHINEBECK, NEW YORK

This is a work of fiction. Names, characters, places, and incidents are either the products of the author's imagination or are used fictitiously. Any resemblance to actual persons, living or dead, businesses, companies, events, or locales is entirely coincidental.

EXCERPT from *The History of Herodotus*, trans. G. C. Macaulay (1904), public domain.
EXCERPT from *The Poetic Edda*, "Völuspá," trans. Henry Adams Bellows (1923), public domain.
EXCERPT from *Carmina Gadelica: Hymns and Incantations*, Vol. 3, "Sun," trans. Alexander Carmichael (1940), public domain. Reproduced from the collections of the National Library of Scotland.
ADAPTED from *The Hymns of the Rigveda*, trans. Ralph T. H. Griffith (1889), public domain.
ADAPTED from *Rigveda Brahmanas*, trans. Arthur Berriedale Keith (1920), public domain.

COVER DESIGN: Domini Dragoone/Sage Folio Creative
IMAGES: steppe © Wassiliy/123rf, Pazyryk carpet, Wikimedia Commons, Scythian glyphs © 123Sidhe/123rf
MAP DESIGN: Daniel Hasenbos/Daniel's Maps
BOOK DESIGN: The Problematic Pen LLC

ISBN: 978-1-966394-00-6 (hardcover) (print)
ISBN: 978-1-966394-01-3 (paperback) (print)
ISBN: 978-1-966394-02-0 (eBook) (eBook)

Printed in U.S.A.

First Edition

WWW.JMELLIOTT.ORG

PUBLISHED BY WARDEN TREE PRESS
6565 Spring Brook Avenue, Suite 8
Box 233
Rhinebeck, NY 12572
WWW.WARDENTREE.COM

For my mother

Brothers shall fight   and fell each other,
And sisters' sons   shall kinship stain;
Hard is it on earth,   with mighty whoredom;
Axe-time, sword-time,   shields are sundered,
Wind-time, wolf-time,   ere the world falls;
Nor ever shall men   each other spare.

—THE POETIC EDDA, "VOLUSPO"
(THE WISE-WOMAN'S PROPHECY)

ORIGINS

ERACLES DRIVING THE CATTLE of Geryones came to this land, then desert, which the Scythians now inhabit; and Geryones, says the tale, dwelt away from the region of the Pontus, living in the island called by the Hellenes Erytheia, near Gadeira which is outside the Pillars of Heracles by the Ocean. As to the Ocean, they say indeed that it flows round the whole earth beginning from the place of the sunrising, but they do not prove this by facts.

From thence Heracles came to the land now called Scythia; and as a storm came upon him together with icy cold, he drew over him his lion's skin and went to sleep. Meanwhile the mares harnessed in his chariot disappeared by a miraculous chance, as they were feeding.

Then when Heracles woke he sought for them; and having gone over the whole land, at last he came to the region which is called Hylaia; and there he found in a cave a kind of twofold creature formed by the union of a maiden and a serpent, whose upper parts from the buttocks upwards were those of a woman, but her lower parts were those of a snake.

Having seen her and marvelled at her, he asked her then whether she had seen any mares straying anywhere; and she said that she had them herself and would not give them up until he lay with her; and Heracles lay with her on condition of receiving them.

She then tried to put off the giving back of the mares, desiring to have Heracles with her as long as possible, while he on the other hand desired to get the mares and depart; and at last she gave them back and said: "These mares when they came hither I saved for thee, and thou didst give me reward for saving them; for I have by thee three sons. Tell me then, what must I do with these when they shall be grown to manhood, whether I shall settle them here, for over this land I have power alone, or send them away to thee?"

She thus asked of him, and he, they say, replied: "When thou seest that the boys are grown to men, do this and thou shalt not fail of doing right:—whichsoever of them thou seest able to stretch this bow as I do now, and to be girded with this girdle, him cause to be the settler of this land; but whosoever of them fails in the deeds which I enjoin, send him forth out of the land: and if thou shalt do thus, thou wilt both have delight thyself and perform that which has been enjoined to thee."

Upon this he drew one of his bows (for up to that time Heracles, they say, was wont to carry two) and showed her the girdle, and then he delivered to her both the bow and the girdle, which had at the end of its clasp a golden cup; and having given them he departed.

She then, when her sons had been born and had grown to be men, gave them names first, calling one of them Agath-yrsos and the next Gelonos and the youngest Skythes; then bearing in mind the charge given to her, she did that which was enjoined. And two of her sons, Agathyrsos and Gelonos, not having proved themselves able to attain to the task set before them, departed from the land, being cast out by her who bore them; but Skythes the youngest of them performed the task and remained in the land: and from Skythes the son of

Heracles were descended, they say, the succeeding kings of the Scythians: and they say moreover that it is by reason of the cup that the Scythians still even to this day wear cups attached to their girdles: and this alone his mother contrived for Skythes.

Such is the story told by the Hellenes who dwell about the Pontus.

—HERODOTUS

CHAPTER I

GIFTS

Gifts are uninvited guests.

THE AMPHORA STOOD on the feasting board as on an altar—a foreign idol awaiting homage. I stood before it in the windowless hall, my palms sweating, fists clenched, defying the itch to smash it on the slates. For I was sure it was an ill messenger marched hundreds of miles across the steppe to our fortress doors.

Gifts are uninvited guests. They bear expectations and impose obligations. They establish bonds as strong as any shackle, which cannot be broken by any hammer but war.

"Is this his idea of a joke?" I asked Father, who came to stand beside me, his arms crossed firmly over his chest.

"I've never known Ariapaithi to be a humorous man," he said, frowning.

"Then, what in the gods' name is he thinking?"

Together, we interrogated the Skythian king's gift, mystified by the squat vessel basking in the torchlight, mocking us in our own court. Father shook his head as he grasped the double handles and drew the unopened jar nearer the torch. At first glance, the amphora's exotic images and delicate artistry were quite beautiful. But then I looked closer.

Glazed and embellished in black, a wide ground of red clay encircled its belly. Against this fiery sunset, two painted figures stood frozen in the deciding moment of battle. A giant draped in a lion's pelt raised a club in one hand. In the other, he brandished a golden cord against the rusted sky. On the ground cowered a figure in trousers. Blood flowed from her brow while she raised her shield to fend off the coming death blow. She was Amazon—what the Hellenes called women like me. He was some hero whose name I hoped never to know, though his purpose was all too plain. The vessel's art masked something malicious, something vile, as beauty so often did. Brush and kiln conspired to join eternal conquest to eternal defeat, sealing them like creatures in amber upon the hardened clay.

Why would the Skythian king send such a thing to us at a time like this? Every gift bore meaning, possessed the spirit of its maker and the place that gave it birth. It lingered as a curse until it found reciprocation—or destruction. Perhaps it was an omen.

"He's proud of his extensive trade," Father offered. "He just wants us to know how profitable this alliance will be."

"Is that *all* he wants us to know?" I asked, raising an eyebrow.

"Anaiti, it has nothing to do with you." He dropped the jar onto the board with a thud. "Don't always be so mistrustful."

"I am the way *you* made me," I said, smirking.

"Heh, you are your father's daughter," he said with grudging pride. "Your mother's, too: quick to bristle at every insult. But it will serve you ill now. She'd tell you that herself. The *hamazan* lays aside her arms—and all that goes with them—when she finally leaves her father's home."

Held captive by the painted scene, I nodded, not meeting his eye. Is that what Mother had done when she wed—surrendered her honor along with her arms?

"Like us, the Skythai are a fearless people," Father rushed to add, striding to his throne and settling himself before his spoils.

"I would wager they flaunt this," he waved his hand toward the jar, "to mock the Hellenes—men unduly frightened of girls."

"If that's true," I said, taking up the jar for closer inspection, "then I will be glad to join them." Father was always ready to feed my dwindling hopes with fresh fuel, knowing how we desperately needed this pact, and I savored every scrap.

Only this past spring, before the festival of fire, our troops amassed along the border with the Agathyrsi, who slavered for tracts of our westernmost farmland. A skirmish ensued, and a band of fifty young Bastarnai warriors were taken captive. Father tried to ransom them with grain from our stores. But the Agathyrsi king, Spargapaithi, had the warriors taken to a grove in his country. There, every man but one was sacrificed to their gods—hung from the trees, speared, and dismembered, their heads mounted on poles around the sanctuary. The lone survivor was a warchief called Dagaric, our tribe's champion, whose right hand they roasted in a brazier of burning coals before sending him home to relate all he'd seen. Father made me sit here in this hall beside him and listen, so I'd know the enemy of our people. He made me look upon the raw, crackled hand of Dagaric that would never again hold spear or sword. Whatever doubts I had about the Skythai, they paled beside what I already knew of the Agathyrsi.

"Skythai manners are strange," he said, "nothing more."

I wondered. Skythai often visited our court to conduct business with Father. No matter the season, they refused accommodation within the safety and comfort of the fort, choosing always to sleep in the fields among their horses. Since I was a girl, I'd been warned to keep clear of such men, deemed little better than predators haunting the wilds. I'd never had cause to speak with them, but I often stole away beyond the walls and watched them from the edge of their camps. More beasts than men they seemed at times, and their unbound world, their feral lives, reminded me of my youth—stirred something buried but not dead within me.

Now that the snows had mostly subsided and the rivers were passable, it was only days until we would depart for Skythia, where I was to be given to Ariapaithi. Perhaps then, the true meaning of the king's troubling gift would reveal itself. The painter's purpose, however, was unmistakable. And I could not shake the image of that dying Amazon, nor the exquisite attention the Hellene had lavished on rendering her downfall.

CHAPTER 2

ARRIVAL

The steppe was an unbreakable horse—
it could not be tamed or enclosed behind walls.

Androktones.

Mankiller. It was the first word I had ever learned in Greek. I had also learned to expect the spitting that followed, as if the word itself was poison in the mouths of men.

Holding my skirt, I glanced one last time for reassurance at Dagaric, my driver, and leapt from the deck of the chariot with a splatter. Cold slurry dripped down my legs as the sodden grass gave way and mud enveloped my feet. Blinking against the wind, I grabbed hold of a wheel-spoke to steady myself as I locked eyes on the spitter.

He was no Hellene, though he loudly proclaimed the word with a perfect Greek accent so all nearby could hear. The short ones were always the loudest. Perhaps they worried they'd be overlooked. But there was no missing him. Not in his caftan armored with gold plaques that flashed in the noon sun. Not with the gold-sheathed sword dangling by his right thigh. Not with his dark hair curled in ringlets after the fashion in the colonies. And somehow, even with the mud and manure all around us, there wasn't a speck on him.

He glared back at me through dark, heavy-lidded eyes. But no matter how practiced his accent or smartly styled his hair, his trousers betrayed him as Skythai. No self-respecting Hellene dared dress that way, not even in this climate. Deeper even than the Greek contempt for barbarian custom was their anxiety about trousers strangling their balls.

I prayed this was not the Skythai king. Surely Father was not that desperate.

Behind him, two more men emerged from the nearby felt-house. Tall, fair, long-haired creatures, and as fit as racing steeds, they were just what I envisioned when someone said *Skythes*, whether in tones of admiration or insult—usually a mix of both. Short swords and axes hung from their warbelts, and bowcases hung at their hips. Horsehair dusted their narrow trousers, and mud crusted their short boots.

"*Oiorpata?*" asked the redhead as he raised an eyebrow at the pseudo-Hellene. Skythian wasn't my native tongue, but I'd heard my fill of that word as well. At least he didn't spit.

Father had gone ahead of my arrival to conclude his negotiations with the Skythai. But as I washed and dressed in preparation for this moment, my misgivings had grown. He had insisted I stuff my tunic, claiming that a woman should always show herself to her best advantage. I defied him. After all, did a woman's chief virtues reside in her ability to delight men's eyes—or other parts? Besides, deceptions were ignoble, and I had nothing to hide. Consecrated through fierce rites and training, I'd earned standing few other women had, and I bore the hamazan's scars upon my breast to prove it. Through these long weeks of travel, it was the trust that these kindred people would embrace me because—not in spite—of what I was that brought me comfort.

Father should have warned me.

To make matters worse, the red one was also pretty for a man. Good rarely came of that. But his bright, blue gaze was calm yet carefully searching. If one of these two men must be the king, I hoped it was him.

Still, I fought a twinge of envy at the sight of his bright hair, my own dull as barley straw. His russet hair and beard were like a soft bed of fallen pine needles, neatly trimmed and combed, with his cheeks clean-shaven in the Thrakian style. This world relegated women to the whims of vanity while nature bestowed its true brilliance upon men. It made the best formidable, daring, and brave. What virtue of consequence did nature allot to women—beyond the birthing and bolstering of consequential men? For what feats did the ages ever remember *us*, if they remembered us at all?

I did not envy the third man. He stood taller than the redhead by a hand, and his eyes were set deep—or they would have been if he still had both of them. Below his tall, fur-lined cap, an oiled leather strap crossed his brow, suspending a pad over the hollow of his left eye. Around his neck, he bore the iron torc of a slave—a bodyguard or bondman, perhaps—though his gaze was direct for a servant. Rolled sleeves of the slave's buckskin caftan revealed forearms writhing with tattoos. A plaited rope of bast hung about his waist alongside a grubby suede pouch and a leather-bound mirror—a curious tool for an unkempt man. No comb or shears had touched his tawny hair or fox-colored beard in some time, though he might have been a handsome man had fate been kinder to him.

Indeed, the Skythai were not the squalid, abject vagrants some claimed them to be. Not the monsters, fanged and fed on gore I'd heard stories of my whole life. Up close, it was clear they were just men like any others. Except for their eyes . . . their eyes were like a summer sky.

"Hamazan," the slave growled to the others from the side of his mouth while his eye remained on me.

None but Father honored me with that title, not even back home. That a slave of all men should do so here left me rattled. I

7

wished to speak up and acknowledge him in return. Embarrassed, I just looked away, swallowing my giddy grin.

The redhead, paying the slave no heed, smiled warmly at me and spoke in Skythian. "Anaiti, daughter of Arianta, of the Bastarnai—"

Still in shock, I could only nod.

He blathered through some formal greeting and then gestured ceremoniously toward the hulking domed tent from which they had just come. "Our father, King Ariapaithi, awaits."

Our. Only princes, then, and thankfully, neither was my betrothed. But I'd been summoned, so terms had been reached. I closed my eyes and breathed deeply to steady myself.

The two princes reentered the looming felt-house. But the grim man with the iron collar removed his worn cap, pressed it to his breast, and drew back the hide draped over the doorway. Strands of hair the color of winter grass swept over his face in the brisk wind. A scowl lurked behind his rusty beard.

My vision blurred and a pounding in my skull drowned out all sound as I shrank before the doorsill. Though I willed it, not a muscle so much as twitched, and I could command nothing, not even my thoughts.

East of camp, a sea of grass waved and shimmered under the noon sun beyond the ominous figure at the door. Not yet the green cloak of summer, embroidered with wildflowers, the pastures were but a thin shawl thrown over the bare shoulders of the earth after the snows had melted away—a patchwork of sparse shoots still fighting frost and flood. But beyond the pitched tents and resting wagons, an unbroken expanse of ripening green rippled in the breeze as far as the horizon. An equally infinite sky of blue, cloudless and crisp, spread overhead. Not since I was a child had I seen such a paradoxical land—so vacant, yet so full. A stiff, chill wind blew in off that prairie, pulling invisible fingers through my hair, rifling through my clothes, bringing tears to my eyes. The air was keen—spicy and sweet with scents unfamiliar.

A warming sun shone down on us, and a bracing wind blew steadily from the east. Around us spread unbroken grasslands as far as my eyes could strain. The riverside was dotted with white domes of felt linked by muddy tracks. Wagons sat at rest, unhitched and chocked in neat rings like skeletal forts. Horses, cattle, and flocks of sheep scattered themselves over the bright green of emerging pasture. And as I stood transfixed, staring into the plain, that deep, incisive eye never left me—studying, unyielding, expectant.

Time flowed thick and slow around me like honey. Why wasn't I moving? How long had I kept them waiting? I had nothing to measure its passage but the pounding in my temples. The drumming tamped down all attempts at thought. If they had called, would I have heard?

Wresting my gaze from the horizon, I turned to the door, daring myself to meet the eye of its sentry. *The slave.* How he prickled the hairs on the back of my neck. Lifting my soggy skirt, I drew myself from the mud and stepped forward. Only two paces remained between us. Looking up into his rough-hewn face, I gazed into his eye the way I would with a rogue horse, showing no fear. That single eye was as deep water—blue, yet somehow also black. It narrowed beneath a jutting brow, fixing me with a cold stare—a wolf who's sighted a wounded doe. If he was trying to frighten me, it wouldn't work. I stood my ground, though my heart bucked against my ribs.

He returned my gaze in stony silence.

But I could not keep my host waiting any longer. I flinched away and focused on the dark opening before me. Inside, I could make out nothing in the blackness but wisps of curling smoke in a single shaft of light. Shivering my tall frame to its full height, I braced my quivering muscles. Then I drew a long, full breath to hone my will and, bowing my head beneath the guard's outstretched arm, stepped over the doorsill and entered.

THE SLAVE LET THE FLAP DROP behind us with a crack. Though

offering a break from the relentless wind, the sudden stillness was grave. The two princes stood just inside the door while a dozen royal guards stood post around the bounds of the immense pavilion, their eyes fixed forward. The slave loomed behind me as I threw back my cloak, the weight of his stare pressing the back of my neck. He was close. So close I could hear his breathing. Smell the pine tar, beeswax, and charcloth in his field kit.

I began to sweat. The air, though still, hung heavy and thick with incense. Four towering wooden pillars propped the bulk of the felt tent's domed roof high above. A great central hearth nestled between them, and the stale-sweet smell of a dung fire filled the vast room. The wind groaned, and the massive tent crackled in its joints like an old woman rising to greet her guests. Above the square formed by the colossal posts, a circle opened to the sky. I followed a curl of smoke as it traveled up into the heights of the dome to dissolve in a single shaft of light, which beamed down over the blazing hearth, blinding me as I peered into the otherwise dark room. Suddenly faint, I slipped my hand inside my sleeve and gouged my fingernails into the flesh of my arm.

Florid carpets met my muddy shoes at the door. I tried to scrape off the filth with as much grace as possible, but it was no use. Giving up, I began to tread gently across the sea of fine tufted wool and hides. Behind me, the princes and the slave all stooped to remove their boots. *Shit.* Too late to turn back, I kept walking.

As my eyes adjusted, vivid tapestries of layered felt and stitched hides emerged. Wolf and bear skulls, stag and elk antlers, leopard and antelope skins hung high upon the beams. Imported pottery, gold and bronze sculptures, and objects carved from wood all lined the floors and tables. Images from nature, wondrous idols, and hybrid creatures I couldn't identify. I'd never seen so much gold in all my life, let alone all in one place.

Over the broad hearth, frankincense burned in a bronze censer hung from a man-sized iron tripod. I recognized the odor with a surge of bitterness. The infamous amphora sent by the Skythian king had been filled with the exotic resin. Now, the pungent smoke obscured my view and choked my lungs. Behind its veil, upon a gilt throne, sat the man who held the tethers of all Skythia's unruly chiefs and clans in his thick, gnarled fist. King Ariapaithi. He motioned for me to approach.

What I knew of Skythia came mainly from stories. Huddled around the hearth at night, the people whispered of a wilderness with no towns nor even huts, but only endless, empty plains. They took a year to cross if one could survive the journey. And the savage people who dwelt there never set foot indoors. Instead, they lived on horseback, in tents and wagons, never settling in one place for long, never rooted to one spot. To outsiders, the Skythai lived a cursed existence. The steppe was an unbreakable horse—it would not be tamed or enclosed behind walls. Nor would its wild people. The greatest armies and empires on earth had all tried and retreated in shame, defeated. Nothing permanent took root here but inedible grasses and noxious weeds. And, perhaps fittingly, their only lasting monuments were to the dead, in the form of ancestral tombs in great man-made mountains that towered over the plain. All else was desert, uncultivated and unsettled, as the gods had made it. And the Skythai dwelt in this wilderness among gods and spirits, undaunted.

Mighty rivers that bound the countries east to west flowed down from ancient northern forests into the Skythian Sea. Beyond the easternmost of these, called the Tanais, dwelt my mother's people—the Rokhalani—warlike and wandering like the Skythai. Only, among them, noblewomen were the equals of men. As hamazan, they rode, fought, and died with equal honor. Further toward the dawn, they said, lay an impenetrable desert inhabited by gryphons that guarded hoards of gold. Above that, a land of ice and ceaseless snow that never thawed.

Only, this was no fireside tale. This was the world in which I now found myself. In this, my tribe's time of need, my father had asked if I could ever live in such a wilderness. *My own father asked this of me.* Truly, who wouldn't wish to see such a place? I'd dreamt of little else since I was a child.

Of course, that wasn't the reason I gave him when I agreed. Our Bastarnai people, primarily tillers of the soil, lived on the northwestern border of the nomads' steppe kingdom for generations, trading wheat and timber to them for salt, leather, and iron, among other things. Much of that wheat made its way to the Greek colonies along the Skythian shore for export—and made us rich. But when the Agathyrsi chose to disrupt our trade with brutal raids, the Bastarnai and Skythai found themselves with a common enemy.

I skirted the hearth to approach the throne, but the princes and the slave remained behind. Father was seated beside the king, and he nodded to me, which I took well. A herald held the king's red and gold trident standard. Opposite them sat an unsmiling, silver-haired woman. In the shadows stood what I thought was another woman, but I soon realized it was a young, beardless man in a skirt rather than trousers. He propped himself upon a thick wooden staff and stared into the flames of the hearth, blind to me as I passed before him. I took my place before the king as the woman raised her head and let her eyes pass over and beyond me.

The king, grey-bearded with watery grey eyes, winced as he heaved himself to his feet. A snarl flickered across his lined face as he fought to straighten his back, and his joints rebelled. Then, serenity overtook his ire as he stretched to his full, imposing height. But his wispy hair, thin skin, and bleary eyes belied his heroic reputation. I had conjured a young and vigorous man consonant with the many accounts of his might on and off the battlefield. Now my heart slumped. He was old. Far too old for me.

Why him? Why not one of the princes, at least? It wasn't fair. The thought of an old man laying so much as a shriveled finger. . . .

The silver woman arose with ease beside him, squaring her broad shoulders and clasping her elegant hands before her. I waited for the king to speak, but it was the young man in women's dress who roused himself from his trance and broke the silence.

"Honored guest," he said in a light voice, "welcome. In good faith, we offer you, Lady Anaiti, a place beside our fire. May the gods grant you peace and good fortune so long as you reside among us." The curious figure handed a small golden cup to the woman.

She turned toward the king, cupping the vessel in her palms, and spoke, her voice deliberate and deep. "Benevolent king, welcome this honored guest into our home and before our hearth. Show her hospitality as befits our greatness." With that, she handed the cup to him.

"Welcome, Lady Anaiti," the king said, "Daughter of King Arianta of the Bastarnai, to Skythia. You will have a place by my fire for as long as you desire it." His weathered face hardened as he let his cold grey eyes slide over me, not lewdly, but as one might appraise a piece of bruised fruit.

"You honor me," I said and bowed slightly, though it felt somehow deficient. I had no idea what I was supposed to say. "I am most grateful, Sura," I said as sincerely as possible, holding myself upright with all the discipline I could muster. I began to understand my father's constant pleas to spend more time at court and less time in the stables.

"I am Ariapaithi," he continued, "Son of Argotas, son of Idanthyrs. King of the Paralatai, High King of the Skythai. And," he opened his hand toward the woman, "Opœa of the Skolotoi, Queen of the Skythai." She took the cup and also drank.

The queen stepped forward and brought the gilded cup filled with kumis to me. I hadn't drunk fermented mare's milk since I was a child, and the memories were less than fond.

I nodded to them both. "I am honored by your welcome, and I thank you humbly for your hospitality." I raised the drink to my lips. It smelled revolting and fizzed on my tongue, like a mixture of spoiled milk and vomit. I held my breath and swallowed a little while doing my best not to gag, convinced that administering kumis was how nomads tested foreigners for weakness.

"Please sit." Ariapaithi waved his hand before him and slumped back into his throne. I looked around me, but there were no benches. I clumsily hitched up my skirt and sat cross-legged on the floor atop my crusty shoes. All my life, I had shunned a woman's skirts for trousers. One did not ride a horse in skirts. But here, surrounded by the world's broadest plains, its richest pastures, and its finest horses, it finally struck home that I would never ride again. Like a fool, I'd rashly traded it all away.

The king's cupbearer now poured out undiluted Greek wine, for which I was desperately grateful. It was more potent than anything I'd ever drunk before. I savored every sip, letting the warmth spread down my chest and through my limbs like sudden rays of sun on a cloudy day.

"You bring the rain, Anaiti," Ariapaithi said in his gruff monotone.

"If that's true, then I beg your pardon." I'd hoped to learn my future now that the pleasantries were fulfilled. Apparently, we would first talk about the weather. The river looked to have flooded its low western banks and swamped the pastures. Everything was a soup of mud and manure.

"A blessing. Maybe you bring good fortune."

"I hope so, Sura."

"You also bring surprises. My son says you ride well. And carry a bow." He cocked an eyebrow.

"How would he know that?" I blurted. I hadn't ridden since we crossed to this side of the river.

"He was your escort throughout Skythia, even if you were unaware of it. Dangerous country for foreigners, I'm afraid. Can you use it?"

"Use what, Sura?" I glanced at Father, my ears and cheeks burning. Father glared back at me. I couldn't tell if he was upset with me for embarrassing him or with the Skythai for spying on us. I set down my cup of wine.

"Your bow."

"Oh, um . . . ," I stammered, now steeping in sweat as I groped for an answer. Words—any words. *Shit. Think!* Why had Father not told them? Did he suspect they, too, would reject me? He must have had some reason, and I might say too much. But surely it was best they knew beforehand, from my own lips. There was no shame in the truth. I stiffened my back and boldly met the king's eyes. "In my youth, I was fostered by my mother's people, the Rokhalani. They taught me to ride and hunt."

"Hmm," the king trailed off, stroking his grizzled beard. "So, you're oior—hamazan?" He leaned back, lifting his gold cup to his lips with a giant, gnarled paw.

"I am, Sura," I answered with a sudden swell of defensive pride.

"That wasn't mentioned," he said, glancing at Father accusatively.

"I never imagined it would be an issue," Father parried.

"A *surprise*." Ariapaithi slowly turned back to me: "My grandfather spoke well of them." He smiled and stroked his beard. "Worthy allies. Helped him win a war . . . ages ago. How many scalps have you got?"

Scalps? I chanced a glance at Father, but he looked as surprised as I. "None, Sura."

"A hamazan with no scalps? Why not?"

I could think of many reasons why not.

"Sura, when my mother died, I left my fosterage with the Rokhalani and returned home to my father's people in Bastarnia before I could complete my training." It was partly true. When I returned home, my father forbade me to train or fight alongside his warriors. "But I am good with a bow, can hunt, and have trained my father's best war horses."

The man in women's clothing briefly met my glance, then quickly looked away. His expression was impenetrable—earnest and unsmiling. As his gaze moved through the room, his eyes seemed distant, unfocused. I'd heard of the *anarei*, the "unmanly," unrivaled seers and healers, but I'd never seen a real one in the flesh. Unlike all the other men here, his pale face was clean-shaven, framed by long earrings of gold and amber. His dark hair hung down his back, and he wore a simple white linen caftan with a long skirt beneath instead of trousers. Given the rumors of the power possessed by such men, I was a little let down—until he spoke.

"The hamazan," the anarei began in a voice high and clear, pausing for the king's attention to settle upon him before proceeding, "are not permitted to become wives until they have killed an enemy in battle. Among some tribes, it is three."

"*Ach*," Ariapaithi spat and grimaced like he'd just eaten a fly. He struck his fist against the arm of his chair. "Damn the law," he grumbled under his breath. "We ended this nonsense years ago."

"Perhaps, but the hamazan are consecrated to Artimpasa. The Suramatai gods are our gods. Their ways are our ways," he said gently. "It is a sacred duty. I mention this only because I know a wise sovereign would never wish to offend the Mistress."

"I am ever vigilant of our sacred duty. Of course, if we knew this *before. . . .*" He glanced sidelong at Father again. Then, his stony face collapsed into a withered pile of flesh.

Father, too, would be despondent. I couldn't look at him. Many long nights, he agonized over this choice to place our tribe within the auspices of Ariapaithi's great confederacy. To save face, it was called an alliance, but in practice, we'd become subjects. His lengthy negotiation was now for naught, and the commitment of a thousand archers of Ariapaithi's famed cavalry for our western border would be gone with it.

I glanced from face to gloomy face. Was that it? Was there no solution? No compromise? On any other day, I would thank the gods for releasing me from this miserable fate. But I was now the reason my people would be raided and ravaged and finally overrun by our enemies. The rank I was so proud of had once again proved a curse.

The queen lifted her eyes to me and leaned over to whisper something in her husband's ear. His brows arched, and his tired eyes drifted to the circular opening in the roof as she spoke. A gust of wind drummed against the felt walls. Ariapaithi bobbed his grey head as he listened. Then his eyes fell upon me.

"King Arianta," he began with renewed vigor. "We still desire this union."

Father leaned forward in his chair. "We also desire this union."

"The gods may yet smile on the covenant between us."

"If my friend sees a way to proceed, I'd be pleased to hear it," Father replied guardedly. Ariapaithi needed us, too. Perhaps it wasn't over yet.

"Like our warriors," the king cleared his throat, "your daughter cannot be wed until she slays an enemy in battle." He stroked his grey beard. "There's a simple solution."

"Indeed?"

"Let her fight."

"Fight?" He raised his hand in protest, but Ariapaithi was quicker.

"She'll ride with our men as they patrol the marches and return when she has a scalp. When she makes her kill, I'll make her my wife."

I rose slowly to my feet. *Could this be happening?*

"Every Skythai must earn his honor before he may take a wife, inherit property, share in spoils, or one day take a seat in the Great Assembly. Let her also bring me the head of an enemy. Only the worthy make their place among us."

"And the unworthy?" Father asked.

"Some do fail." Ariapaithi gave a weak shrug.

"You mean they *never* wed?" I asked, working to conceal my mounting excitement.

"Some die. Some grow old trying."

Some grow old trying.

"Anaiti, do you wish to keep the rites of our men—of your mother's people?" Ariapaithi asked.

"I do," I said. "Though I don't know if I have the skill."

"You're good with the bow, you say. You ride. Can you use an akinaka and sagaris?"

I'd never had cause to use a sword or battle-axe. Mostly, I hunted in the woods and fields around the fort. "I can handle a spear, sling, and lariat. The rest I can learn."

"Hmm. . . ." Again, he stroked his grey whiskers. "Arianta, my friend, what say you?"

"I don't like it." Father shook his head. "She's already a young woman, far past the age to learn such things now. It's too dangerous." He leaned back in his chair, eyes shifting between Ariapaithi and me.

"Life is dangerous. Soon, even your homeland will not be safe."

Was it a taunt or a threat? Either way, Ariapaithi knew where to stick his dagger and twist it. Father looked at me like a man about to slaughter a calf. I nodded. He looked away and sank into his chair ever so slightly. He'd decided.

"Who will look after her? Train her? Safeguard her . . . chastity? A woman, among so many men? If I am to agree, I need assurances."

"Come, my sons." Ariapaithi raised his hand and waved over the men standing behind the hearth. They came forward and stood beside the fire. "My dear friend, it's in both our interests to see she's well guarded. Before this holy fire that burns perpetually upon my hearth, I swear by Tabiti and Thagimazda that I—with my faithful sons as my agents—will be her protector wherever she travels throughout my vast realm." He lifted the cup still in his hand and drank.

"My eldest son, Skyles." He gestured toward the one with ring-lets in his dark hair and oil in his black beard. *The spitter.* "Warden of the South March, he oversees trade with the colonies."

A glorified merchant. No wonder he was such an arrogant prick. Father had always warned about allowing merchants influence in the court.

Skyles acknowledged my father with a curt nod but did not look my way. "Couldn't she just kill a slave," he asked, "and be done with it?"

"Good gods!" the anarei exclaimed, thumping the end of his heavy staff on the floor. "It must be in honorable combat, by hallowed law. Flouting this would surely bring affliction upon us all."

"*Too late,*" Skyles mumbled.

The king sighed deeply, ignoring their bickering, and turned again to me. "My second son, Oktamazda." He gestured toward the handsome redhead. "Warden of the West March. Thanks to him and his seasoned army, your tribe's grain, furs, and timbers make it to the southern markets."

Thanks to him, they were also heavily taxed. But then, with the addition of his men to our border, we might just repel the next Agathyrsi assault.

Oktamazda lifted his cup to me. "My sword is yours," he said, smiling, and I could not be sure in the flickering light whether he winked as he sipped his wine. I decided it was probably a trick of the shadows. I stood up a little straighter and nodded solemnly back. It could be far worse. If I were to ride out with his forces, maybe I would be close to home, helping defend my own tribe. I liked the thought of that, at least.

"My third and youngest son, Aric, is Warden of the East March and *Kara-Daranaka* of the kingdom's most sacred warband."

There was a third son?

All eyes turned to the last man, the ragged one with the iron ring—the slave.

What a fool I'd been. How blind. But how could this creature be the son of a king?

Ariapaithi stroked his beard thoughtfully, his eyes shifting between grinning Oktamazda and glowering Aric. I held my breath.

"Her experience is . . . limited," the king mused. "Novices should train among the warband. Aric, you've seen her ride?"

The third son stepped forward and stood over me. His thick, marked arms folded across his chest, his drinking horn gripped in his large hand. Pinched between his brows, a chasm formed as he stared down at me with his solitary eye. I stared back at him un-wavering, though my legs swayed beneath me like boughs in a gale.

He said nothing but only clenched and unclenched his jaw, studying me like an eagle sighting its prey—its ability to flee or fight, its frailties and strengths. That single glance from him seemed to measure me fully. There was something chilling in that—and fascinating. What did his hunter's eye see? The tent creaked around us in the waiting silence.

"She smiles too much," he said, a rumble of thunder from a dark cloud.

Did I? My face fell slack. I would never smile again. And for an agonizing moment I was suspended somewhere above the earth— the rabbit in the raptor's talons. I held my breath. His keen eye, now shining, remained locked on mine.

"But if she will, she may ride with us and fight like the men do." He held his hand over the fire. "And, by Gœtosura, with my own life, I will shield her from death and dishonor." Raising his drinking horn, he drained the rest of his wine in a single swig, wiping his red-bearded mouth with the back of his hand.

CHAPTER 3

INITIATION

*You don't yet know what you are. What you truly
love or hate. What you'll kill or die for. Not until
you've been out there.*

ARIAPAITHI'S ANAREI LED ME to a tent near the western
edge of the encampment, though for what purpose I couldn't
imagine. One had to be wary of holy men, especially those close to
power. They often proved sanctimonious. And cunning.

Men scurried past, carrying amphorae of wine, skins of kumis,
sacks of grain, and freshly slaughtered carcasses. Such a fuss to
make for my arrival, I mused, before I remembered this was the
Eve of Eramandin. There would be a celebration tonight having
nothing to do with me. The start of summer and the first day of
Pasture Month were occasions for drinking and feasting, as well as
contracts and unions. Just south of their nomad capital at Gerrhi,
the sprawling camp of courtiers—warriors and herdsmen alike—
prepared to begin their northward journey in pursuit of summer
pasture. But though the camp hummed with activity as countless
Skythai strode about the grounds and rode by on their horses, I
did not see a single woman among them.

The anarei labored to pull himself across the mucky camp

with a thick staff, his right foot dragging ever so slightly. Under his left elbow, he'd tucked a cloth-wrapped bundle. As he walked, he splashed through the ruts left by wagon wheels the way a child stomps through puddles after a rain shower, careless of his skirt hem and oblivious to the muck. As I followed, I tried to guess what had left him lame. With no other signs of disease, I decided he was likely kicked or trampled. Nevertheless, he seemed to have prospered. Unassuming though he looked, he must have been gifted to earn himself so high a station at a young age—another reason to be wary.

Two paces behind, I kept my eyes forward as I dodged mud puddles and piles of manure, conscious of the stares. What I wouldn't give to be ignored for just a day. I was no stranger to attention, but it was not the kind of attention most women receive. I was not beautiful. Tall like a man and more interested in chasing game than mates, I was neither feminine nor flirtatious. I much preferred the feel of reins or a bowstring against my fingers than gold rings, and my hair was usually done in a simple plait on the days I wasn't being betrothed to a king. I never managed to care much about such things. When a girl is too pretty, she's disinclined to cultivate any other qualities—if she has any.

While I may not have been beautiful, I possessed a unique grace—one peculiar to life on horseback. Each true horseman recognizes another by it. The inexorable forces of nature cannot move us, for we've ridden the winds. The horseman's world is a secret society; its spells, rites, and rules are known only among its initiates. Most women knew none of its arts, and that was their misfortune.

A smaller felt-house stood beside the eastern banks of a shallow stream near the outskirts of camp. Beyond it, the sun descended over a deserted plain, empty but for the silhouettes of birds fleeing their shelters in the swaying grasses. Outside, we shook the mud from our skirts and scraped our shoes before entering. He set his staff inside the door, and I saw then it was no ordinary walking stick but the weaving beam of a loom. An impractical choice, cumbersome under the best of circumstances, not to mention in the slender fingers of an effeminate cripple. I removed my boots and placed them beside his soggy shoes of woven bast. His bare feet somehow emerged clean and dry.

We stood face to face. More slender than I, the anarei stood nearly my height. He was young. Or maybe it was just his clean-shaven face that made him appear deceptively boyish. Yet there was no mistaking the man beneath the dress, and he made little attempt to hide it. The anarei were men who shunned manly duties, never riding or hunting or fighting. Some claimed Artimpasa plagued Skythian men for some ancient offense, which deprived a chosen few of their manhood and burdened them with foresight. Others whispered that the anarei were eunuchs, though such tales were hearsay. The anarei were reclusive, and few knew anything about them at all. Standing before one now thrilled me more than it should. No perfumes masked the scent of masculine sweat, though he did smell faintly of cannabis and honey. In the dim light of the tent, his pale skin, free of lead paints and kohl, gleamed so brightly I could think of no earthly substance like it. Perhaps fresh beeswax, like that from a new, clean honeycomb, buttery and sweet. His long hair was as black as the rich, dark soil beneath the pastures across this country. And his eyes—those great, uncanny eyes—were the pure, bright blue of flax blossoms, at once beautiful and unsettling.

"My lady, you may call me Erman," he said, speaking the language of my mother's Suramatai people, his voice resonating like the middle string of a fiddle. He wiped his nose on his sleeve.

"Thank you," I replied in kind. I hadn't spoken my mother's language aloud since leaving my fosterage. It felt strange to speak it now. "Please, call me Anaiti."

He turned his back to me as he smothered the dung fire burning in the hearth and raked the ashes over their clay base until they were smooth. Upon an altar against the western wall, he unbound the cloth bundle he'd carried under his arm. He held a dozen dried willow wands about the length of a man's forearm in both hands.

Standing before the hearth, arms outstretched, he whispered an incantation to himself and dropped the twigs on end into the ashes. They dispersed with a scuffing clatter. A soft puff of ash whiffed over the hearth, enveloping them where they lay. He stood in silence, reading some meaning in their pattern of fall, or perhaps the marks they wrote in the cinders, or whatever signs seers place their trust in.

He then stooped and arranged each one, examining it as if it told a story. Satisfied, he collected them one by one, brushed the ash from each with his fingertips, and smoothed the cinders again. Then he rekindled the hearth with a wooden fire drill instead of flint, whispering an unintelligible prayer.

The anarei were said to perform necromancy and to possess the two sights—all gifts gained through their strange form of devotion. I knew I should keep my distance from such a creature. But he was nothing like I imagined a sorcerer to be.

"You understand what you are here to do and why?"

"I believe so."

"Is there anything that might prevent you from fulfilling your duties?" He blinked hard, tilting his head inquisitively.

I hesitated. "I don't believe so." There was nothing I dared speak aloud.

"Yet you're concealing . . . *something*."

"I—I am?" Had he guessed? Or had he *seen*? I waited for him to speak, but he simply regarded me serenely. The silence stretched between us. *He knew.* By casting some sticks into an empty hearth, he'd seen it. He truly had the sight or spirits had whispered in his ear. My throat tightened so that it became hard to breathe.

One day, a girl in the village below our fort fell into a trance, speaking of an odor and strange visions before collapsing and writhing as if on fire. People thought it miraculous, regarding her with both suspicion and awe. Some brought her gifts and sick beasts to heal; others begged for portents from spirits. Then, as harvest approached, a sudden thunderstorm descended on the country. Hailstones ruined half the wheat. The villagers gathered, seized the girl, and drowned her in the lake.

I don't believe I have ever writhed upon the ground, and I knew better than to tell anyone about the other signs that plagued me. When I smelled the unearthly odor or felt the terrible presence of darkness approach, when time pulled the earth from beneath my feet, I fled far from the eyes of others. I hid for my life.

But where would I hide now?

I cleared my throat. "This day has been a bit of a shock, that's all," I said.

"You don't seem happy about being a wife—about taking the hand of a king."

That hardly required a seer to uncover. "It's an honor to unite our tribes," I offered. "And I've always dreamt of returning to the steppe one day. This is the most wondrous country in the world."

"Ariapaithi repels you." He smiled wryly.

Was that obvious, too? I suppose I hadn't thought about what wifehood would really mean and all it would entail until I saw the king. He looked at me, not even lustfully or cruelly, but like one more obligation or asset to be valued and managed among a hoard of others. A cow prized so long as the calves come each spring and the milk flows.

I chose my words carefully. "The king is legendary even in my country. The stories do him justice. And he does great honor for my family and me." That wasn't even a lie. Despite my noble birth and generous dowry, I was not in high demand as a wife. And, with twenty winters, I was long past my first flower. It was true that women of greater use were kept at home longer, while less valuable girls were sold off as quickly as possible. My family artfully maintained the illusion that they kept me because of my great worth and lack of *worthy* suitors. An offer like this would come only once. They leapt at it, assembling horses, heirlooms, gold, and jewels for my dowry. Rumors flew that Father even looted tombs to make a respectable settlement. But I never put much stock in such talk.

"I understand," he said solemnly, though the corner of his mouth curled upward as he appraised me. "He can seem coarse. You'll not get pretentious language and pompous displays from the Skythai; it is not our way. We speak as we live . . . plainly. But something deeper disturbs you."

We stood in silence for a long while. I wound and unwound a loose thread from my sleeve around my finger. Was it a trap? It could do no good to speak up, and it might do harm.

"I have all day," he said. "But I doubt Aric or Ariapaithi have that kind of time."

"I don't know what you want to hear."

"As you wish." He clasped his hands and remained eerily still.

"There is something I don't understand."

"Ask."

"The prince, Aric, watched our approach. He saw me riding. Knew I was hamazan. Why did the king bother with the negotiation if it was bound to fail?"

"Aric mentioned you could ride; he never told the king you were hamazan."

"Why not?"

"I guess you'll have to ask him. Maybe he didn't notice. I understand you didn't notice him either."

Unlikely. Aric did not seem like a man who missed things.

"There is more?" he pressed.

"Well, when my father told me I was coming to Skythia with a dowry of our finest horses, I suppose I envisioned a different life—a different place."

"What did you imagine?"

"It's just," I nearly whispered, as if it were a secret, *"there are no others like me here."*

"And you thought there would be?" He frowned.

"I hoped," I conceded, feeling foolish. "The Paralatai and Rokhalani are like cousins. Our manner of living is the same." I swallowed past the lump in my throat. My voice strained as I continued to speak. "I guess I just assumed that a woman like me would have a place here. Would be welcome. But not a single woman here shows her face in the sun. They all seem content to hide themselves away in their wagons. Do none of them ride, or hunt, or help with the herding? I can't understand it." It wasn't until after I'd spoken that I knew I'd said too much.

"I see. I regret it's not as you imagined. Truly, I do. It was not always so. Times change, and not always for the better."

"Where have they all gone?"

He lowered his eyes. The silence was worse than any story he might have told. Against all restraint, I began to sob.

"Fear not, Anaiti. You shall find your place."

I forced a smile and wiped my moist eyes. "That's all I wish."

"Why then do you weep?"

"Because I can ride and hunt, it's true. But raids, heads . . . scalps? I don't know if I'm able."

"Why not?"

"I am no killer."

"You don't yet know what you are. What you truly love or hate. What you'll kill or die for. Not until you've been out there." He raised his arm and pointed through the tent wall toward the dawn. "Until then, it's all words."

I sniffled and nodded, staring at the empty spot on the wall.

His serene, gentle manner darkened, and his tone became stern. "Your heart is the fire; it must become the cauldron."

I nodded dubiously, pretending to understand. This was why

people disliked poets and priests. They could never just say what they meant.

Reaching forward, he seized me by the arms, his thin fingers biting into my flesh. Bright, calm eyes trapped me there as if sunk in a well, looking up at a small window of sky. *They are not like us,* he said. He released me and turned to go, shaking out his skirts as he went. Limping to the door, he slipped on his shoes and grabbed his staff. Then, as the door swung open, he disappeared into a flash of light, leaving me in near darkness as it swooped closed.

Us?

I ASSUMED IT BEST not to wander the strange camp alone, so I waited in the secluded tent where the anarei left me. But when no one came, my mind began to churn. Had I said too much? Was the seer conveying my words to the king? What did he mean by the things he spoke? Surely, there was some knot I was meant to untie. I wandered the tent as if searching its contents might provide me answers.

Above the altar, a tapestry caught my eye. A richly dyed mosaic of layered felt depicted a horseman at the end of some quest—or maybe the start of one. A hero or king, he rode before his goddess, seated on her throne, and offered forth a drinking horn in hopes of receiving her blessing. In one hand, she held a round vessel, in the other, the Great Tree. Behind her, a sacrificial horse skull hung from a sun-pillar. A herald raven sat on her shoulder, and a guardian wolf at her side. All around them, the world morphed into a swirling chaos of cavorting animals and warring monsters, songful birds and hungry vultures, blooming flowers and choking vines.

Brightly dyed leather rugs and woolen carpets were arrayed over the floors. The walls were hung with more felt tapestries. Smooth leather panels, carefully stretched over wooden frames, were delicately painted with strange creatures locked in savage battles. They were the most beautiful things I had ever laid eyes on.

I brushed my fingers across the tapestry, every detail exquisitely made. Reds, blues, greens, yellows. Vibrant hues so rare, the dye alone must have cost a small fortune. And the delicate fringe of fine golden threads along the edge. Too fine to be horsehair, it had to be silk. Marveling at a master craftsman who could bind so many strands of silk, I ran my fingers through it. Then I saw the silk was fixed to thin strips of glistening white hide. I snatched my hand away, and a chill skittered up my neck. Only one creature grew a pelt so fine and long. It was a scalp. My fingers were twined in strands of someone's long, honey-blond hair.

Were there more? I scanned the room and spotted no other scalps. Instead, I found greater horrors. The decorated animal hides. Pigment penetrated both sides of the leather, and I should have realized that it was not paint but ink embedded deep in the flesh. These were not paintings nor from animals. The flayed skins of men had been cured and stretched over frames to display their elaborate tattoos.

I tugged at my collar as my skin began to prickle with goose-flesh. My mouth went dry, and I needed air. These people were bloody savages. Like all the stories said, the kind who drank from the skulls of enemies. Alliance or no, I couldn't live among brutes like this, who displayed the hides of men like trophies and wore them like garments. Father would understand, and he would just have to make other terms. It wasn't yet too late.

I have to get the fuck out of here.

THE DOOR FLAP SUDDENLY WHOOSHED OPEN, and I startled violently. Aric ducked through in a sweep of tawny hair, then stood, filling the entrance with his terrible bulk.

No longer sporting grimy clothes and crusty boots, he had washed, combed his hair and beard, and put on fresh garments of crimson summer wool, embellished with embossed golden plaques down the sleeves and outer seams of the trousers. He still wore his sword and warbelt, the broad central plate of bronze polished bright.

"The sun sets," he said gruffly.

"Shouldn't I—we—wait for the kings to finish their negotiations? Perhaps this can wait until morning," I said, hoping to tease out some more time before the ceremony—planning my escape.

"We leave for the East March at dawn," he said. "The day closes. You must be sanctified under the All-Seeing Eye. Less than an hour remains."

"What must I do?"

"One does not venture into the wilds without first seeking the blessing of the one whose domain it is," Aric said. "There are rites. To join the fellowship of warriors—the kara—you must swear an oath to me, its daranaka, and to Gœtosura to whom we are devoted."

"What oath must I swear?"

"To be faithful to our order and to uphold our code of honor."

"That's all?"

"It is everything. If you cannot swear to uphold these decrees, speak now. Deceivers, cheaters, false witnesses, and oathbreakers shall all wear the noose."

"If I cannot swear?"

"You cannot ride."

The massive stone lifted from off my chest, and I could breathe again. The answer had shown itself. If I could not take the oath, there would be no scalps, no union. Father would be furious, of course, but even he would not wish me to pledge falsely—not at the risk of my life. And there was no way I could swear to any laws or oaths by which these cruel savages lived.

"Time is against us," Aric said. "Are you ready?"

I swallowed and bowed my head in something like assent.

"Come, then. The day is fast closing its eye upon us."

BESIDE THE TENT, a broad, shallow stream flowed toward the

Borysthenes River, still in flood. The western sky reddened as the sun prepared to set. Someone had lighted a fire within a ring of stones. Across the stream, on the opposite shore, another small bonfire burned. A dozen or so rugged, armed men, young and old, had gathered in a half-circle around it. Each warrior wore a wolfskin draped over his shoulders.

The eyes of the men were upon me—a living fortress of flesh, iron, and scowls. Should I smile and greet them, or would that be unseemly? Should I present an impassive face, or would that be haughty? What did it matter, anyway? I wasn't staying. I'd never see them again. So, I turned away and held my hands over the hearth to stare into the fire, letting the heat and flames entrance me away from this moment into a thousand others before it when I stood staring absently into a blaze like this—when I was not here.

Beneath the vaulted canopy fading sky and emerging stars, the assembled warriors stood in solemn silence, their breath misting in the cool evening air. The fire crackled low, casting flickering shadows across their faces as the leader stepped forward. Aric broke my trance as he began to speak.

"If you would stand among us," he began, "you must pledge yourself to the Twelve Virtues, the sacred pledge of our brotherhood. Speak these words with your whole heart, or not at all."

He then began to recite, his voice measured and reverent:

I swear by the stars above and the earth below,
    By the flame that endures and the winds that roam.
Courage shall be my foundation,
    Mastery of spirit, triumph over fear.
Resilience shall be my armor,
    Endurance through hardship, fortitude of mind.
Excellence shall be my pursuit,
    Skill at arms, grace in horsemanship, wisdom in verse.
Honor shall guide my deeds,

Integrity unbroken, truth unwavering.
Loyalty shall bind my heart,
　　To king, to kin, to tribe, and comrades.
Order shall be my charge,
　　The keeping of Arta, the warding of chaos.
Duty shall be my purpose,
　　To uphold the balance, to sustain the world.
Justice shall be my sword,
　　Opposing the destructive, guarding the productive.
Discipline shall guide my spirit,
　　Restraint in action, diligence in toil.
Generosity shall open my hand,
　　For none stand alone in the circle of life.
Humility shall temper my pride,
　　For none achieve without the aid of others.
Gratitude shall dwell in my heart,
　　For gifts received, both earned and unbidden.
This I swear before the eternal flame,
　　By Wind and Sword, I am bound.
To these virtues, my life is given.
　　'Til the earth reclaims me, I shall not falter.

Aric's voice faded, leaving a profound silence that seemed to echo beyond the gathered company. The men lowered their blades but did not sheath their swords. Their expressions were serene, and their eyes remained fixed on the fire burning in their midst. A terrible dread surged up in me. I was expecting something bloodthirsty and depraved from a people who used the skins of their enemies to adorn their walls, some cruel decree to which I could easily object. There had to be something to fault, to dispute. Something that might disqualify me—or them—so I could walk away and forget I ever saw this place.

I pored over Aric's words for something, anything, that would release me from the oath I was about to take; I couldn't denounce a word of it. I was falling into a trap.

Aric towered before me. "Anaiti, I speak to you now as a daughter of a king and a future queen. You acknowledge that your station provides no immunity from loss of honor or punishment?"

I nodded.

"Neither your name nor kin will win you pardon should you overstep the bounds of the law. Our nobility must be an example for all. We must be vigilant, striving to excel in our wisdom, courage, and discipline. For if we prove undeserving of the rank bestowed upon us, everything you see around you falls." He stared expectantly at me, the amber light of the sinking sun gilding the contours of his damaged face.

"I understand."

"Will you swear to the gods to uphold this sacred code?"

I drew a deep breath and held it long before exhaling. It didn't stop the trembling.

"I will."

"Repeat these words after me:

I will defend our altars and tend our fires.
I will further Arta daily in my words and deeds.
I will honor all covenants, keep all oaths, and speak only the truth.
I will honor the rites of our fathers
    and the ground in which they rest.
I will respect the wise rulers, submit to the established laws,
    and oppose any who would disobey or destroy them.
I will not dishonor my sacred arms with use upon whims.
I will not abandon my comrades at whose side I stand.
I will not leave this land diminished
    but greater and better than when I came.
Witness this my sworn oath,
O Thagimazda, O Papahio, O Gœtosura, O Eraman,

O Artimpasa, O Tabiti,
and the sacred bounds of this land.

Tears welled in my eyes as I repeated every word of the oath back to him. My voice strained as my throat constricted. A roar swelled in my chest, and my eyes spilled over. They'd think me womanish for weeping, but I'd longed my whole life to say such things aloud. They were only words, but even as intentions, they were nobler than any purpose I had ever set myself to. "With all my form and will, I swear."

"Then let it be so," said Aric. He unwound the coil of hair at the back of my head, grabbed my long braid in his fist, and, with his dagger, sliced it off at the nape of my neck. I gasped. Stunned, I didn't move or speak—a lifetime's worth of my hair was gone in the swipe of a blade. He dug a trench in the earth with his dagger, laid the braid in it, and carefully covered it, mumbling some words silently to himself. The ragged remains of my one beauty lay in tatters about my face.

Aric then instructed me to strip off my skirt and caftan. My hesitation only provoked more glowering, so I shuffled my clothes off as modestly as possible, covering myself with my arms as I stood in my undergarments before the men. He waded into the center of the stream. Confused and wary, I followed him into the icy water, no deeper than my ankles.

"Now, place this over your head."

It was a hood of black wool. Feeling queasy, I looked at the men prowling the shore, but I breathed in deep and slipped it on. It stank of sheep and made my nose itch, causing me to sneeze inside it. The water splashed and swirled around me as he moved, then looped something over my head and around my neck. Another sneeze was coming on when, suddenly, a rope tightened about my throat. It yanked me off my feet, and my toes strained for the streambed as I tried to pry it away with my fingers, clawing, kicking with my heels. Then a gentle voice whispered in my ear, "Don't fight," and my mind's eye closed. All went black.

I LOOKED UP AT A DIM, STARLESS SKY. Nearly naked, I lay in the icy stream, soaked through, with my back to the pebbly streambed as the dark waters slipped over and around me. The rope still hung loosely about my neck. A rush of anger coursed through me. I shot upright, and my head began instantly to throb.

How long had I been gone? It was hard to say. I stood slowly, testing my balance in the rushing water. The evening breeze was sharp against my wet skin without my clothes, and I began to shiver. My skirt and caftan lay only a few paces away by the hearth on the western bank. On the eastern bank, the grim warriors stood before their bonfire with swords drawn—and Aric stood out among them like a bull among the herd.

It was warm before the bonfire despite their cold looks. I pulled the noose over my head and thrust it into Aric's hands as he presented my new trousers, tunic, and caftan. The tunic was of delicately woven hemp cloth resembling linen—the trousers and caftan of the finest woolen twill. There was nowhere to conceal myself as I dressed, but the men all seemed to cast their gazes respectfully away. I could belt the caftan tightly as needed, but the trousers, made for a man, were too loose in the waist and a bit snug in the hips.

"The best we could do on such short notice," Aric offered almost contritely as I tied them as best I could around my waist.

The sun sank low, and the evening air crept in with a bite against my damp skin. I rubbed my arms for warmth and eyed the men warily.

"Almost done," Aric assured me under his breath, holding forth a large silver cup filled with wine.

I reached out to take the drink, but he sliced at my wrist with his dagger, catching the drops of blood as they splashed into the silver cup. Holding it to his breast, he stepped back and set the cup upon a stone. I pressed the wound with my fingers to halt the bleeding, careful not to get blood on my new clothes.

"Henceforth, you shall wear, not torcs of princely gold, but this iron ring," Aric said, lifting something from the same stone, "as a symbol of your bondage to the Lord of Hosts, Father of Inspiration, Light of Truth, Pourer of *Haoma*, Keeper of Oaths." He slipped an iron torc, like the one that made me mistake him for a slave, around my neck. "With this girdle, you shall be bound to the fellowship of the kara." He placed a stout rope of golden linden bast in my hands—the same one I had put in his hands only a moment ago. I looped its hangman's knot around my waist.

Next, he placed a single arrow in my hands. "Break this."

The men scrutinized me, their faces red with the bonfire flames. I handily snapped the shaft in two.

He handed me a bundle of a dozen arrows. "Now break these."

I tried them over my knee. Hard as I wrestled the shafts, the bundle wouldn't budge.

"A single arrow breaks easily, but a bundle of arrows is unbreakable. You are bound to a fellowship now, and nothing can break that."

He lifted an akinaka on his palms. It burned in the light of the fire, and an orange glow flashed over its mirror face. But it was the hilt that made my heart skip. A grip of antler from a massive hart set between a guard and pommel of gold. A doubly royal blade, waxed from years in storage but still sharp. I clipped its worn leather scabbard, lined in sheepskin, to the right side of my belt and tied it loosely around my thigh as the others wore theirs. Then Aric placed the blade into my bloody hands, the heft of it potent, dangerous. The last rays of the sun turned the burnished blade red.

"This is the first sword I was honored to carry. I do not have the time to relate all of its deeds, but know that it is a noble sword and a slayer of unjust men. Never unsheathe it without bathing its blade in human blood. May it bring you the strength and luck it brought me."

His sword. Its demands filled me once again with dread. "You honor me. I pray I may do it justice." It was a beautiful weapon. Well-forged and made, though smaller even than the short sword that now hung by Aric's side. I wondered how much blood it had seen before retiring. How much he expected it should see again.

He carried the cup of blood and wine into the circle. The men dipped their blades into the mixture one by one, wiped them lovingly with a cloth, and sheathed them. At last, he brought the cup to me and instructed me to anoint my new sword. I did as told and, wiping the blade, sheathed my akinaka. Aric cast the cloth into the fire. Then, he blew three times into the cup and whispered verses in a speech I did not recognize. Finally, he passed the cup to me, and with bloody hands trembling, I gripped it and lifted the mixture to my lips. He nodded, and I drained it to the last drop.

Aric stepped forward to place a wolfskin across my shoulders. As the sun slipped below the horizon, he said, "Now you belong to Gœtosura."

CHAPTER 4

FEAST

The gods themselves have given her thorns.

Dark fell fast once the sun had set, and immense bonfires lit the broad plain like stars risen in the field of night. The smell of woodsmoke and roasting meat filled the raw night air. We left the fires beside the stream to burn themselves out and crossed a narrow plank bridge behind the tent, following the glow and smoke trails of torches along a squishy path. Here, we encountered Erman, staff in hand, bound in the opposite direction.

Festivities had begun in our absence. Far off, in the fields to the north, flutes and voices joined in strains of haunting music like a chorus of dying birds.

Erman nodded approvingly and flashed an awkward grin when he spotted me in my new attire. "I must take my leave of you for now," Erman said. "May the Mistress bless and keep you. Remember my words."

He quickly departed in the direction of the unearthly music. Part of me ached to follow him and that sound, to discover its source just over the horizon. But I had my own company to keep now. My feet to the path, I followed the warriors southward.

REED MATS LAY SCATTERED OVER THE GROUND in a rough circle, surrounded by embellished felt cushions. In the center were strewn the first flowers of the field, gathered fresh that afternoon by their looks, and plates and drinking cups were set around the edge for a feast. Nearby, torches staked in the earth cast their shuddering light over the festivities. Out beyond, in the fields, the cattle-herders spread their own tablecloths upon the ground. From turning spits and great cauldrons came the scent of roasting beef, venison, wild boar, boiling mutton, and sides of horse meat. I had to avert my eyes. Holy sacrifice or otherwise, I had never reconciled myself to the eating of horseflesh. They ranked alongside humanity in nobility and were my closest companions, so it felt like the worst kind of betrayal to seek their trust only to one day prey upon them.

Guests made ready to take their places. A sumptuous cushion of crimson silk embroidered with gold sat beside the circle. To its right stood the queen holding a round pitcher of gold and to its left stood Father. How his eyes widened when he saw me. Soon, every eye in the room turned my way. And what a sight I must have been, with my cropped hair, Skythian trousers, the iron collar, and a sword at my side. Hopefully, Father would not inquire into the fate of my new dress, as it had been costly.

The royal princes stood beside Father while the head of the king's royal guard and various dignitaries filed in beside the queen. The warriors from my rite took their places beside the princes. All arranged themselves in order of rank. Though youngest, Aric took the position nearest the king. The herald guided me to where I would be seated after the eldest, Skyles—the spitter—third among the brothers.

Queen Opœa seated herself cross-legged upon a cushion, and the guests began to do the same. I dreaded an evening trapped beside Skyles, but it was only one meal, and then I'd be gone. I could ignore him for an hour or two.

Before I could sit, Aric suddenly pushed in beside me, displacing

Skyles and upsetting the order. Chatter dipped and swelled around the circle as he settled onto a cushion and set his cup of wine down before him on the mat.

"You're good with a horse," he said.

"Thank you, my lord." I kept my eyes forward, focused on a burning lamp in the center of the circle.

"Call me Aric. I'll not call you 'lady' after today."

I nodded. He scooped up his cup of wine and turned to me, a half-grin twisting his lips. "Is that fear or hate I see in your eyes?" he asked.

I sipped my wine without tasting it. "I hate being watched," I said over the rim of my cup. I could feel him incline closer.

"Get used to it. Nothing hides on the steppe. Not even in the Wild Fields. Not from me."

"That's where we're going?"

"It is."

When I was a child among my mother's people, I'd heard stories of the Wild Fields. A no-man's-land in the borders between the steppe kingdoms inhabited by roving bands of wild men, beasts, and outlaws. My curiosity aroused, I turned to look at him. "Is it as dangerous as they say?"

He leaned in closer, resting his elbows on his knees. "You've never been in a real fight, have you?"

"I am not afraid."

He grinned. "You will be." Then he guzzled his wine, tilting his half-full cup at me. "Everyone is, sooner or later."

The queen and guests suddenly rose to their feet around us as the head of the tribe arrived. I stood, grateful for the distraction. Followed by Erman, Ariapaithi strode toward his wife, who waited with a golden pitcher in her hand. Standing before her, the king withdrew a gold-plated drinking horn from his belt and held it forward.

Filling the king's cup with mead, she said in a loud, clear voice:

"Great King Ariapaithi, see how brave and honorable men come to join us on this blessed day! The unworthy dare not show their faces to you. Rejoice in your friends. Be content partaking of this sacred feast, be cordial to your people, and be hospitable to your guests."

"Good wife, noble Opœa," he said, turning to face those gathered. Nothing shall please me more!" Amid cheers, Ariapaithi raised the cup to his lips and drank.

The queen then made the rounds of the table with her pitcher and mead, bestowing a blessing upon each as she went. Pouring out a cup to Father, she placed it in his hands, and he raised it to his lips.

Before he could drink, a middle-aged man from among the ranks of the warband stood forward. "King Ariapaithi," he said, "grant me permission to speak."

The king nodded, flicking his hand indulgently at the man. He was of average height and slight, with greasy, hemp-colored hair combed back from his low forehead. A scraggly beard like hazel twigs sprouted from his narrow chin. His small eyes narrowed to slits as he scanned those whose attention he now held, and a satisfied grin overtook his face. I recognized him as one of the warriors at my initiation.

"Most of you know me. But allow me, King Arianta, to introduce myself. I am Rathagos, son of Akasas, *vazarka* of the Paralatai, and rider of the East March," he said. "I wish to voice a protest on behalf of my brothers."

I looked to Aric, but he was unmoved, watching, as were the others.

"I have to wonder," he continued, "how it is, King Arianta of the Bastarnai, that any man—and indeed a king so wise as yourself—allows his own daughter to ride and bear arms like a man? And now you send her out with us into the path of harm. It is unfeminine and surely an insult to the Lady Apia. Likewise, it is an affront to Thagimazda, Gœtosura, and the honor of the kara. Is this not a sacrilege to your Bastarnai gods as well?"

I looked to the queen, but she stood solemn as the man spoke. Ariapaithi, too, remained impassive. I turned to Aric, and his face was cold and still as stone. My cheeks began to burn. Would no one intervene on our behalf? Would they permit this man to insult and challenge the king's guest—a king himself? Would the rest of the warband not defend me after having just called me one of their own?

Father appeared unperturbed—even amused—by the insult, though he must be raging inside. He turned and addressed his so-called ally Ariapaithi, ignoring Rathagos entirely. "Dear friends, the Bastarnai people are grateful for the warm welcome and generous hospitality you have bestowed upon their sovereign and his beloved daughter. With immeasurable pride, I give my daughter to the noble Ariapaithi and join our two great houses.

"I wonder, have any of you daughters?" he asked of all those present. "Have you sisters and wives? Your people are herdsmen, so perhaps your ways are different. But my people are farmers. I, too, am a farmer. I love to watch things grow. And what a farmer fears most is to plant a seed and see it drowned by storms, starved by drought, ravaged by insects and animals, or cut down before it is ripe. My daughter was a beautiful, tender flower from the day she was born. I wanted to shelter her from all harm. To give her good soil, water, and sunlight and watch her grow.

"But no garden wall could keep out all storms, or beasts, or men. So, instead of building a stronger wall, I cultivated a stronger flower. A gardener, no matter how vigilant, must close his eyes sometimes. I don't have to build a wall around this flower. The gods themselves have given her thorns. Who am I to challenge their wisdom? By their will, Anaiti is fearless and strong. And I would have it no other way."

I'd never heard Father say such things. My eyes stung to listen to the words spoken now. I blinked and swallowed hard, hoping no one would notice. Heads nodded their assent around the table, though Rathagos seemed unimpressed.

"Well said, my friend," Ariapaithi finally spoke up, "well said."

The queen blessed Father with a smile and her cup and came at last to me. She stood rigid before me and looked me up and down. "Welcome, Princess Anaiti, hamazan of the Rokhalani, daughter of Arianta of the Bastarnai. Thanks to Papahio and blessings of Tabiti upon you," she said flatly.

"Thank you, Sura. Blessings upon you," I repeated like the others. I paused with no thought of what to say next. I should offer an oath, something to do with my impending union, but I was never a good liar. "I come to this place with one desire: to benefit both my people and yours. Let me do honor to that wish in my time among you or let me fall trying."

Her eyes softened as she nodded subtly. I took the cup in both hands and drank, the mead thick and sweet.

"Thrive and prosper here, Anaiti," she said quietly as she took the cup from my hands.

She returned to sit at the right side of Ariapaithi, and the feast began. Servants brought meats of every kind, assorted river fish, sausages and blood puddings, cheeses, lentils, flatbreads, bowls of kumis. The Skythian-style wine was spicy but warming. Talk and laughter resumed, and I soon found the nomads were like any others when gathered around a table of food and drink. Passionate and funny. Generous and full of mirth. I listened and did not speak as the warriors around me joked together over their meat and wine.

The guests stood and drifted from the tables to stretch their legs, digest their food, and converse before being served the final course. Father took his leave of the Skythian king to pull me aside and question me about my initiation and impending departure. We spoke in our own Bastarnai tongue, and I tried quietly and patiently to reassure him that he need not worry—that I could take care of myself. He disguised his doubt behind sips of wine.

At the table nearby, the royal family had ceased speaking Skythian and began to debate amongst themselves in Greek. They spoke almost in whispers, so I had to strain to hear until the conversation became heated. Skyles, the pseudo-Hellene with the too-black beard, turned to his father. "I cannot believe you consider union with a *mankiller*," he said, unable to conceal his disgust—or not even trying. "This is an outrage. They dishonor us by offering her, and it will be a scandal if we accept."

Oktamazda, caught in the middle, eyed Aric, who folded his arms across his chest, his features hard in the torchlight. Aric glanced at me, and though I pretended not to notice, something like panic coursed through me.

"Why such enmity for Amazons?" Ariapaithi asked Skyles in Greek.

"Because, Father," Aric answered for his brother, "if women take up arms, Skyles might be humiliated by one in battle."

I bit my lips to suppress a smile.

"A man is far more likely to be humiliated by a woman he weds than one he fights," Skyles said.

"You speaking from experience?" Oktamazda jabbed with a smirk, his ruddy face blushing as he and Aric both indulged in a good chuckle.

"Enough! All of you." Ariapaithi's face twisted in a snarl.

"Father," Skyles pleaded, "the Rokhalani covet our lands. She cannot be trusted."

"Eh," Oktamazda waved him off, "she's also Bastarnai, and it's with them you've made your pact. The Bastarnai have long been our allies. We can't lose any more profit to Agathyrsi raids. The girl would not be my first choice, but the hamazan are said to be honest. She is tall and strong and has good hips for childbearing. One could get formidable sons from a woman like that." He shrugged, adopting an aloof air, which was even more striking than when he smiled. It was hard to scorn him entirely, even if he was sizing me up like a broodmare.

"Lest we become effeminate like the Hellenes," he added with another smirk as his gaze flashed back to Skyles, dressed in his Greek-made finery.

Skyles's face reddened. "Oh, heaven forbid the Skythai should become civilized," he hissed in a loud whisper.

"*Civilized*, ha!" Aric taunted him. "Is that what it's called? When men in the streets swaddle themselves in bedclothes? Pen themselves up inside living tombs? When hungry ships crowd our shores to stuff their hulls with slaves and grain? They can mock and scorn us all they like, but you and I both know the truth. If that's what 'civilization' is, I want no part in it."

Skyles clenched his fist and slammed it down on the plate before him, shattering the dish and turning the heads of the diners. But before he opened his mouth, the king raised his hand, and Skyles bit his tongue. The brothers fell still, glaring at one another in taut silence. Opœa, seated beside the king, raised her eyes and briefly caught mine, but in a flash of panic, I looked away, worried she might have realized I understood everything they'd said.

CHAPTER 5

BONFIRE

Skythia was the last country to be populated
by men. Before that, this entire land was desert,
inhabited only by spirits, winds, and wild beasts.

THE CAULDRONS WERE REFILLED, fresh carcasses hung over
fires on spits, and amphorae of wine poured into buckets for
serving, but I'd had enough of feasting for the night. I excused
myself while Father busied himself with trade and politics. Taking
another horn of wine and a hunk of cheese, I slipped away, seeking
a quiet spot far from the noise of the crowd.

Out in the field, I found the forgotten remains of a bonfire.
Stoking its embers, I threw some logs into its glowing center and
stood in the cool grass, losing myself in the play of the flames as
they began to rise again. Reedpipes and drums played a frantic
tune for dancers in the pasture, their harsh drone resounding up
the low slope of the plain like a thunderstorm.

A half dozen massive fires still dotted the horizon. There was
wood—a lot of it—but no trees in the plain. A small forest must
have been imported just for this night. When I was home, I loved
nothing more than the open fields. How limitless they felt, running unhindered toward the horizon. But smelling that bonfire, I

missed the trees. The forests were only budding when I'd left and would be nearly in full leaf now, the fruit trees blossoming and the birds nesting. Oak, ash, and willow lined the streams where I watered the horses.

A colossal linden stood in the courtyard at the center of our fort. No one knew whether the tree or the village came first. Some said the tree was ancient long before the first hut ever stood and that the town sprang up around it. My father's fathers built their fort on the hill generations ago and were all crowned at the foot of that tree. Father, too, before I was born. She, too, was called "The Lady"—Lady Linden. And each year, when the tree was in flower near Midsummer, the Assembly of Bastarnai came from far and near to meet beneath her spreading canopy, for it was said only truth could be spoken in the shade of her branches.

As a child, I clambered up the nooks of her craggy bark and nestled into her swaying limbs, rocking to half-sleep from the vantage of the birds. Like the dappled sunlight that would bathe my skin in summer, her leaves would turn golden, crisp and fall, warning of the night season. And she'd abide, naked and barren, through the storms and trials of winter. No moon was as perfect and pure as that which, on a cold night, lay cradled in the bare branches of that tree. Here, stark and unadorned, the moon was just a sliver—a bright scythe sweeping across the field of night.

A half-furlong away, a dance circled around another fire. I'd spent most of my youth avoiding the ludicrous duty of public dance, and I hoped no one would see me and try to make me join them. The night had settled in now, and the dancers melted into the dark, invisible but for the glimmer of their gold adornments in the firelight, each a constellation unto himself.

The warmth of the wine and heat of the flame spread through my blood like a fever, and I closed my eyes to shut out the chaos whirling around me. I hardly knew what to make of all that had transpired since I stepped off my chariot this morning. Nothing had gone to plan. I'd walked straight into an ambush. Did Father know how much these men would scorn me when he chose to send me here? He'd promised that my duty was not to seduce the king—not that I could even if I tried. I was to keep my eyes open and convey what I learned. His intentions were plain, without the need for words: I was to probe the Skythai—and Ariapaithi—for anything that Father might seize upon or exploit for the good of our tribe. There must be rich plunder here, as the three princes couldn't sit down to a meal without almost coming to blows. They made no attempt to hide it. Yet, the Skythai spoke fervently of oaths, and Aric's words sat ill with me. A man I'd never met, who owed me nothing, swore today before the gods to sacrifice his life for mine? Men were sometimes mad, and perhaps the Skythai were doubly so, but such a seasoned warrior couldn't be so reckless. That had to be the kind of grand, empty talk men made at court. But what kind of man makes a solemn oath knowing it to be hollow? *What kind of man makes such an oath and means it truly?* I wasn't sure which was worse.

"So, you're off again already?" said a voice beyond the bonfire, approaching from outside the firelight. Prince Oktamazda stood opposite me, where I could clearly discern his fine features in the flickering light. I could just make out a small group of a half dozen men, lured like moths by the now-roaring bonfire. Their approach wakened me from my reveries.

"First thing," came the low rumble of Aric in response, as if I'd summoned him with my thoughts.

"Too bad. We only see you at festivals and funerals."

"You say it like it's a bad thing."

A third man joined them. "Ever met one before?" he asked. By his burly outline, I thought it must be Bornon, a bristly man with a badly scarred face but soft cow eyes who'd been among the dozen men at my initiation.

"A hamazan? Thought I did once," another interjected too

loudly, "but it was just a pretty boy!" That one they called Olgas. Through the smoke and flames, I could make out his rangy silhouette and tousled black hair cut in a fringe across his brow. He laughed heartily at himself, revealing the gaping hole where all the teeth on the left side of his mouth had been smashed out.

"Bet you tried to fuck him anyway," burly Bornon said, slapping him on the back. More laughter from the group. "No, you'd know it if you met one. There's no mistaking it. I met many when we traded for horses with the Aorsi across the Tanais."

"You've traded with them?" Oktamazda asked. "What was that like?"

"Best horses in this world. Raided from the very pastures of heaven."

"Do they really learn to fight," Olgas asked, "and go to war like men?"

"The best among them," Aric replied. "Like us. They're just training bitches instead of dogs."

Slender Olgas shook his shaggy black head. "Well, what's it got to do with us? Women aren't meant to see and hear the secrets of the kara. Others have died for this. The fuck you thinking?"

"I'm not so sure it's wise either," Bornon said, "taking her into the Wild Fields." A deep frown furrowed an already deeply scarred face.

"Eh, she'll do," Aric said gruffly.

"*She* might. But what about us?" Bornon asked. "You don't turn a mare loose among stallions."

"Heh, so you're a stallion now?"

"You know what I'm saying."

"I do," Aric said, "but you're men, not beasts."

"You hope."

"She looks soft to me," Olgas said, "with her doe eyes and dewy face. She won't last a week. Won't even last the ride out."

"We'll see," Aric said. "What looks hardest is often most brittle

49

and breaks easiest. Besides, her mother was Suramatai. She's practically Skythai."

"*Hardly*," a fifth man, who'd been silent till now, interjected.
That haughty tone would be forever seared into my memory. *Skyles.*
"Any peasant can sit on a horse and shoot a bow, even the girls."

If I stayed, I would have to listen to their bullshit for the rest
of the night. So, I gathered myself and stood to skulk off and
find another fire to warm myself at, squinting angrily through the
smoke and flames at the men who disturbed my peace.

"Ah, see? Look how she scorns us!" Aric said, meeting my gaze
across the fire. "She'll do just fine." He waved me over. "Anaiti, come,
join us for a drink." Ladling a cup of wine from the bucket they'd
brought, he held it up in offering.

Shit. Did I have to? I just wanted to be alone—to sleep. But it
was too late to hide now. I dragged myself around the bonfire to
them. *One drink.*

Aric handed the horn to me as the other men stepped in closer.
Their clothes all smelled of cannabis. Another man stood with
them. Stormai. He'd also been at the ceremony and feast, but I'd
not heard him speak. Tall and powerfully built, he was younger
than the others and boyishly handsome, with sandy hair and a firm
jaw. When I nodded to him, he looked at his boots.

"Blessings on becoming a fellow of the warband." Oktamazda
raised his horn and gave me a kind smile, his red beard glowing
like polished copper in the firelight.

"Thank you." I tried to hide my weariness. "I hope to prove
worthy of it."

"What do you think of Skythia?" Oktamazda asked. "I expect
it's strange for you, coming from farm country?"

"It's strange in some ways but familiar in others. I was fostered
among the Rokhalani, as I told the king. I've missed those days.
I've always dreamt of returning to the steppe."

"I understand. I was fostered in Thrake among the Odrysai with my uncle Sitalk before he took the crown and have just returned from there this morning. I have seen this country from within and without. It can seem strange and formidable to foreigners," he said. "But I hope you'll come to appreciate it as we do."

"Indeed," Skyles stepped in, "outsiders often misunderstand this place. They think we live poorly, but it is just the opposite. There is opportunity for great wealth if one knows how to seize it."

I gritted my teeth and swallowed. There was nothing I despised more than a one-man cock-measuring contest. I tried to let him win. "I imagine that's true. The Skythai seem well equipped to do so."

"The Skythai?" Skyles said, inexplicably affronted. "Who said anything about the Skythai? We Paralatai are the first men to inhabit this land and the first kings of this country. All others dwelling upon the steppe do so by our leave. You would not be here otherwise."

If Father were here, he would have told me to be diplomatic—to not let him provoke me. "We are honored to be allies of the Paralatai and friends of King Ariapaithi." Actually, he'd have told me to keep my mouth shut. "But we do quite well for ourselves. It seems our merit is mutual, as you depend on us and the grain we supply to feed yourselves and your markets. Without tribes like ours, the colonies and trade you value so highly wither and die. And your tariffs with them."

His muddy eyes narrowed, and his jaw muscles tightened. "Then perhaps King Arianta did not enjoy the gifts I arranged for him on the occasion of this covenant? Are such exquisite treasures so common in your backwater that they merit no thanks? Tell me: what fate would await your little tribe without our favor, our trade—and our protection? I'll tell you: rape and murder by the Agathyrsi," he said through a forced smile.

Oktamazda stepped forward and interrupted: "Let's not *joke* and *tease* each other on a night like this. It's Eramandin! Tonight, we celebrate! Our tribes are soon to be joined. And let's not forget

51

that our respective nations were founded by brothers . . . more or less."

"Brothers?" I asked, welcoming his distraction before I got myself into real trouble.

"Not this bloody story," Skyles groaned.

"What's wrong with it?" Aric asked.

"It's revolting." Skyles sucked in deeply through his nose and spit a wad of phlegm into the fire. I stifled a gag.

"It's our history," Oktamazda said, "and I quite like it."

"So do I," Aric said to the assent of the others. "It seems you're outnumbered." He grinned mockingly at his brother, raised his horn, and finished off his wine.

"I'd like to hear." I glanced around at the men, and none would meet my eye. But Aric's eye gleamed, and he methodically refilled his cup, then smiled at me as he filled mine, the crowd waiting, watching in silence.

"Well, you see," Aric began, "Skythia was the last country to be populated by men. Before that, this entire land was desert, inhabited only by spirits, winds, and wild beasts. Like those beasts, it is a fierce, untamed place unsuited to cultivating crops or building towns. The first man to settle here was Targitao. The son of Papahio and a priestess of Apia, he was no ordinary human and walked the earth a hero among men.

"One night after he had been raiding cattle, a terrible blizzard descended upon him as he drove his spoils through the Wild Fields. He made camp beside his chariot and lay down to sleep. But when morning came, he awoke to find his horses gone. He hid his cattle in a narrow valley and followed the horses' tracks in the snow south to the Woodland of Hylaia. There, he came upon an ancient willow within a grove. Beneath its roots, a cleft opened into the earth revealing a cave, and, peering inside, he was greeted by a wondrous creature. Above the waist, she was a woman; below, her legs were like twin serpents which writhed and coiled about as she slithered along the floor of her cave," he said, making serpentine motions with his arms.

"He was mystified as he watched. 'I am Apia, Lady of the Waters,' she said, 'and your horses are now in my possession.'

"She was the daughter of Targitao's adversary, none other than Volos, the Encloser. Wrangler of Cattle, Gatherer of Clouds, and keeper of the Great Swamps of the Volosdanu, which the Hellenes insist on calling 'Borysthenes,' because they can't pronounce our words."

We all laughed, except for Skyles. "You would not find that so funny if you knew how dreadfully you all speak Greek," he said.

"Did she give his horses back?" I was eager to know.

"Ah, first, she wanted something from him in return." Here, Aric paused to refill everyone's wine, but I had forgotten to drink the cup I had. "She said: 'I have your horses. And I will return them to you. But only if you will lie with me.'" At this, the men all grinned and nodded knowingly at one another. I couldn't help chuckling to myself. "He agreed, of course."

"*Of course.*"

"So, Targitao spent the rest of the long winter in the hollows of her chamber. All the while, she kept his horses hidden so he might forget them and remain with her longer."

"Heroes," Skyles interrupted, "are supposed to *slay* monsters, not lay with them." His eyes narrowed and fixed their cold stare upon me across the waning flames.

"Well," Aric said, "be grateful he didn't, or none of us would be here."

Skyles's face twisted in disgust.

"How would horses survive in a cave all winter?" I asked, ignoring the hateful glare.

Oktamazda spoke up. "They say that the cavern reaches deep below, into the realm of Volos himself, where there are wide pastures and a bright, clear spring at the roots of the Great Tree."

"Are you going to let me tell my story or not?"

Oktamazda gave an audible sigh.

"Anyway," Aric continued, "she soon gave birth to three sons by him. After the snows had passed, Targitao prepared to leave with his horses and continue his journey. Apia asked him what she should do with his sons when they were grown: 'Shall they remain here in my kingdom, or shall I send them off to you?'"

"Well," I asked, "did they have feet like their father or snake legs like their mother?"

Frowning deeply, Aric hooked his thumb in his warbelt and just stared at me for a long moment. "*Feet.* Do you want to hear this or not?"

"Never mind, please go on."

"You're as bad as him," he said indulgently, tipping his drinking horn toward Oktamazda and taking a long draught. "Well, Targitao gave her his bow and warbelt. And he told her that when the boys were grown, whoever could string the bow should also wear the belt. That son would receive her vast kingdom. The others she should send off to seek their fortunes elsewhere. The older two were called Agathyrs and Gelon, and when they were grown, they could not string the bow, so they were forced to make their way beyond the borders of this land. Agathyrs went west into the fertile plains. Gelon went north into the forests. The youngest son, Skyth, succeeded in stringing his father's bow and inherited the steppelands, founding the nations of archers. From him descend the Paralatai and all the kings of Skythia."

"It's a wonderful story," I said. "Is that the end?"

"I certainly hope not," Aric said, grinning wryly.

"Speaking of women and their mysterious caverns," Olgas said, his voice mushy with wine, "it grows late. . . ."

Aric scowled at Olgas as he glanced toward me. Olgas shrugged sheepishly, "Pardon, my lady."

I smiled and nodded, having never really minded men's talk.

There was no point in feigning squeamishness. I'd said far coarser things myself.

"The rest of the tale," Oktamazda smiled charmingly, "should wait until you return safely from the Fields!" He raised his cup. "Anaiti, blessings of Targitao, Volos, and Apia upon you and your road. May you return to us in honor, glory, and health!"

The lot of us clashed our drinking horns together and drained them.

Aric clapped Olgas on the back. "Don't be late."

"Never," he said, downed the last of his wine, and refilled his horn before marching off beyond the firelight.

"We leave at dawn," Aric said, turning to me. "You should get some rest."

"Of course." I thanked the men and took my leave. Even the quiet one, Stormai, smiled reservedly as I left, though he spoke not a word in my presence all night.

I went to make my excuses to my hosts, exhausted but relieved to have the day done. After so much wine, my own legs nearly writhed beneath me, and I longed for the dark quiet of my wagon and the oblivion of sleep.

CHAPTER 6

MARCHES

Beyond the bounds of camp lay a sea of wild
prairie under the dominion of gods and spirits,
both terrible and benevolent.

WINDS TRAVELED TIRELESSLY OVER THIS COUNTRY, not
resting, as gentle creatures do, with the fall of darkness. But
what cause had the wind to seek refuge? It flew and bore with it
the song of nighttime pastures, trod by hoofed and shod creatures
who hummed along in muddled whispers and lilting cackles as
they passed by my wagon. Cold, clean moonlight spilled through
the chinks in the windows and door, thwarting my sleep. It was
still dark when I finally awoke, leaving me time to ready my horses before the spectacle of sunrising over the broad plain and its
boundless horizon.

Only, my head throbbed, and I could scarcely swallow. I washed
quickly, the basin water cool in the damp spring air. The thought
of food sickened me with my stomach still sour from too much
wine, but I tried to drink a sip of milk and eat a crust of bread.
The clothes I'd been given the day before lay on the trunk beside
my cot. The clamor of camp grew more hectic outside, and little
time remained before I must meet the others to depart. But even

as I shivered in my underthings, I could not bring myself to dress. None of these garments were mine. Not really. I ran my fingers over the iron torc around my neck and shuddered. *I can't.*

A wave of nausea possessed me, and I bent over a pail to vomit. As I stood, I felt *it* coming. In my right ear, it whispered to me. *Anaiti.* My skin prickled, and I covered my ears, though it was no use. The voice knew no bounds, for it spoke from within. I could neither run from it nor hide. *Anaiti*, it called. It had a keen sense for when I was most exposed. That was when it chose to strike. That was its upper hand. Even through the foul taste lingering in my mouth, I could smell it—the fetid but familiar odor it came cloaked in—as a terrible foreboding stalked into the cramped wagon, raising its shadow over me, flooding every corner with doom. Heralding its portents, revealing its signs. Suddenly, *I knew everything* that would happen in the coming hours, days, months. Dire things, momentous things, which filled me with dread. All this, I saw from the bottom of a dark pool, obscured. And if I tried to speak, I'd drown. I could never articulate this knowledge—not even to myself. Then, a moment later, it would be gone. Wiped clean from my memory, but for the lingering dread it left in its wake.

But that was not all it had come for, and there was little time.

My vision swimming, temples pounding, I rushed to latch the wagon door and sat on the bed, burying my fingers deep into the coarse wool of the sheepskin blanket, eyes wide as the flood of darkness washed over me.

———◆◆———

THROUGH A HAZE of ebbing shadows, grain by grain, I sifted back into myself. Like a sleeper awaking with a numb hand, fingers moved by a stranger, I observed with that same detached curiosity, awaiting, not the return of feeling, but memory—who I was, where, and why I was here. Worse still, I knew not where I had gone when I left this flesh, though I had my fears.

All the better that I could never recall what I had seen or met in these travels. I tried instead to forget. Whatever wretched message it sought to impart was now lost to my waking mind. No doubt for the best. But though the dim room where I sat was unfamiliar, oddly, I was not afraid. I searched the space for the source of the muffled sound reaching my ears.

It was a rapping on the door. A man's bellowing voice broke through, irritated and insistent. "Wake up!" He thumped again, harder. "What in the Lady's name are you doing in there? Open the door!"

I knew the voice. I knew the anger in it. *Father.*

I rubbed my eyes and blinked hard as if it might clear the shadows obscuring my mind. "I'll be right along," I said to the oaken door, finding my voice, my memory. One by one, my thoughts returned from wherever they had wandered. The dread was gone. The Skythai were waiting.

"I'm almost dressed." Standing unsteadily from the bed, I dragged on the new trousers beside it. I unlocked the door.

Father shoved his way in, searching the wagon in exasperation. Then he looked at me, and his face fell.

"You've had another one of them—one of your spells." He ran his hand over his face and exhaled.

Though I had become skilled at hiding them, Father had seen them before. He called these spontaneous trances "spells" as if I had suffered a bout of lightheadedness—nothing that couldn't be cured with a bite to eat and some rest. He never asked to know more, and I never offered. He chose to see them as a mere nuisance, and I chose to let him do so and not worry. Still, he knew they were cause for caution. Others might not be so understanding. I hardly understood them myself. Perhaps I might have consulted a priest if, from an early age, Father had not instilled in me a deep distrust of divine mouthpieces as, he warned, holy men seldom shared the interests of either the monarch or the misfit. So, I never told anyone.

"It was just a little one. I drank more than was wise. You know I can't handle much wine."

He filled me a cup of water from the pitcher, and we sat together on the bed. "What if one of *them* sees?"

"I'm just thirsty and tired," I tried to reassure him—and myself. "They are hunters, too. Surely, they segregate women during their monthly time."

He frowned and placed his hand over mine, giving it a firm squeeze. "You may be able to conceal yourself during the dark moon—when you expect the spells. But the moon is *waxing* now. Your nerves are getting to you."

I couldn't fool him. With the new moon already passed, it should not have come now; something was amiss. Perhaps I had let my guard down and let it in.

"What if it happens again?" he asked. "Where will you hide then? I do not trust that man—that beast in man's clothing."

"Which one?"

"Take your pick."

He was right, of course. We could not afford to test the Skythai any further—not now. It was one more worry I couldn't afford today, and like a buzzing insect, I tried to stamp it down into a dark corner of my mind.

"Then, you must trust me." I smiled, trying to convince him. "I will find a way. I always have." What other choice was there?

He scoffed faintly, but I embraced him one last time before he could disagree. There was no point in arguing. I was going, and I had better not be late.

DEW VEILED THE SUMMER GRASS, shimmering a ghostly white under the iron grey of early morning. Just a weak spark, the sun struggled to ignite on the horizon we would soon ride toward. A sharp wind from the east stirred a spirit within the horses that made them lighter than air. They danced and sprang with their necks arched like swans, and their tails flagged high like banners in the breeze, snorting like trumpeters before battle. We smiled to watch them at play as they tossed their heads and shook their manes with the spirit coursing through them. The Skythai, being the finest of horsemen, spoke soothing words to them and stroked their necks to quiet their fury, for we had a long ride ahead.

Each horse was richly outfitted with colorful woven or appliquéd woolen saddlecloths stitched with fringes, furs, bands of silk, or beaded baubles. Their bridles were plated with intricate golden ornaments, and tattered tresses hung down from the lengths of their reins like a second mane, proof of their riders' prowess in battle. With Aruna's conspicuously plain leather bridle and sheepskin-padded saddle secure, I fumbled with the buckles on Sakha's pack saddle in the murky light, my fingers blind and numb with cold. My mouth was dry, and my head throbbed. I could have drunk a river if only the thought didn't churn my stomach. How the Skythai survived on the quantities of wine they drank was a wonder.

The tribe's women had finally come out to see off the men and boys leaving for the East March. Some, I expect, had also come to gawk at me. They came bearing gifts of food, woven clothing, charms, and talismans, but there were no tears. They raised their voices in unison and shouted a rough kind of encouragement, exhorting them all to be brave, to keep their honor, to bring back heads of enemies and rich spoils from their raids—*or not return at all*. I wondered if my father harbored a similar sentiment.

As Aric had ordered, I chose my two best horses to take to the Wild Fields. I loved all the horses in my charge, but Sakha and Aruna were more than superior mounts; they were faithful friends I had raised from foals. I could hardly imagine passing a day without seeing them. With my horses and packs ready, my old bow and new sword at my side, I said my goodbyes quickly and checked my girth one last time.

Father approached Aric. They gripped right hands and

embraced. "Often have I heard your name spoken these many years, Lord Aric."

"You mustn't believe everything you hear," Aric replied without irony or humor, which sent an odd twinge of foreboding through me.

"You are a man of your word. That is all I need to know." Father stepped back and forced a smile toward me. I grinned back, trying to reassure him. His worry for me was sweet but less than inspiring. I was scared, too, but I could take care of myself. Better than he imagined.

The men had already mounted. Most of them had trained their horses to kneel, a handy trick when one is burdened with shield and weapons, but one I never thought to try. I grabbed hold of Aruna's chestnut mane, but my legs threatened to give out under me. Aruna tossed his head impatiently. None of this had seemed real last night. The others sat quietly in their saddles, waiting, watching. Their unforgiving eyes on me. Gripping Aruna's mane and saddle, my arms went limp, and my legs went wooden. If I tried to vault up onto his back now, I'd slide down his side in humiliation.

Drawing a deep breath, I tried to steady my clouded vision. I'd be damned before I gave the men a reason to ridicule me. I knotted my fingers deep in Aruna's mane. Summoning every bit of muscle I could muster, I heaved myself onto his back. As I swung my right leg over, my new sword nearly got hung up on my saddle. At the same time, I jabbed myself under the ribs with the pommel. Sitting up as straight as I could, I made my face a mask of serenity as I nodded to Aric, relieved to be settled and safely aboard.

THE SKELETAL REMAINS of burned tree limbs and cattle bones stood silver and black against the reddening dawn. The great twin heaps of cinder and ash, remains of the previous night's bonfires, loomed about half a furlong apart at the edge of the camp. Weakened livestock had been driven between them during the festival to be purified of the dark season's lingering sickness and ill fortune before moving on to the summer pastures. Now, we rode between their still-smoldering remnants as a red glow peeked from the embers, and the mounds hissed and crackled, steam rising like wraiths in the chill morning mist.

Beyond the bounds of camp lay a sea of wild prairie under the dominion of gods and spirits, both terrible and benevolent. Beyond the shelter of society's laws lay their majestic realm, untamed and merciless. This was where the kara dwelt.

Nudging up into a brisk canter, we rode headlong into the unforgiving wind across a flat, desolate plain. At the head of the party, Aric set the pace, rode hard, and never looked back to see if I kept up. I had hoped to take in the sights of the steppe and get my bearings, but the ride was a whirlwind, and I struggled to keep my horses together. Warriors of highest rank rode at the front, while novices like me kept to the rear of the field. Neither of my horses much liked being at the back, and they fought me with every step to race ahead, stretching my arms and tearing my hands as I struggled to hold them. We were spattered with mud and pelted with clods from the many hooves before us. I saw little but the backsides of other riders and the blur of grass between my horses' ears. When I did look around me, much of the country was featureless—flat or gently rolling and yellow-green to every horizon. If not for the sun moving overhead, one might think we'd made no progress at all.

We broke at midday to graze and water the horses beside a shallow, wide creek that ran clear and cold. Exhausted, I wanted to take off my boots, soak my feet, and lay on the bank in the sun. Worried I might fall asleep, I only drank, quickly splashed water on my face, and hurried to rejoin the men. I ate ferociously, being beyond the reach of manners already.

We rode on after swapping tack to fresher horses, passing through more pastures, floodplains, and shallow valleys. The day warmed despite the wind, and the sun shone brightly in a deep, clear sky. Every so often, I caught a glimpse of flashing lights on the horizon, though the sky was cloudless. I wondered if oases or springs were catching the sunlight. The plain was vast and mostly unwatered. Any decent horseman keeps a mind map of water along the routes he rides and never sets out without knowing where his horses will drink. But it was hopeless, as I was utterly lost.

Most of the open country was empty but for red deer, foxes, and other wildlife stirred up by our passage. Some of it was camped by dispossessed clans in shabby wagons and tents and grazed by scattered cattle and sheep. All looked like they were living at the mercy of the wolves and reavers. Some, perhaps, were reavers themselves. But everywhere, the country was the same—lush, vast, and unscathed by man's cultivations. It was magnificent.

Walking at times when we reached rough ground or boggy floodplain and occasionally stopping to rest and graze the horses, the journey took a full day of hard riding. Finally, after dark, we arrived at what the others called the *buna*, where their camp was made. Men patrolling in the night's watch greeted us silently as we rode by. Most of the camp was already asleep. Sun- and windburned, aching in my saddle-weary bones, and tired beyond reason, I fumbled my way through caring for my horses, washed and watered them, and put them out to graze, fitting their foreleg hobbles for the night.

"Hobble your horses well," Aric admonished as he gently scrubbed the dried sweat from his own horse's back. "At least until they grow familiar with this place and learn to stay with their new herd. There is a wild herd nearby. If one should run off after them, he will surely die."

Rubbing my bleary eyes, I tried to make sense of his advice. "Isn't it better he joins a herd than taking his chances alone against the wolves?"

He kept working along the back of his black horse with a coarse hemp cloth. "A wild herd will not allow a tame horse within its midst. It will be attacked—killed or driven away."

"But why?"

He shrugged. "I could guess. But only they know."

I patted my horses' necks and checked their hobbles three times before leaving them for the night. Then I rolled up my trousers and waded up to my knees in the calm waters of the river to wash the dust from my face and soothe my saddle sores and blistered hands.

IN THE HOWLING WIND before an open hearth, I sat beside Aric, the dozen warriors, and the fifty or so novices who rode out with us. Some of the novices were nearly children, and all their heads had been shaved bare, so I suddenly counted myself lucky that only my braid had been sheared off. We had a few moments to eat leftover stew, barely warm, in the cauldron before retiring for the night. One of the warriors—Tarana was his name, I think—played his lyre and sang softly as the rest settled into their suppers. Two burly watchmen joined us to talk briefly with the men as they ate, sharing the camp's news. The boys and men chattered quietly, but no one spoke to me.

A young man came to stand behind Aric, seemingly waiting. He wore plain clothes of grubby sheepskin, vegetable dyed hemp, and a greasy, pointed cap of red felt on his head. He had a goryt by his side and a long knife in his belt, but he was not a warrior like the others; that much was clear. After quickly finishing his stew, Aric arose, greeting the young man like an old friend, stepping aside to speak with him alone. They leaned close, holding a private counsel outside the firelight, with furrowed brows and frustrated glances. Then Aric clapped him on the back, and he departed.

"So, you can ride, hamazan," Aric said, sitting down next to me as he dug into his second bowl of stew. It was a good, broad grin that dimpled his cheeks and deeply crinkled the skin around his eyes. I think it was the first time I'd seen him look content.

64

"I usually manage to stay on," I replied, a little flutter of pride bringing a smile to my own face.

"Tomorrow, we'll see if you can shoot."

He got up to leave and squeezed my knee so hard I almost cried out. I was sure it would leave a bruise. *Shoot?* I wondered if my training would begin immediately or if he had something else in mind, but asking too many questions seemed unwise. "I look forward to it," I said boldly, rising to my feet and resting my hand on the bow at my hip. "I should get some sleep. Could someone show me to my tent?"

"You will be my guest."

I could only stare at him, gaping stupidly. In *his* tent? That couldn't be right. "You—you mean until mine is prepared?"

He stepped in close, and even in the near-total darkness, I could make out the stern lines of his face as he stood over me and stared down. "I can only look after you if I can see you."

"Then, you do not fear the taboo of a woman's blood?" That was all the discouragement most hunters needed.

"I do not fear blood. I fear only to break the oath I've made."

I'd never lived among men before. Back home, I had my own tiny hut within the bounds of the Bastarnai fort. As my mind flashed across all of life's daily necessities, from washing to dressing to the things far more guarded, I did all of them away from the prying eyes of both family and strangers. I stood mute, trying to think of proper reasons why I couldn't possibly be his guest or sleep in his tent. Reasons that were not insults. Trying to phrase a demand or—or what? I was in no position to make demands. Negotiations had ended, and I was far from home. He ruled here. I couldn't refuse his hospitality, no matter how unwelcome.

"ANAITI, I OFFER THE SHELTER OF MY TENT," he said stiffly, removing his fur-lined cap and pressing it to his breast. The emerging crescent of moonlight touched softly on the crown of his golden head while tousled hairs lay scattered across his brow, cast askew by the lifting of his cap. He pulled back the hide doorflap. "You shall have a place of honor by my fire."

"I thank you for your hospitality; I am honored to be your guest," I replied as I nodded and bowed back, placing my fist over my heart. Then I ducked under his arm and entered. Freezing in my tracks, I caught my breath. Another man was already inside—a good-looking, well-built man with warm, walnut eyes.

"So, this is the girl," he said flatly.

Aric grunted. "Anaiti, our steward, Antisthenes."

A Greek name. A Hellene here among the kara? Was truly nothing sacred even in this last untamed portion of the earth? Was there nowhere in this world left undefiled by their insufferable touch? And I was now forced to sleep beside one. I'd rather sleep in a nest of vipers. Indeed, perhaps I was about to. Any hope I'd felt in coming to this place was now doused. His pallet was on the left, nearest the door, and without even a word of greeting, he turned to remove his weapons and began to take off his caftan for bed. Embarrassed, I looked away, unaccustomed to men undressing before me.

"Your steward," I whispered to Aric. "Am I . . . safe?"

"Antisthenes?" he whispered as he stepped in close, the pungent scents of sweat and leather filling the space between us. He pinched his brows patronizingly as if I'd asked something outlandish. "You needn't fear him. He's a most honorable man and my most trusted friend. And besides, *you* would not be to his liking."

No, I imagine not.

IT WAS A SILENT PLACE AT NIGHT—eerily so. As loud as the outdoor gatherings were, all became hushed once we moved inside. Aric and his steward lit a low fire and spoke in careful whispers once within the confines of the tent.

The felt-houses here were smaller, simpler, and boasted no

furniture or decoration. But the refuge from the wind was a mercy. I peered out the door. No light of human habitation, nor even
the faint spark of a distant campfire, was visible on any horizon.
Unlike the fort where I grew up, where torches burned along the
palisades all through the night, there were no defenses or lights
here. Darkness was not just a notion; when the torches were snuffed,
it had weight you could all but feel, thick and black before your face.
Cooking fires were allowed to die, while those for warmth were
concealed inside. The only light came from the moon and stars.

Tents were arranged in concentric circles. From what I could
observe, the twelve vazarka slept paired in six tents at the camp's
heart. The remainder of the three hundred kara slept four to a tent
arranged in four rows of eighteen. The fifty or so novices—or pups,
as they were teasingly called—slept in the several wagons circling
the whole encampment. An open space about thirty paces across
stood at the center, bearing the communal hearth. Our tent was far
enough away from the others for some comfort—about ten paces
by my eye. Still, anytime I needed a piss, the world would know.

Aric warned that one never entered another's tent without an
invitation. To do so could prove fatal. Each had a unique signal
upon entering their tent. Aric and Antisthenes used their own
coded knock upon the doorframe, which he taught to me.

"Lay your pallet here next to mine," he whispered in his deep
rasp, handing me a stack of sheepskins and felt blankets and pointing to a neat bedroll laid over in a worn doeskin blanket on the
right. "You'll be closer to the fire."

He first hung up his bow inside its goryt, then unfastened his
warbelt, which he hung from an antler hook over his bed. I did
as told and prepared my pallet of sheepskin while he tended the
hearth. But I could not bring myself to undress and lay upon it
while he was so near. My back soaking up the warmth of the fire,
I clasped my hands before me, wringing the blood from them, and
just stood there dumb.

"Undress," he insisted, becoming impatient. "It grows late. Remove your warbelt, girdle, and caftan," he gestured with his hands at each item as if explaining to a child. "But keep them close. We sleep in most of our clothes."

Staring at me, hands on his hips, he waited as I stood paralyzed by the sheer audacity of his request. My modesty was foolish. All I really wanted was to sleep. So, with Aric glowering before me, I willed my hands to do as he instructed, though I felt as if I'd just drunk a flask of vinegar. As he watched, I fumbled with the buckles and laces of my clothes, slipping off my warbelt and caftan but leaving on my tunic and trousers.

Satisfied, he grunted his assent and peeled off his tunic, hanging it on the antler beside his weapons. I looked away into the fire.

Outside the tent, footsteps approached. A dozen or more, they encircled the tent. Muted voices babbled in whispers and jabs, questions and gibes.

Aric raised his chin to the upper dome of the felt-house, its smoke-hole open to the night sky, and roared in a voice that I was sure could be heard, not only through the walls of felt but through the whole camp. *"In the morning."* The deep, thunderous rumble of it shocked and even frightened me a little. *"Now, go to sleep!"*

The chatter and laughter fell silent. I held my breath. Then the footsteps shuffled away. I began to breathe again, but Aric looked unfazed. "They've heard of your arrival by now," he said. "They will be curious." He continued to undress. "Lay down," he pointed at the pile of blankets I'd made.

Dropping clumsily to my knees, I sat on my heels, sweaty palms on my thighs, looking up at him senselessly. His body was a maelstrom of scars and tattoos, formless and fierce as it sank into the shadows lurking against the wall of the tent. Staring down on me, brooding and grave, he reached for his sword, drawing it slowly forth with the muffled hiss that iron makes within a sheepskin scabbard.

"The dagger you have under your pillow?"

Caught off my guard, I had no words. I thought his back was turned, but somehow, he saw. I never slept without my dagger close, and this place made me want it more than ever.

"What of it?" I managed defiantly, the tremor in my voice belying my boldness.

"You won't need it while I'm near," he said. "But it's a good habit to keep—even better if you can use it." He flashed a crooked grin. "Out here, we sleep facing our homeland," he said, nodding to the western wall of the tent. With that, he touched the sword's blade to his forearm, slicing into the skin until a streak of blood welled up along its edge. Then he placed the bloodied sword between our two beds, the hilt to our heads, and lay down atop his blankets, mere inches away.

My heart settled into a steadier rhythm. I wiped my clammy hands on my trousers, drew a deep breath, and lay down, too, pulling the felt blanket up to my chin. Turning west, I felt his eyes upon the back of me as we lay in the profound silence of the sleeping camp. After a day in the open—the rush of wind, the thunder of hooves, the chatter around the hearth—the stillness exposed my frayed nerves. If not for the wind gently ruffling the tent flaps and the soft breathing beside me, the quiet might have induced panic. It was too hot under the blanket. But I lay there and sweated, like prey gone to ground.

Antisthenes, the steward, began to snore softly.

How did he know about the dagger? He couldn't have seen. He couldn't know if I was a Bastarnian assassin any more than I could know if he was a defiler of women. There was nothing to stop me in the night from taking that dagger or the sword between us and cutting his throat. His head was a most valuable prize. How he rested it so comfortably on his pillow, I couldn't imagine. And now I must rest my head beside it.

CHAPTER 7

GIRL

The same is true with a snake: it may be harmless or venomous. It takes practice spotting the difference. But if you aren't sure, it's wiser to be on your guard than be bitten—it's even better if you know how to cut off its head when it strikes.

ARIC'S BOW, BOOTS, AND SWORD were already gone. The Hellene was gone, too. A bowl of clean water for washing and some porridge above the hearth had been left for me. I lowered the cauldron chain to warm breakfast over the fire while washing myself and my wounds from the previous day's ride. Every part of me ached. But I could finally remove my new trousers. They fit too loosely and rubbed my legs as I rode, causing oozing sores inside my calves and knees. The twill cloth had fused with the flesh in the night and scabbed there. Pulling it free and cutting away the new skin left me in no shape to ride. The sores on my hands were also deep and raw. Gripping reins or weapons today was inconceivable.

Still, I hurried into the rest of my clothes, tied up what was left of my hair, and choked down what I could of the slop in my bowl. Then I strapped on my weapons, retrieved the dagger from under my pillow, and set out into the morning. Outside, all was quiet. The sun was barely up, and no one was around. Not knowing anyone, I decided to search for my horses to see how they fared after a night in their new home. As I headed out to the pastures, I heard the stirrings of a small rabble behind me.

"No wonder Aric looked exhausted this morning. He's been riding all day *and* all night."

The mob laughed heartily at that one. I kept my head down and kept walking.

"Hamazan, eh? Are we supposed to fight her or fuck her?"

More laughter. Riffraff was the same everywhere, and it didn't take long for the crassness to take over. And the vulgarity only increased as they grew more enthusiastic.

I tried to outpace them and reach the pasture before them, but my legs were aching from the previous day's ride, and they gained on me. I refused to turn and look, so I had no sense of how many were following. Clearing my throat, I gathered myself to stand my ground and get the unavoidable confrontation over with. I turned to face them. Nearly two dozen warriors hounded me.

The mob all froze in their tracks and went silent. Could I have shocked them into submission? No, they weren't looking at me but past me. I turned and, coming over the knoll by the pasture, Aric rode his black gelding and led my horse Aruna by a rope halter. He kicked his horse into a canter, rode before the crowd, and ordered one of the young men at the back to run and summon all the kara.

LIFTING THE SPEAR LIKE A SCEPTER, Aric spoke over the pack in a deep, calm, and commanding voice. "Hear me," he called so all three hundred kara could hear. "I will say this once only: This woman before you is Anaiti, daughter of King Arianta of the Bastarnai. She is betrothed to our most noble sovereign. As you see, she wears the iron ring and sacred girdle of our Lord, having sworn her oath in blood before the gods. Indeed, she is one of us until she makes her tally. She is also my guest—and has the protection of my hearth." He paused and let his eye rest on the warrior throng. "Offense to her offends hospitality, the Bastarnai, your king, your karadar, and your oaths to this kara. I trust I need say no more?"

Like scolded dogs, heads dropped. But the crowd issued not a word.

"Speak if any of you object."

There was only transfixed silence, no dubious looks, no murmurs, no whispers. Their eyes were trained upon Aric when he spoke, like loyal dogs upon the words of their master. If any objected, none dared voice it here.

Good enough. I didn't expect the warband to like me. For now, I just needed them to not hurt me.

The men dispersed. Aric had gathered five men around him and called to me as well. Like him, they wore no armor but for the shields slung over their backs. I recognized Olgas, Bornon, and Stormai from the night before. Another warrior, Gohar, joined the party. The fifth was the same scruffy young man who had spoken to Aric beside the hearth when we arrived. He called himself Skopas.

"Ready for your first raid?" Aric asked.

My stomach dropped. "What enemy do we ride against today?" I asked, trying not to sound scared.

The other men looked at one another, then at me, incredulous.

"It comes to us to settle a grazing dispute," Aric said. "We have cattle and other belongings to confiscate, and those we go to rebuke will not give them up easily. Saddle your horse."

"I—I will make myself ready."

"Good. Try not to get yourself killed on your first day." He smirked, and the others chuckled, then turned to gather their horses.

I didn't blame them. I wasn't ready to go out on a raid. But "grazing dispute" didn't sound too ominous. I tacked Aruna, and we set off north with the band upriver at a brisk canter. Aric asked me to ride at the party's head beside him, though he spoke little and not at all to me. The day was warmer than the last, and the ground had dried like a stone underfoot, making the going quicker than on the floodplains. The howling wind had calmed itself to a soft whimper.

There were more flashes of light on the horizon, this time from the north. Aric took the polished bronze mirror from the case on his belt, angled it northward to where the flash was last seen, and, catching a ray of sunlight, flashed a beam of light back. I marveled at this small triumph of ingenuity while we stopped to rest and water the horses briefly. We resumed as the day began to warm, and the morning dew was burning out of the grass.

I'd watched Aric ride all morning as I had the day before. His hands on the reins were firm but forgiving. His seat was natural, neither posing affectedly nor jostling carelessly. He pushed his horses hard but was fair with them, giving them ample water, grazing, rest, and grooming. He saw to their needs before his own, as a good horseman should, and didn't employ a groom though he had many to command. They were settled and calm in his presence and worked hard for him despite how much he demanded of them.

I'd come to the grudging conclusion that he was a good horseman. That was a surprisingly rare thing, let alone for a man whose occupation was slaughter. Many live by horses but understand them little and show them even less regard. A man might feign a good character, but it's a far more difficult task faking the trust of a good horse. Both kings and commoners often went to great pains to learn the horseman's art, for a rider's rank matters nothing to his mount; horses can make fools of all men equally.

I never knew my mother well, but she lived by a simple rule: Know a man by his hands, for mouths may say anything, but hands seldom lie. Watch them long enough, and their actions and deeds will reveal the spirit that guides them. Perhaps no more so than when people handled beasts, where no law but conscience governed them.

THE COLD DAWN had given way to a day gentle and warm—good for hunting. We'd spotted the Tokhari's makeshift campsite, recently abandoned, near the banks of the river. The men had deemed this the final moment to wash their faces and make their invocations before the hunt began in earnest. I should also wash if I was here to take quarry.

"The winds favor us this morning," I said as I led my horse down to the river to drink.

Gohar squinted his deep-set green eyes up at me, his wet face and ruddy beard glistening in the early morning light. "Why, then, do you cover your face with your scarf?" he asked.

His first words to me since my initiation caught me by surprise, filled as they were with genuine curiosity. He wasn't a big man, shorter than the others, but there was something in the measured ease with which he moved that told me he could handle himself— and he knew it. Though his hands were scarred and coarse, witness to countless clashes, his smooth, shining face bore scarcely a mark.

"Well, I'm the only one here without a beard," I said, glancing around before withdrawing the scarf to reveal my own face. "I thought it best to hide the fact."

The raiding party—Gohar, Olgas, Bornon, Skopas, and even the shy one, Stormai—all shared a hearty laugh. All except for Aric, who scowled and, fixing his single, shrewd eye on me, crossed his thick arms over his chest.

"What's so funny?" I asked. "Is that foolish?"

"Beard or no," said lanky Olgas with a wicked grin, "any man can tell you're a woman from miles away."

"What's that supposed to mean?" I said, louder than I intended.

"Ha, what do you think it means?" Olgas said. They all snickered.

I failed to see the humor, and it unnerved me to even think

of it. The last thing I wanted in this place was to stand out—not like that. I had no armor to speak of, and convincing myself of the invisibility the scarf afforded had allowed me to venture this far into the steppe with little thought for my welfare. Only, instead of rendering me inconspicuous, it had done just the opposite.

"Where are we headed, anyway?" I asked, changing the subject.

"The night before we arrived," Bornon said, swiping the water from his bearlike cheeks, "there was a raid a few hours' ride upstream in Skopas's spring camp." He nodded at the quietly smoldering young man who had joined our party this morning. "They didn't just lift cattle and horses. They came into the camp and took a girl—his sister. Men died in the skirmish. Their elder brother among them. Their father, Chief Kasagos, was gravely injured."

"Why would they do this?"

"We had a bad summer," Skopas spoke slowly, restraint in his voice, "then a bad winter. The pastures were bare, and much of the hay that was made molded in the fall."

Silent since we rode from camp, Aric finally roused himself from his brooding and spoke. His tone was solemn, his words deliberate, as if passing sentence. "These many acres of grazing are given into the stewardship of two clans. When the land was granted, both were small households and humble, but they have grown fat over the years through breeding and raids. Too fat. Last summer, I ordered the chiefs to cull some of their stock before winter so neither would overgraze the pastures.

"A wise man knows not to summer more than he can winter. It is the delusion of plowmen to believe the earth's abundance is boundless, but hunters and herdsmen should know better: only by death is life sustained. The chief of the Tokhari refused. Kasagos, foreseeing the misery to come, enacted my decree and slaughtered the excess stock."

"Then, the Tokhari not only defied the law, they sought revenge?" I asked.

"It is so. They tried to seize their rivals' lands—and failed. Now, there will be justice."

"But I thought raiding was permitted?"

"The Skythai raid enemies," Olgas said, "not our own. No new territory or stock will be gained from our tribesmen. What good would it do if the king must feed the bereaved from his own herds and stores come winter?"

"All this over a few head of cattle?" I asked. I knew it was a brutal country, but it seemed an undue amount of blood to shed over a handful of beasts—a dispute which could likely be settled for silver. These men seemed quick to anger and slow to forgive.

"Cattle are wealth," Aric said, "they are life. But *how* a man gains and keeps his cattle decides his honor. Whether traded for honestly, won honorably by conquest, or bred with the blessings of Papahio, one too many can still break a pasture. Soon, all who graze it starve. One is richer today; all be damned tomorrow. It could take years for the land to heal—if it ever does. Even now, the grazing is thin and choked with weeds. To make matters worse, we are cursed with drought. The fields will not support the stock they once did."

"So, the Tokhari broke their covenant. Surely men do not invite anger from the gods and dishonor among their people unless something far greater is to be gained?"

"What is greater than the gods' favor and honor among men?" Aric asked incredulously. "No, greed is the father of improvidence. And some men are simply soft," he said bitterly, and though his face contorted in a kind of grimace, he sounded more disappointed than disgusted. "Weak and self-serving men never fight to expand these borders nor cull their herds so all may thrive. If this land holds pasture enough for just one, who should it be: the weakling or the warrior; the upstanding man . . . or the outlaw?"

I STUDIED ARIC as he stooped to divine some meaning from the faded tracks in the dry grass. Furrowing his brow, Aric squinted into the west. I was a decent tracker, but as I scanned the expanse from the camp into the vast sweep of steppe, I saw nothing on this unyielding ground to betray their route. It's also true that we can scarcely move through this world without leaving some mark, try though we might. What did he see that I did not? I followed the line of his gaze until I spotted it: the faintest hint of a trail, or rather many trails, fanning out across the plain, weaving and winding their way through the soft blades of the field. Watching the wind slowly erase the last traces with each gentle breath. The trail was just a whisper, but it betrayed its makers as they moved deeper into the western steppe, away from their home range.

Aric pointed behind the distant hill on the horizon and said he expected them to take the high ground. They knew we were coming.

I separated from the men to find a secluded place to relieve myself before heading into the open steppe. Skirting the tangle of brambles, I made my way toward the shore and tied Aruna's reins to a branch. As I unfastened my trousers, a shriek shot up from within the brush, nearly stopping my heart. The men came running, their swords drawn, as a disheveled girl of about twelve or thirteen winters broke cover and ran. She didn't get far. Olgas and Gohar rode her down until she threw herself to the ground and cowered with her face in her hands. We gathered around her, and the girl, frozen in shock or terror, gaped at me like a ghost. Whatever the men said, I should have kept the scarf over my face.

Skopas jumped down from his horse and ran to embrace the girl who, it took me a moment to realize, must be his missing sister. Either she had escaped or had become more of a burden to their flight than any ransom could warrant, and they cast her off. But when Skopas drew near, his joy turned to rage at the sight of her scratched skin, bruised face, and bloody dress. His anger seemed more potent than his relief at finding her alive. She flinched at the sound of her name and scurried back under her shrub. Skopas looked genuinely bewildered, but Aric scowled with irritation. He waved his hand at the shrub and signaled Skopas to mount up, reminding us that the Tokhari were gaining valuable ground while we were wasting time.

"You." Aric jutted his bearded chin toward me. "See to her."

Me? "Is this why you brought me?" I demanded. How dare he? And what did that even mean, *see to her*? Did he think I was some kind of nursemaid?

His arm stretched ominously as he pointed upstream toward Skopas's distant encampment. "Be inside before dark. There are wolves about."

I opened my mouth to protest, but Aric and his men had already pulled at their reins, put their heels to their horses, and galloped away west, abandoning me by the river with the pillaged girl.

The only small mercy was that I wouldn't have to take part in the bloody hunt about to ensue. Taking Aruna's reins in hand, I dragged the squirming, squealing girl out from the brush where she had scurried, took her firmly by the sleeve, and marched her down to the banks of the river. There, I pulled what was left of her tunic over her head. I lay my warbelt with my bowcase and weapons on the shore, took off my boots, and waded into the icy water with her, washing her face, arms, legs, and hair with water cupped in my hands.

She had stopped fighting me and slouched, staring into the clear, bright water. When I had cleaned away the blood and filth of her ordeal as best I could, I stripped to my linen tunic and gave her my belted caftan to wear. Then I sat her on the bank in the sunlight, and we both stared into the distance in silence. I couldn't imagine what thoughts, if any, went through her mind.

It seemed as if hours had passed, though I knew they had not, and I watched anxiously for a sign of the men returning over the rise, but there was none.

I tried speaking to her to pass the time. "Those brutes will be punished for what they did. They'll never be able to hurt you again," I said.

Silence.

"I'm sure your mother told you this when your courses began, but if you can find some seeds of wild carrot, you should eat them before you sleep tonight. Even better, drink a tea of rue or pennyroyal in the next few days. A midwife in your clan should have what you need."

The girl just stared as the river flowed by. This was useless. What was I even doing? I didn't belong here, and there was nothing I could do for this girl. I'd done my part, and I imagined just leaving her there. She could find her own way home. Behind me, Aruna cropped the sparse grass. It would be easy just to mount up and go. Find my way back to camp or pick up the men's trail.

I stood up and brushed the grass from my backside.

"Is it hard to kill a man?" the girl broke her silence. She turned her expressionless face up to me and waited, unblinking, for a response.

Not ever having killed, I didn't have an honest answer. "It's easier than dying." That was what my mother had told me when I asked her the same question. "You can do it if you truly want to live."

"If I could fight like the men do—like you—I would."

"I know you would. You're tough. I can see it."

"But how? They are so strong," her voice quavered as she spoke. "Don't we need them to protect us?"

"Men only guard us against other men." That was the simple truth. "There are many good men—most, I think. But not all can be trusted, as you know too well. The same is true with a snake: it may be harmless or venomous. It takes practice spotting the difference. But if you aren't sure, it's wiser to be on your guard than be bitten—it's even better if you know how to cut off its head when it strikes."

The girl nodded.

"Men may offer us protection. But it's good if we can protect ourselves, too. It's never wise to rely on others for the things you need to survive. Here, take this." I handed the girl one of my daggers.

"I don't know how."

"Let me show you." We stood on the bank, face to face, my other dagger in my hand, as I kept the habit of wearing one in my belt and one concealed in my undervest. "Hold it like this, with a firm grip, but not too tight. Keep it close until you're ready to strike. It must be a surprise. And do it quickly. Here," I touched the dagger's tip to my body, "under the ribs, into the lungs or heart—but any organs will do. Then you run. Don't wait for them to die. Just run. Do you understand?"

"I do," the girl nodded vigorously.

"You can do the same in the back, under the ribs, or into a kidney. You have butchered a deer or a goat? A man is much the same inside. A quick, hard thrust, here or here," I pointed to my flanks. The girl was eager and caught on quickly, so I showed her where to strike an armored attacker and what to do if she had no weapon handy. Things my aunt among the Rokhalani taught me when I was near her age training to be hamazan. "It's trickier, but slash the neck here if you can." I drew the blade across my own throat. "Inside the collarbones. The underarms, or the thighs here, where the arteries are shallow. Hamstrings are good as well. Untrained men always forget to defend their legs. You see?"

The girl nodded again.

"Come, show me how you'll do it."

We practiced under the heat of the noon sun. I knew none of these things would have saved her from the horror she'd already faced. But there is no worse feeling than surrendering before the fight even begins.

"Good. You've got it now."

We cupped our hands and drank mouthfuls of cold water, then sat down once more on the riverbank in the tall grass.

"You're a woman today," I said after a silence.

"Because I'm not a maiden anymore?" She frowned.

"No," I shook my head. "No, not that. No one else can make you what you are. You can be a woman with nine winters or a girl with ninety. You're a woman today because now you know how much you can endure—because you can look after yourself. Nobody can give that to you or take it from you."

She smiled to herself and nodded. "Here is your knife."

"It's a dagger. It belonged to my mother, who was a great warrior. And now it belongs to you. Keep it close and use it wisely."

"Mine?" She beamed at the weapon in her hands and appraised her reflection in its mirror face as she slowly turned the flat of the blade to and fro.

I suppressed a smile of my own. "You've earned it. Keep it sharp and practice every day," I added in my best schoolmaster's tone. "Now, let's get you home."

I LED ARUNA by his reins as I followed the girl down the valley to the small farmstead of her father, Kasagos, where a camp of six covered wagons and a felt-house clustered beside the shallow, pebbly river. Sheep and goats grazed a lush patch of pasture, but a wide black swath slashed across the damp soil where hooves had churned up the earth. A freshly made grave stood open on the low hill above the camp's edge, awaiting a funeral.

The family invited me inside the felt-house, giving me the seat of honor beside the altar, a nearly shapeless hunk of stone upon which sat a three-footed wooden bowl with fixed handles carved in the shape of the bronze cauldrons found on most altars. They offered me kumis, and, after some pleasantries, we sat about in pained stillness. The girl's mother sat sobbing quietly to herself as an older woman dressed the girl in her own clothes and gave me back my caftan. Behind them on his bed lay the wounded clan chief, Kasagos, who did not rise or speak.

"Your accent is strange," the girl's mother commented, rousing herself from her sobbing and wiping her eyes.

"Is it?" I pretended ignorance, but I knew I didn't speak Skythian as well as I should.

"Where do your people come from?"

I wasn't sure how much I should tell strangers. My instinct was to be guarded. Since I was a child, my parents had drilled into me to trust no one: speak little and say less. "I was born in the west but fostered in the east." Gripping my cup like an amulet, I dared not look up from its contents. I hoped they would take the hint.

A soft, steady voice broke the silence. It belonged to an elderly woman who sat opposite me and studied me since I arrived. "So, you are Aric's wife?"

"*Me?* I'm—uh, no." That was a staggering thought; I could only begin to imagine the sort of women who populated that man's bed, but I hoped I bore them no resemblance. "I'm here to make my tally." That was what they had called it.

"Hmm, that's too bad. Can't be many fighting women left in these parts."

Left? "Do any remain?"

"A few here and there, though they must be on in years by now. The custom has died out."

"That's unfortunate. I was hoping to find others like me here."

"Unfortunate for us all." She leaned in close, lowering her voice between us to a whisper. "Children forsake their elders and call themselves wise. Heh! Years ago, we all fought. Maybe not all proper like you, but it makes no matter to the wolves who draws the bow. And when the reavers came, I daresay I got a few!" She smiled a broad, toothless grin, and her leathery face crinkled like the palm of an old, worn glove.

"Those must have been harsh times."

"What times aren't? These fields were always filled with stock, and every hand was needed. My brother taught me to shoot and hunt after our father met his end. All the girls rode. None of this sitting inside the wagons like children. No wonder we are prey."

No wonder, indeed.

"If I wasn't so old, I'd still. . . . But we should be thankful for the help we have, such as it is."

I didn't know if she intended an insult as she referred glancingly to Aric and the warband—to me. After all, it seemed it was only after stock was lifted, homes destroyed, victims kidnapped or killed that we were called upon to intervene. By then, the damage had already been done. The band did its best but could not be everywhere.

I don't know how long I sat there with them, waiting. The girl now slept soundly. Dark had fallen, and the men of the warband still hadn't returned. I grew restless sitting in this modest tent with strangers, listening to the moaning, to the sad stories. The old grandmother placed her hand over mine.

"Don't worry for them, my child. Aric and his band have seen worse." She rubbed the little wooden figure of twined serpents that hung about her neck between her thumb and forefinger. "Apia, give them strength."

I hadn't let myself think it until she spoke it aloud. They'd been gone too long. They were only six against the kind of brigands who would rape, rob, and murder their neighbors. What if something *had* happened to them? Not to mention the bleak prospect of finding my way back alone in the dark. I'd wait till morning. Finding the route to camp along the river wouldn't be too difficult if they didn't come by daybreak. But what then? Suddenly, I was so cold and tired that I began to shiver. I rested my weary eyes against my palms and tried to think of other things.

JUST BEFORE MIDNIGHT, Aruna whinnied loudly outside, and a distant horse answered his call. I flew to the door to see the raiding party descending the valley in an easy trot. They drove a small herd of cattle and a few horses into the camp. Kasagos clutched his side as he stood. Peering through the eye that was not swollen shut, he gingerly limped out to meet the warriors, propped on a spear shaft.

Aric brandished a handful of sticky scalps by their long hair, a half dozen by my count, which he thrust into the fist of the chief. I should have been sickened by the sight but was overcome with a perverse sense of satisfaction. Skopas, the son of Kasagos, raised the severed head of a man I could only assume was the Tokhari chief. Though young and unseasoned as a warrior, Skopas appeared sound as he dismounted and embraced his weeping father.

I approached Aric as he dismounted his lathered horse. Filthy, he stank of fermenting sweat and blood.

"Are you all right?" I asked, my weary voice shaking as I surveyed the expanse of gory, torn clothing.

He reached for his side. I held my breath and cringed as he turned to face me. "The bastards, they broke my best whetstone," he said as he plucked it by a leather thong from its holder on his belt and raised a fractured piece on his palm toward my face, the gold-capped end catching the faint moonlight.

"Then you're not hurt?"

"Don't sound so disappointed," he said with a sardonic grin stretched across his face.

I glared at him as hard as I could, but he only laughed. I longed to tell him to fuck himself, but I was afraid he might leave me here in this forsaken place—or worse. He had been charged only with keeping me alive and undefiled. It bore no explicit constraint on punitive measures, and that was a boundary I wasn't eager to test just now.

The chief embraced him, then invited the men, all bloodstained and reeking, to the cramped tent for a drink before departing, hanging the scalps on a hitching post outside the door. Aric and Skopas followed as Kasagos brought the head of the slain chief inside. The other men of the warband gathered around the open door like dogs at dinnertime.

I just wanted this awful day to end. My muscles were still raw from the long ride the day before. Saddle sores split open and wept. Every part of me ached. I needed to wash away the stains of the day from my face and hands and sleep. It was after midnight, and the cold had set in deep. We'd still a few hours ride back in the dark, and camp seemed impossibly far away. I made an excuse of tending the horses.

When it was finally time to depart, Aric found me watering the horses at the river.

"They told me what you did for the girl," he said. "It was a great kindness."

I shook my head furiously. "No," I said, shoving past him to untie Aruna. My eyes filled with tears. "It would have been a greater kindness if they had killed her."

He grabbed me hard by the arm and spun me around, nearly jerking me from my feet.

"*Why would you say such a thing?*" His fingertips bit harder into the flesh of my arm as I tried to wrest myself free.

"Because," I went limp in his grip, "she'll be broken. Haunted by these nightmares the rest of her life."

He drew a hissing breath and frowned as he released me from his grasp with a shove.

Turning away, I mounted my horse and pulled my cloak around me to no avail. Shivering in the dark, tears streaming silently down my face, I waited, desperate to begin the long ride home.

Aric didn't say another word. None of the men spoke. We rode the distance in eerie quiet, with only the horses' weary snorts to break the silence. We cared for the horses and fell into our tents an hour or two before dawn. Pulling off my boots, I threw myself onto my bed without even undressing. Everything hurt as I sank into my pallet, waiting for the last hours of darkness to wash over me.

"You are wrong," Aric's low rumble summoned me back from the brink of merciful oblivion.

"Hmm?" I mumbled groggily.

"I think you're wrong . . . about the girl. In time, she will mend. She may have nightmares, but she knows now how to fight them. You gave her this."

CHAPTER 8

LESSONS

I blinked, and my eyes were blade sharp.
They saw only him.

THE HEARTH BURNED LOW, and the remnants of cheese and lentil porridge simmered in the cauldron. Outside, the camp was humming with activity. Voices rose and fell past the door, iron chinked and clanked, horses whinnied, and every so often, gruff shouts rang out. Peering out the door into the midmorning sun, I saw nothing and no one. I quickly washed and ate, half-afraid of what I'd find once I set foot on the other side of the door. I didn't have the stamina for another expedition.

The men all made their way toward the western pasture. Others had gathered on the knoll, and a commotion rose from their direction, but I could see nothing. With my warbelt bound tight and my weapons by my side, I followed.

Mounting the slope, I climbed up the rise behind the others and traced the sounds of clanging iron. At the top of the rise, I met a wall of men, their backs to me, watching something in the field. I shouldered through the crowd to find brawny Bornon clashing swords with a pup of maybe sixteen winters. I asked the man beside me what was happening. After giving me a long look up and down, he informed me that it was a training day. Raids themselves sufficed for most of our training, but when there was no pressing business at hand, veterans treated younger members to more formal education. Surveying the field sent a little thrill through me. Though I saw no sign of Aric or the Hellene, further afield, men fenced with swords, boxed, grappled, practiced archery. Boys and young men lined up to watch and take their turns. It seemed a ripe opportunity for me to take mine as well.

Before me, Bornon demonstrated guard positions with a sword to a group of young men. I stood with them, listened to his instructions, and watched as he allowed each youth to stand across from him and try his skills. For a stout man, Bornon was surprisingly quick. I'd never seen anyone faster with a blade. When they'd all taken their turns, I stood before him and reminded him of our introduction, when Aric had bestowed his own sword upon me, and humbly asked if he would instruct me in its proper use.

He stood and squared his thick shoulders as he stared at me with his soft brown eyes. Meaty hands gripped the hilt of his short sword. The young men around us glanced nervously from one to the next. He said nothing. Instead, he sheathed his sword and walked away.

I found the same everywhere I went. I approached, but the instructors retreated. I watched and listened, but none of the tutors would train me when my turn came.

WALKING TO THE CENTRAL HEARTH for dinner, I passed a vazarka called Mourdag coming back from the pastures, his linen tunic spattered across the chest with blood. His square face, cut and bruised from fighting, was framed in thick waves like oak bark, and his pale eyes shone like two silver coins.

I looked him in the eyes and nodded, an attempt to be cordial, though he'd been a prick to me earlier, refusing to train me in the boxing square.

Glowering at me, he mumbled, "hamazan witch," as he passed.

"Go fuck yourself," I said, and I intended to leave it at that. But as I walked on, a swell of rage surged up in me. I turned around, marched over to him, and, with a closed fist, bashed him upside his thick head. He swung at me and missed as I ducked. We grappled for a bit, both refusing to let go of the other, and I tried to kick him in the balls. He was too quick, leaping back out of reach. He snarled, drew back his fist, and held it at the ready.

I leaned in and stared him in the face, waiting. "Go ahead, *I dare you*," I goaded him.

He drew his head back, his eyes grew wide, and his face fell slack. "No." He wagged his head and went meek like a scolded boy. "I won't strike a woman."

Still gripping his arm, I dug my nails in as hard as I could. "*Do it!*" I screamed at him, trying my best to rattle his massive frame. "I fucking dare you!"

He released his hold on my arm and thrust me away.

"Coward!" I taunted.

"Oiorpata," he said and spat at my feet. Then he spun around and stomped off, his fists still clenched.

"I thought you were men here!" I shouted after his retreat. "Cunts!"

"YOU'RE DOING A SHITTY JOB OF MAKING FRIENDS," Aric said at our evening meal when I related the incident with Mourdag, wanting him to hear it first from me.

"I'm not here to make friends," I said, holding my bowl out to him as he scooped a revolting brown slop from the cauldron. "I'm here to train—so I can learn to fight enemies." I slumped beside him on a reed mat spread over the grass with my bowl of slop.

"These men are not your enemies."

"Has anyone told that to them?"

He stared ahead and chewed.

I dropped my spoon into my bowl. "How am I supposed to learn or grow stronger if no one will train me?"

He turned to face me, his hand propped on his thigh. "*You* need *us*. We don't need you. Look," he gestured to the others seated around the fire, all engaged in their own talk. "Who sits with you now? Who speaks with you? They don't care who your father is or why you're here. You want their fellowship, you'll have to earn it."

His words stung because he wasn't wrong. "How?"

"You'll try again tomorrow. If you're sure you're ready?"

I looked him in the eye. "I'm ready."

"We'll see."

"NO MATTER HOW STRONG YOU ARE," Aric said, his fists raised, shoulders like a bull's, forearms knotted like the cords of a rope, "most men will be stronger."

He stood opposite me on a flat patch of ground just after dawn, stripped of weapons—as was I. Dew soaked the grass, and the morning smelled of wet wool and cooking fires. A crowd of spectators swarmed around us.

"This is simply a fact," he said. "Even men who are small and thin might still surprise you. Don't think, because you're tall and fit, it's enough."

"I understand." Disconcerting as his words were—unfair as they were—I knew he was right.

"In battle, skill with a horse and a bow level the field. But a man's size and muscle are his advantage on the ground. Learn yours. Keep him at a distance as long as possible. Know where he's vulnerable. Always keep your dagger and sagaris close. If he is one-quarter bigger, you must be smarter or quicker by half. These are your advantages. Most of all, *be ruthless*. Never hesitate. Never flinch. Never yield. Is this clear?"

"It is."

"A man is more vulnerable than you in other ways. Use that."

"You mean go for the balls?"

A smile broke his grim expression as he nodded. "He'll guard them well, but," he chuckled, "go for the balls. And the eyes."

I cringed, finding it hard then to meet his eye.

"Anything delicate you can get your blades, fingers, fists, knees, or feet into. Be ruthless. You must remember: In battle, the prize is life. Never expect mercy from your enemies. Are you ready?"

"As I'll ever be. . . ."

"Then come and strike me—if you can." Aric circled slowly around me like a wolf late to a kill. I moved around him, too, but striking him without cause felt ignoble. My hands were dead.

"Come on! Make your move," he said, his rasp more forceful.

This is what I asked for. If I couldn't do it, I'd never earn the men's respect. I stepped in and swung at him with all my strength, which he easily sidestepped. Quicker than I imagined. *Shit.*

"All right," he said. "But a big move will be seen and ducked. Punch from the center of your chest. There's no dodging that. Try again."

I circled a half turn and tried again, darting forward and landing a good blow to his breastbone before he could duck. I didn't want to hurt him. But the sensation was profoundly satisfying— the impact shuddering through my hand, up my arm, into my ribs.

He swung his fist and caught me hard in the shoulder, throwing me back a half step. A murmur rose through the crowd.

"Quick, come again," he barked as I recovered my footing.

I stepped forward and jabbed again from the center, this time catching him in the jaw.

As the first blow glanced off my browbone into my right cheek-bone, I turned away. But the next flew so fast, I barely saw it coming. Square into my nose and mouth. Before I could block. Before I could blink.

Pain didn't frighten me, nor injury. Living around horses all my life, I'd had more than my share of broken bones and bruises. I'd been knocked about, trampled, kicked. Not to mention all the falls. But nothing could have prepared me for the feeling of a powerful man throwing his fists into my face. Of waiting in expectation of it. Of seeing it come, unable to duck fast enough. The force and sting of it. Radiating across my whole face and into my stomach. The loss of equilibrium. The way my teeth rattled in my skull. Seeing my own blood spatter across my breast. The taste of metal. All this in the space of a breath.

I reeled backward and, staggering, caught myself before I fell. I blinked, and my eyes were blade-sharp. They only saw him. His eye locked on mine, his fists poised. He nodded his readiness almost imperceptibly. I lunged. Seized his beard with my left hand, pulling him to me and me to him. With my right fist, I shot three sharp punches to his nose, his eye socket, his mouth. I leapt back, still clutching strands of his beard in my fingers. He didn't budge or flinch. His nose was bloody, his lip split and a cut on his brow bled down his cheek. He grinned broadly, blood smeared across his teeth.

"Ha, ha, that's it!" He stepped toward me.

I retreated as he advanced, fists up again. He spat a mouthful of blood and held up open hands in a gesture of peace. I braced myself as he came near and grabbed hold of my hand.

"You can strike here," he said and pressed the edge of my open hand to his windpipe.

Like the mane of a well-groomed horse, his beard's copper hair was fine and soft to the touch. But he was still speaking, and I quickly shook off such distractions.

"Also, when you punch to a bony place, especially the nose, you can use the heel of your hand."

He turned my hand over in his and pressed his great palm to mine. My hands were by no means small or delicate, but they were still dwarfed beside his. I then understood just how much injury he could have inflicted if he had truly wanted to hurt me.

"It does more damage, and you won't harm your hand. You can throw all your weight behind it."

I swallowed the blood in the back of my throat. "Thank you."

"You've made a good start today. Go and clean yourself. We have a patrol to ride." He slapped me hard on the back, and I tried not to wince. "Next time, Bornon will show you swords," he said pointedly.

When I turned to see the men assembled, they were all gaping. Blood still poured from my nose and mouth, which I wiped on my tunic sleeve. Some frowned; others looked bewildered. But none probably more bewildered than I.

RAVENOUS BUT NOT EAGER to face the others, I dragged myself to the hearth for our evening meal when we returned from our patrol. Worn and battered, Gohar was the first to approach, his expression grim. I slowed and braced for whatever came next.

He handed me a drinking horn full of mead. "You look like you could use this," he said, a grin slowly spreading over his weathered face. "Ha, the woman who stood against Aric . . . and lived!"

I sighed in relief. "Thanks."

"I can't decide if you're brave or stupid," Gohar said.

"Ask me tomorrow?"

"Heh," he jabbed at me with his elbow, spilling my mead. "Look here!" he shouted to the other men. I was about to protest, being too tired for whatever bullshit was about to be hurled my way. I just wanted to eat and maybe drink in peace, then fall into my bed without any more strife. But before I could stop him, he grabbed me by the arm and, spilling more of my precious mead, dragged me into the circle of the firelight. I was too weary to resist. "Look who's shed her first blood of combat today." To my great astonishment, most of the men stood and began to shout a cheer as they raised their horns.

I looked up from my half-empty horn and saw them all drinking to me. *To me.*

It was foolish, but the sound of it warmed me from within and made me hum inside like a tree full of bees. For the first time all day, I forgot my swollen face and the sting of my bruises—forgot the sting of the day before—and downed my first cup of mead with them.

AS I PREPARED FOR BED, a little drunk from all the mead, Aric called me over to sit beside the hearth.

"Here, let me see." He squeezed the bridge of my nose.

"Ouch." I winced hard. "That hurts."

"You're fine," he said softly.

I didn't fool myself that the quiet in his voice was the product of sympathy but rather the protocol of nighttime.

"It's not broken. Your eyes will swell and blacken, but it will heal."

"I don't mind," I whispered and looked at the floor, unsure how to say what I wished to. "I'm grateful, truly."

"Grateful?"

"Not for the bruises. But that you don't treat me like . . ."

"Like what?"

"A girl."

He furrowed his brow and regarded me a long moment. Then turned to stare into the fire. "It's nothing."

CHAPTER 9

HORSE

*The noble horse was a great appraiser of man's
character, which is why so many went to such
pains to break the proud creature in body and
spirit—to spare themselves the truth.*

AFTER A MORNING SCRUBBING LAUNDRY in the river, my reward was to join Aric and his Hellenic steward, Antisthenes,
on an outing beyond camp. Aric and some of the kara had been
away the past few days on raids. I'd stayed behind with Bornon and
the pups, studying the ancient art of sword dancing. I relished the
rigors of training but also welcomed some rest. Today, we would
ride northwest with a small party into the uplands, searching for
deer in the early evening.

I'd just stuffed my gloves in my belt, taken down my goryt, and
added arrows to my quiver when a guttural bellow rose from the
direction of the pasture. "What is that awful noise?" I asked in
horror, knowing the answer: it was a horse's anguished cry.

"Tarana captured a stallion from the wild herd last night. He
and some other men have been trying to break him all morning."

I ran beyond the circle of tents and wagons to see the source of
the commotion. Sure enough, a gathering of men stood around a

light bay who'd been haltered and lashed to a post. They'd hobbled him, though that did little to prevent him from bucking off the rider clinging desperately to his back.

"They're never going to break him that way," I said to Aric, who had walked up beside me.

"No?"

"They might wear him down. Get him to submit for an hour, a month, a year. But one day, he'll turn. A horse broken like that can never be truly trusted. They should turn him loose."

"They'll kill him first."

Not if I could help it. I marched to where the beast stood tied and called out to Tarana, the man with the rope in his hands. "Let me have a turn. I want to try."

A wiry man with dirty blond hair and a deep scar on the bridge of his nose, Tarana was a vazarka, though there was nothing remarkable about him that I could see. Why Aric had promoted this scrawny creature to the fellowship of twelve who served as his council and bodyguard was a mystery to me. Was he clever? Insightful? Loyal? Brave? It clearly wasn't his competence with horses.

"Heh, you think you can break him?" Tarana refused to turn and look at me when he spoke.

"I know I can."

"Bullshit. We've all tried. You'll get your taste tonight. Let us have our sport in peace."

"Afraid I'm right?"

"He's not even fit for the fighting arenas. He'd kill you."

"What's it matter to you?"

"It doesn't. You wanna kill yourself, it's not my problem. But Aric won't like it."

"Ask him." I glanced back to where I'd left Aric to see him standing with his arms folded across his chest. "He'll agree. I want a turn, like all the others. If he kills me, you all get a good laugh. But if I ride him, he's mine."

He paused to consider my offer. "All right, then. Suit yourself. Looks like someone's gonna get broken today after all." Tarana looked back at Aric, who waved his hand in acquiescence, if not exactly approval. His confidence in me was heartening.

"And just what makes you think you'll be able to break him," Rathagos, my gadfly, asked, "when none of us could?" He'd been attempting to help Tarana with the horse and had a fresh lump growing on his low brow to show for it. It made him look even more brutish than he did the night he tried to humiliate my father and called my presence here an insult to the gods. With his many years of experience, Father made swatting gadflies look easy.

"I only asked to try. I've trained all my father's best horses."

"And riding a king's finest steeds makes you a breaker of horses, does it?" Rathagos punctuated his statement with a thrust of his bristled chin.

"Wild or captive makes no difference," I said. "Horses are horses."

"Horse training is hazardous work. It's not fit for girls."

"We'll soon see."

It amused me what a tenuous proposition gallantry often was. Whom did it seek to protect? Back home—in secret and openly—people called me stable boy, groom, horsefucker. I wore those unladylike names as a mark of honor—an armor. And they could hate me for it all they liked, but I was a horseman, and that was all I ever wanted to be. Partnership with a powerful, unrestrained creature brought mankind deep into a primal dance with nature. When harmonious, nothing was more sublime. When transgressed, nothing was more brutish. The noble horse was a great appraiser of man's character, which is why so many went to such pains to break the proud creature in body and spirit—to spare themselves the truth.

I approached the sweating horse tied to the post gently, eyes lowered in truce. He had a burnt ocher coat, long black legs, a thick black mane and tail, and a crooked blaze like a lightning bolt running down his long, sharp face. His flanks heaved, and his nostrils flared as he rolled his eye and turned his ear to me, but he stood square and firm on all four legs.

Bound to a post by a rope halter, his front legs were hobbled. Rope burns cut into his neck, fetlocks, and above his hocks. Raw and oozing, they drew flies. Dried sweat whitened his neck and back. A thin, tight cord like a noose gelded him. No wonder the poor creature was ready to fight. All morning, they said, he'd been tied and whipped, hobbled and mounted. He'd battled, bucking, rearing, throwing his whole body to the ground to rid himself of his riders. Man after man took his turn, trying to wear him down.

I admired his rebellion. It's easier to submit to force and fear, and tyrants don't celebrate the will; they lay siege to it. This was a fierce and brave creature, indeed.

They called him Vatra after their god of obstruction—a name usually spoken like a curse. As I approached, his neck arched and ears flattened to create an elegant arc from nostril to wither, like a serpent ready to strike. I came slowly at his shoulder, outside the range of feet and teeth, and gently touched his tense and sweating neck. His expression softened as I stroked his neck, but he remained wary.

"No more stalling," Tarana said. "Time to ride." He and Rathagos moved forward with a lariat.

"No, don't," I said, motioning them away.

"Second thoughts? I told you she was all talk." Many of the men laughed.

"I'm going to untie him. No ropes. No hobbles."

"That's madness. He'll get away."

"He won't," I said, untying his lead rope from the post. "We're going inside the wagon fort."

INSIDE THE RING OF WAGONS and tents was a circle about thirty paces across. The hearth where we dined stood at the center. With the entrance closed, the wagons made a high wall around the circle's perimeter from which nothing could enter—or exit. The horse would be corralled inside with me. I took the doeskin gloves from my belt and slipped them on as the men gathered around to watch. Their eyes bored into me from all sides. But if I acknowledged the weight of expectation, I'd collapse beneath it. I must become blind to all but the horse.

Once inside the clearing, I unfastened his hobbles. Stepping back, I allowed him to run to the end of the long rope tied to a simple rope halter. I stood quietly at the center and watched him run, remembering what freedom felt like. Free for the first time all day after having been lashed to a post and tortured, he tore away and let loose with a series of bucks and shrieks, galloping madly around the perimeter of the space.

When he'd got all his bucks out, he settled and began investigating his surroundings. Blowing out through his nose and flagging his tail high as he pranced past, he was shy of the tents and the noisy men, and so his interest gravitated closer and closer toward me, the quiet human who stood at the center. He came gradually nearer, picking at tufts of grass, snorting at the ashes in the hearth, and spooking himself knocking over a cauldron. Few animals are as curious—or downright nosy—as horses.

Finally, he approached me. Then retreated. And approached again. I stood still and let him decide if I was trustworthy. Letting him come to me. Soon, he came close enough to sniff at me. When he didn't spook, I spoke quietly to him and let him smell my hands. Then touched his shoulder softly until he no longer flinched. Then I began to stroke his neck and scratch his withers with my fingertips. With his lip, he ruffled my hair.

He balked and bolted in short bursts a few times, but I let him flee from me and gently reeled him back in, petting and speaking to him. Though anxious, he soon quieted. He walked briskly, and forward motion seemed to comfort him, so I used the rope to keep him in a small circle around me, always staying just behind his shoulder to herd him forward and keep him from turning.

When he had settled, I gently applied pressure to the rope, asking him to bend his head and neck toward me, and then released it. Just enough to turn his eye to me. As he relaxed and stretched, I gave him more rope to widen the circle, continuing to loosen his tense neck with the rope. I kept speaking to him to accustom him to the commands of my voice. "Walk; trot; halt."

Soon enough, he stretched out his frame in a long, easy walk. Then I clucked and asked him to trot, swinging the end of the rope toward his tail, and he moved around me in an easy jog on the full circle and shook his mane. He was a fine specimen once he settled. Tarana would be loath to lose him, I mused with a smile.

When I reeled him in on a smaller circle, he lost speed. I stepped in front of his shoulder, and when I said, "Halt," he came to a quiet stop, letting me approach to stroke his neck and rub his mane. He touched his soft muzzle to my cheek.

Suspicion, intelligence, and a great desire for tenderness lay beneath his fierceness. Horses want only to understand what's expected of them so they can go through their days without confusion or pain. To do their work and retire at the end of the day with their companions and a full belly. They want to be good, not because it's right, but because it makes life tolerable. Maybe, in the end, that's all "good" is.

Working slowly and patiently, it all took an hour or two. The men watched quietly as I worked, mainly at a walk. I stopped him often to stroke his neck and speak softly to him. I looped the other end of my rope through his halter to make reins. He stretched his neck for another rub, and I lay across it, patting him. He didn't flinch, so I then lay my body across his back. Still no reaction. I swung my leg over and sat upon him, keeping my chest low to his withers and rubbing his neck.

Around the circle, all the men—even Tarana and Rathagos—were silent.

I sat up straight. "Walk on," I said, and Vatra walked a tiny circle, led by the rope reins and halter. "Halt," I spoke to him, and he stopped in his tracks. I slid from his back, patted his neck, and let him rub his sweating face on my caftan.

In the silence of the onlookers, we walked to face Aric, who stood mute and indifferent, his arms crossed over his chest, his jaw set, his narrowed eye fixed on us.

I held the reins out to him in an offering of peace.

He eyed me up and down. "Keep them. A deal is a deal: Vatra is yours. But, tomorrow, you teach this to me."

THE HELLENE EMPTIED THE BASKET of fuel bricks into the fire as we made ready for bed. The scent of burning grass filled the room.

"We're running low on fuel," he said to Aric and ducked out of the tent.

Aric waved him off and chuckled as he unbuckled his goryt and hung it on the peg above his bed. "That was an impressive trick today," he said.

"It's no trick."

"Where did you learn to handle horses like that?"

"My father had a lot of horses through his stables," I said, placing my saddle against the wall behind my pallet. "I always felt for the ones too wild or sensitive to be ridden—they suffered terribly and eventually became food. So, I would take them on."

"Why would you bother?" He shrugged off his caftan and folded it neatly beside his pallet.

"And do nothing?"

"Maybe some are better off as food."

"I've begun to wonder if you're right. It's unkind teaching animals to trust us."

He stopped undressing and turned to me. "How do you mean?"

"I'm fair with them. So, they forget their wariness." I hung up my warbelt beside his. "But they should be wary. The next man won't be so kind. It feels like a cruel deception."

"At least they know *some* kindness in this life," he said, pausing to peel off his tunic. I looked away. "Which is more than most get in this world. Perhaps, having taught them to do their duty and be reliable, others will find no cause to show them unkindness. Is it not the same with children?"

It was possible. I never counted much on the goodness of people. But I hoped, for their sake, he was right.

"How would you normally break in a young horse?" I asked.

"Me? I take a colt into the river, where the water is as deep as its chest, and the current is strong. Then, I mount it against the current and hold it until it stops fighting me, letting the water do most of the work. When it submits, I ride it to shore."

"Isn't that dangerous? What if the horse panics and you are swept away by the current?"

He shrugged. "I can swim. And then I find out early which are the untrustworthy horses."

I had to admit there was a grim sort of pragmatism to it. Any horse that would rather scuttle itself in a river than be ridden probably wasn't worth much out here.

"Why didn't they just do that with Vatra?"

"Maybe because the river is low with the drought. Or because, though they are my brothers, they are fools," he snickered, and I laughed louder than I should have. He cocked his head and looked at me, his brow scrunched in bemusement. "You love them."

"Horses? They're honest. To have two minds, two wills, two forms—and somehow unite them toward a single purpose. Only the pure heart of the horse makes this possible."

"You don't believe humans capable of this?"

"A human who is kind and fair to a horse or a dog can trust in that animal's loyalty for life; can the same be said of the human?"

"Then, you trust no one?"

"Do you?"

He chuckled. "I've never heard anyone say the things you do."

"No? Then you must think I'm mad."

He chewed his lip and squinted at me. Then smiled inscrutably as he drew his sword and nicked his arm before laying it between us. "I think you'll drive *me* mad."

CHAPTER 10

SWORDS

*If they should capture her, it will be far worse
than anything you or I could ever do.*

H E LOOKED TENTATIVE, unconvinced, as he weighed the wooden sparring sword in his hand. I adopted a defensive stance and took up the ox guard, the hilt of my own sparring sword gripped in my right hand and raised to my right cheek, the point facing outward over my shield, toward his face, and waited. He didn't move.

Short swords like the akinaka were easy to carry on horseback, but they meant fighting in close. An unhorsed Skythai meant a desperate Skythai. His bow was his weapon of choice, then his spear, then his sagaris—the light, spiked axe, best wielded from a horse's back or as a projectile. He was likely in dire straits when he found himself on foot with a sword in hand.

I made a slight advance, which he mirrored but did not strike. So, I attacked first with a test cut, which he deflected easily. We traded a few simple thrusts and parries. He struck weakly, allowing me to block each blow with my shield.

He was playing with me. I watched for an opening, but none came. His form was perfect, and, for a big man, his movements had an effortless grace that made it seem almost like a dance. Round and round we went, trading blows, blocking one another, to the music of clashing swords.

"You don't have to go easy on me, Bornon. Really, it's all right."

"I just want to show what you've learned," he answered. "Close your stance and remember to face front." He made a circle with his fingers in front of his belly as he faced me. "Belt toward your opponent. Your feet and shoulders may move, but never your center. This is your balance. Your strength." He resumed his side guard.

"Right." I adjusted myself, eager to perfect my skills.

"Good work, Bornon," Aric said, smiling. "You've put her through her paces."

He picked up a sparring sword from the box beside our make-shift arena and, without delay, lunged at me, stabbing down at my chest. I leapt aside just in time and came around with a strike toward his flank, but he turned aside and checked me with his shoulder, nearly toppling me. I stepped forward and around him instead of back and struck again, almost catching him across the hamstring. He leapt clear and put some distance between us.

"Good!" Aric said. "You nearly had me." He was beaming, a rare sight that caught me off guard.

He came for me more quickly than I predicted and struck hard from above. I deflected the first strike with my shield, but he was quick to close any openings, and again he was moving. He left me a space, but it was too obvious. I knew well enough by now it was a trap. I didn't take it. Nor did I let up, but feigned a step to his right, only to strike on his left, catching him sharply across the cheekbone with the pommel of my sword. While he reeled, I pushed in with my point, ready to slip my blade behind his shield and stab down above his exposed collarbone. And withdrew my attack.

"Excellent," he said, massaging his jaw.

My head swelled with his praise so that I nearly failed to block a swift blow from above. He rushed me and checked me hard with all his weight. My feet flew from under me; I spun and fell hard, face-first on the ground. Gasping for air, I lay prone, cursing myself for stupidity.

Struggling to my knees, Bornon ran to my side and offered his hand. Hunched, with my hands braced on my knees, I fought to catch my breath. Aric barked at me, but I didn't need his reprimand to make me feel even more of a fool. I averted my gaze from him as he shouted in his restrained way, but I could feel my face burning with anger—at him for his scolding and at myself for my mistake. I already knew where I had gone wrong. Bornon warned me time and again about falling into the trap of perpetual defense. *Stupid.* I'd let one good stroke go to my head.

"You're too hard on her, Aric! Back off." Bornon showed none of Aric's restraint when he shouted. He stood face to face with Aric, though a head shorter, and let his displeasure be known. His manner softened as he turned to me. "Are you all right?"

"The enemy will not be forgiving," Aric said. "If they should capture her, it will be far worse than anything you or I could ever do."

"It's fine," I gasped, still aching in my chest. "I'll never progress if he doesn't test me." I wanted another chance to prove myself.

"Still, I don't like it," Bornon said. He was kind, and I respected him as a tutor and swordsman. But he never coddled the boys this way. It was clear: he thought me weak.

"Come for me again," I said, struggling to my feet. I raised my eyes to Aric, breathing steadily in and out to calm the burning in my chest and focus my thoughts. I braced myself for another blow, determined to show him just how tough I could be. But before it landed, I saw Bornon in the corner of my eye turn and walk away. In my distraction, Aric knocked me to the ground again.

THE DAY DISSOLVED SLOWLY into an indigo twilight. Only a pale, rosy glow lingered at the edge of the western plain. Already, the moon and stars rose in the east. We'd only moved to this new buna many miles south and made camp by late morning. With tents packed on the wagons, we drove herds down the valley just after sunup to a quiet place on a sweeping bend in the snaking river. Here, the pasture was fresh, and the climate was cooler. This buna stood midway between our last camp and what would eventually be our midsummer camp further north across the highlands above the Pantikap River valley, where trade and raiding were sure to pick up toward the end of the season. Gohar and Olgas had gone hunting while the rest of the three hundred warriors and the young novices chocked the wagons and erected the felt-houses. It took only a few hours with so many hands. We spent the rest of the day in sport while we waited for the hunters to arrive so we could build the fire and start the evening meal.

When Gohar and Olgas finally returned with their kill, they were greeted with much pomp. The stag they shot was carried to the site of the future hearth, where it was butchered. Its hide was stripped and placed in a cauldron, mixed with its brain for tanning. Its head, which was not permitted to touch the ground, was mounted upon a pole at the center of camp. Its heart was buried in a pit in the earth. Over this, the vazarka Galati, who seemed versed in the ways of sacrifice and proper invocations, spoke words of thanksgiving, and a prayer was offered to the spirits of the place, asking permission for our stay. Then the site where the heart lay was heaped with dried grass, the stag's bones were arrayed over this, and the whole thing was set to light.

Soon a great fire roared at the center of our new camp where those not on watch gathered for their evening meal. Tonight, the venison Gohar and Olgas shot roasted in a cauldron over the fire. The liver went to the hunters, tender backstraps to the kara-daranaka and the vazarka, and the remaining cuts were dispensed according to honor. A stew was made from the rest. Being new and unproven, I ate stew with the other novices.

"Your training is progressing," Aric said as we sat down to eat, much to my surprise after the disastrous showing earlier that day.

His lip was split, and he had a shadow on his cheek where I struck him with the pommel of my sword. It would probably bruise. *Good.* I smiled secretly. I would have plenty of bruises from him. It made the soreness in my muscles a little sweeter.

"I'm trying."

"And you're getting on with Bornon? He's not neglecting your education?"

"No—I mean, he is not. He's a good teacher. Very patient with me."

"Good. He frightens a lot of the pups. And a lot of women," he added with a little chuckle.

"Not me. Bornon has a kind eye."

"Ha," he laughed now in earnest—a deep, rich rumble from within his chest as his cheeks dimpled and his eyes crinkled softly, "you speak of men the way others speak of horses."

"Do I?" I asked, a little embarrassed. I had shunned most people most of my life; animals were all I really knew. "Everything you need to know about a horse is in the eyes. I reckon a person is no different; there is a beast inside every man."

"And what do you see in my eye?" he asked, fixing me in a soft-eyed gaze. "What manner of beast dwells within me?"

"You think me a fool?" I accused jokingly. "Even if I knew, I wouldn't dare say." The truth was, I had no luck in reading him. He confounded me, and that was rare.

He tilted his head back and let out a soft chuckle. "Fair enough! Though, one day, I will have my answer."

"Answer me this: what did you mean when you spoke of my capture?"

"Just that *you* must be especially careful here in the Wild Fields. Counting all the beasts and men that walk the earth, the hamazan have more enemies than friends."

"When I was young, my father warned me nearly every time I left the hall about the slavers lurking in dark corners waiting to capture and sell me. I always thought he was just trying to frighten me into minding him." I smirked, remembering his wild stories of scoundrels who snatched little girls and sold them to dirty old men in foreign lands—the irony of my present circumstance not lost on me. "Is that what you're doing?"

"No, he was right. Being captured could get you sold along to a slaver rather than ransomed if the price is right. Maybe I *am* trying to frighten you; you should be afraid."

"But the Skythai also sell prisoners captured in battle."

"It is so. The Skythai may sell a man—or woman—but we never buy one. We often send our enemies far from our lands if anyone will pay for them. But we have our honor. And we will not be served by any man but that he does so willingly. It ensures that both the work and the men are equally honorable—a wisdom won long ago through sore treachery and disgrace. The man who purchases a woman for sport is most pathetic of all; he is twice dishonored."

"What's wrong with men that they do these things?"

"If I knew that. . . ." He raised his brows and smirked as he speared his venison with a tiny bronze trident and sliced off a small piece. The kara believed that meat provided by the gods and spirits of the wilderness should be treated with a certain reverence, and after being cooked in the sacred fire, it might be defiled by hands, so must be eaten from knives, spoons, or prongs. Aric set the slice between his teeth, chewing thoughtfully.

"You spoke of ransom?"

"Dangerous enemies are killed on the field. Less dangerous captives are sold. However, where peace may be bartered, valuable prisoners are usually ransomed."

"You'd pay my price?"

He grinned with one side of his mouth like perhaps it was an unprofitable option. "We take care of our own," he offered at last.

"And the ones that don't bother with ransom?"

He stopped slicing and turned to fix me in his gaze. "I will

OF WIND AND WOLVES

not let that happen. Besides, our enemies know our wealth, and we keep our word. Any man who raises the cry of *Zirin* must be granted safe passage as a ransom-bearer. It is a law as old and sacred as the stars. But if I should fall in battle, seek out those twelve men you met that first night. The vazarka are sworn to protect me. They are bound also to protect you."

I searched around the fire for their familiar faces. Perhaps Aric gave them too much credit. It seemed unlikely that any group of men, much less this feral pack, would feel compelled to protect me in the absence of their lord's command. I did not doubt their loyalty to him, but they couldn't be expected to give up their treasure for me. A few might even look to sell me themselves. "And if *they* should fall?"

"Then, you must decide a fate for yourself."

"I know which I would choose." I clutched my sword hilt. Hardly a choice.

"It's easy to make bold claims, but many—most even—choose otherwise. The slave markets are full of men and women who chose life. There's no shame in it. There can even be honor—look at Antisthenes. No man bore his servitude with more dignity and fortitude than he."

"*Antisthenes was a slave?*" I whispered as if it were a secret. I looked at him, seated among some older novices across the firepit, smiling and chatting. Though I was loath to admit such a thing of a Hellene, I'd met few men of such forbearance and grace. It was impossible to imagine.

"He was." Aric sliced off a juicy piece of his tenderloin and offered it to me. "But that's his story to tell."

110

MAN-EATERS

No one has a right to be innocent in this world.

THE RIVER BROKE TOWARD THE DAWN, and the plain before us stretched barren and empty into the north. We pulled up our horses before a line of a dozen or so mounds—some large, some small—which stood along the western bank of the river. Taking each grave in turn, Tarana led the men in a recitation of the names of each chief and warrior who slept beneath the barrows, along with each man's deeds of renown. The novices were encouraged to repeat these names and verses so they should not be forgotten. When this remembrance was through, Aric nudged his grey gelding, Tura, out before the trading party and faced us.

Addressing the company, he explained that we had cattle, salt, and a little gold to trade for timbers, charcoal, grain, and fine furs, which were valuable for exchange further south. But there was an expanse of unwatered steppe to cross before we reached the easternmost Geloni settlement. We'd have to pass through a lower portion of Mardia, the territory held by the savage Mard-Khwaar—the Man-Eaters.

I didn't know what they called themselves, but that was the tribe's name in every other country. They hunted men for sport and consumed them with gusto. Rumor of them was enough to ensure children everywhere were home before dark. But to see one? Actually meet a Man-Eater in the flesh? That was something I'd not prepared for in coming here.

Once we crossed beyond these mounds and into the lightly forested region, we'd be in the domain of the Man-Eaters. Aric explained that, as part of an uneasy truce made in his grandfather's time, we could travel their realms and use their wells and streams, but we could not unbridle our horses or allow them to graze freely, for that was considered a claim to the land. We must assume we were being watched, keep the cattle moving, water and feed only as needed, and hurry to the nearest Geloni trading station.

THE FIRST STOP OF OUR JOURNEY across this cursed territory was a well. The land was poorly watered; there were no rivers or streams for many miles, and the cattle, in particular, needed water along the journey. There was but one road to travel and one well to water at. Amid the riverless valleys, it sat in a depression surrounded by low hills on which yellow broom was flowering. We reached it around midday, and the animals were desperate with thirst.

We dismounted and let the horses come to the well first, our eyes on the horizon for signs of movement—of dust stirring or branches quivering on the hillside. One by one, the horses lowered their heads, sniffed the water, snorted at it, and refused to drink.

"Something is wrong," I said. "This well is fouled." A dog will drink from any filthy puddle. A horse will only drink clean water.

"There's no other water for miles," Olgas said, sounding more angry than worried.

"Could it be tainted?" Gohar asked, squinting his deep-set green eyes.

"Does it matter?" Mourdag replied. "If we push on now and do not overtax the horses, we'll just make it. The cattle might be a little worse for it, but they'll live."

"It matters," Aric said. "We must know what we ride into."

"It could be the drought," Bornon suggested, wrinkling his brow and peering down the well shaft.

Hoping the water had just grown stagnant, I turned the wheel to bring fresh water to the well's low trough. When I drew up the bucket from the depths of the shaft and tipped it, spilling its contents back into the trough, the source of the water's foulness revealed itself as the water drained away. The bucket contained a human skull.

RETURNING BITTER AND EXHAUSTED from the failed trading expedition, we gathered for our evening meal: more beef or mutton stew. I couldn't tell the difference anymore. There had been no wheat or barley for two days, and the lentil and onion stores ran low. The men ate in silence. We had plenty of bay salt but no one with which to trade it. The scrap iron we had left from Ariapaithi's famed mines was better than any bog ore we could get from the north, but it was not enough for new weapons. And with no wood or charcoal, there would be no blacksmithing—neither repairs nor tools nor weapons made.

There were other places to trade if we moved camp farther south. But my thoughts kept returning to the well. I knew little of the tribes in this place or the conflicts that drove them. It seemed a leap to assume the Man-Eaters had poisoned the well when several bands might have passed that way, and many had cause to stir up trouble. But then, who else might it be? The uncertainty gnawed upon the calm of the mind. Tired as I was, I had no appetite.

I was not alone. I'd never seen the men so morose. Even Aric was more sullen than usual. Though, being a wise leader, he saw that the camp always had enough drink on hand. This bitter turn of events called for something sweet, and Antisthenes had prudently produced the stores of mead. I grabbed a jug and brought it to Aric to refill his drinking horn. He looked up and smiled curiously as I held the jar toward him, then raised his horn to me. In the sudden silence, all chatter had ceased. I looked around to find the men's eyes were on me, having stopped in their eating, and now I felt very foolish for serving Aric like a common wench. I filled his cup, and then he spoke.

"I am Aric, son of Ariapaithi, Warden of the East March, protector of the Skythai, bane of oathbreakers, and I will see these outlaws punished," he said to me and then lifted his horn, let his eye pass over all those gathered, and drank of the mead.

The men were stunned, expectant even, and they seemed to be waiting for something as they stared in silence. Then, the vazarka all set aside their meals and rose to their feet with their drinking horns clasped in their hands. I couldn't guess what rite I had unintentionally initiated, only that I must now serve the rest of them. Glancing nervously toward Aric, I saw the corners of his mouth curl ever so slightly as he gave me a nearly imperceptible nod. I went next to Antisthenes, who offered a pledge as he held forth his horn, then to smiling Bornon, and down the line of vazarka until all had been served. Then, when the jugs of mead had been passed among all those gathered, I filled my own horn, raised it to all the kara, and drank as well. The meal resumed, and with it, the lighthearted chatter and mirth I was accustomed to hearing around the hearth soon returned.

"You don't eat?" Aric seemed offended when I left my bowl to get cold.

"I'm not hungry tonight." I didn't think I could eat any more stew. "Is there any cheese?"

"You've eaten your portion of the cheese—and some of mine. Not till we can trade for more."

"Well, I can forage vegetables and mushrooms. Set some fish traps and rabbit snares."

"Good," he said between bites. "Do it."

"I miss bacon," I said. "Do you never keep pigs here?"

"Have you ever tried to herd pigs?" he raised his eyebrow as he chewed. "Besides, like horseflesh, we may eat pork only rarely, on sacred occasions. But there are wild boars in the woodlands and marshes south of here along the river. We could hunt them."

"I suppose. But it's not the same."

"I wouldn't know," he looked out into the darkness and chewed thoughtfully.

"Truly?" It sounded like an accusation. "Well, one day, I will take you to my home, and the cooks will make you a proper feast. I don't know their secret, but the bacon . . . ," I trailed off, suffering a sudden pang of homesickness.

He smiled indulgently at me, and I realized what a foolish thing I'd said. He would never have cause to visit my distant homeland. And neither again would I.

Olgas poked his black head into our little circle and jabbed Aric with his elbow. "Did I hear someone mention a boar hunt?"

"Forget boar," eager Azarion said, glancing sidelong at me, his dark eyes gleaming. "It's been too long since we had a *real* hunt."

A murmur arose from those gathered around.

"It is so," Rathagos added, fingering his slick hair back from his low brow as he leaned in. "Or have we gone meek with a woman among us?"

A chill shivered through the silent camp.

Aric sat eerily still and stared, unblinking, with his one cold eye. He looked to the sky, then at the horizon. "Not tonight."

An angry grumble pulsed through the company.

"Two nights from now. When the moon is full," he growled, set aside his empty bowl, and moved closer to the firelight. Hunching over his goryt, he withdrew a needle and thread.

"Good, I've always wanted a Man-Eater scalp to wipe my ass with," said Olgas.

I gave him a stern, disapproving look, but he only winked at me and laughed.

"We're going after the Man-Eaters?" I asked Aric. "Are you even certain it was them? That they did it out of malice?"

"They call themselves the Mokhsa," he said. "And who else would have poisoned the well—the Geloni traders?" Aric asked. "You saw with your own eyes. It violated our agreement and must be punished. And because you were among that trading party, you will also be part of the raid."

My first real raid. I'd been training for weeks, but since joining them to find the girl, Aric had kept me away from the small expeditions the warband had undertaken. Some part of me resented his coddling, his suspicion that I couldn't handle myself as well as even the younger boys. But the greater part of me was relieved. I didn't want to go on any raids where I might have to use those skills they taught me. Where I might actually succeed in my wretched mission. And I would be damned if ridding the world of even one vile Man-Eater meant returning to a life at court. I couldn't give up my place here. Not when I'd come this far.

"So, this will be your first raid?" asked Siran, the young red-haired vazarka sitting opposite me as we prepared. "Is it true the hamazan live in camps like this? That they train the girls the way we train boys?"

"It's true," I said. "Among the Rokhalani, girls of the warrior clans also spend time in the wilds, learning to hunt and fight to prepare them for their duties guarding the camp while the men are away raiding. Some join them."

He only grunted, then went back to fletching his arrows. The others had called Siran "plowman," and he always wore a shabby, ill-fitting coat, unlike the other kara who dressed neatly and took pride in their presentation, even if we must often go dirty and rough out here. The vazarka had means enough to outfit themselves well, so the tattered, sloppy coat was conspicuous. Father always said that those who made themselves conspicuous "with aught but able deeds" could not be trusted. But Siran seemed mostly harmless.

Stormai shyly held out a jar of salve to me. He was said to be a cousin of Aric's, and it was easy to see the physical likeness. His hair, like raw linen, and his eyes, a hazy sky, caught the last rays of the sun.

"What is it?" I asked.

"Beeswax and bear fat. For your boots." Not since I met him that first night at the court camp had Stormai spoken a word to me.

"You're very kind." I smiled at him, and he blushed as I took it. "My feet are soaked every day." Despite the lack of rain, the flood-plains were still soggy, and I waded into the rivers often.

He'd dumped the arrows from his goryt, made a pile, and began to whittle and carve at a shaft. "Have you marked your arrows?" he asked.

"Mark them? How?" I scrubbed the dried mud off my boots and wiped them clean.

He slotted the arrow back in the quiver and began another. "With your *tamga*—a sign of your clan, of yourself." He held up the shaft he'd been sawing with his knife. He had etched a crude, linear symbol resembling a soaring bird. My clan had no such sign that I knew, though the stag was sacred to our house. "How will you know where your arrows strike if you don't mark them?"

"Why would I want to know that?" I asked, smearing the wax on my boots with my fingers, working it into the stitching.

"So you can claim your spoils from the field." He shoved another arrow into his quiver.

"I want nothing from the dead." The idea of picking over the corpses of the battlefield like a vulture revolted me. But Aric looked up from his sewing, and I knew I'd insulted them by his pained expression. I tried to cover myself. "I only mean that, spoils, should I win any, belong to my kara-daranaka and this fellowship. For your hospitality."

"That is an honorable trade," Aric replied, smiling. "I accept and will distribute them as I see fit."

I smiled and nodded graciously, hoping the matter was satisfied. But I could see I would be required now to mark my arrows.

"Take a handful of poisoned arrows as well," Bornon warned, removing a few brightly striped shafts from his goryt and carefully passing them to me. "Should a Man-Eater strike you down or capture you, prick yourself with one. If one of us falls, by Gœtosura, have mercy and shoot! They eat men to deny their spirits a life in the next world."

"That's *monstrous.*"

"Kill the goatfuckers before they can digest you. Poison your flesh, and your spirit will burst forth from their vile guts and remain free."

It relieved me to hear the Skythai speak this way, as perhaps it meant they disdained the practice themselves. "Are there more eaters of the dead about?"

"The Saudaratai are much like the Mokhsa in their traditions," Aric said. "But the Issedoni, who dwell in the east, believe that by eating the dead they keep the spirit of their ancestors alive among them. Or so my swordmaster, Ispakaja, told me. He ate his father—he and his brothers made a stew of him when he died and swore it was their father's dearest wish. The greatest fear among the Issedoni is to die of sickness and be buried in the earth."

"It's true," Olgas added, "they keep the gilded skulls of their elders on an altar in their homes and revere them daily. They'll pay almost anything to ransom a head taken in battle." He shrugged.

"Then who is right—the Mard-Khwaar or the Issedoni? Does it preserve or kill the spirit?"

"Maybe neither," Aric said. "Who but the gods can know? But I don't intend to find out." He pulled a handful of arrows halfway out of his goryt, revealing their viper-like stripes.

As the sun set, we repaired our tack and clothing, fletched arrows, and sharpened blades. Aric sat bent over his goryt, working. Always at our sides, the combined bowcase and quiver received relentless abuse and needed constant repair. I'd long admired the design of his goryt. The face of it was covered in the most unusual material. It had the appearance of fish scales or fine, glossy feathers. I wondered if he'd covered it with seashells.

"May I?" I asked as I reached out to touch it.

He nodded. "Fingernails."

I snatched my hand away and wiped it on my trousers.

"Why do you make that face?" he looked bewildered and then made an absurd imitation of my horrified expression.

"Those are from . . . *men?*"

"What else? From the right hands of my enemies. It took me a while to cover it." He beamed as he held it up to show me.

"It isn't right to defile the dead."

"Defile? You wear leather, fur, horn. . . ."

"But those are from animals."

"So are these."

"You don't *eat* men?" *Did he?*

"I have plenty of other food."

I could only stare at him, speechless.

"We are all animals. Make no mistake. And this flesh," Aric touched his fingertips to his chest, "is hide like any other. I protect yours; you protect mine. And that horse of yours . . . ," he pointed to Sakha grazing out below us with the herd, "you'll protect his hide because he's yours. But if you were naked or starved, you'd skin another man's horse."

He presumed a lot of me. "But why . . . *those?*"

"The warrior is the right hand of his people. Without him, the tribe's strength is diminished. Never again shall these wield a weapon against the Skythai." He raised his right hand, his last two fingers folded toward his palm. "Papahio, just Lord, grant me power over my enemies."

I SAT UP THAT NIGHT, marking my arrows with a little symbol

like antlers. I wasn't going to get much sleep anyway. I'd heard from the others that not all raids were bloody. Most amounted to little more than cattle rustling. They seemed almost a competitive, if violent, sport between rival tribes. Those were the good days. The men seemed to respect Aric because he had a talent for choosing fights they could handily win, and he never rashly put his men or horses at risk. Surprising a poorly guarded camp and stealing off with a few head of cattle or sheep and no life lost was not only possible but common. However, one never really knew how it would go until it was over.

The bloodier raids took on legendary status. Those who fought and died were celebrated around the fire in tales and songs. But only if the cattle were won. It was only heroic if the men got their prize. Dying in vain rarely got anyone a ballad, and riding home empty-handed was the worst fate of all.

I had gone to the pasture to catch Sakha and returned to find Aric holding his horse's reins, staring into the fire. I summoned the courage to speak what had been troubling my mind.

"Why do you let Rathagos goad you into this? You are daranaka. *You* command *them*."

"I do. But I also listen. The men are right; this cries for justice." He turned from the fire to throw a saddle over Isiras's back. "Our stores dwindle. But worse still, we've suffered an outrage. A covenant was betrayed. These men are not just hungry in their bellies; their spirits wither without reckoning."

"And those you raid must pay for that?"

He stopped cinching his girth and turned to face me. "If you learn only one thing during your time in this place, learn this: war is about hunger, nothing more. It's about deciding who eats and who starves. Like all precious things, this world is finite. There is only so much pasture, farmland, and forest. Only so many rivers and springs. So many fish in the waters. Not every man will get to drink and eat of them. Who will you feed? Because you *will* have to choose. Will you choose foreigners over your own—people who mistrust, or hate, or wish you ill? I choose *my* people; I choose *our* children. I choose our faithful friends. And I make peace with that because if I don't, we die. If we don't master these lands, others will. Their stock and houses will fill these fields, and we'll be gone like those before us. You don't have to enjoy it, but you need to accept it."

I shook my head and threw my saddle over Sakha's back, tightening the girth. "There has to be a better way."

He lifted a long spear that rested against the side of the nearby felt-house, leaning on it like a staff. "What way? Tell me. This is nature's plan. The animals accept it. Still, some wretched weakness in man refuses. When the deer are too many, the wolves cull the herd; when the deer are too few, the wolves cull their packs. If the deer have a god, it must be the wolf. Perhaps the wolf worships the deer for the same reason. Only man worships himself. How can such a creature survive?"

"I didn't say—"

"Ask yourself this: Are you the hunter or the prey?"

"I don't want to be either."

Using the spear, he vaulted up onto Isiras's back. "Then you will be dead. Your kin will be dead. Your people dispossessed. You have a heart that seeks justice, and that's noble." He tilted the head of the spear at me. "But preserve what's best for your own people first. For those you can trust. For those who love what you love. Then let us see what's left for the rest."

I stood defenseless, stumbling over my thoughts for a way to refute him.

"You baffle me," Aric continued. "You wish to be a warrior, yet you think you can remain innocent your whole life?" He took a swig from his wineskin, extended it to me, and then shrugged and took another swig.

I lowered my eyes. "I am no butcher."

"You fool yourself. Everyone is a butcher, even if their hands are never bloodied. We all thrive by violence—done by our own hands, by warriors burdened with our protection, or by our ancestors who won our very existence with war and conquest. Don't pretend otherwise. Some may never know the stain of blood on their own hands, but our lives have been purchased with the blood of others. To disavow this is to tell ourselves the worst kind of lie. No one has the right to be innocent in this world."

"What if some have no stomach for blood?"

"But everything they love is bought with the very things they hate. It's paid with *our* grief, *our* flesh. Yet they have the gall to judge—to renounce us! We wring our hands clean each night so they may rest their delicate heads in peace and forget—or, worse, condemn. It's selfish. And weak." He took a long drink from the wineskin and let his far-staring eye come to rest somewhere beyond me.

His words gave me a heavy feeling in my chest, like a great stone had lodged there that I couldn't budge. All the while he spoke, my mind scrambled for a defense. An explanation. A justification. But if there was one, it eluded me. Maybe I had been foolish, believing I could come to a brutal place like this and never soil my hands. I could play at being a warrior while hiding from my first duty. But I didn't want to become like him, collecting the heads and hides of enemies like plunder. Maybe I didn't belong here after all.

"This upsets you." He turned to fix me in that terrible gaze, his eye narrow and sharp. Was it disappointment I saw there? Or anger?

"It upsets me to be heartless."

"Why are you here? Why are you *really* here?"

"You know why."

"I know what you told my father. But if you're not here to defend this land, don't waste my time. Don't waste theirs," he swept his arm toward the camp. "You're going to get somebody killed."

Killed? Waste his time? Did he believe me that pathetic—that dangerous? I looked away as angry tears filled my eyes. I should tell him to go fuck himself. That I had as much right to be here as anyone. But that would be another lie.

"For fuck's sake, are you crying?"

I couldn't look at him. "I didn't realize you thought so little of me." The sobs began, and suddenly, I was reduced to a scolded child.

"Don't you *dare*. Have you heard nothing I've said?" There was rage in the growl of his voice now, and I worried the camp heard him shouting at me.

I worked up the courage to glance his way. His face burned an eerie, bruised red in the torchlight, and his voice lowered in volume but raised in intensity as he squeezed the wineskin nearly to bursting.

He reined his horse in close to me. "No one owes you a place in this world. You must claim it. If you want a place here, *fight for it!*"

I wiped my face and blinked stupidly at him. "You're not sending me back?"

He shook his head. "I won't beg you to stay. You want to go, take any scalp of mine and go."

I wiped my nose on my sleeve and summoned the nerve to face him as he towered over me on his black gelding.

What if I did? Just take a scalp and go back. From this day forward, live out my days as a lesser queen among the royal court where, with any luck, I'd soon be forgotten once my *wifely* duties were done.

Or I could press on. Even if it meant becoming the things I feared. Or the things I was perhaps fated to be. Did it matter whether I left or remained, biding my time and prolonging my days of liberty? Either way, my destination would be the same. Sooner or later, it would likely end with me bringing a scalp to the king. But, would it be a scalp of *my* taking? Whose would it be? Or would some warrior get the better of me and take my head instead? Somewhere on this steppe, a man's fate and mine were intertwined; my life and his were bound. I would leave this field either in marriage or death; only respite in this wild, holy place made either prospect bearable. How could I ever know my true fate unless I followed this road to its end?

"Give me the wine."

He stifled a grin as he passed it to me.

I drank a longer swallow than perhaps was wise and hoped I wouldn't regret it. "You speak like a priest," I said.

"Fuck off," he scowled and snatched back the wineskin.

"I meant it as a compliment."

"I prefer to fight my battles in *this world*."

It seemed I would have to learn to do the same, and it began tonight. I didn't know if I was ready to become a killer, but neither was I prepared to be a wife.

WE RODE OUT TO A COVERT deep in the forest-steppe just before midnight—the heart of Man-Eater territory. The central reaches of Mardia were not nearly so barren as the eastern part we'd tried to cross just days ago. We spent the day before traveling to within range of their main camp—for they too were nomads—and made our own rough camp nearby. We then slept the morning and set out to make our raid at nightfall. Once we arrived, it would be straightforward as raids went—catch them unawares, lift the stock, and drive them off as quickly as possible, hopefully before anyone noticed or could get hurt. But it required camping in the territory of the Geloni, which meant if we were successful, we'd have to share a portion of the spoils.

We forded the flat, muddy banks of the lower Mokhsa River, the full moon high in the sky. The riverbanks were flooded, and the land was sodden, with the mud a thick and sticky slog. The horses struggled with each step over the floodplain, slowly picking their way through the mire.

Emerging from the floodplain onto solid ground, I felt a hitch

in Sakha's stride. I jumped down to check his legs. The tendon of
his left fore was tender to the touch and had begun to swell. It had
not yet bowed, but it was in a bad state. If I pushed him any harder,
he might be severely crippled—perhaps permanently. Too far from
home, I couldn't turn back, and I couldn't wait here alone. Instead,
I packed his leg with some cool clay, around which I wrapped fresh
grass and bandaged it with strips of linen from my tunic. I prayed
it would hold, silently reciting an ancient hamazan charm over it
that I had learned from my mother:

> As the wagoner fits the parts of a chariot,
> May the gods fix joint to joint,
> Join bone to bone,
> Join marrow to marrow,
> Join sinew to sinew,
> Join flesh to flesh,
> Join blood to blood,
> Join hair to hair;
> May all be united and sound,
> Join what was broken,
> Stand up, go forth, and run.
> Stand upright!

Aric watched in wordless silence. Once again, I became aware
of slowing him down. I mounted up, feeling guilty toward Sakha,
and said a little invocation to the spirits of this unforgiving land
to please let all survive this night.

"Now," Aric said, as the raiding party drew round, "the Mokhsa practice rites under the full moon. We are more visible, but
they are more vulnerable. Most will be intoxicated with potions
and absorbed in sacrifices. We strike silently. Things will move
quickly once we're in sight of the herd. Have your bows ready," he
said, looking at me, "but don't shoot unless they shoot first. Their

flocks will not be well guarded. They are not accustomed to raids in this country."

"I've not seen any signs from the Ravens," Gohar added, "but they'll alert us of any trouble."

I scanned the horizon futilely for signs of our young novices who, as part of their training, spent time in the fields employed as scouts, dressed in sooty grey. Scavengers of the field, we relied upon them to be our spies over the steppe. Always stealthy, at this time of day, they would be invisible. In the wilderness, a hunter knows that the best trackers of the field are wolves. They sense things invisible to us, and their endurance is superior to any human's. But ravens are the wolves' all-seeing companions. Unlikely allies, ravens will follow wolves from above, anticipating the leavings of the hunt and leading them on to their prey.

"Staurin has scouted this valley," Olgas said. "What say you?"

Staurin, one of the oldest novices who had already made his tally, urged his horse forward to report to his vazarka commanders. "It's shaped like a shallow bowl," he said, outlining it with the sweep of his hand over the horizon. "At night, the flocks should be down near the stream. They don't use scouts, but they keep dogs. Mean ones. They will bark like mad when we get close."

"All right," Gohar said, "we'll have to be quick about it."

"Remember, don't let them capture you alive," Bornon added, holding up one of the striped arrows from his quiver. "It's bad enough to steal *this* life. But to rob you of the *next* life and shit you out the next day is a triple death."

The men frowned and nodded, then tugged at their reins, perhaps eager to get it over with. I shared that sentiment with them, at least.

We divided into two parties, riding from opposite directions along the stream, and waited for the scout's signal that the men below had left their posts. When Aric gave his sign, we crept down into the bowl to scoop up the flocks and herd them out of the valley.

There were six Mokhsa herdsmen on guard. Or, they were supposed to be. We found them eating on the shallow banks beneath
a tree. I cringed to imagine what they might be snacking on, but
the thought quickly left me when one of the guardian dogs began
to bark, and they sprang to action. Wilder men I had never seen.
Squat with bald faces and piercing dark eyes, their clothes were all
of hides, their cloaks pinned together with the canines and claws of
animals, and on their breasts, they wore unmistakable long-haired
pelts of men. Their caps were topped with animals' skulls strapped
under their chins with thongs. Plumes of feathers and tufts of hair
floated behind them as they darted into action, screeching like
mating foxes. They sprang to the backs of their mongrel ponies as
they heard us thundering down the valley.

They were outnumbered. We fled quickly, our plunder snorting and bleating before us in confusion. The Man-Eaters didn't
confront us directly but waited until we were in retreat with our
spoils, then shot arrows at our backs and harried our flanks. I
watched the kara for a sign. Did they turn to shoot? Should I? But
they just charged ahead. I knew I needed to keep up—to keep the
flock together and ahead of the riders behind me.

We rode hard toward the river. The riders behind were not
giving up their chase. Ahead, the mud would slow the flock and
us, as we'd be mired for a slow race to the ford and a plodding trek
out again on the other side. The pursuers were bound to catch up;
I didn't see how we'd make it. The goats and sheep sunk in the first
of the floodplain and slowed a little, slogging frantically as they
lurched forward through the boggy banks. The horses slowed, too.

The moment Sakha entered the mud, I felt it. He flinched and
then faltered as the tendon gave way. I stopped pressing him, but
I knew that if I dismounted, I'd be bogged down in the muck, too.
I could only let him struggle as I pulled six arrows from my goryt
and fitted one to my string. The herdsmen closed. With the sheep
lost, they weren't coming for the stock. They were coming for blood.

A loud twang rang out like a chord strummed upon a great lyre, and several arrows whizzed past my head. The six men fell from their horses—dead or alive, I couldn't say. I spun round in my saddle to see Aric, Gohar, Olgas, Bornon, Staurin, and Stormai with bows in hands while the rest of the party kept driving the sheep ahead. They rode on as Aric circled back to me.

"Climb on," he said as he pulled up his horse beside mine and thrust his spear into the soft earth.

I grabbed his hand and swung over behind him, my arms around his waist. With his burden eased, Sakha followed, limping bravely home.

EVEN AFTER SHARING a portion with the Geloni, we won a respectable prize from the field and safely made it to camp. The men cheered that the raid had been a great success and that we hadn't lost a man or a horse. But though I wanted to revel in the victory with them and hail the success of my first real raid, I knew they were wrong. Sakha, my trusted friend, would take weeks to heal, and even still, he'd never be the same again.

There was no epic battle, no stunning feats of courage to be seen for all their talk. Not by any man, at least. Beforehand, I had envisioned a perilous fight, bathed in gore and bravery, and all of us lucky to escape with our lives. Yet the raid was none of those things. I suppose I should have been grateful. But after steeping myself in fear and doubt, I craved something more. Something to justify the anguish I'd suffered. The hurt I inflicted on Sakha. What, after all, was the purpose of this expedition?

I had believed it was merely punitive—an act of reprisal for the spoiled well and a chance to seize some booty for our troubles. Though perhaps warranted, that was hardly the noblest undertaking, and all we gained were a few measly sheep, scarcely worth the risk. But Aric hadn't spoken of spoils; he talked of survival. If the Man-Eaters had turned hostile toward the Skythai, then the Man-Eaters had become an obstacle. And obstacles must be dislodged.

Among the Bastarnai, the first story every child learned was of the three-headed dragon that dammed up the river of heaven with a great stone, causing a terrible drought over the earth, and of Taranis, the one who battled the dragon and smashed the stone, setting the waters free again. We learned how the hero battles endlessly against such forces to free the rain in the clouds and the minerals in the earth for our benefit—that no agent of obstruction, however great or terrible, was immovable if it threatened our survival.

In the light of morning, I saw the raid with clearer eyes. It wasn't vengeful but strategic. The raiders hewed away at the obstruction while their rivals weakened, starved, and were forced to cede territory—or come to terms. They seldom lost man or horse, but those they struck continually lost ground, sustenance, perhaps able bodies. Battle was a slaughter, but raiding was a knife in the dark, a slow bleed. All the warband had to do was pick its fights wisely and be strong enough to guard its own when others came.

CHAPTER 12

WILDS

I fought back the sleep that came for me
after long days of riding.

I'D SURVIVED MY FIRST WEEKS OF TRAINING, an actual raid, and even cannibals. I'd endured meals like fermented horse milk, salted meat, and curds. Too-infrequent washing. The latrine—dubbed "the shit pit." The ubiquitous belches, body odor, and smells even fouler. And spitting—constant spitting. I would never understand why men spit so much, but there was certainly not a more disgusting habit. The marches—and its men—had proved trying, but not intolerable.

In the day, there was no escape from the sun's glare. There was either constant wind or unbearable stillness, which meant flies—relentless flies—and midges biting wherever they found bare skin. The fields were full of nettles, thistles, and something I called bristle grass. The patrols were unforgiving. Hours and hours on horseback, riding over rough, monotonous terrain, or just sitting under the sun and watching the horizon, then riding back to do the same the next day. Finding trails. Abandoned reaver camps. Cold campfires and the bones of poached stock. If we were lucky, tracking them to their source. There was the ghostly unease of riding night watches under the blue moonlight, able to see almost nothing but shadows, but hearing everything in the darkness, twitching at the creak of every animal and insect, all my hairs standing at attention. Listening to the eerie howling of the wolves after a hunt.

Breaks came on trading days or visits to clan encampments, few but welcome, when I could meet with local clans or the minor karevans passing through the steppe. Though I woke each morning painful and stiff, I wore my cuts and bruises like a crown, having earned them honestly. It was the way I felt when I was training horses. I relished the ache in my muscles after a long day. It felt like accomplishment. It had purpose. And I knew it meant I was growing stronger.

Most of the men were kind, generous, and forgiving as I came to know them, especially considering my greenness and the strangeness of having a woman among them. Many were green themselves. They were young men—boys, really—also here to collect their scalps before they could gain their rights at home. They would become familiar faces to me, but most without names.

Once the torches were extinguished, no words were spoken in the darkened felt-houses. Aric was always gone before I awoke. When not on patrols by his side, we trained after dawn, and he went off on other business with a small guard, leaving me in the care of the warband to work with the horses until nightfall. After eating, he'd nod off beyond the light of the fire. But I knew he was always watching, and I was never far from his sight.

Foul as they might be, I was delighted when the other men felt easy enough to relate their most repugnant stories in my company. And when, during my instruction, they didn't rush to help me up. When we could all laugh at the day's mishaps—including my own—over cups of kumis or mead by the fire.

About the hearth at night, they were quick to laugh, full of wild—certainly exaggerated—accounts of martial feats and sexual conquests. In the flicker of the firelight, swathed in darkness, in the middle of nowhere on this forsaken plain, I fought back the sleep that came for me after long days of riding to sit under the stars and listen to them tell their stories and sing their songs. Clapping their hands in unison, beating upon drums of skins or pots, bowing and strumming their lyres, and chanting their poetry. The persistent rhythm was like a potent elixir working its way down my spine and into my chest like a second heart. Unlike wine, it cleared my thoughts. And the winding melodies were a balm that smoothed the ends of my frayed nerves. Voices joyous, strident, and plaintive sang words of beauty, heroism, and longing deep into the night. Their stories were eloquent and bold. Heroic and funny. Romantic and sorrowful. They were noble and rude, and some of them quite filthy. They were wonderful. I hated the moment when Aric would say goodnight, and I must retreat with him to his tent. The music and laughter would continue without us into the forsaken hours while my ears strained to hear until I finally drifted off to sleep.

CHAPTER 13

TARANA

In this life, we can have pity or respect—
but not both.

A BRUISING WIND BLEW over the dry grass. Since I arrived, no
rain had come, and the drought stirred whispers everywhere
through the parched blades. But the sky remained silent. White
clouds drifted through, followed by grey ones which came to stay,
throwing deep shadows over the fields. The pastures were thirsty,
but I hoped a storm wasn't brewing.

After working the horses, I undressed to my tight-laced linen
undervest and breechcloth and climbed down the bank of the
sluggish river. It had receded to almost a trickle, but nothing was
sweeter after the sweat of a workday than lying on the smooth
stones of the riverbed and letting the water wash over me. I closed
my eyes, stretched out my arms, and let my head fall back into the
cooling current.

I drifted there, weightless, the crisp, clear water slipping over
my skin, the warm glow of the sporadic sunlight seeping through
my eyelids, the burbling current mumbling in my ears. A long cloud
shadow passed over me, and the warmth faded. A quick series of
splashes startled me from my peaceful daze. As I opened my eyes,

hands gripped my outstretched arm, flipped me over in the water, and forced me under, pinning me down to the riverbed. With eyes clamped shut, I braced my hands against the stones. Pushed with all my strength. But a frightful weight bore me down—the weight of a man on my back.

My lungs burned, and my ribs were about to crack when I was lifted, dragged to the bank, and thrown face-down on it. He was impossibly strong, like an enraged bear. Still, I thrashed against him as he restrained me. He grabbed me by the back of the head and, with a growl, smashed my face into the stone-hard ground. Dust and blood mixed on my tongue.

Desperate to scream, I coughed up water and gasped for air. But more than I wanted words or breath, I wanted a weapon in my hand. My dagger was with my clothes up the bank. *Stupid.* No rocks or sticks were nearby, even if I could free my hands. Even my bare feet were mired in slick river mud.

Body pressed against mine, he released his right hand and slid it down between us where I could feel it working. He began to untie his trousers.

Panting on the back of my neck, his breath was thick with the odor of wine. My thoughts blurred. *This can't be happening.*

But while he worked, my right arm was free. Pulling a scream from deep within my chest, I planted my foot on the bank and shoved back with all my strength, flailing my elbow at his face so violently that he fell back into the water. Then I scrambled up the bank, grabbed the dagger from my pile of clothes, and ran for my life. I think I was still screaming.

Azarion, Bradak, and Stormai appeared at the top of the low hill, galloping toward me with bows in hand. I tried to cover myself with my arms. They pulled their horses up in front of me.

"We heard screaming," said Azarion, annoyed and with his brow cocked skeptically. "What's the matter?"

"Oh, shit," Bradak calmly answered his brother as he pointed at the man clawing his way up the riverbank, the front of his trousers still open. From atop his horse, Bradak looked down his crooked nose at me in understanding, sable hair blowing across his face. I turned back toward the river. Now that I had a chance to look at my attacker, I should have guessed. *Tarana.* He bore a grudge against me since the day I won his horse from him. Probably long before.

Azarion shouted to him to halt as he reached the shore, but, like a hurled stone, Tarana threw himself from the bank into the river with a loud splash. Kicking their horses on, Azarion and Bradak cantered across the water toward him. The riders were on him in no time, shouting at him to stop. Tarana spun round in a whirlwind and let forth a growl like an angry beast. Then he drew his sword and began thrashing at them, his movements sudden, senseless, tenacious. The two brothers called his name, but there was no recognition in Tarana's eyes. Bradak fitted an arrow to his bowstring, and Azarion flanked him and pulled his own sword. A cornered animal, Tarana lunged at Azarion's horse, sword raised and shrieking. Azarion wheeled his horse around and deflected the strike just as Bradak swiftly half-drew and released his arrow with a dull twang, shooting Tarana in the back of his thigh. The bolt barely slowed him in his rage, but it gave the two brothers enough time to dismount and wrestle him to the ground, where both men struggled to subdue the thrashing madman. They sat upon him like an unbroken colt and bound him tightly as he bucked and writhed. Yanking the arrow shaft from his leg, they hitched him with their lariats like a sledge behind their horses and dragged him away screaming.

With hands trembling and fingers fumbling at the ties and buckles, I dressed as quickly as I could. I still clutched the dagger in my hand. My legs were muddy under my clothes. Blood flowed over my tunic and caftan from my nose. My head throbbed. Sweet Stormai, who'd remained behind to watch over me, didn't speak. He couldn't look me in the face even after I'd dressed.

STORMAI ESCORTED ME TO CAMP, and I rushed back to the tent to find Aric and dry clothes, but there was no time to change. News had arrived ahead of me, and a riot was breaking out at the center of camp.

"What's happening?" I asked of Antisthenes as he emerged from our tent. Since my arrival, we'd barely spoken beyond daily formalities and courtesies. Mostly, we avoided each other. But, once an outsider here himself, I hoped the Hellene could, if not muster approval, at least help me navigate this treacherous new terrain—even if only for Aric's sake.

"A trial," was all he said as he pushed past.

That sounded ominous. Would *I* be accused? No doubt Tarana would try to say I incited him. My only witnesses were Tarana's sworn brothers.

I followed Antisthenes toward the western pasture where all were gathering. "Have no fear," he said. "The Skythian sense of justice runs deep."

That was precisely what I was afraid of. "Will Aric send for a lawspeaker?"

"We kara have our own law."

After arriving here, I'd learned that, outside the boundaries of court and the farmsteads of cattle-herders, a karik was *eka*—an individual, independent and free from the bonds of society to act according to his own will. Unlike ordinary citizens, he lived according to the *svadha*, or self-law. Each was to govern himself by his own sense of honor, in keeping with the oaths he had freely sworn to the gods and the agreements he made with his fellow Skythai and foreigners alike. He was judged accordingly in the eyes of gods and men. It sounded virtuous, but I had no idea what that meant in practice.

"There are no prisons on the steppe," he continued, "and no karik will be made a slave. Justice will be swift and final."

"What justice?"

"A fine in wealth, a fine in flesh, death, or exile."

"What is Tarana to be accused of?"

"Several crimes, perhaps. A man must only pay for the worst of them—in this case, perhaps breaking his oath. But forcing himself upon a free woman—and a noblewoman who is his lord's guest, no less—is most grave. It is strictly forbidden to molest a woman against her will. That alone is punishable by death."

"Death?" I stopped and looked at him, incredulous. *Impressed.* "I've never heard of a man being killed for violating a woman."

Three riders galloped past us toward the trial.

"Oh, truly, the Skythai are jealous of their holdings and take great offense at anyone who does not approach their women with proper respect."

Holdings? That was a disagreeable term for it. I resumed walking.

"A man's honor is bound to that of his women."

"As is a woman's to that of her men."

"Indeed. *Character is the thread with which the Fates weave,*" he said in Greek. "Our own as well as that of others. Usually, there is not a trial, though. If a man lays hands on a woman against her will, he will be simply beaten or killed by her kin or husband on the spot."

We were nearing the western pasture, and I slowed, not eager to arrive. "But he is a vazarka?"

"Tarana has transgressed an oath made before the gods. The Skythai hold that to break one's word disturbs Arta and incurs the wrath of the gods. The murderous must suffer iron; the hedonistic must suffer fire or water; the oathbreaker—enemy of true speech—must be punished by the noose."

"Then . . . he is doomed?"

"It would seem so," he said with a shrug. "Are you not pleased?"

"Do the Skythai not believe in mercy?"

"What do you believe Tarana would have done when he was finished with you?"

I took a moment to consider what he asked, and the answer chilled my heart.

"If there is leniency for Tarana, others will transgress their oaths. But we must see what the trial reveals. Unlike in my homeland, there are no inscribed contracts, no fences, no walls, no fortifications here. A Skythai would say, 'There is only the truth.' One's true words and deeds are all he has. They are worth more than gold."

THE SKY GREYED, and the air became drenched with the weight of coming rain. As we pushed through the mob, Aric sat upon Isiras, his black gelding, looking down on Tarana at the center of a silent crowd of men. Rope still bound his hands before him, though he knelt passively now—drowsy, even, as though he'd just been roused from a deep sleep.

"What have you to say for yourself?" Aric asked.

Tarana bowed his head and refused to speak.

"What man of honor raids his own?"

Tarana's face burned red, but he would not look at Aric.

"The woman is not your prize to take. She is one of us. And in seizing her, you have made a raid upon your king. And King Arianta. Understand?"

At this, Tarana drew a deep hiss through his teeth and raised his head, glaring up defiantly at Aric. "I have pledged myself unto death. If now my life is forfeit, so be it. I have served my brothers and my kara faithfully. But who is this girl to me? What does *she* serve—besides Aric's cock?"

An uproar seized the crowd.

Aric dismounted Isiras and drew his dagger as he strode to the center of the circle to stand over Tarana. "You also slander my name and impugn my honor?" He cut the prisoner's bonds. "Stand, then, and make your accusation against me, brave Tarana."

Tarana lowered his eyes, and the crowd fell still. Aric struck him across the face with the back of his fist, knocking him flat to the ground, and took him by the throat. His back in the dirt, a knee on his chest, Tarana went limp beneath Aric.

"That's what I thought," Aric snarled as he released the man and stepped back. "You are a ravisher, a slanderer, and an oathbreaker."

The wind picked up, flattening the grass, and thunder rumbled in the distance.

"Why?" Aric asked. "Why this woman?"

Tarana squirmed to his feet and shook his head. "I might ask you the same." He aimed his quivering finger toward me as his craggy face scanned the crowd for sympathizers and found more than a few to nod along with him. "Maybe my blood is hungry," he said. "A man's heart craves glory. Is that not what you all beg me sing of beside the fire each night? Beside the tombs? Where is glory now? We grow tame in the company of this woman." Gathering himself up, he raised his heavy head and spoke out to them. "What's happening to us? A woman joins our ranks, and we don't raid like we used to. Just these pathetic hunts a few miles from camp so Aric can rush back to his mistress. I'm a noble son of the Paralatai and a vazarka. Weeks into the season, I have nothing to show for it—a mangy scalp and a few scrawny goats. We should be buried under mounds of gold and beef by now! Instead, this—this *sorceress,*" he clenched his hand into a fist, "has seduced me into folly. To lead me down the path of my destruction, just as she is leading our kara-daranaka."

I could sense Antisthenes's firm, calm presence beside me. I desperately wanted to glance toward him as I watched a wave of support for Tarana spread across the faces of the other men, but I held myself still.

"Lies," Aric said. "Look at her wounds. Someone has been harmed here, but it is not you." Aric called out to the crowd: "You swore an oath by the sacred fire. Before Tabiti. To Gœtosura. By Papahio and Eraman. Thagimazda sees—and punishes—all deceptions. You have been a great champion of the vazarka. But now you've betrayed not only me, your kara, and your king but all the gods. I won't ask again, brother, *why?*"

He shook his head.

"Your future life depends on your answer. It is no time for lies."

Tarana lifted his eyes to Aric's, grit his teeth as his face reddened, and again shook his head.

"I recall none of it. I—I was walking along the river. She was in the water. Just lying there." His eyes welled with tears. "Then, the fog. When it cleared, she was gone, I was in the river, and Bradak and Mourdag were hunting me with swords and arrows." He scrubbed his hands over his face and rubbed his red eyes with the heels of his palms. Pulling the words from his lungs like arrows extracted from his chest, he whispered, "*I was possessed.*" Then he collapsed onto his knees with eyes raised to the sky and chest heaving. "The fury," he murmured, "just took hold of me. I—I was powerless to stop it."

The gathering of men let out a long, low moan, like wind blowing through a hollow tree, their eyes fixed on Tarana as if in a trance. I didn't understand what was happening.

Aric turned to the men assembled before them and asked, "How do you judge the acts of this man?"

In silence, most men in the gathered crowd bowed their heads and raised their right hands, the last two fingers folded toward the palm. Rathagos, the man who had spoken out against me the first night at the king's feast, fixed his eyes on me and folded his arms across his chest.

Aric drew a long, slow breath and nodded to him. "It is time."

Tarana fumbled to take Aric's hands in his. "So be it," he said longingly, his eyes spilling over with tears. His demeanor began to change. He seemed almost joyful. "I wish to see my father again."

"I will miss you, my brother," Aric said. "But we shall meet again. Death is but the center of a long life."

"Thank you, my lord. The greatest honors have fallen to me in the service of Gœtosura and my karadar."

Beside me, a man began to weep.

Aric stepped in front of him and looked him in the eye. "You are a vazarka and a fellow of the kara. I will hear your wishes."

"Raise a mound over me beside my fathers. My possessions all go to my sister. She is a widow. When he's old enough, my nephew will make a fine karik. See that my bow and the dagger with the horn grip go to him. My lyre, sword, and the chestnut gelding rest with me."

"I swear it will be done."

Tarana nodded solemnly, strands of greasy hair falling about his face.

"Any final words?"

Tarana sighed. "The poet's words are reserved for praise. Silence shall be my song now." Then he smiled and raised his eyes once more to the sky. "I can't see the sun," he said with a quavering voice as he searched the clouded sky for the glow of the dim orb behind its veil. Fixing his sight upon its muted light, he drew a long, deep breath and held it. On his knees, he stretched himself tall and waited.

"O Apia, to whom this flesh is hallowed, I give this man to death. O Thagimazda, All-Seeing Judge, Upholder of Arta, Keeper of Oaths, Wielder of the Noose, grant him justice. O Gœtosura, Lord of Wide Pastures, Creator of Speech, Father of Inspiration, he is your faithful servant. Give him peace in your kingdom and a place beside your holy fire. I send Tarana to you, O Great Lords."

Then Tarana took the bast girdle from around his waist and handed it to Aric, who tied it around his throat like a noose. Tarana stared vacantly ahead and clenched his fists but remained still. Wrapping the cord over his hand, Aric lifted and pulled it tight while seizing the man's throat in his other hand, squeezing beside his windpipe with a terrible pressure, crushing the life from him.

Tarana gagged, his tongue protruding and his eyes bulging, and then was silent. His limbs jerked and convulsed and then were still as his staring eyes went dim, and his weight slumped forward against Aric.

I looked on in detachment, like seeing from within a dream. There was no solace or glee in it. Just a sense that I needed to watch—to take part. That somehow, it would not be complete without me. Aric's expression was blank—jaw clenched, eye fixed on some distant point, no emotion crept into his face. The veins in his hand and arm swelled, and the sinews strained. Aric braced the weight of Tarana against his own body and kept his hand and the noose tight for another minute before allowing the body to fall limply onto the ground. As the rope loosened, hisses and gurgles emanated from Tarana's lungs like water dropped onto a hot iron.

I stared at Aric's hands hanging at his sides, the rope still twined about his fingers. They'd given me little pause before. If anything, I always thought them rather gentle. Eager to share. Skillful with reins. Surprisingly deft with a sewing needle. But to see a man stand before another and squeeze the life from him. To know such raw violence lay dormant in those hands that rest peacefully clasped across his chest each night. The hands that trained me. That passed me my cup of kumis at dinner. That brushed innocently against mine as we passed one another at the door. What other terrible deeds had those hands done? What more might they do?

The sky was now iron grey, and the thunder's rumblings drew closer. Aric ordered the novices to deal with the body, which was to be loaded on a wagon and driven back to his clan for embalming and burial. The crowd dispersed, and Aric walked calmly away toward camp.

Antisthenes turned to go.

"Is that all?" I asked.

"What more do you want?"

I shook my head. I wanted none of this. Still, something had been troubling me for some time, and it only now occurred to me what it was.

"How do the Skythai say *metamelomai*?" I asked, using the Greek word for *I regret, I feel remorse*. I was still learning a few words, and some subtleties of meaning eluded me. But *sorry* was something I'd never heard uttered since I arrived. Could a man not even apologize for his crimes? Would he not try?

Antisthenes frowned, scratching his chin through his dark beard. "There is no such word in the Skythian language."

His answer took me aback. "But then how does an offender express his feelings of remorse when he has committed some injury or wrong?"

He grimaced like I'd just proposed something obscene. "His feelings are irrelevant."

I'd lived among the Skythai for some time now, and I'd known them to be a sensitive and passionate people, full of both kindness and sympathy. I was sure I was not insane. Maybe he didn't understand my question. I tried a different tack. "What do *you* say, then, in those circumstances?"

"Well, if I felt guilt or shame, I would never ask for pity or beg for quarter, if that is what you suggest. This would only deepen my dishonor."

"Honor? What about humility? Doesn't a man relieve the burden he bears in his spirit to speak this aloud?"

"Relieve *his* burden? This is not humility. Trying to cast off his burden—and onto the very one he has wronged! This is the antithesis of humility."

"Then what's to be done?"

"A man takes responsibility for his deeds, both helpful and hurtful. He makes even restitution to those he has wronged—not with mere words, but with blood, sweat, or gold. Sentiment is cheap and, therefore, worthless. Self-pity is the cheapest sentiment of all. A worthy man seeks neither pity nor pardon; he redeems himself through true speech, right conduct, and kept promises. In this life, we can have pity or respect—but not both. We must choose."

I FLED THE CAMP, needing space to clear my thoughts and possibly my stomach. With my guts churning and sick rising in the back of my throat, I headed down by the river. There, I would not have to see or speak to anyone.

This was not the life I'd agreed to.

What kind of place had I come to where these men could watch their own be strangled with such serenity? With joy, even? Regardless of what he'd tried to do to me, Tarana's head was not the trophy I came here to win. I was going to hunt down that brute and demand he send me home. There was a karevan leaving tonight, even if I had to go with a corpse. I'd take any scalp he had and go. The others were right—this was no place for me. What ever made me think it could be?

An outcrop of rushes near a low marshy bank would provide me some shelter and quiet. The reeds glowed an eerie gold against the iron clouds forming behind them, and the sunburnt grass waved a fiery orange above. Slipping down to the shore, I surprised a man crouched in the mud. Aric.

We both froze. He narrowed his reddened eye and looked up at me as if to say, *don't*. He stood, kicked some thatch over a puddle of vomit, and wiped his bearded mouth with the back of his hand. Staring coldly at me, he drew a long, steady breath, then shoved past. I watched numbly as he marched toward camp, a speck disappearing into the flat horizon.

THE LIGHT RAIN CONTINUED into the evening. I left the river and wandered the pastures until dark. With everything that had passed and the weather turning, I had no desire to be out at night. But I returned to our tent with my innards in knots. Antisthenes had already left to drive the funerary wagon bearing Tarana's body to his clansmen. He'd be gone a few days at least, and I'd be left alone with Aric.

At the door, I stopped and considered sleeping outside. Thunder rumbled in the distance as the storm grew in strength, and even if I felt uncertain about Aric, I didn't trust anyone else. Not tonight. I knocked on the doorframe and peered inside to find him sitting before the hearth, staring blankly into the flames. He motioned for me to sit beside him.

"Let me see," he said, lifting my chin and feeling the bridge of my nose. Though tender, I tried not to wince. "Still not broken."

I searched his dispassionate face in vain, still finding him impossible to read. In my weariness, I gave up trying. My body would bruise, my eye would blacken again, and my lip was cut and swollen, but miraculously, I was unharmed.

"I'll be all right." *And you?* I wanted to ask but thought better of it. I would heed Antisthenes's words, keep my feelings to myself, and assume he wished the same. Instead, I went and poured a cup of wine and handed it to him. He took it without acknowledging me and did not drink. I filled one for myself as well. Standing before him, I braced my spine, clearing my throat softly. "My presence has caused grave strife in the ranks of men. My karadar has been unselfish, and I have been careless. Today, I was heedless of my surroundings despite your warnings. Henceforth, I promise to remain vigilant." I swore in earnest.

He clasped the cup with both hands and held it before him, his expression grave. His eye met mine for the first time since I entered the tent. He nodded slowly. "As will I," he said softly, raising his wine and waiting. I realized I must drink first. I lifted my cup solemnly and drank, and he likewise sipped from his.

Over our heads, the rain finally let loose, hammering on the felt roof. He patted the carpet beside him, and I sat before the hearth. All night, we drank in silence, staring into the flames and listening to the drumming of the rain.

CHAPTER 14

TRAPS

I never made plans for a long life.

I AWOKE TO A BRIGHT, damp morning with a coolness in my blood and a crispness in my mind. Aric, as usual, was already gone. The earth yielded softly underfoot, and the dewy pasture glistened in the morning light. Small bands dispersed for their patrols while others set off on the hunt or busied themselves with repairs to the camp. But with no training, no trading, no raiding today, a strained silence had settled over the camp.

As I walked, bridle over my shoulder, saddle slung against my hip, backs turned to me. I kept my head down and hurried to the pastures to check on the horses. It pleased me to see Sakha's leg healing so nicely. Then I quickly tacked my chestnut gelding, Aruna, and rode off in search of Aric.

I found him down by the mouth of a small, swollen stream that emptied into a pond, checking and resetting willow fish traps near the shore. I hobbled Aruna alongside his horse and stood on the bank in the sun, watching. His boots, warbelt, and caftan lay on the bank, and his trousers were rolled past his knees as he slogged through the reeds.

"Can I help?" My hands hated being idle, especially today.

He didn't look up. "Almost finished."

"You don't build weirs to catch fish and eels?"

"Who would be here to collect them once we move camp? Instead of fish traps, they would become fish tombs." He worked furiously on a knot tied to a stake in the stream bed.

"I hadn't thought of it like that."

"Indeed, in this country, tombs are the only permanent things we build. Only the dead have ceased their wandering—their bodies have, at least." Very close to untying the knot that was perplexing him, his expression took on a serene focus. "Heh," he remarked coolly, sliding the cord free of the stake and lifting the trap from the water, "I got it."

I wondered how long he'd been at it. Knocked around in the storm, the trap was full of sludge and debris.

"That's a good funnel. What do you use to hold your bait?"

"Hold it? Nothing. I just throw it in before I tie on the cap."

"I like to hang the bait inside so nothing can pick at it from outside. I'll show you," I said, as I cut a handful of green willow shoots and began weaving them.

"You've done this before." He finally stopped what he was doing and looked up at me.

"You sound surprised. Everyone must eat."

"All right, let's try one your way and see which the fish prefer," he said, grinning.

It warmed me to see him smiling again. To have someone in the camp speaking to me.

He set the trap on dry land and sat beside me on the bank, squinting across the water. "And you? You're good?" he smoothed a white pebble he'd snagged from the shore between his fingers.

"Like you said, nothing broken. Just some bruises."

"You had fitful dreams in the night." He cast the stone back into the water.

Did I? I didn't remember. But if I had, it was rude of him to mention. My dreams were none of his concern. "Who doesn't have strange dreams from time to time?"

"You've had a fright," he called after me. "No one would fault you."

Wouldn't they? Returning with my bundle, I dropped down beside him, his legs still wet and his feet muddy from the stream bed. "I know the men are upset with me. I understand why, but it isn't fair either." I passed him a handful of reeds.

"No." He began sorting them. "But it will fade."

"Will it? They already resent me."

"I don't believe it's resentment so much as fear," he said, splitting a reed with his knife.

"Of me?"

"Of losing control."

"That's what men fear?"

"That's what fear is."

"Huh." I tied off the last rib in my bait cage's skeleton. "Well, what's that got to do with me?"

"A woman can unsettle even the most indifferent man at times." He handed me neatly trimmed strips of reed. "You remind them their control is . . . limited."

Good. "Still, Tarana thanked you," I said. Something about the trial made no sense to me. It had disturbed my thoughts all night. "It almost sounded like he was grateful to die?"

Bracing the reed strips between the balls of his feet, he began to plait a cord. "Out here, we live on the sword's edge. We thrive by being bold—able to summon awful fury in the blink of an eye. The bravest among us owe our victories—our very survival—to this. But the violent passions that give a warrior his terrible power don't belong to him—don't reside inside his breast—or they would consume him and all those around him." He tied off the cord and prepared another. "No, to live in the world, he must make his flesh a fortress and keep such daimons at bay. Only when battle calls may he open the gates. But you should know they also come unin-vited. When a man is drunk, weary, or lets his thoughts stray into darkness, he leaves his gates unguarded. Those unable to govern their actions may not remain among us—they go to dwell with the gods, who incite the fury. It is said the Lord of Frenzy chooses sacrifices thus, and his servants gratefully accept. It is an honor, a duty, a blessing."

I drew a deep breath. "It is a lie."

He stopped his plaiting and frowned, fixing me in an accusative glare. "How so?"

"You say a man fears losing control. How, then, is losing his wits—his life—a blessing?"

He resumed his plaiting. "A man possessed does not lose con-trol—he gives it up to something greater than himself—a mixed blessing, to be sure. But one to be deeply desired. And to give his life at his lord's will? There is no greater glory."

I gaped at him in disbelief—in reproach. "You use these men to your will and dispose of them when you can no longer trust them. You drive them mad with zealousness and rage, then when they lose control—when *you* lose control of them—you convince them the gods willed it, and their execution is an honor." I braced myself for his wrath.

He looked up once more from his reed-plaiting, seeking my face, and gently smiled. "Clever Ana. How clearly your eyes see."

I didn't want to look at him but forced myself to meet his cold eye. "So, you don't even deny it? Do you believe a word you say?"

"Oh, do not doubt me, I believe. From the moment of our ini-tiation, we are dead men. We live in this realm as wraiths, at the mercy and whim of Artimpasa, mere branches that grow and with-er at her will. Only by her leave and Gœto's protection do we last even an hour here. Under the all-seeing eye of Thagimazda. How could this be unless we somehow serve their purposes? With our pledge to Gœto, we become little more than storms that blow at his command. Name it what you like, but the things that stir men to excellence sometimes drive them mad. What stands between inspiration and destruction but the will? Passion is the horse and will the rider. A heedless rider is often run away with or unseated. Every one of us is on the brink of losing our grip. On ourselves, on those around us, on this place. What would become of this warband—of Skythia—if we let madmen and rogues who lack restraint run wild among us?"

After finishing my bait cage, I removed my boots. "I honestly don't know," I said, wading into the bracingly cold stream.

"Nor do I. And I hope neither of us ever find out." He reached out his hand to me to pull me to shore. "Come, help me with the next set of traps."

THAT NIGHT, the mood in camp remained somber, with the men eating quietly and dispersing before dark. Tarana's lyre would be missed. But I was grateful for the quiet. I had watched the moon's phases with trepidation all my adult life. And as the moon dwindled, my dread grew. Tonight was a new moon, and that heralded something dire. Knowing when it would come was like foreseeing the coming rain—part observation, part intuition. Something one saw in the skies and felt deep in the bones. Mostly, it came in stealth, with the dark of the moon, just before my monthly time. Or else in times of thirst or pain or distress, when my defenses were weakest.

And if these men mistrusted me before, they must surely never learn of this now. Aric had warned of the dire consequences of possession. I had seen them with my own eyes. I could not afford to reveal the truth now. Not if I hoped to avoid Tarana's fate.

After sunset, I stole away from the gathering and made like I was going out to the pastures. Instead, I broke right on the outskirts of camp, over the rise northwest of the river. I found a hollow in a copse of trees, where I pulled my cloak over my head and tucked myself beneath the brambles. Concealed in the dark, I waited for it to find me—to make its presence known. Like no earthly thing I could name, the familiar odor was fetid and sweet, like burnt hair and rotten fruit decaying in a tomb. It always sparked the giddy wave of panic now fluttering in my gut. Something, or someone, watched me from within; looked with my eyes and felt with my skin, but was not myself. Then came recognition; I had somehow lived this exact moment, as if my spirit was dislocated, moving back and forth through hours and places I had been and had yet to go. For all I knew, I was not sensing but remembering. Or *something* was, as it showed me omens I was meant to apprehend.

In that moment, the sky grew heavy, pressing me down, squeezing the air from my lungs, threatening to crush my skull. Flashes of a punishing hunt flooded my mind. Men stalking men. Figures obscured by night. Panic seized me, and with it the searing, liquid light surged into my brain as vomit rises to the mouth, blinding my mind's eye.

Around me, the plain evaporated in faint wisps as shadows seeped in from all sides. My heart thumped. Fingers dug into the earth. And I opened my eyes wide against the inrushing darkness. But the dark was not before my eyes—it came from inside me. In rage, in terror, a futile voice inside my mind cried, no, no, n—

THE SHADOWS RECEDED, and I roused with a start. A one-eyed man towered over me, clutching a dagger in one hand and an amulet in the other. It was quiet now, but I thought I had heard chanting. He crouched down upon one knee and stared gravely into my eyes.

"Were you . . . *singing?*" I asked, utterly confused.

"What have you summoned?" he demanded, frowning anxiously.

I drew a deep breath and lowered my eyes. "I do not summon it. It summons me."

"Is it still about?" He allowed his gaze to shift from me to glance over his shoulders into the dark night surrounding us, squeezing the amulet in his fist.

My memory was missing. Of this place, of my name, my past. Confused but unafraid, I peered out onto a broad plain covered in night, and I didn't recognize any of it. I didn't know my own skin. Or the calloused hands with dirt-caked fingernails. Men's clothes. Only the troubled face before me somehow seemed familiar and safe.

"Was I gone long?" I asked.

"Long enough. Hard to tell in the dark. A minute or two, maybe."

"Aric."

"Hmm?"

"That's your name," I said triumphantly. My own name still eluded me.

"Have you lost your mind?"

"It's returning, thankfully." I exhaled deeply and considered my next words carefully.

He let the arm gripping the dagger fall to his side, though his fingers were still pale. "What is all this?"

"I—I don't think I can say."

He stared down at me in the faint starlight. "You'd better try."

Besides Father, I'd never told anyone about the spells—not even the priests. Certainly not a foreigner. It was probably a terrible mistake to tell Aric. But he'd seen. What point was there in hiding now? "Mad as it sounds, I think I die."

"I know how death looks. Your breath never ceased, and you mouthed strange words—to whom did you speak?"

"Truly, I don't know. I wish I did."

Aric's revelation was both a relief and a new worry. He asked questions neither of us could answer.

He shook his head. His expression softened into a bewildered smile as he sheathed his dagger, tucked the amulet into his belt, and knelt before me. He took my hands in his and squeezed them a bit too hard. "I have heard of this. Seen the anarei send one of their several souls to flight in their rites. Your *manah* has journeyed to the realm of the shades while your living form lies waiting. That is why you believed you had died." His eye widened with wonder. "It takes most anarei years of training to accomplish this, yet you do it freely. What did you see?"

"Nothing. It's all dark and silent. Not even dark; empty. Black and empty like the spaces between the stars."

He leaned in close. "Tell me all of it."

I wouldn't know where to begin or if I even should. I was too confused. I might say the wrong thing and make matters even worse. "Ask me another time?"

He was clearly dissatisfied but nodded.

"Wait," I shook my head, suddenly disturbed, "you followed me here? For fuck's sake, do you follow me to the latrine as well?"

"This was the other direction. I thought you might be . . . meeting someone."

"Meeting? What do you take me for?"

"Well, you wouldn't be the first. Besides, you shouldn't be wandering about at night."

"I don't need your supervision!"

"Have you forgotten where you are? Even the men know better than to stray out of camp alone after dark. We all need protection."

We sat in awkward silence. It was quiet here, and the moonless night was unusually still. Even the nocturnal creatures lay dormant.

"I understand if you wish me to leave the kara," I said. He would surely tell the king, and now that everything was revealed, the pact between our tribes would be dissolved.

"You swore an oath to god," he said, his voice toneless and grim. "I cannot send you away."

Then it was too late. "Will—" I swallowed hard, "will Tarana's fate be mine, also?"

"Why would it?"

"Because," my voice cracked, and my eyes began to sting, "I, too, may harbor some unruly daimon." There was no place in this world

153

for those who could not master their own bodies and minds. He had made that quite clear.

"This is . . . *different*."

"How do you know?" The night was warm, but I pulled my cloak close around me anyway.

"Because I've seen madmen. You harm no one." He drew a deep breath and took my hands in his once more. "And I have need of you."

"Need? What need?" I searched his face through the darkness, but he remained a menhir to me, immovable and unreadable.

"Anaiti, the gods gave you a gift."

Only fools spoke so fondly of things they didn't understand. "It's no gift, I promise you."

"There is a fine line between gift and curse," he chuckled, "I will grant you that. But I've never had a seer in my council."

"Me? I'm no seer. What do I know of such things?"

"You speak the language of beasts. Look into their minds as if looking through the waters of a spring. And now I witness you in congress with spirits—or even gods. I don't comprehend it. But the gods must grant you the two sights for some purpose. Why would they have sent you here if not to reveal it?"

How was I supposed to answer that? Already, I felt like a fraud in this place, acting the part of a warrior to eke out a bit of life before wifehood usurped my remaining days. But I wasn't what he imagined. I couldn't pretend to be.

When they first began, I also thought the spells conveyed hidden prophecies. They felt so momentous, so urgent, so consequential that they must be messages of cosmic import sent by those with sight and power beyond this world. But when I searched their contents, there was nothing there. Long ago, I decided my spells were tricks played upon me by some cruel or callous force of nature. A test, perhaps, but nothing more.

But Aric had so far been good to me and fair. If he believed

I could help him somehow, I should, even though I couldn't see how. I had nothing else of value to offer, though I longed to be of use. I knew in my bones there was nowhere else I belonged more than this inhospitable world I had stumbled into. It was an alien sensation for me, wanting anything of my own. But after I'd tasted pure freedom, how could I choose any other fate?

I never made plans for a long life. When I looked into my future, I never saw an old woman. I didn't fear death, and maybe in some bald logic, it made sense that I should be joined to an old man. All my life, I tried to keep my attachments few and thin. Mostly, I kept to myself. But if my time was to be short, I wanted to live—really live. Not just survive but be alive. I'd given up all hope of that before I came here and tasted it, swept across the plain under these dizzying skies. A brief respite before I either returned and wed or took an arrow to the heart. Those fates I'd reconciled, too. But what was I supposed to do now? I wasn't prepared for someone I hardly knew to stand at my back. To keep and defend me, even after what he'd seen of me—of what I was. And it filled every part of me with regret.

"If you truly believe I can be of use," I said, "I will try to help you in any way I can."

He squeezed my hands, and a smile warmed his whole face, dimpling his cheeks and crinkling his eyes. "I knew you would do me good. From the moment I first saw you."

"The others will not look so favorably on this."

"That's why it will be our secret." He grinned slyly. "Now, we should get back before the rest of the camp begins to talk."

CHAPTER 15

VISION

It was winter, and blood stained the snow—
mine and hers.

Antisthenes plucked the stones from the fire with iron tongs and set them into the bronze brazier, which, like a miniature altar, had a tripod base and a turned wooden handle for grasping when hot. Then he slipped through the flap of the leather tripod tent. Aric beckoned me to follow.

Inside, Rathagos, Stormai, Bradak, and Mourdag were stripped to the waist, waiting. Sitting cross-legged on the ground, our knees touching, we huddled around the brazier. Rathagos sat opposite me, and his scowl bored through my skin. Never my champion, I'd learned since the trial that Tarana had been Rathagos's blood-brother. After that day, wherever he was, I strove to be somewhere else. But he was a vazarka, and I could not avoid him forever.

The cramped, murky space had warmed quickly, and I began to sweat. Aric then dropped a handful of dried cannabis flowers upon the heated stones of the brazier. "We thank you, Tabiti," he said, "for the potency of your fire; Apia, for the gift of your rich bounty; Gœtosura, for the inspiration and vision we pray you grant us tonight; and Artimpasa for the wisdom and grace to enjoy the fruits of all."

Soon, a vapor rose and filled the steamy tent. I had to close my eyes against the potent fumes of the incense. I waited uneasily, but nothing happened. Blinking against the smoke, I looked around at the others, and they, too, sat in silence with their eyes closed, breathing deeply of the vapor. Confined in the stale, unlit space, the heat made me groggy, and my skin prickled with sweat. The acrid smoke drew tears from my eyes. My arms grew heavy and slow as if moving through water, and the faces around me began to recede into the shadows. The more I concentrated, struggling to keep hold of my thoughts, the more they slipped through my fingers, like trying to catch fish with my bare hands.

Rathagos opened his eyes to glare at me through the smoke. I quickly glanced aside, blinking to clear the stinging vapors. One by one, the men began howling like wolves. I sought Aric's face and tried to focus on him alone. But amid the howling, from the corners of my eyes, I saw the faces of the others transform horribly. I had to look away. In the dim light of smoke and shadows, I saw a vision I could not bear. An inner voice begged me to stand up and throw the whole tent down. Release the vapors to the wind along with their howls. Casting my gaze into the stones and embers, where only seeds and ashes of the incense remained, I breathed deeply to calm myself and thought of sand along a riverbank—clean, dry sand sifting through my fingers—to clear my mind. A savage headache spread over the crown of my skull, and I rested my head in my hands, palms pressed into my eyes, until the ritual was over.

When the men dispersed from the tent, I rushed to the river to wash my face and drink the cold water. The first sliver of moon had risen overhead, and the sky was clear and full of stars.

Aric followed. "Did you not enjoy the holy vapor?"

"I did not." I couldn't see why they would intentionally subject themselves to such a horror. But he seemed unusually lighthearted.

"What's distressing you so? The incense is meant to cleanse the spirit and bring peace. And the others were respectful. I didn't invite Olgas. He can get carried away. And he always farts in the tent." He laughed heartily at this and needed a moment to catch his breath. "But I wanted you to enjoy your first time."

"It was kind of you. Perhaps it was the heat. My head aches and I just need fresh air."

"Were you given visions?" His eye grew wide at the prospect. "The visions are what make the vapor so cleansing. I thought it might encourage yours."

So, visions were part of the ritual? Should I relate my horrid daydream about the wolves? How they set on him and tore him to pieces. He would think me ridiculous. But what if it was a warning?

"I feel silly, but I think the wolf howls of the men upset me." I told him what I saw. "It probably means nothing, but that's why I was afraid."

"Bless you, Anaiti," he smiled, took my hands, and kissed them. "You've shared your first portent! But you've no reason to worry. I've no fear of wolves anymore."

"Anymore?" I asked as I sat on the riverbank and let my feet dangle in the cold water. The moon's faint glow made us little more than shadows.

"When I was young, the sound of wolves howling at night terrified me," Aric said, sitting beside me and pulling off his boots.

"It's one of the most chilling sounds in this world."

"Not according to my father," Aric gave a wry smile and set his feet in the water. "He said the howling of wolves was the music of the steppe—the voices of our ancient fathers. But I'd cower near the fire beneath a blanket, put my hands over my ears, and hum to myself whenever they were about."

It was nearly impossible to reconcile the hardened and scarred warrior beside me with a frightened little boy tucked under his blankets in hiding.

"Any child would be frightened by wolves," I said. "Most adults, too, I think. The sensible ones."

"Well, this only angered my father. No son of his would be so cowardly, even if I had only six or seven winters."

"He was angry?"

"Ashamed, I think. He dragged me out into the wilderness in the middle of winter with him to hunt wolves, telling me, 'The wolf can smell fear,' and that I must be unafraid, or they would come for me."

I leaned back and pressed my palms into the grass. "This was designed to encourage you?"

"Heh, I suppose. We stalked a small pack along a deer trail through the snow for half the night until they made a kill—a doe. He made me kneel below a rise downwind and watch as they fed. I crouched there with my bow in my hand, afraid to breathe. One of the wolves tore off its portion and dragged it beside my hiding place to feed. In the faint light, I saw the shine of the wolf's eyes. It looked straight at me. I held my breath and drew my bow." He looked away downriver.

"You killed it?"

"I shot it dead with a single arrow straight through the heart," he said dryly, speaking into the darkness.

"That's incredible."

"Truly, it is," he turned to face me. "It's also complete bullshit. But that's the story the king tells of that night." He hesitated, his voice softening. Slumping forward, he drew a deep breath. "I shouted for my father, fell in the snow, and dropped my bow. I was certain I would be food for the wolves. I even pissed myself." He chuckled, and a sardonic smile turned his features.

I tried and likely failed to hide my shock at his candid revelation. But my heart broke for that little boy. "That must have been terrifying. Did the wolf attack?"

"Something even stranger happened. It spooked and ran."

"You didn't kill it?"

"No. But my father was waiting nearby. He shot her as she fled and dragged the carcass before me, his arrow piercing her side. She was still breathing, whimpering. It took her a while to die. I cried watching her suffer, but he refused to end her pain. He strode forward and struck me across the face. I remember tasting blood. It was winter, and blood stained the snow—mine and hers.

"Then my father slit open her belly and removed her heart. He squeezed the blood from it over my head and held it out to me. 'Eat,' he said. He took my hand, thrust the warm heart in it, and stared down at me. I knew he would not ask again." His eye glazed as if he were conjuring the image behind its veil. "I ate. The blood sticky on my hands. The raw flesh like iron on my tongue. The chewy gristle in the center. I nearly puked up my guts."

He sat upright now, hands resting on his thighs as he looked at the flowing waters.

"He made me wash in the frozen river before we could return home. I sat naked before the campfire while my clothes dried, shivering through the night." He shook his head and drew a long breath through his nose. "All these years, I've kept the true version of that story to myself. It's strange to tell it now."

I still didn't know all the unspoken laws, but I gently rested my hand atop his. He didn't flinch or pull away.

"It is forbidden for a warrior to eat the flesh of a wolf or dog. It is akin to cannibalism. But my father thought it the only way to put my fear to rest. I've kept that wolfskin to this day—to remind me."

"I can't believe your father could be so cruel." The same heartless man I must one day wed. "You were just a child."

"They say the wolf pup is born dead. It is only awakened to life by the sound of its father's howl." He took my hand in both of his and looked me in the face. "I was born a king's son. I was never a child. But after that night, I made a choice. I would no longer have fear. Not of any beast, nor man, nor of the dark."

CHAPTER 16

VIGIL

*When the moment came, I could neither save
him nor follow him to the grave as I had sworn.*

JOLTED FROM MY SLEEP, I lay as still as stone, afraid even to
breathe. Eyes wide in the fading light of the smoldering fire, I
struggled to make sense of the sounds beyond the felt walls. A
muffled rustling stirred the dry grass like the grazing of sheep.
Should I wake Aric? If it was nothing, he would be angry. But my
instincts cried out to be wary. I peered across the dimly lit tent, and
Antisthenes was not in his bed. Reaching over the sword stretched
between our beds, I gently but firmly gripped Aric's wrist. He
slowly turned his head toward me, blinking. I clutched my dagger
and rolled my eyes toward the sound. He nodded, slowly pulling
his blade to his chest and curling his fingers around the handle of
the sword between us.

Something scraped against the felt. My heart pounded furiously. Blood rushed in my ears, and I could no longer hear. Awaiting
a sign, I fixed my eyes on Aric. Would he raise the alarm? Rush
out to fight? Or wait for *it* to come to us? Maybe it was nothing—a
deer or loose horse.

He held up three fingers close to his chest. Three prowlers.

Fuck.

There was only one way into—and out of—the tent: through the door. Going through the felt and lattice walls would alert us and others. Our advantage was in knowing of their presence and getting to the door first. Aric placed his finger over his lips, then pointed to himself and the door's left side, then to me and the right side of the door. I followed his lead as we crept on our bellies to the door, crouched with weapons drawn, and waited. Aric, I knew, could handle himself even if we were outnumbered, but I wasn't prepared for close combat. Where the fuck had Antisthenes gone?

When the assassins entered, they came softly. The first one through the door, Aric pounced upon like a leopard. Seized him from behind with an arm around his neck and, with one swift motion, cut his throat. It was not what I imagined killing would be. The man did not linger, whimper, or gaze at us in dread like the heroes' tales all told. He gasped and fell limp across the doorsill in a spout of blood.

The next followed fast on his heels, stumbling over the body as I thrust my long dagger hard under his ribs. This one did not die quickly. He turned and fell on me, and we both crashed to the ground. I seized his wrist as he stabbed with his dagger, diverting it into the mats beside my head. He thrashed, unable to pull free, trying to punch and claw at me with his free hand. Aric rushed to pull him off me. Grabbing a fistful of his hair, he pulled back the man's head and sliced open his throat, spraying me with a shower of hot blood.

The third man rushed in. Wrestling the heavy dead man from atop me, I pulled myself free from the corpse, but my dagger remained stuck under his ribs. Aric spun around with his akinaka in his hand, the stabbing point down in the confined space. The walls close, the man circled the hearth, stepping over the bodies already littering the floor. On my feet but weaponless, I readied myself to pounce. The third man lunged at Aric before I could move.

He charged, avoiding Aric's sword, knocking him to the wall and pinning him. Aric fought to wrestle the dagger away, the man's wrist locked in his grip. I leapt upon the beast's back and grabbed at his throat but could gain no hold on his strained and bulging neck, thick and sweating as it was. I wrapped both my arms around his windpipe, squeezing with all my might to choke his breath from him. I felt a strange, sharp pinch in my left forearm, and I realized with horror that the man's teeth were sunk deep into my flesh. Releasing my hold, I instead reached for his face and dug my fingers into his eyes. I clawed with all the ferocity in me. With horror, I saw the assassin's dagger was stuck in Aric's ribs. My fingers burrowed into his eye sockets, his bulging eyes squishing like boiled eggs in my angry grip. I probed and scraped until he screeched like a woman and abandoned his assault, releasing Aric to pry my hands from his face.

This gave Aric the chance to push the beast back, toppling him over on me and driving his sword down through the assassin's body, the point piercing his side.

I relaxed my clutching hands but did not move until I was sure he was dead. With my last remaining strength, I shoved his bulk aside and struggled to my feet, wiping my hands on the thighs of my trousers.

Aric stood, his back to the wall and both hands upon the grip of his drawn sword. As blood streamed down his brow and into his eye, he blinked furiously and stared, unseeing, into the shadows of the tent. I stepped toward him, and he braced the sword and made a threatening cut. "Name yourself!" he demanded, his voice strained but controlled.

"Aric," I said calmly as I could manage, "it's me, Anaiti. They're all dead." He blinked hard, but his eye still had not focused on me. I stepped closer, approaching slowly, speaking softly. "I am here," I said, touching his quivering arm. He didn't flinch but relaxed and lowered his sword, releasing a hand from the hilt to wipe the blood from his eye. Blinking furiously to clear his vision, he looked at me as if for the first time, exhaled deeply, thrust an arm around my back, and crushed me against him, his hand resting softly on my head.

"Ho! We heard a struggle," Olgas shouted through the doorflap.

Aric released me with a brusque shove.

"Help us!" I called to Olgas, and he rushed in, sword drawn.

"Oh, fuck." Stormai stood beside him, eyes wide, mouth gaping. "The Man-Eaters have come." He ducked his head back outside and shouted for the vazarka to rally around the tent and the other men to disperse and search the surrounding fields for more hostiles.

I turned to see if Aric was all right. He braced the fingers of his left hand flat against his ribs around the dagger and slowly withdrew it with his right. The blade seemed to have glanced off the bones themselves and lodged beneath the muscle. He sneered at the knife and tossed it toward the dead man at his feet.

"Ana, are you hurt?" Aric asked.

"No," I said. "But one of the bastards bit me." I pulled up my sleeve and showed him my arm.

"Ha! Your worst fear! A cannibal ate you," he teased and eased himself back against the post for support.

"The white crow has claws," Olgas said, pointing to the eyeless man on the floor.

"What?" I asked, confused once again by their odd expressions. "You're a bit late. But now you have three Mokhsa scalps you can wipe your ass with," I said as I placed my foot against the dead man's ribs and yanked my dagger free. Strange how readily flesh accepted iron and how unwillingly it released it.

"Did you kill any?" Stormai asked.

"Strictly speaking, Aric slew them all," I noted. "You're bleeding badly," I said to Aric, eyeing his wound. "Sit, let me look at that."

"I'm fine," he said, waving his hand dismissively, and promptly collapsed where he stood.

I fell to my knees over him and used my tunic sleeve to wipe away the blood so I could examine the place where the short, narrow blade had pierced his side. The wound was not terribly deep, but it bled a lot. I wasn't sure, studying the weapon more closely, but I thought I could smell something off.

"Stormai!" I shrieked, unaware he was already beside me.

"I'm here," he said in his deep monotone, but the worry was written on his creased brow.

"Please, sit with him. Put pressure on this cloth—as hard as he can bear—and I'll return with water and salve to clean this."

TWENTY MORE MAN-EATERS were killed in the fields before they could inflict any more harm or steal any stock. Their bodies we burned on the opposite bank of the river, and we buried their ashes under a pile of black stones. They'd never harm the Skythai again, in this world or the next. A massive raiding party immediately set out for the Mard-Khwaar territory to finish what perhaps should have been done that very first night. The Man-Eaters would now fall under the terrible vengeance of the Paralatai. Many would die, and the rest would be driven from those lands forever when the Skythai laid claim to their territory. No more would they terrorize the tribes of the north or dam the flow of trade down its rivers.

I wished I could have ridden with them, but I was determined to remain with Aric, helping tend to his wound. Antisthenes rushed back to the tent when he got word of the attack, though he said nothing of where he'd been. We spent an entire day scrubbing the walls and carpets clean and replacing the mats soiled with blood until no trace of the invaders remained.

No trace but one.

Unsurprisingly, Aric was a terrible patient. He'd allowed the camp's healer—a vazarka called Galati—to anoint the blade of the Man-Eater's dagger with a healing balm and then recite verses over him to exorcise the malignant daimon introduced into his body on the point of the blade. The healer was a good-looking man of middle years, tall and slender with long flaxen hair, long beard, and dusky blue eyes. A savage-looking scar ran the length of his face on the left, from his temple to his chin. Galati banished us from the tent for an entire day and night while he performed a clamorous rite with a drum and cast various sweet and noxious herbs onto the fire, chanting all the while. I peered through the cracks from time to time to observe the rites, which I didn't understand. He moved quickly for a tall man but not hurriedly. With a smooth grace, each long, slim limb rose and fell with the fierce, sharp precision of a whip's lash.

In the morning, when he emerged, Aric looked brighter. But after that, he could not be persuaded to rest nor let us summon a healer from court. Instead, he salved the dagger's blade several times a day and never let it from his sight. Soon, the cut was severely inflamed, rimmed with traces of blue-black rot from the evil. Galati continued to feed him a cure of herbs and fermented fruits. It smelled sweet, and he said it would counter the venom.

"Perhaps I should have taken my father's advice," Aric chuckled listlessly as he propped his back against a freshly scrubbed post, "and let that wily anarei poison me." His eye looked almost bruised, so dark was the shadow that encircled it now.

"Why would he do that?"

"The king has Erman poison him each day with every manner of toxin, in small amounts, to harden his flesh against their effects. He claims to have built a tolerance for every venom and disease known to the Agari, the greatest sorcerers and poisoners in the world."

"And how does Erman come to possess this skill?"

"He was born of their tribe. They learn to harvest deadly plants from the moment they can walk."

His head lolled back against the post, and he closed his eye.

All warriors feared—and decried—poison as treacherous and cowardly. It was a double death, for it took both life and honor.

Yet few shunned it entirely. The Mard-Khwaar, I learned, were known to dip their arrows and blades in venom, feces, noxious weeds, and corpses before attacking their enemies—which, to be fair, we had done before our raid as well. Unlike the poisons used in hunting, which killed instantly, these brought a slow, horrific death meant to instill weakness, inflict torment, inspire fear. Instead of defiantly facing down the jaws of an enemy's weapons on the battlefield, poison's lingering incapacity bestowed a shameful death upon the proud warrior. There was no telling what kind of rot was now coursing through Aric's blood. I clenched my hands into fists to keep them from trembling. Much as we all respected Galati's craft, I feared his intercession with the spirits might not be enough. Though what I could possibly do, I had no idea. Perhaps only stand and watch as Aric's chest heaved with labored breaths or listen to the wheezing that rasped past his dry lips like the wind rattling through the door of an abandoned house. I was glad he closed his eye so he could not see the panic on my face.

He was overcome with a fever in the night, and his limbs swelled. At least in his weakness, he had no choice but to allow us to care for him, though now we feared it might be too late. Antisthenes mixed a potion of willow powder and Apia's tears—the poppy's amber resin—to help him sleep and ease his pain. With nothing to lose in trying, I mixed a warm poultice of mashed plantain leaves to draw the poison. Then, in the morning, I soaked some bread in buttermilk, left it to curdle in the sunlight, and then applied this poultice to the wound. For two days, it seemed to slow the rot. The blackness ceased to spread, and his condition improved. Then suddenly, the fever returned.

His skin burned, and he lay in sweat-soaked rags. His thirst was terrible, though he wouldn't eat. His pale skin clung to his bones like wet cloth to a rail. Nothing we tried to feed him—not any potions or nourishment—stayed in his stomach long. He slept, seeming to remember nothing.

When his fever worsened and his skin went dry and hot like an iron stove, the men wanted to call a priest to perform divination and offer sacrifice. Galati and several others said I was killing him. And maybe they were right. I was no healer. The only medicine I knew was for horses. It was a foolish risk to take if he should die. But how could I not try? In his few waking moments, I begged Aric to let them summon help. He refused.

When I demanded to know why, Antisthenes explained that—even if Aric would tolerate such healing, which he would not—we were far from a friendly village or farmstead of any substance. With the court a hundred or more miles away this time of year, finding a trusted healer with these arts—or getting one to make the long, slow journey by cart, as they did not ride—was impossible. And he was far too sick to travel.

We were stranded, then. Abandoned like a boat without oars. But I would be damned if I would stand and watch him suffer another day. Listen to him mumble in his delirium. Feel him convulse with fever under my hands as I sponged the sweat from his burning flesh. Look into his fierce but weary eye and wonder when the fire would finally burn out.

I knew of only one more thing to try. It was an ancient cure I learned from an old hamazan healer and once used on a beloved horse that tore its leg in a chariot mishap and was too far from the sea to be steeped in the brine. I'd seen wild garlic in the meadows, but it was still early for onions. I might find some, but they wouldn't be ready to harvest. I would have to gather what I could and hope for the best. I spent the better part of an afternoon wandering the fields collecting the bulbs I would need. Crushing equal amounts in a mortar, I mixed the mash with a cup of undiluted wine. This mixture was then steeped in a cow's stomach for three days while suspended in a cold, flowing river. I only prayed he had three more days.

While I waited, we carried water from the river for cooling

cloths to bathe him, and I sat with him almost night and day—vigilant, though for what I couldn't say. Sitting cross-legged at the head of his bed, I looked upon his grey skin in dismay and watched his breast's laborious rise and fall. Day and night, he lay in a state more like death than sleep. When he roused, I would take his hand and speak softly to him, gently combing my fingers through his damp hair until he grew quiet. I'd never cursed an entire people, but I cursed the Mard-Khwaar. Man, woman, and child, I cursed them.

EACH DAY, AS I SAT VIGIL, some of the vazarka would come in shifts to sit with me or take my place while I slept. We still feared another strike while Aric was weakened, so guards were posted day and night.

Bornon came and sat with me one day outside the felt-house, and we spent the better part of the afternoon brushing up my technique with daggers. I was determined that I should never again be caught off guard. When the lesson was through, we sat to refresh ourselves with kumis and sharpen our blades. A stolid man, he was unusually chatty as we sat together plying our whetstones. Dawdling about camp was getting to everyone.

"Were you really eaten by a Mard-Khwaar?" he asked, screwing up his face in revulsion.

"Well, just a bit."

His expression transformed into childlike curiosity. "Can I see?"

I pulled up my sleeve to show him the wound. Two neat semi-circles cut into my forearm in the unmistakable shape of human teeth. He cringed.

"Is it bad?" I asked him, my well-concealed worry rising to the surface. "Will I become like them now?" With bigger concerns, I'd tried to put the fear from my mind.

His face contorted as he worked to suppress a smile. Then he burst out with a hearty laugh. "I don't think that's how it works," he said, slapping his thigh with amusement.

"Well, I don't know how they get like that."

"And you thought being bitten . . . ?"

"Don't laugh! When a rabid animal bites another, it goes mad. I thought maybe men go mad the same way."

"Have you been troubled about that all this time?"

"Maybe a little. . . ."

He erupted with laughter again.

"I'm glad this amuses you."

He snorted and caught his breath, then stopped sharpening his blade and looked at me in earnest. "Did you really pull out the man's eyes?" He blinked his own soft brown eyes at me in disbelief.

The memory of it still sickened me.

Grinning, he gripped my shoulder, shaking me gently. "Next time we train, I will teach you proper grappling. If you like."

"I would. Very much."

He nodded his shaggy brown head and went back to polishing the nicks from the edge of his sword. "You've been standing watch every day since?

"If they want him, they'll have to fight me."

"I'd not tangle with you," he nudged me with his elbow and smiled. "Did I ever tell you that my old tribe used to cross the Hamazan River to trade with the Aorsi for horses?"

"I think I heard you mention it. Did you know many hamazan?"

"A few. There was a girl . . . Leimeia. You remind me of her. A bit shy, *very stubborn*. A smart mouth on that one, too," he grinned.

"I like her already," I kidded, giving him a playful shove.

"She tamed horses, too. They have a way with horses, the hamazan. They can pacify them with a word or a touch like I saw you do with that bay gelding of yours. I never saw horses like that anywhere else, and I would go on festival days to trade for them with the band. We'd meet up, Leimeia and I, after the fairs and ride into the fields. After long, we even talked about leaving our bands behind to join our houses. We were both rich enough in stock. We argued, though. We just couldn't decide which side of the Tanais we'd settle on. She couldn't imagine leaving her homeland. And my people thought it a disgrace for a man to settle in the home of his wife. But I decided I didn't care. One year, for Midsummer, I crossed the river, determined I would go to her side if she'd have me. But she was gone. Killed in a raid that spring."

"Oh, Bornon, I am so sad for you," I said clumsily. I wanted to put an arm around him and pull him close, but he kept working at his blade with steady, even strokes. I studied him as he worked. Beneath his bristly beard, his face was deeply scarred. Rows of scars lined his cheeks, crossing the bridge of his nose and forehead. He was missing half of his left ear and his left hand's last finger at the second joint. "You've seen so much fighting," I said. "More than I ever will. May I ask . . . if it isn't out of line? Who could have done such terrible things to you?"

He set down his whetstone and looked me squarely in the face. "My lady, may you never know the thing that has done this to me."

I shook my head in regret. "I meant no offense."

"I've taken none. I will tell you this much. Before I came here, I was a karik in the warband of another tribe. My beloved lord was slain. When the moment came, I could neither save him nor follow him to the grave as I had sworn. I had other vows yet to keep. But this life—and my lord Aric—promised me vengeance."

"Did you get it?"

He looked wistful, his eyes going glassy as he stared at something inside his mind. "A thousand times over."

"Yet, you remain."

"What else is there for me?" He tested his blade with a piece of leather thong. It sliced through like an oar through water. "All these men are here because they could not find satisfaction in the world. We're exiles, by chance or by choice. We remain in pursuit of something. Honor. Justice. Purpose. Redemption. Gold and cattle can't buy these things." He nicked his arm, drawing blood, then sheathed the sword. "What do wealth, rank, kin—even sur-vival—mean in the face of service to this? To the lord we serve?"

"Aric?"

"Gœtosura."

MORE DISTURBING THAN DEADLY, my wounds were mostly healed. Though eager to help, Antisthenes seemed preoccupied with maintaining order in Aric's stead. As steward, it was his duty to take charge in Aric's absence. But he'd been acting strangely since that night, and more than once, I stopped myself from asking why he wasn't in his bed when the assassins came. I assumed he had gotten up to take a piss. Was there more? I lacked the authority here to question him, and we both had more important concerns just now, but I kept a close watch on the Hellene as we went about our tasks, unsure what I was even looking for.

The time had come to try my potion. I knew it wouldn't work instantly. I just hoped it would work. The blackening around the wound's edges, indicating the presence of poison, had subsided, but a feverishness and ooze had lingered. Soaking some clean bandages, I pressed the mixture into Aric's festering wound. Holding the flat of my palm over the soaked cloth and gazing down at his listless form, dread filled my breast. What if this should fail? Unwilling to entertain that possibility, I lifted the bandage and poured some potion into the open wound. Then soaked another clean cloth and held it again to his rattling ribs.

What would become of me in a place like this if he were gone? And what of these men? What would become of the warband? He was the pole at the center of this great tent, keeping the whole structure aloft; if he fell, it all fell.

Antisthenes left the tent to fetch more butter from the lar-der wagons for our breakfast, and I was alone with Aric. It was the first time I'd seen him without the patch. In his delirium, he could no longer prevent us from removing it. Tentatively, I leaned forward and pressed my lips to his burning brow. "Aric, don't you dare die," I whispered. "I know you are weary. Rest. But don't go. Please don't go."

Antisthenes tapped his brief signal on the doorframe and slipped back through the door. I bolted up straight and still, staring at the wall until I heard him settle into chores behind me. Closing my eyes, I exhaled slowly, and a word formed itself in my mind. *Please.* Over and over, I chanted it like a prayer. *Please.*

The following morning, Aric's fever broke. As I laid my hand on his cool brow, the clenched fist within my chest relaxed, and I let the weariness rise. My touch awakened him with a scowl, and he swatted away my hand.

"Woman, don't fuss over me," he grunted and turned his face away.

"Fine, go to the crows then!" I snapped.

"You should thank Anaiti," Antisthenes chided him. "You have been quite ill. Her skill has healed you." He was busying himself over the hearth, cooking barley cakes and mild millet porridge. Aric hadn't eaten in days.

Aric frowned, bewildered. "How long have I been sleeping?" his voice was raspy and thin.

"Nearly a week," Antisthenes replied as he lifted a barley cake from the fire and set it aside to cool. He came and knelt beside Aric's bed, his hands clasped before him. "When they came, I was not there for you, my lord, because I had forgotten my duty. I am humiliated." He bowed his head and spoke in Greek, "*Dikēn aitoumai ektisai:* I ask to pay the penalty."

"You have never failed me before. And you are here now," Aric said weakly, "and so am I," placing his pale hand over that of Antisthenes.

"I prayed, and the gods were merciful," Antisthenes nearly whispered, his voice cracking. He cleared his throat. "They heard my prayers; you shall survive."

"Doesn't feel like it," Aric attempted to chuckle and clasped his side, his face contorted in agony.

"You had a fever," I said in understatement.

He just shook his head. "And your wounds?"

"It turns out being eaten by cannibals sounds worse than it is," I forced a smile. "Do you think you can eat a little?"

Antisthenes retreated to fetch the cooled cakes and porridge.

"It appears I owe you a great debt," Aric said.

"You'd have done the same for me," I boldly assumed.

"I owe my life to you twice over—when the Man-Eater overcame me and again when his foul poison nearly did. With Antisthenes as our witness, by Thagimazda, Gœtosura, and all the gods, and on this day, whatever day this is, I pledge you, Anaiti, daughter of Arianta of the Bastarnai, two lives." He pointed to a wicker chest on the back wall beside the altar. "Fetch me that chest."

He winced as he struggled to prop himself upright, wheezing harshly with the effort. Antisthenes, seeming eager to be of use, rushed him the chest, and Aric rooted through it until finally drawing out a small leather pouch. From it, he pulled two golden rings, each the size of a man's fist and made of three slender gold bands twisted into a rope.

"My pledge." Aric held the rings out to me on the palm of his hand.

"But I would do it again freely."

"Take them, my lady," Antisthenes urged.

"What does it mean?" I glanced between them, confused.

"They are yours. As is my gratitude. I owe you two lives—your own or any others of your choosing."

ARIC SAID HE NEEDED to see the sun rise. Indeed, it would probably do him good. He dressed just before daybreak. Moving slowly, he managed to get into his trousers, though Antisthenes and I had to help him into his tunic and caftan. At the door, he slipped on his boots and grabbed his cap. We made no mention to any of the others that he'd be venturing out so there'd be no crowd of well-wishers.

I held the doorflap for him just as the first hints of gold glowed in the east. Facing toward the dawn, before the door of the felt-house, he took his cap from his head and pressed it to his chest, then waited for the sun to break over the horizon.

As the disk came into view, he began quietly, almost to himself, to chant an incantation to the rising sun:

> Eye of the Great God,
> Eye of the God of Glory
> Eye of the King of Hosts
> Eye of the Lord of the Living,
> Pouring upon us at every season
> Pouring upon us gently and generously
> Glory to Thee, thou noble Sun,
> Glory to Thee, face of the God of Life."

As he finished, the great disk of the sun cleared the horizon. No longer able to look on the brightness of it, I turned to face him, and he smiled gently, the red-gold glow of first light emblazoned across his joyful face.

CHAPTER 17

HAMAZAN

*In the dark age of my tender youth, after
countless failed efforts to explain, I decided I
didn't need to justify my existence to anyone.*

I N THE FOLLOWING DAYS, Aric remained close to camp while
he recovered his strength. Antisthenes and I argued over whether
he was up to making the long journey to Gerrhi for the Midsummer festival, though it seemed unlikely anyone could stop Aric if
he wanted to do something. I may not have been able to dissuade
him, but I kept a close eye on him, worried about all the things I
couldn't control.

On a warm, sunny morning, I suggested he looked well enough
to ride out with me and check traps and snares in the field surrounding camp. It was fruitful work but not overly taxing on the
body. He'd agreed and even led my horse in from the pasture for
me. But I observed how winded he was upon his return. We walked
our horses out to the hunting grounds, enjoying the leisurely day.

"Look what I got!" I shouted across the field to him. A deadfall
trap I had set the day before near an outcrop of rock had taken
a good rabbit. I'd be happy to give that to Bradak for our dinner.

Aric whistled back a cheer.

I put the rabbit in my pack, reset the trap, and ambled down the field to meet him. He gave a faint smile at my approach and looked away. He'd been quiet all morning.

"Is it Midsummer worrying your thoughts? I'm sure no one will mind if you miss the festival this once. I won't mind missing it, either."

"The men are uneasy. Now is no time to tax their faith." Kneeling in the grass, he was untangling a snare that had snarled in the underbrush, as they often did from the fierce winds over the plain. "They fear you, you know."

Was it me he brooded about? "That's ridiculous. Bunch of grown men—warriors no less—afraid of a woman. Is this about the potion? I healed you, that's all."

"Some of the men say the hamazan are sorceresses. Others say you're not human."

A cackle burst from me, but I could see he was serious. "What are we then?"

"Mourdag said that you're the maidservants of Artimpasa, spirits which lead men into the wilds and drive them mad." He flashed an inscrutable smile.

"Oh no, you're not going to blame me. I found you like this. You were already in the wilds—and already mad."

"Heh, I can't argue there," he chuckled and finally pulled the snare free. His laugh warmed me, as did the way his big, boyish grin crinkled the skin around his eyes. Even with the patch, his eyes were expressive, especially when he was happy. Aric looked up from the snare in his hand, quiet and thoughtful. "Why do you do it?" he asked, brow furrowing with what seemed genuine curiosity, free from the disgust that so often tinged the questions of strangers.

"Oh, that." I knew his meaning. I laced my undervest snug to avoid the questions, but sooner or later, they asked. Men invariably noticed breasts—or their absence. I'd long ago ceased retelling the lore I learned from my mother and hamazan tutors. It wasn't what outsiders wanted to hear. It had made me an oddity among the Bastarnai, where such customs were unknown. And though I had once hoped women of the Skythai shared in the hamazan tradition, they seemed to have abandoned it with the coming of the Hellenes. In the dark age of my tender youth, after countless failed efforts to explain, I decided I didn't need to justify my existence to anyone. Still, part of me needed him to see.

"It is forbidden to reveal its secrets. Any man who witnesses the sacraments or learns their mysteries is put to death," I warned him. "But you have welcomed me into the rites of your order; I will trust you with the secrets of mine." *Some of them, anyway.* His earnestness deserved honesty. But would he understand or be horrified? I drew a deep breath.

"As you know, we dedicate ourselves to the Mistress of Beasts and of the Wilds. Among the Suramatai, where I was fostered until I had nearly twelve winters, it is to Artimpasa that fellowships like this are devoted. The rite sets us apart from other women and is a source of strength and pride for the hamazan."

"But not to you?"

I shrugged. "A hamazan's arm must be hardened to draw the bow and strike deadly blows like a man's, so its weakness must be negated if we would be equal to the task of battle. When the right breast is sacrificed, all its force and power is channeled into the right shoulder and arm, imbuing it with the strength necessary for the rigors of combat. But outside of our homeland, this makes us misfits . . . monstrosities even."

"And among your own?"

"The wise mothers say it is our first union. We need no other."

His brow wrinkled with confusion. "To whom are you joined?"

"There is no one to speak of. Like two sides of a coin that cannot be divided, they say all opposite things must be joined to become whole. In this way, the sky is united with the earth, day with night. And female must be reconciled with male. Even before we come of age, the hamazan are made whole in this way." I instinctively pressed my closed right fist over my breast. "This—not her first blood, union with a man, or birth of a child—is her moment of maturity. Unlike other women, she does not need a husband to find completion, for she is full within herself—woman and warrior."

Aric stared at me, dumbfounded and, I think, a little unnerved. Did he really wish to know all this? Once I had opened the door to this secret world and allowed him a glimpse inside, might I lose the trust and friendship I had so grudgingly conceded and so foolishly craved?

"Though, my mother told me another story when I was just a girl. I doubt if it's true, but I always liked it. She said that when Artimpasa was a young goddess, she dwelt in the wilds of her secluded river valley. She would spend her days and nights in solitude as she hunted and swam in the river or ran through the fields and forests like a deer, with the beasts as her only companions. She refused all suitors and had no desire to belong to any man but treasured her liberty above all else.

"But the more she refused them, the more the gods pursued, desiring above all what was denied them. They spied upon her one day as she went to bathe. As she undressed, they became inflamed with lust. She saw them approaching the riverbank with lascivious intent, coming to ravage her and carry her back to their palace.

"She reached the bank before they did. There, she drew her dagger. They only laughed, thinking she would try to stand and fight them all. She knew she'd be no match for their numbers and strength, but what she did next disarmed them all the same. She turned the dagger upon herself, and with it, she severed her right breast and offered it up to them to soothe their vulgar passions.

"With their object of desire in hand, so to speak, they were satisfied—spellbound by its beauty. They departed, and she was able to slip away unmolested. They left her to her wild kingdom and never troubled her again.

"See? So little given; so much gained."

"I think I understand," he said, chewing his lip thoughtfully. "So, how is it done? Is there much pain?"

"A small tool of bronze like a spade is heated and put to the right breast. It's done when we're young, so it never fully forms. I remember little of it."

"Do you regret it?"

My eyes swept over the contours of this boundless place, with no dwelling or mark of human hands upon it but only the unbridled winds bending the grasses beneath them. I met his earnest gaze and smiled. "Not here."

———— ◆◆◆ ————

AS THE MOON RECEDED, I knew the next spell would soon come upon me. Having made a pact to guard me during these spells, Aric agreed to help me in both concealing the fact of them and reaping whatever benefits might be gained by them in the way of prophecy. I was dubious about the latter, but I was more than ready to try for the sake of the former.

The solution he proposed was that we should venture into the cannabis tent when I sensed one was imminent. This would arouse no undue suspicion. Here, we could be alone, away from prying eyes and ears. The tents were meant for a divinatory purpose, anyhow. Simple tripods of light wooden poles draped in leather or felt, most of the men owned personal smoking tents. Being conical and about chest height, a private tent allowed one or two people to sit cross-legged inside around the burning brazier. Space within was held sacred by all Skythai, and if anyone suspected indecent behavior, they dared not speak their thoughts aloud. I hoped the tent's heat would bring on the spell more rapidly, as thirst and stress often did.

After the first experience with cannabis smoke and my night-marish vision, I asked Aric not to burn it, fearing it would only confuse things. He acquiesced but suggested we light the fire and heat the stones, offering to burn some dried juniper for protection instead in hopes of cleansing away dark spirits. With the heat inside the tent, wearing only a minimum of clothing was necessary. Boots, stockings, and tunics were left outside, as were our weapons.

In the glow of the small brazier, I sat across from him and watched the curls of juniper smoke rise before his face. He grinned awkwardly at me, a little nervous, I guessed, as was I. The glow of the brazier was faint. Out of the shadows, the orange light glanced off the broad, angular sweep of his cheekbones, the long, straight bridge of his nose, and the smooth, subtle arcs over his brows, interrupted only by the leather strap. I dipped into the deep well of my thoughts, searching for something to say, but came up dry. And if I stared at him any longer, the silence would crawl inside me and begin its dance—the slow, throbbing procession along the nerves of my body. The scent of juniper and Aric's own strong, not unpleasant, smell filled the tiny space. A light wind drummed against the leather. He had his amulet set before him on the leather carpet's colorful appliqués of swirling shapes and twisting animals, but he looked only at me, his angular face eerie in the shadows thrown by the glowing brazier.

"What is it you wish to know," I asked, "if I should be so blessed?"

He leaned forward, his brow worried, his mouth strained. "Will the drought last? When will the rains return and the pastures recover? Is it time to increase our stock or continue culling our herds?"

I nodded, a pang of distress biting at me. What did I know about the rains? I closed my eyes and listened to the sound of his breathing and found it matched my own. Slow, steady. "That smell. *Did you. . . ?*" I asked, my eyes snapping open.

"Certainly not!" he snapped back, clearly offended. "Who am I, Olgas?"

It must be something else, then. "Do you smell it?"

"I smell nothing but the incense." He looked bewildered.

"Nothing at all?" I asked again, panic creeping into my mind.

"It comes," he said soberly, taking me firmly by both hands. "I am here."

I met his steady gaze and squeezed his hands with all my might as his face was swallowed by the darkness.

ARIC INTERROGATED ME about the content of my visions for some time after I recovered my senses, though, as before, I had little to offer him. As all had faded to black and the panic overtook me, I was oppressed by an ominous sense that a momentous, violent clash was imminent, but from where or with whom I couldn't say. I only knew I was afraid. But I was always scared when the spells descended, so I disregarded it as a fearful hallucination, a remnant of the previous days' distress. Enemies were everywhere. These men knew it better than anyone and faced it with courage. I would keep my dark impressions to myself.

Aric wanted knowledge of the drought and the pastures, and on that matter, I had answers from neither the living nor the dead. Still, he pressured me for insight. I told him what I would do in his stead—or, rather, what I imagined my father would do. It was not yet Midsummer, and conditions would only worsen if the rains did not come. Where pastures weren't recovering, he should prepare gifts of salt for the herdsmen and order that they cull a portion of their herds now to spare the fields for next season. To my surprise, he agreed. And though I craved his good opinion, I was filled with dread at the realization that, with my obliging words, I had likely decided the fates of men and beasts I had no right or wisdom to govern—all of it based on a pretense.

CHAPTER 18

MIDSUMMER

*The forces that order this world have erected
barriers to keep mankind from knowing the
gods, the mysteries of life,
our purpose, ourselves.*

THE WILD MEADOW FLOWERS were now in full bloom, and the first haymaking of the season was underway. As we made our way west, herdsmen waded into the meadows with their long-handled scythes to cut the tall grass and let it dry under the broad, clear sky. Others already raked theirs into windrows, soon to be stacked as a bulwark against the snow through which the sheep and cattle could not graze. Like our Bastarnian farmsteads, they, too, fought to hold their own against the unknowns of ever-coming winter.

Aric was determined to journey to court for the Tardin festival with the cattle and horses the band had garnered from raiding and the sheep and goats we'd lifted from the Mard-Khwaar. In truth, they were a liability to us in the Wild Fields and cost us pasture and time to herd. Additionally, the Skythai favored polled cattle, typically trading or slaughtering horned beasts right away. If they were not brought to Gerrhi now and exchanged for gifts from the king, we would have to wait several months until the next festival.

We left three days early and took our time, driving nearly a thousand head, I reckoned, through the lands of various smaller tribes and clans along the way. We wore our wolfskins and carried our arms all along the route, more in procession than expedition, as there was little prospect of attack here. But I was grateful for the leisurely pace. Sakha remained at camp with his swollen tendon mending, meaning this would be Vatra's first long journey.

As we rode through the territories, each clan raised a cheer for us, spreading flowers before us as we passed. They brought us kumis to drink and meals of cheese, smoked meat, and bread. In return, Aric bestowed upon each chief a curious gift: a small pouch of pinkish salt over which he first spoke a blessing. A pinch sprinkled over the food of any creature promised to ward off sickness and make it thrive. The chiefs revered this gift like a holy treasure and guarded it like a sack of gold, more valuable even than the great sacks of salt given to them for curing their meat. The tribes also received an unofficial tax in stock as we passed, Aric generously granting each chief their choice of fifty goats or sheep for the privilege of passing through his lands.

"Isn't your father king of these tribes?" I asked him as we rode away, confused by the odd extortion I'd witnessed from the chiefs. "You are the protector of these lands, yet you must pay a toll to cross them?"

"Ariapaithi is King of the Skythai," Aric said, "not King of Skythia," he explained. "We are not tyrants. We rule by their leave . . . and would keep it so. These are men we may yet need to fight beside us. If our presence in their territory damages the grazing, we repay the loss with interest. The fidelity of one's countrymen is worth far more than any riches." He grinned wryly and crooked his eyebrow. "Certainly more than a few sheep."

ON THE LAST OF THESE LONG SUMMER DAYS, we arrived at Gerrhi, the seat of Ariapaithi near the marshes of Gerrhos, the ancestral burial ground of the Paralatai. Gerrhi was a twelve- or fourteen-day journey from the mouth of the Volosdanu to this spot. Court was wherever the royal camp and its followers happened to be, but important festivals were often held in the capital. Since we'd left them at the last festival, the court had been slowly pushing their herds northward, halting to camp and graze as it made its way toward the semi-fortified camp on the low dawn-facing banks of the Volosdanu. At a bend in the river, ramparts comprised of banks, ditches, and timber palisades created an island of defense at the confluence of the Volos, two smaller rivers, and a large salt lake. Wagons, tents, and even livestock by the thousands had space to shelter within its massive three-thousand-acre enclosure. Beside the ford rose great dunes like those of the sea. Above these lay the grand rapids where, upriver, the broad Volosdanu became impassible for a stretch of some fifty miles.

Here, the Paralatai kings had made themselves something like a citadel at the site's southern edge, on the highest rise overlooking the river and plain. Simultaneously, the fort below enclosed great ironworks where the countless weapons, armor, and cauldrons that maintained his innumerable soldiers were forged. A semi-permanent residence of farmers, herders, and craftsmen seemed to occupy the site, supporting this production. Less than forty miles away, across the river, were Skythia's abundant iron mines, where quality ore lay close beneath the surface. They were skilled excavators, having practiced on the many tombs and barrows that graced the countryside. They were also skilled carpenters crafting the frames of countless felt-houses clustered about the plains as well as the most sought-after wagons and chariots not only on the steppe but exported across the known world. Timbers were floated down the rivers from the nearby lowland forests to keep the wheels turning and the forges burning.

Artisans from across the steppe and even the colonies came to ply their crafts for King Ariapaithi, not least because his court had a reputation for its wealth in gold. And, of course, it drew the country's best fighters—some for the same reason. With the billows of smoke from furnaces, forges, and cooking fires rising from the busy camp, we rode toward the sounds of clashing hammers and bleating sheep in the tent-filled fields between the rivers.

STANDING BESIDE A SMALL STREAM beneath a willow, the anarei's felt-house stood atop the deck of a wheeled oxcart, which meant it never needed to be disassembled for travel. The door already open, I peered inside. Sparsely outfitted but spacious, the place smelled strongly of coriander, artemisia, and something spicy I couldn't name. His thick staff stood propped beside the door. A small fire smoldered near the center of the room. Against the wall, a low, narrow table bore a three-legged altar of bronze. A weighted loom held a half-finished multicolored cloth. A meager pallet of dry grass and blankets lay upon the floor. From pegs in the latticework hung sundry clothes and robes, and beside them, jars and bottles of various tinctures and potions lined shelves and cubbies.

"Aric said you wanted to see me?"

"I do," Erman said, raising his dark head briefly to acknowledge me before returning to folding a pile of washing in a reed basket near the hearth. "Come in."

His invitation lacked the formality and ritual I had come to expect, so I hesitated, waiting for more. When nothing else came, I tentatively stepped over the doorsill into the spacious room. As I ducked through the low door into the dim space, something dangling from the ceiling brushed against my forehead and over my hair, sending a chill down my spine. Flinching away, I gave it a swat.

"Don't!" the seer shrieked. "It's for luck."

I stood back and tried to focus on the thing that had struck my face as it finally came to rest on the end of its cord. A dried horse phallus dangled in the doorway like a solitary wind chime. Lucky or not, I gave it ample clearance as I turned to remove my weapons.

Suddenly, Erman stood before me, smiling. Beneath our feet was a carpet, the richest item in the room, tufted with a pattern that was a kind of gaming board. I pulled off my boots and placed them beside his bast shoes by the door.

Erman poured a cup of mead for each of us and gestured to a place on the carpet. "Please, sit," he said, wiping his palms against the front of his skirt. With legs crossed, the gaming board between us, we sat regarding one another in silence for a long, agonizing moment. "It's good to see you well . . . and whole. I heard that cannibals had eaten you."

"Did you really hear that?"

"They say a Mokhsa chewed your arm clean off, and then it miraculously grew back, good as new." He smiled mockingly. "You are quite the wonder. And there's talk about other arts you have been practicing in the Wild Fields."

My cheeks warmed. Gossip seemed to easily cross the steppe for such a vast and empty space. "I train. That is all."

"I hear differently. They tell me that you saved Aric from a poisoned blade."

"Anyone would have done the same." *They?*

"But not everyone could. Where did you learn such a cure?"

"It's a poultice I've used on the horses."

"So, you used *horse* medicine on a royal prince?"

Shit. I stared at him, dumbfounded. If there was a correct answer, I didn't know it. A burning rose in my chest and ears. I must be glowing red before his eyes.

He chuckled, his blue eyes glistening with impish glee. "I see no harm. Unless you find him in the fields munching the grass and mounting the mares."

"I hope not," I said, stifling a giggle at that image in my mind. "I don't know a cure for that."

"*Indeed.*" He smirked. "This sounds like a miraculous medicine. You must teach this recipe to me."

"Of course."

"He says you saved his life twice—first when the Mard-Khwaar came for him, then with your potion."

"He'd have done the same for me."

"Perhaps, but it took mettle. It took skill. You proved your worth. You're to be marked."

I gulped. "Marked?"

"Tattooed, as one of the tribe."

Right now?

He chatted idly as he prepared some equipment. "And the others? Antisthenes is well?"

"He speaks little to me. I think he'd rather I had not come." I caught myself. I should not complain about Aric's steward to this anarei. "Not that I blame him. It is crowded, the three of us in one tent. He limps when no one is looking and rubs wild cabbage oil into his knee at night. I think it must pain him terribly. But otherwise, he seems well enough."

He reached for a clay jar on one of his shelves and carried it to me. "Give this to him for his aching knee. Don't tell him you mentioned it to me." He flashed a conspiratorial grin and returned to his preparations as I set the sealed jar aside, wondering what I would tell the aloof steward about the anarei's gift.

Erman turned to me and indicated for me to bare my right wrist. He spoke a verse over me, then dipped a sprig of myrtle in a bowl on the altar and sprinkled me with drops of mead. Next to me on the carpet, he laid out several iron needles, pots of pigment, and hemp cloth.

"What are you going to mark upon me?"

"First is the sign which every Paralatai bears." He pulled up the sleeve of his tunic. I had seen the trident symbol upon many of the men already. "Raised to the sky, it is the scepter of Papahio himself. But I will tell you a secret only spellcasters and seers know," he grinned as he thrust his hand outward to hover over the earth.

"Cast over the ground, it becomes the Crow's Foot. Use it wisely. Shall we begin?"

With this tattoo, I would become indelibly Skythai, for good or ill. If given a choice in the matter, what would I choose? I nodded.

He handed me a long white robe of bleached linen. "Wear this."

"Can I not just pull up my sleeve? There will not be much blood."

"For a rite sacred as this?" he asked, raising an eyebrow.

Abashed, I took the offered garment and looked for a place to undress. The room was open, and I had nowhere to hide from his gaze. I turned my back to him as I removed my trousers, tunic, and undervest, clutching the loose garment tight to my chest. I told myself it was proper to show modesty. In truth, since leaving the Rokhalani, I'd never let anyone—male or female—look upon my chest.

"I am a healer; I've seen scars before," he said.

"Perhaps," I said as I slipped the robe around my shoulders, "but men may bear their scars with pride; women must rue theirs."

"Why do you say this?"

"We're but the vessels of men's desires; we're meant to be pristine." I tried to keep the bitter sarcasm from my voice, but I could practically taste it. I cinched the belt and turned to face him.

He shook his head.

"You deny it?"

"Ideals are lies."

"Are they not the gods' design . . . or something?"

"You repeat the Hellenic horseshit that pollutes everything these days. An ideal, by definition, can never be real. It is a mirage. Only the truth is truly perfect—it needs no enhancement. It is our desire to exceed truth that is flawed. Those who create ideals above nature sanctify not Arta nor the divine but themselves. They hunt gryphons for gold."

When people spoke around the edges of things, it was usually to avoid being candid. "You're horrified."

"No, surprised." He smiled. "I have never seen a living hamazan. The masters told us stories, but I wondered if they were legends. Fuel for the Hellenes' nightmares." He chuckled.

"Ha, a worthy cause," I said, sniggering, imagining the demented mind that would concoct such a tale just to torment the Hellenes.

"In their paintings, you're always whole."

"As if they'd show us otherwise . . . our reality could never meet their lofty standards."

"I never thought of it that way." His smile fell, and his brows drew together. "The Hellenes who keep their markets and workshops in Tyras, near my birthplace, have a temple within the city walls. We traded wool, milk, or cheese with them each market day. When I was stricken, my mother brought me to ask for their god's blessing. But she was forbidden to enter the temple with me. They don't allow anyone with a defect inside their holy places."

As if one needed more reasons to dislike them. But it wasn't only them. Many harbored an intolerance toward the infirm and crippled, believing it to be proof that they'd been born of sorcery or corrupted by malicious spirits. "It's just like them to be cruel. But who has more cause to address the gods than the afflicted?"

"It's all right. Later, I snuck inside," he said, "just to see what was so special about their fastidious gods. But they were nowhere to be found. It was silent and empty as a tomb. That is, until the priests discovered me, and they came throwing stones, chanting, and fumigating the place." He grinned his mischievous smile once more.

I couldn't help smiling with him.

"Ready?"

I nodded. He gripped my wrist tightly and dipped the tip of his needle into some pigment.

"This will hurt."

I gritted my teeth as he began stabbing away at my skin in small strips. I was determined not to show any sign of weakness, no matter how much it hurt. And it did hurt. He stopped only to wipe away the blood and excess dye. In time, a pattern took shape. As he worked, we talked a little.

"How are you finding your time in the Wild Fields? I hear you've run into a bit of trouble."

He had collected every scrap of gossip, hadn't he? "That was regrettable. But I will manage."

He stopped working and rose gracefully to his feet, then shuffled to the wall where he kept all his potions. He stood motionless before the shelves, transfixed by their shapes and colors. I stared, too. Suddenly, like a snake striking its prey, his hand snatched a vial from a cubby, and he shuffled back to his place on the carpet beside me.

"If any man should ever succeed," he paused, allowing his meaning to take hold, "*drink this,*" he instructed, depositing the small wax-sealed bottle into my palm. "Such mysteries are not for men's eyes. Keep it *secure.*"

I cupped my hands delicately around it like a hen's egg. "I will. And thank you," I said, carefully placing it aside.

He nodded and resumed working.

"When I first arrived," I wondered aloud as he focused on his design, "you said: 'They are not like us.' Why do they despise us so?"

He set down his needle momentarily to hold me in his gaze. "There is something you must understand, Anaiti. Like me, you are a white crow. Something rare. Unexpected. The forces that order this world have erected barriers to keep mankind from knowing the gods, the mysteries of life, our purpose, ourselves—invisible boundaries between the realms of earth and sky, night and day, life and death. But what are these borders to envoys such as us, who unify all in our very being?"

I barely understood his words, but they quickened my pulse and stirred my mind. "I wish to learn about these things."

"Aric said you would be a worthy apprentice. But these are not practices one takes up lightly," he said, resuming his work with the needle, punching away at the delicate skin of my wrist, "out of passing curiosity or boredom. They are a life's work—a commitment. If, when you are done with your time in the Wild Fields, you still have a keen interest, I will teach you whatever I am able."

I didn't want to wait. I was hungry to learn now. Not only to better fulfill the promise I made Aric, but because I was curious about the strange wisdom of the anarei.

"Won't my duties as wife of Ariapaithi prevent my studies then?"

"Ah," he tapped his needle against the inkwell without looking up, "but isn't that what secrets are for?"

CHAPTER 19

COURT

How I despised the court's dance.

ARCHERY CONTESTS WERE ALREADY UNDERWAY in the northern pasture when we'd arrived, and the members of the warband rushed to take their turns, even before unpacking and setting up our tents for the evening. Riding back from the tent of the anarei, I joined them to cheer on my fellows. I had no intention to compete, but as I sat on the sidelines watching, the men badgered me about riding the course as well. Whether it was genuine encouragement or morbid curiosity, I couldn't say. The feast was not for several hours, and I enjoyed archery. Amid the cheers and jeers, I finally agreed.

The course consisted of crude targets staggered across the field like a karevan of scarecrows. Already mounted upon Vatra, I set out at a brisk canter for the first target. His training had progressed nicely, and he was becoming an excellent hunter. I barely needed to touch the reins. He always knew where I wanted to go just by where I looked, and I could guide him entirely with my seat and legs if I wished. I dropped the reins to his neck and fitted an arrow to my bowstring.

The Skythai were masters of shooting from horseback and

rightly feared for it. The trick lay in releasing the arrow when the horse had all its hooves off the ground. Timing was everything. That sweet moment of suspension only happened at a canter or gallop, so speed was of the essence. But there was only a breath in which to aim and release. Accomplishing all of that while managing the half-wild animal thundering beneath you, over uneven terrain, with the wind rushing by, was a minor miracle.

I released my arrow and buried it deep in the heart of the first target. We cantered past and handily struck the next five before turning back. The most distant target was covered in armor, a helmet on top. Dozens of broken arrows were strewn at the foot of the dummy. In a heartbeat's choice, I took a risk and aimed for the eye slits. The shot hit home, piercing the target cleanly through the narrow gap in the dented old bronze helmet. We rolled back and, in full gallop, struck five more in the heart.

I rode by the last untouched target in a blur, grinning to myself. Laughter roared from the sidelines. "You forgot one, dear," someone shouted to me as I fitted the last arrow to my string, swiveling around in my saddle and stretching my bow. I shot the final target over Vatra's tail, turned, and galloped past them.

The sidelines erupted in a chorus of howls. I'd hit every mark. As I rode in from the course, my wrist aching and sore from my tattoo, I stupidly thought I might receive an honor. But I received neither prize nor praise. They awarded the win to another man, claiming I crossed the course's finish line before completing my final shot.

"Bullshit!" bellowed Olgas, thrashing his gangly arms in displeasure. "I'll show you the fucking finish line!" he shouted, dropping his trousers and bending his ass toward the judges. I wasn't sure exactly what that meant, but I appreciated the sentiment, nonetheless.

Laughing, I begged them to let the matter go so we could return to our camp and attend to more pressing concerns, like the unopened amphora of wine we'd brought for ourselves. It was only a worthless contest, after all. And finally, after some convincing and the lure of drink, the kara threw up their hands in disgust and walked away, mumbling to themselves. I returned to the wagons to help unpack and set up camp, waiting until sunset when we'd all gather for the feast.

"YOU DON'T EAT," the king barked from the soft cushion where he sat before his guests. "The food not good?"

I had spent the evening avoiding his gaze and trying my best to escape his notice, but it seemed even my avoidance was noteworthy. Strained as the effort felt, I knew I had to be gracious.

"Oh, no, the food is excellent, Sura. I am afraid I am just not hungry." I wasn't, though I had my eye on some sweet, ripe cheese to grab and spirit back to camp for later. "The wine is appreciated, though. We don't get much of it in the marches these days."

"From now on, we'll see you do!" He raised his cup and smiled kindly. "You like music?"

"Very much." What kind of unimaginative person disliked music?

He held up his hand and closed his eyes. The whole table fell silent as the musicians struck a tune on crane flute, goatskin drum, and Skythian fiddle—which looked like a tiny ship with strings in place of sails, strummed with a bow. They played a haunting, plaintive warble that rose like a tide. A single high note trembled above the rest and quickly fell again, and the music resumed its pattern as before. The king's face lit up as he opened his watery grey eyes and beamed joyfully. In that moment, much as I hated our arrangement, I could not hate him.

Across from me, a dark-haired, dark-eyed woman in a Hellenic gown of bright imported cloth and gold reclined languidly on a pile of cushions. She appeared young, barely more than a child, but she looked over the hall with the sneering manner of an old gorgon.

Like an insect, she was composed entirely of sharp edges, jagged points, and harsh lines. She must have torn her way out from her mother's womb the way a lizard does from its egg. Balanced on her frail frame, her head was huge, and sitting atop her upswept hair was a headdress that looked like a gilded bucket overturned and draped in a tablecloth. With her skeletal features, she squinted sidelong at me, lips pursed like she'd been waiting all her life for a kiss that never came. She'd liberated an entire tray of fresh, golden honey cakes from the center of the low table and was already working on her third.

"What manner of divinity compels a woman to desecrate her flesh?" she turned to say to her handmaiden. "Worse, what manner of man would have her?" With an exaggerated delicacy of her bony fingers, she extracted a crumb of her honey cake and set it between her lips. Then loudly sucked each of her fingers in turn, each sharp, moist chirp raking up my spine. I cringed with each repugnant bite she took.

Women were ever the harshest critics and enforcers of conformity upon other women. Good sense told me to ignore her. But I felt my neck stiffen as I stretched taller where I sat.

"I don't think we've been introduced . . . ," I began.

"Who are *you* to speak to *me*?" she snapped.

Bitch. "I believe I was in the middle of clarifying that very thing. Should I speak more slowly—use smaller words?" I enjoyed watching the color rise in her face before adding: "And, just who are you?" *And why do you have a chamber pot on your head?*

"You've come here with a lot of demands, *androktones*. You should remember: the Bastarnai serve us; we do not serve them," she squinched her hard eyes and moistened her withered lips, puckering her mouth like a horse's anus.

Taken aback, I caught myself about to defend my tribe, but the arrogance in her impudent face and the venom in her tone made me catch myself. I'd done nothing to offend her, and my people had nothing to apologize for. "You're mistaken," I said flatly. "The Bastarnai serve no one. And I am not here for you—whoever you are. I am a guest of King Ariapaithi."

Delicate ladies were worthless. Mouths without hands, taking without making. What of value did they contribute? Studying the bucket, I figured with enough force I could shove her entire head inside. How easily I could smash her dainty little nose. Break the teeth behind her venomous smile. I wanted to so badly; I could feel my heart pound faster with the mere thought. And why shouldn't I? Any man would defend himself against such affronts to honor. Why shouldn't we? Why must women's weapons be confined to seduction and manipulation or words of spite and malice? I had two hands and the will to use them. I needed only to be unbridled.

This was the court's dance I'd long sought to escape—the performance demanding a subtle balance of learned disdain, affected fragility, feminine manipulation, and false modesty. I'd never mastered the art. Or rather, I never cared to try. The entire gathering had been a blur of faces and names I would never remember. They came in and out of focus as I moved through the crowd, and I struggled to find care for any of it, though I knew some part of me should. Men and women who mattered to the king would one day have to matter to me—but not yet.

She glared down her narrow nose at me and leaned across the table to whisper. "I hope the Skythai rape you bloody."

"Is Ligeia sharing her depraved fancies again?" Aric boomed as he pushed in beside me. Her face soured, and I nearly snorted my wine. "She's got quite the imagination."

"That's Skyles's wife?" I asked in horror but not disbelief. Ligeia was the perfect match for the vain Hellenic prince.

"Mmm," he leaned close to whisper, "In Olbia, she partakes in all manner of wild orgies in the name of her god. Thankfully, I've not seen it myself, but word is she shares herself around like a wharf whore and runs intoxicated through the fields beyond the city walls, naked and raving, dismembering living creatures with her bare hands. She offers herself to any man who'll have her, slave and noble alike. She claims her god demands it." He rolled his eye sarcastically.

"That's too vile to be true," I whispered. "Does Skyles know?"

"He joins her."

CHAPTER 20

EYE

The more I learned, the more questions came
than answers.

I REMAINED BEHIND with Antisthenes to begin breaking our little camp while the others made final visits to the wagons housing
the karevan of whores who, like flies after a herd of cattle, flocked
to the kara whenever they came within reach of a settlement.

"Aric has business with the king this morning," Antisthenes
informed me as we prepared breakfast before starting. "But he
will join us soon to help."

"He doesn't join the others?"

"Aric? He never indulges in," he paused to clear his throat, "*in-
tercourse* while he has warriors in the marches."

"No? Why not?" I kneaded the barley flour with milk, honey,
and lard and shaped it into a neat little cake on the baking stone.

"Like many warriors, he believes it saps his strength for battle."

"And when he is not fighting?"

"He is always fighting." He dripped a spoonful of stew into the
fire and spoke something under his breath, then poured some into
a bowl for me.

"That must be difficult, I mean, given men's . . . *appetite?*"

"It depends on the man. It could be worse. It is not like hunger. After all, a hungry man cannot just rub his belly and be satisfied." The corner of his mouth drew up slightly, and I felt my face flush with embarrassment. "Maybe he just does not want some whore showing up with his bastard one day when he is king, claiming compensation or rights."

"Aric? King?" Those two words had somehow never joined themselves in my mind.

"Who else?"

That was a good question. "I've never really thought much about it." I prepared to place the stone slab bearing the cake into the fire, but Antisthenes stopped me.

"Offer a portion," he said, pointing to the flames. "To the gods."

"I don't know how the Skythai do it." I'd never watched the men prepare our food before, worried all such women's work would eventually fall to me.

"The fire is the mouth of the gods, who consume our sacrifices. Drop a little butter or flour into the flames and speak the name of the gods to whom it is offered. It is the Skythai way."

"You pray to Skythai gods?" I asked. I'd never known a Hellene to adopt barbarian gods.

"I recognize my own gods here, as you will do in time. They just go by different names, as all things do in foreign tongues."

"And to which gods do you sacrifice?"

"There are many, and they change day by day. I am always sure to remember Gœtosura, of course; he is Apollo to my people: the wolf, slayer of serpents, lord of winds, of archers and arrows, of healing and plague, of music and prophecy, of the hidden and manifest, of the fire which does not consume—the light which casts no shadow. Eraman is Hermes, the keeper of observance— of rites, customs, traditions, and hospitality to men and gods; I owe special devotion to him in this land. Papahio is Zeus, the almighty father of heaven, keeper of law, and dispenser of justice.

Even Targitao, the thunderer, is much like Herakles. They are the patrons of warriors. Some of the men frown upon the worship of the gods of the earth, patrons of herdsmen, but I see no shame in it. Apia is Gaia, Mother Earth, its bounty, and queen of all that lies beneath. Tabiti is Hestia, 'the burning one' whose fire shelters us and accepts our sacrifices. And of course, Artimpasa is not like any one Greek goddess. She is like Artemis, the Huntress and Mistress of Beasts, or Athena, my homeland's wise patroness and protector. Likewise, Artimpasa is the patroness of Skythia and its kings. There are others, but these I hold most dear."

Most of the names he spoke were foreign to me, but I think I took his meaning, and it seemed harmless enough. I did as he instructed, breaking off a small piece of the cake and tossing it into the flames, repeating the names of the gods before placing the stone for baking.

"You're certain it will be him?" I asked, still skeptical. "Surely Aric's elder brothers have a stronger claim? Oktamazda looks the part. Though, of course, Skyles is eldest." The thought sent a shudder of revulsion through me. I hoped the Skythai had the sense never to make that man their king.

"It does not work like that among the Skythai. In their view, no one is owed rule, or land, or status purely by birth. They choose the worthiest man. A father assesses his sons and determines who will best manage his household and defend his legacy. The people do the same with their chiefs. Time favors the firstborn, but this is by no means assured. Their ancient traditions favor the youngest. But no one inherits the kingship. They earn it."

"So, Ariapaithi chooses his favorite."

"Ariapaithi chooses an heir. Then, the gathering of the Ældar of all the Skythian territories chooses the best man from among all the clans' chiefs, with the help of their gods, to be king. Due to their prowess, powerful heads of clans are deemed favored by the gods. The Ældar could choose any chief of any tribe, but they will shrewdly choose the one with the greatest warriors, wealth, and allies. It is always one of the Paralatai tribe."

"And they will choose Aric? Skyles must make many of them rich, maneuvering their wares for trade in the colonies. And Oktamazda can call up a formidable militia to fight for him and seems well-liked."

"Skyles makes some of them rich, this is true, but mostly it is the colonial governors and farmers who benefit from his dealings. The colonies of the Hellenes and farms grow at the expense of Skythai pasturelands. Not everyone is pleased about this."

"No, I imagine not." But Antisthenes was a Hellene. Surely, he'd be pleased?

"And Oktamazda has been Ariapaithi's ambassador abroad, but it means his allies are mostly foreigners these days."

"I see." My father was among them.

"And Oktamazda is a little too well-liked," he added. "He has managed to bed the wives and daughters of nearly all the chiefs in Skythia—and the gods only know who else. Every time a red-headed child is born, they laugh that Oktamazda must have paid the lady a visit. It is only half a joke."

"So, Aric is just the last choice?" I took a bite of my stew. It was awful. I had no idea what manner of service Antisthenes did as a slave, but he was certainly no cook.

"Oh no, far from it," he said, taking a hearty bite of his stew. I cringed. "The king is not just a man who ensures prosperity and conducts the tribe's business, for any husbandman or merchant could do that. And he is not just a war leader, for any warchief could do that. He is not just the intermediary between the people and the gods, for any priest could do that. The king must do all these things at once. But you know this already, being the daughter of Arianta."

"Indeed. It's a lot for one man to carry."

"The Skythai believe his success or failure depends on the favor of Artimpasa. He becomes her consort . . . if she wills it. Only a king or chief who is prosperous, courageous, and wise can win her grace. Without her favor, he will never be able to sustain his people, bring health and prosperity to the land, win victory in battle, or protect them from harm."

When he said it that way, Aric did indeed begin to feel like a king. "Aric is among the noblest men I've ever seen."

"Aric is a noble man but not a whole man. That is perhaps his greatest liability. Your cake is going to burn."

"Oh, shit." I grabbed the iron tongs, pulled the stone from the fire, and then pried off the slightly singed cake with my knife. It looked mostly edible still. "He could be passed over because of his eye?"

"Rumor is some assembly members fear the Mistress will reject a marred man."

That seemed like petty wool spinners' gossip. Unless there was more to the story. I had always wondered, and I finally summoned the nerve to ask: "How was he wounded?"

"That was before my time here. He never speaks of it, but I have since heard the story from men who were there. I believe it is why they do not leave his side to this day, though they have made their tallies and are rich beyond their dreams.

"When Aric was young, about fifteen or sixteen winters and rising through reputation as a warrior, the kara embarked upon a long campaign against the Melanchlæni—the Black Cloaks—an eastern tribe who call themselves the Saudaratai. They have forever been hostile to the Paralatai, and a fierce rivalry exists between them to this day. Following a devastating raid, the bereaved tribe sought retribution, and the warband was pursued. Many were captured, including Aric. In an act of great treachery, the captives were not ransomed to their countrymen, but, with the aid of certain Greek merchants, secretly delivered to the king's greatest rival, Spargapaithi."

"The Spargapaithi who harasses my people now?"

"The same. With his enemy's youngest son and heir in his possession, Spargapaithi tried to incite a war between the tribes. Ariapaithi would not fight. He offered payment and hostages instead; he offered a peace treaty in good faith; he offered land. But Spargapaithi refused to accept any terms but war. Ariapaithi still refused. They had reached a stalemate. Growing desperate, perhaps Spargapaithi thought he could provoke him if he humiliated the royal hostage. Or perhaps he thought he would appeal to his gods for victory over his enemy. There is a grove in the country of the Agathyrsi, which is consecrated to their divine patroness. It is to this place they took Aric to offer him up in sacrifice. As the tribe gathered, he had Aric bound and prepared to dismember him, which is the savage rite their goddess demands. They pierced him with blades and burned him with irons. But Aric, though little more than a boy, never pleaded. He never flinched. He never made a sound."

"I can't even imagine it," I said, trying my best not to.

"This silence angered Spargapaithi, who wanted to break his rival's son before his people. So, he snatched the blade from the hand of the priest, determined to do the deed himself. Still, Aric showed no fear. After weeks of hunger and abuse by the Agathyrsi, he only stared back. They say Spargapaithi's face turned white as death. But with so many watching, he could not desist. So, he began the sacrifice and cut out Aric's eye."

"No," I gasped, and my hands flew to cover my face, dropping my bowl in my lap. I looked on the results daily, and yet to hear it told—to know how it came about—was more terrible than the sight of it could ever be.

"They say Aric was deadly still and silent through it. And a terrible panic rose through the crowd. The people became so terrified by his silence that they feared he possessed some sorcery. That his gods or dark spirits protected him. When they saw how the people took fright and turned against the ritual, the Agathyrsi priests intervened, prophesying grave misfortune would descend upon them again for executing an inauspicious rite. They proclaimed that their goddess was appeased. Whether inspired by the gods or good sense, they called a halt to further sacrifice of prisoners, offered up fifty horses and cattle, and demanded the Skythai be expelled from the country. To save face, Spargapaithi demanded his ransom, Aric's and his companions' bonds were cut loose, and they were driven from the territory to march home."

"I never imagined it was so awful," I said from behind the hands clasped over my mouth. "Poor Aric. He was just a boy."

"If he was a boy when it happened, he was a man when it was done. They say Aric did not stop to rest until he crossed the Istros—he would not bathe his wounds or wash away the blood until he'd reached his own land. And for a year from that day, he refused to let shears touch his hair and beard and did not utter a single word."

How little I knew Aric. The more I learned, the more questions came than answers. I had surveyed him like I did this landscape. I began to recognize its features, and I was learning to navigate the terrain. Yet I knew nothing of how it was formed, the storms that shaped it, who left the strange, silent landmarks that cropped up across the plain, and what might be buried beneath.

"Spargapaithi is a monster," I whispered. "Why does he despise Ariapaithi so much?"

"They both made claims on the throne when their father died. Ariapaithi was made heir, and Spargapaithi and his followers challenged him. It was an ugly battle. Spargapaithi was defeated and cast out from Skythia."

"They are *brothers?*"

He nodded and stirred the cauldron, scraping the sides of the pot and tapping the ladle's handle against the rim. "He and his followers had to travel far to find a new place to settle. Ariapaithi had allies in nearly every neighboring tribe. They passed a long, harsh first winter exiled in the wilderness before finally settling among—well, conquering—the Agathyrsi. That first winter, they ran short of food. Many died of hunger. The rest, like frightened rabbits, ate their own young. He has resented Ariapaithi ever since."

"Their children?"

"Desperate times," he said flatly, spooning more stew into his mouth.

"This is a terrible story."

"He is a terrible man."

"Still, to be tortured by your own kinsman in cruel vengeance. What must something like that do to a person? Scars like that must run deep."

Antisthenes absently combed his dark beard with his fingers. "From what I have seen, it does different things to different people. Some it makes hard, and some soft; some hot and some cold; some bright and some dull; some it purifies, and some it poisons."

"What did it do to him?"

"Aric? I did not know him before, but he has a firmer footing than most. Though it can shift day by day."

"So, he chose an ascetic life in the marches?"

"He was married once."

"Married? I can't picture that either."

"No one could," he mused. "Not even his wife."

"What happened to her?"

"You should eat that stew before it gets cold," he said, scraping the bottom of his bowl.

I wasn't hungry anymore, but I picked up my bowl and shoveled a spoonful into my mouth. It was already cold. I hadn't imagined it could get worse than that first bite. How wrong I was.

"That was just after I arrived. Aric was still very young. His father thought a wife would settle him. She died a month or two after he led her home. No one expected her to survive, if you take my meaning."

"He . . . *killed her?*"

"No, not with his own hands. He barely saw her. Though there is always speculation. The Skythai believe man harbors many souls within, which all depart for different realms upon his death, as well as ancestral daimons that watch over him during this life. Some say that a malevolent spirit attends Aric, sparing him from harm and giving him his terrible strength. Some of the Ældar fear that as well."

"Is that what you believe?" The barley cake had cooled enough. I broke off half for him.

He took a bite and made a painful face but crumbled it into his bowl and ladled another scoop of stew on top. "Me? I think it was the climate," he continued between mouthfuls. "It drives foreigners to despair."

"Not you, though." I took a sip of water from my skin to wash down my dry cake.

"We Hellenes are made of better stuff than that," he said without pride.

"Indeed," I smiled. His resilience never ceased to impress me. A life like his would have broken a lesser man long ago. Or, at the very least, he would have starved. "You don't have to stay here with me. Don't you want to join the others at the karevan?"

"There is nothing for me there."

"There is someone, though?" I gently prodded. Many nights, I lay awake with my eyes closed, pretending to sleep as he crept out of the tent and sometimes didn't return for hours. I warmed to see someone so stolid blush.

He lowered his eyes and sighed. "I cannot say. Such things are no longer permitted once a novice has made his tally. He'll retire from this place at the festival of Yamadin."

"Oh, Antisthenes." My heart sank for him.

"Say nothing of it," he raised his eyes to me, pleading.

I nodded. I understood. Among our Bastarnai warriors, such

things were accepted until the young men were of age to take wives. But those who neglected to take wives became the subject of scorn and ridicule. "No one else knows?"

"I take a woman occasionally to keep the other men from talking."

"Men talk. You are a vazarka. Why should you care what they say?"

"For myself, I don't. But if neither Aric nor I am seen among the women . . ."

"Oh, I see." Antisthenes's sense of duty was touching. But Aric's discipline had placed an undue burden on his friend. "And what of the young man?"

He gazed absently at the grey felt of the tent's western wall. "He will have a chiefdom, eighty wagons or more, good grazing lands, hundreds of horses and cattle one day. He will have his pick of wives and sons of his own. And I will maybe train them, too, if I live that long."

"Couldn't he choose to remain a karik?"

"Give up all that?"

I nodded. "Why not?"

"That is woman's talk. No, this is as it must be."

"If you say so." I slid over beside him and pulled him tight to me, my head resting on his shoulder. "But I'm sad for it—for you both."

"Anaiti," he said, shoving another spoonful of cold stew into his mouth, "do not imagine that any of us gets what we want in this life."

CHAPTER 21

KAREVAN

Here, on this humble spot,
we stand at the very center of the world.

Mourdag whistled. "Mount up. They're coming."

We'd come southward down the valley to the karevan road hoping to catch up with a certain Median merchant due to pass, perhaps inspect his wares, and maybe do some business. The men always had hides from hunting and spoils from their raids to trade if they found something they fancied, and though we'd managed to assemble most of what we needed since, we were still low on a few supplies after our foiled expedition north to the Budini.

We'd stopped to graze the horses while we waited to meet the karevan from the east as it reached the Raiding Road, a route in the southern territories used for driving home cattle from raids on eastern tribes. When the karevan was due, Aric not only liked to examine their wares but add a few more bowmen along this stretch of the route as they passed through, though the traveling troop was sure to be heavily armed. Indeed, most men who marched with it were mercenaries hired to protect its goods from predatory raids.

I pulled myself up from the grass and rushed to Aruna's side to unbind his hobbles. Familiar flashes moved across the horizon.

Mourdag took the mirror from his belt, angled it toward the sun, and flashed a signal back.

I still couldn't say how many men might be stationed at border encampments like ours or just how long the border extended, but it was clear there were camps of the Suramatai across the Tanais to mirror our Skythai ones. There must be women among them like me. After all, they were my mother's people, and it would not have been uncommon for noblewomen to be among the warriors guarding the border. Only a few miles separated me from a world so like this one—and yet so different.

Just across that river, not so long ago, my mother had been a young warrior. There, she had earned the right to wed by killing her tally of enemies. When a wealthy foreign king came calling to trade for six of their finest breeding stallions and three hundred brood-mares for his herds, he also took a fancy to a young hamazan—the second daughter of the Rokhalani queen—and bargained for her as well, sealing the friendship between our tribes. She joined the horses in the long journey to Bastarnia and became their keeper until her untimely death, never to see her homeland again.

In the distance, a long train of wagons and carts pulled by oxen, pack mules, and asses—flanked on all sides by hundreds of armed riders and foot soldiers—snaked their way along the valley floor beside the river. Our able band might ultimately defeat such a force with our speed and numbers, but we would surely lose more in horses and men than we would gain in goods.

"ARIC, WHAT IS THIS YOU HAVE HERE, MY FRIEND?" The kare-van leader approached and took hold of Aruna's bridle. Long and lean, with suntanned skin and a woolly black beard, his extravagant but road-worn clothes hung off his wiry frame like rags. "Is this your wife?" He raised an eyebrow. "*Your concubine?*" Then indulged in a long, lewd grin.

"She is not. Takhmaspada, this is Anaiti, of the Bastarnai." Aric dismounted Isiras, his black gelding, and approached the merchant. I wished he would not give my name to strangers.

Takhmaspada leaned in close to Aric. *"Name your price."*

I crossed my arms and gave him the foulest look I could manage.

"She is not for sale," Aric replied, looking more amused than outraged, as he should have. I was waiting for him to strike the merchant or draw his sword. Something appropriately threatening. But no such defense ever came—just friendly chit-chat.

"I have a buyer looking for just such a thing. He will pay . . . *handsomely.*"

"No, my friend, not for any price."

That wasn't entirely true, or I would not be here. But I suppose it was good of him to pretend.

"Trust me, you don't want this one."

"No? Is she . . . unclean?"

"No, but I wouldn't fuck with her if I were you," Aric warned in his most earnest, stern manner. "This one is a white crow. She was eaten by the Mard-Khwaar and lived."

Takhmaspada's jaw fell open. "The *androphagoi?*"

I rested my hand on the hilt of my akinaka and struggled to keep a straight face, avoiding eye contact with any of the other men. My fierce facade could crumble at any moment.

"It is so. The savage nearly chewed her arm off," Olgas added.

"Truly," Bornon said, "she tore the eyes clean out of his skull."

Takhmaspada stepped back, releasing my reins.

"I owe her a blood debt," Aric added solemnly.

Takhmaspada held up his hands. "I meant no offense, my friends—my lady." He gave a reticent little bow. "As you please."

"No worries, my friend," Aric said jovially and clapped him on the back. "What have you got for us today?"

He glanced warily over his shoulder at me before taking his leave. "Be my guest." He made a dramatic flourish with his arm, the wind fluttering the folds of his voluminous sleeve. "We usually have more precious metals and jewels, textiles and carpets, spices and delicacies. Not so much now. These days even Hellenes want iron, copper, and tin. Weapons. Warhorses. Slaves. Wood for ships. Chariots. Charcoal for smithing. Food that will keep. But look at the craftsmanship of this sword," he said, placing a beautiful akinaka in Aric's hands.

"Athenai is hungry," Antisthenes added. "We hear similar requests."

"If war comes, will it last long?" Takhmaspada asked. I couldn't tell if he was hopeful or worried. I got the sense that business was good. Rumblings of war in the Greek mainland had everyone on edge, and many looking to score ever greater profits.

"Who can say?" Aric answered. "I hope for our sake it ends quickly. Wine is getting expensive, my friend."

IT WAS A SHORT RIDE to the seashore from the road where we met the karevan. When Aric suggested the detour, the men leapt at the prospect. The change of scenery did us all some good, and the scent of the sea air was something I hadn't known since I was a child. The height of summer now, salt wind whipped through the grass atop the bluff, tugging at our hair and clothes.

"Interesting friends you have," I said to Aric as we sat and gazed out over the sea.

"The karevan driver? Don't let him bother you. He's all talk."

"He's ill-mannered."

"What, will you execute everyone who insults you?"

"No, but he offended me. Should I just accept this?"

"And you offend him and lots of other people. The world is built of such abuses. You are not responsible for his soul, only for your own. Tend to your ways, your thoughts, your duties. Let him attend to his."

Repugnant to me as his friend was, I could see the good sense in Aric's counsel. "He has been your friend a long time?"

"It pleases him to call himself my friend. He is a decent enough man in his way, and he has always kept his contracts with me over the years. That is a kind of friendship—a valuable kind. But I don't know if I'd go so far as to call him my friend. Not truly."

"Why not?"

"He believes his wealth buys him honor, and therefore friendship."

"He's an obnoxious man, but that seems harsh even to me."

"Is it? He profits from the lies he tells to sell his wares. What does he produce? What does he create?"

"He transports the goods, though."

"Indeed. And the horse breeder helps guide the stallion's cock into the mare, but he doesn't make the foal. Rest assured, though, he will take all the credit for it when it is born, and he will take all the profit when it is sold."

"Father says something similar of merchants and traders. They peddle the swords but never fight the wars."

"Precisely. One day men like these will rule the world," he said with a heavy sigh. "Keep them always at a spear's length."

WE SAT ON THE BLUFF, watching the west wind ruffle the silken sea for the better part of the afternoon, lulled by the surf's gentle attack and retreat. The karevan carried jars of *aschy*, a tart, rich syrup made by hermits in the east. Each, they said, lived beneath a flowering cherry tree, which he guarded with his life, nurturing and tending the tree as kindly as it sustained him. The hermits swaddled the trees in thick white felt and burned fires in the orchards to keep them warm in the winter. They slept beneath the trees' branches and sang songs to keep them happy and fruitful. When the trees were content, their fruits ripened sweetly. The cherry juice, pressed and boiled, turned thick and dark like congealed blood. We bought the karevan's whole store of the delicacy and passed it among the nearly three hundred of us to spread on the barley cakes and cheese we'd brought from camp as we enjoyed the salt breeze on our faces and the men lazed in the grass, gorged on the treats, or gamboled along the cliffside, laughing among themselves.

A great eagle flew into view from behind us, golden bronze in the light of the sinking sun. Aric sat up straight to watch her swing over the water, stretching her broad wings and riding a gust of wind high into the clouds.

"I haven't kept eagles since I was a boy. But they're perhaps the best hunters of all," he said, shielding his eye from the sun with his hand. "Ispakaja, my tutor, would take me up into the highlands to scramble into the cliffs and, while the mother eagle was away, steal a young chick from a nest to rear myself. For hunting eagles cannot be bred in captivity but, like all the best things, must be found in the wilds. She was beautiful, my eagle. I wept bitterly the day I returned her to Artimpasa."

"She?"

"We only hunt with females. Far bigger and fiercer than the males."

Then, the eagle dove.

"Look!" Aric gripped my arm. Like a thunderbolt, the raptor shot down toward the waves. Her talons skimmed the water, and in a blink, she was beating her broad wings against the sky, rising with a little, young dolphin in her grip.

"If I could be a creature other than a man, that's what I'd be," he said, pointing toward the sky.

"An eagle?" Of course. The supreme raptor—spirit of Papahio himself.

"The dolphin."

I glanced at him and back at the eagle, the immature dolphin in its talons, flapping away into the distance with her catch. "Prey?"

"Sooner or later, we're all prey for something. But, though young, think of all he's seen. The depths of the sea. The shores of this land. And now the view from heaven. What man of any age may say all that?" He rose and brushed the dried grass from his backside. "We should be going. The eye of day is closing, and we're far from home."

WE'D ARRIVED AT CAMP just after sunset and rode to the pastures to put the horses up for the night. The last rays of the sun caught on the river below, turning it into a ruddy serpent twisting its way down the shallow valley toward the sea we'd just left behind.

"You've been quiet all afternoon," Aric said as we untacked our horses for the night. "I hope the karevan driver didn't ruin the day for you."

"Not at all," I said, hobbling Aruna. "I enjoyed it and had a chance to pick up a fine new dagger." I'd wanted to replace the one I gave away for some time, as I always carried two. "But you didn't have to do that. I mean, make up those stories."

"I merely embellished a little." Aric flashed a twisted smile. "Besides, it was fun."

"It was, actually. The look on his face . . ."

"That reminds me. I have a gift for you," Aric said as he fixed hobbles on Isiras's forelegs.

"For me? What for?" I placed my saddle beside his and studied him anxiously. A gift from him put an undue burden upon me. I had nothing to give in return.

"As a token of our new partnership. And to apologize for Takhmaspada." He pulled the bridle off the black gelding's head and let him graze.

"It's all right," I said, taking a straw wisp from my pack and running it over Aruna's sleek chestnut coat. "It was good speaking to someone who travels as he does."

"That's the beauty of our country."

"The misfits who roam it?"

"Ha, you're more right than you know," Aric said, rubbing the sweat from the gelding's black back with a stiff hemp cloth. He paused and pointed to the ground at his feet. "Here, on this humble spot, we stand at the very center of the world. All springing from the same heavenly source, our broad rivers flow across the country to the sea. Every manner of trade passes through our borders. We meet diverse tribes of men and hear every wisdom thinkable. Like fishermen," he spread his arms wide, "we stretch our great net across the steppe and catch and keep the best of each for ourselves. And we trade our many inventions far abroad."

"This is why I have come to love living in this place."

He grinned so broadly that his eye nearly disappeared. "Do you? Love this place?"

I ran my fingers through the tangles in Aruna's tail, smiling to myself. "You said you have a gift for me?"

"I have." From inside his caftan, he produced an amulet the size of half a walnut shell. Balanced on his fingertips, the deep blue stone was flecked with gold, polished bright, and set in a thick bezel of gold. It was like the dome of the night sky glittering with stars.

I couldn't think of a good enough word. It was mesmerizing in its beauty.

"It's lapis lazuli. Mined far away in the mountains at the scorched edge of the earth where the sun rises. Takhmaspada said it was destined for the queen of Mudrayam, but I persuaded him to give it to me."

I didn't know what or where Mudrayam might be, but it had to be a place of consequence by the way he spoke. The gift was too generous. What had I done to deserve it? But how could I refuse it? Tentatively, I opened my hand, and he set it gently on my palm.

"I have nothing for you," I said despondently.

"You've given more than you know," he replied with an inscrutable smile, gently closing his fingers around mine and the amulet.

CHAPTER 22

TICKS

*Had I just sparked a war in the dry tinder of
Aric's tempestuous heart?*

OUR SMALL SCOUTING PARTY of six rode down from the
highlands in the early morning, following the river's course.
At times, we passed the small encampments of other clans, who
came forth to greet us with timid smiles, offering cups of kumis
and gifts of flowers. For most of the day, we trekked through dry
summer fields, which opened gradually onto a lush lowland plain.
Here, we cut inland and ascended a steep hill, winding our way
above the valley floor.

"Why are we going this way?" I asked Aric as we left the riverside behind. He ignored me and nudged his horse along faster. We
pulled up our horses on a hillcrest above a settlement straddling a
narrow, shallow stretch of the Lykus River. Below in the valley, I
could make out the edges of farm fields as we climbed the hill. It
was no nomad camp of felt-houses and wagons, nor even the log-
built settlements of the few Skythai farmers nestling themselves
into tranquil river valleys; this was a proper village. A dozen or
so huts of wattle, turf, fieldstone, and fresh thatch were hemmed
in with willow wickets and bramble. Wattle fences, ditches, and

drystone walls crisscrossed the pastures. In the pens were pigs, sheep, and a few cows. Beyond, a patchwork of fields shimmered gold in the afternoon sun with nearly ripe wheat and barley. From the mucky pens and slick, black pathways between the houses, the wind wafted the scents of excrement and urine, thick and pungent.

"What tribe lives there?" I tried again. "It does not look like a camp or farmstead of the Skythai."

"Hellenes. From Alsos and Kremnos," Aric offered grudgingly.

"They're far from home."

"They are. New settlers."

"This far north?" I'd never heard of a colony beyond the shore.

He grunted.

"And we're not permitted to pass there?" I sensed I picked at a scab, but such deference to Hellenes irked me. The Paralatai should have access to all the lands under Ariapaithi's domain, including the colonies that resided and traded in Skythia at the king's pleasure. If they chose, the Skythai had the power to dislodge the foreigners at any time, and the Hellenes knew it.

"We made two hard raids against them last year. That ditch-and-bank around the homes is new. They've fortified it since."

"They dare defy you? Why have you not ousted them?"

Aric explained that he never imagined the colony would survive after punishing raids, a harsh winter, and the lingering drought. But I saw crops ready to harvest and new cottages under construction. Two big storage barns. Grain pits. The plantings were vast. They would have enough surplus to last another year—or export.

"They must have support from someone powerful." He shaded his eye and squinted down at the makeshift huts being replaced with permanent cottages and barns, walls and fences, irrigation and fortifications. "Which likely means my brother."

"I see." So, this was the real reason for his reticence.

"What do you see?" he asked pointedly, turning to face me. "Does your sight reveal anything when you look upon this place?"

His question filled my chest with a burning flutter, like a lamp flame near a drafty door. But I was reluctant to answer, knowing the misery my dark instincts could bring. "*You* are Warden of the East March," I said instead. "Have they a covenant with you or the king?"

He turned away without an answer.

"Then, they are no longer colonists. They are invaders."

He shot a disturbed look my way but still said nothing. I thought perhaps I'd misspoken. Then he drew a deep breath and sighed. "I'd not thought of it like that. But this land was grazed by a productive household of some fourteen Skolotoi and their small flock of sheep, cattle, and horses. It was a good pasture, and they never disturbed the dead. Last spring, they returned from their winter camps to find their pastures plowed up. Now, look at it."

"The dead?"

"That hill amid the barley is a barrow, built long ago." Aric pointed to a shallow mound amid the nearly ripe grain. "As was that one, beside the road. These farmers have no idea they are sowing in a graveyard. Or they don't care. The bones of our ancestors are now plowed under to grow crops on which to feed foreigners."

My breath came faster, harder as I looked down over the muddy section of river, snaking across the naked steppe. Something was so incongruous about the sight of those rude houses piled upon one another amid the pristine plain. In my mind's eye, I could envision crops, fences, and stone houses stretching over the steppe from horizon to horizon, with nowhere left to graze. It was like a nightmare that I knew to be an illusion, yet it felt like a warning.

"But," he continued, "these men are cursed already. They've disturbed the dead where they sleep."

"Those crops look ripe enough to me," I shot back. "And I've never seen the dead rise to defend themselves—that duty is left to the living."

"Their presence here angers you?" Aric said, raising his eyebrow.

"Their presumption angers me. Does it not anger you?" He had to see they were burrowing in deep. There would be no eradicating this parasite from the body of the steppe if they survived another winter. And if Aric did not confront Skyles and these settlers' open defiance, he would forever be diminished in the eyes of his men, his kin, and his people. Even I could see that. If he would seek my counsel in the vapor tents and by the dark of the moon, then I would give it to him now as well, come what may. "What is a settlement, if not a discreet invasion?" I prodded. "They've overrun their own lands. Now they overrun ours. Why should the blood and bones of your fathers nourish these outsiders?" My outrage surprised me, but it was too late to tamp it down.

His eye widened as he regarded me with raised brows and a gaping mouth. "I've never known you to speak this way." Was it amazement or horror that had seized his features? "But it's true. We've let them live here and grow prosperous, and they still despise us. Insult us at every turn. We don't need their trinkets. Their wine to blunt our minds. Their filthy cities on our shores. *They* need *us* to survive; we don't need them. If they fell into the sea, life here would continue as it always has. How would they fare without us? Especially with Athenai once again on the verge of war. They are unwise to test us."

"You asked about my visions?" I said. "When I look on this place, I see destruction: theirs or ours. The poison the Hellenes bring with them and how it seeks to extinguish all that the Skythai love."

The audaciousness of my own words stunned me. Perhaps it was not my fight, but when I looked out over that settlement, I felt the threat of the Hellenes' vision for Skythia viscerally. If he really believed I possessed the two sights, then this ossified future to which every sign pointed—of walls and wheat fields, of towns and temples, divvying up and trampling over these heavenly pastures, of wives trapped within their husbands' homes like prisoners—must never come to pass.

"Then we must destroy them," he said with grim finality.

"*We* must? I never said that!"

"Who then?"

"I don't know. Skyles brought them here. Let him oust them." Even as I said it, it sounded idiotic. "At least let the parties speak."

"That time is passed. They struck the first blow."

"Perhaps, but is now the right time to strike back?"

"When will be better? You say you see only destruction for our people. Will you let this plague spread over us? Or, when you find ticks gorging upon you, do you pick them off and crush them?"

I began to regret speaking my thoughts so freely to him. Had I just sparked a war in the dry tinder of Aric's tempestuous heart?

He combed his fingers through his beard as he watched a shepherd below herding a flock of sheep into one of the pens near the muck-filled byre. "I have hesitated and equivocated too long," he said. "But you are right to goad and shame my reluctance. There is wisdom in your words. It was the same with the Persai when my great-grandfather ruled. They wished to raid us, rape us, and erase us from this land. They came suddenly, like an eclipse. The Hellenes come subtly, like nightfall. They would both plunge this country into a darkness and destroy us." He clenched his jaw and nodded solemnly to himself. "If we cannot hold back the darkness, we will light such fires that the gods themselves will think it day."

WE CAMPED BELOW the farther crest of the hill. The hour had grown late, and the ride back to camp would be too far in the dark. I sat near the light of the hearth, enjoying the sweet, burning grass scent of dung fire as I attempted to repair a tear in the seam of my linen tunic. Sewing had never been my best skill, but I was doing a decent job of it, considering how little practice I had. I held the seam to the light, admiring my handiwork, and gave it a good tug to test its hold.

Aric came and sat close beside me. The deep crease between his brows said that he was still troubled. I set aside my sewing and fetched my wineskin, filled with mead. He sat in silence beside the hearth, and I added more fuel to the fire.

"What will you do?" I asked after a while, wondering if I had made a mistake in speaking so freely. If I had pushed him too far.

"I don't yet know." He took the skin, gripping it in both hands close to his chest, but didn't drink.

"Can a treaty be made?"

"We have a treaty. The settlers broke it in coming here. As you said, only Ariapaithi or I can grant lands in the East March. Skyles had no right to offer them those tracts, yet they refuse to leave. There is no peace where covenants are not kept. We've traded honestly with the Hellenes, honored them as guests in our lands, and not begrudged them their cities and even parcels of farmland to sustain them," his voice rose in frustration. "But it's never enough. You're right. We've been hospitable. Yet, they denigrate us endlessly on our own soil, disrespecting our ways and dishonoring our fathers. They take more than they are owed, usurping our pastures and pushing our people aside. There is no end of them in sight," his fingers clenched around the goatskin as if he were trying to crush it. "Am I wrong?"

Something about the sight of all those fences and walls crossing the open steppelands had cast a shadow in my mind that I could not shake. Discordant and unnatural, they foretold something ugly and ominous to come.

"No." I exhaled slowly. "If you give this settlement leave, others will take it as a sign. It will become a great invasion."

"That's what my heart tells me. These Hellenes don't respect us—don't show us courtesy in our own land. They are the needy ones, yet will never look on us as their equals. Why allow those who despise us to profit from us? We must rein them in: they need not admire us, but they will heed us."

"You think it calls for something more than a raid?" I asked, already knowing the answer.

"Skythia has borders made not of walls but of words, not of stone but of men. It relies upon covenants, oaths sworn, and the trust that binds them."

He spoke of the world I had come to love—the intangible world I had seen the good men around me try to speak into being and keep alive with their sweat and blood.

"But no one honors promises, or keeps his word, or tells the fucking truth anymore." He sounded more weary than angry. "And so, it must be like this now. Suspicion, mistrust, a fence, a wall, and a guard on the wall, and soon the whole land is divided."

"Dishonorable people need walls between them."

"We have never had such a need before. The eyes of the gods bound us to our words, and honor bound us to each other. There was a time when the greatest gift a man could offer was his oath. It proved his worth. Today, he thinks he's worth more unhindered by it."

"Who needs such corrupt men?"

"I agree," he said. "Next year, they'll only encroach further."

"They're nearly fortified. How will you uproot them now?"

"I fear we've waited too long." He pulled up a plug of grass and tossed it into the fire. "We haven't the men or time to starve them out. We're spread too thin out here, and their crops are lush. It would take a coordinated effort of several tribes' warbands. They know this. Which is why they're so brazen." He drank a deep draught of mead.

"Then you have your answer." I'd never seen them fight, and I struggled to imagine how Hellenes fought and rode in battle, draped and swaddled in their bedclothes.

"But these aren't the Mard-Khwaar," he said. "They're just common farmers."

"Then all the more shameful that they've made such fools of

the Skythai," I said, already growing weary of this conversation. I failed to apprehend the reason for his misgivings. A man who did not scruple to raid his neighbors and put his loyal brothers to death for their crimes was suddenly squeamish about evicting foreign invaders from his own tribe's land? "This isn't my country. But, for what it's worth, it feels like my home. And if someone came into my home uninvited, helped themselves to my property without offering thanks—while insulting me and dishonoring my ancestors, no less!—I would not sit idly by."

He rubbed his tired face with an open hand. "Then war."

War. There was resignation in his voice as he said it. Yet, spoken aloud, the word had such momentum to it. Like a sorcerer's spell, it had power all its own, and the world bent around it.

"Do you have a plan?" I asked, feeling the pull of that momentum.

"That's why I've come to you," he leaned forward eagerly, his elbows braced on his knees, the wineskin clasped in both hands.

"Me? What do I know of war?" I took the skin and drank.

"What will happen if I pursue this?"

I shook my head. "I can't tell you what will be, only what could be." I wouldn't try to foretell the future or pretend I could. I had a knack for seeing paths before me; often, they were paths no one else had thought to look for. But as far as I knew, there were no sure paths, only better choices. I suffered the curse of choices.

"That's all I ask. What have you seen—do you see?"

Had I seen anything at all? I didn't know how to make him understand that my spells didn't show me the kinds of signs he sought. Before the last spell in the cannabis tent, I sensed the approach of some kind of battle. Could this have been what it pointed to? I hadn't told him about those silly hallucinations. Now, if I did, there'd be no turning back. I might still try to stop it, but to what end? To keep my own hands clean? Cruel though it be, we had a chance to kill a rival in its cradle.

"The signs are silent on our path forward," I said.

"Can't you cast some rods or search the flight of birds and give me something? There was the eagle—was it a sign? I could make an incense tent, and you could fall into a trance. . . ?"

"You know that's not the way my sight works. Impressions come to me of their own volition. I cannot summon them." I had to offer something to placate him for the moment. "I see things as they were, as they are, and as they might be," I repeated the words a fortuneteller in the streets of Bastarnia once said to me when I paid her a bronze coin. "The future holds three paths: I see what can happen and what should happen. Not what will happen."

"Any man can do that," he rocked back, sighing in exasperation. "*I need answers.*" His frustration with me was mounting, though he remained composed. He grabbed the skin from me and drank his fill, wiping his mouth with the back of his hand.

"Then I'm no good to you," I said pettishly, though, in truth, I was relieved. Perhaps Aric began to see reason. I had also wasted my coin that day on fruitless answers. "If any man can do what I do, some other man should. I don't have the experience of your vazarka. You should have *them* give you war counsel."

"You twist my words. I only wish to learn our fate," he said, pulling at his beard as he did when he became agitated. Something portentous comes in these hours ahead." His voice faded to a whisper. "*I can feel it.*"

His impassioned plea burned away the fog of my foolishness, and I saw him clearly for a brief moment. He hadn't come for counsel—he came for comfort. He was frightened, not of the battle, but of forces beyond the reach of his weapons. Unlike clashes with swords and arrows, that was a struggle I knew something of. I took the tunic I had been sewing in hand. It was threadbare in places, the fine weave of the light cloth exposed along the shoulders and elbows.

"Fate is a strange thing," I said. "I don't know about the Skythai, but the Bastarnai believe that our fate is continually woven as if on a great loom, bound by the strands of people, places, deeds, and events in our life. As each of these moves across the warp of time, they become interwoven with one another until their pattern becomes inextricable, as it is here." I stretched the cloth before the firelight and exposed the pattern of the weave. "Fate is like this."

"Then, there are no choices? We are but threads being pulled along by another's hand?" he frowned deeply, his hands going slack.

"I used to think so. When I was young, I didn't understand listening to stories about the unseen beings who spin and weave our lives. But I've thought of it often as I've grown older, and it finally feels clear. Your fate is determined by the time and place of your birth, the people who surround you, and the choices you—and they—make. But not all these things are fixed. The quality of any fabric rests in the quality of its threads and the skill of its weaver. Your cloth is still being made. It cannot be unwoven, but it can be altered from this point onward. You cannot reset the loom, which was done at the beginning of time. But I believe you can alter some of your life's future design. Change the people and places who become bound up with your life's cloth. Unbind some of them if you wish. Some change is within our reach. But we must choose it carefully; cut or pull or change one thread, and it will forever change the tapestry's design."

"So, we still have a hand in our fate?" he asked, meeting my eye.

"Of course. We must."

"Then, the gods have not decided everything?"

"We have our will, don't we?"

"And the gods have their will. If they deny us victory in this, does that mean they scorn us—reject our cause?"

"That I can't say."

He rubbed his face in both his hands. "Would you? Scorn me?"

I placed my hand on his arm. "Never."

"And would you ride with me? Into this battle?"

Did he doubt me still? "I would."

"You hesitate." He jabbed absently at the fire with an iron.

I wished I could say I wasn't afraid. That I was eager. But that would be a lie. "I—I just hope I am ready. That I acquit myself well."

"You've trained and tested. Mastered the skills for battle. Have you mastered the will? Because a warrior cannot fear death."

"How? How do you not fear it?"

"Well, it's one thing to say and another to do. But I think of it this way: we lose nothing but this here when we die. Time owes us nothing. The old and the young lose but the same thing: this moment. The past is gone; the future belongs to no man. Tomorrow does not yet exist. And one cannot lose what he does not possess. If I die now, I have lost only this. That is all I have earned thus far. Seldom has it served a man to hide away and hoard his hours out of fear."

One cannot lose what he does not possess. Such a Skythai thing to say. Also, jarringly true. "What is it really like? Battle, I mean." I knew the raids I'd seen were tame compared to actual war.

"There are no gentle battles. No friendly fights. No kind ways to wage war. You can only end it quickly. Brutally, if you must. The short war is the most humane, like the quick death. A lingering conflict, mild or brutal, is torture to body and soul. Most battle is faster than you'd think once it's upon you. It's over almost before it begins. It comes like a summer storm. There is a thunder of hooves, a shower of arrows, a flash of spear tips and swords, and it is done. It rumbles over you with thunder and lightning. You're soaked in a downpour, but you feel each raindrop, cold and hard. It nearly drowns you. And then it's gone, quick as it came. And the sky clears the next moment. But the earth is muddy where it was just firm. And it was so sudden, you wonder to yourself if what just happened was real. But you still hear the thunder in your ears. You feel the static still in your blood. And you realize how pitiless gods and nature are."

CHAPTER 23

BATTLE

*From above, I watched my own form, as one
looks into the reflective waters of a flowing river,
helpless to retrieve it.*

THE DEAD TREE STOOD against the darkening sky like an ant-ler stuck into the ground. No wonder it had died; it had no business in this place. The howling wind blasted incessantly over grass withered to a parched and dusty brown. On the uppermost branch of the tree, a crow spread its wings but did not take flight.

We camped a mile upriver from the settlement. Our ranks had swelled with kara and novices until our number was over three hundred. We swarmed around the fire as a small, red-glazed jug was unsealed and poured into a golden bowl upon an altar. Each of the warriors unclasped his warbelt and held its bronze or gold clasp before the bowl. Into the face of each clasp, in what had seemed an ordinary circular design, the vazarka Peraka—*haomapaithi* of the kara, maker and dispenser of the sacred drink—poured out a measure of liquid, which the warriors caught in the hollow depression of their broad buckles. I, too, raised the bronze plate of my warbelt to be filled. It looked like ordinary milk, but I knew it was not. Tentatively, I lifted the *haoma* to my lips as they all watched, then guzzled the bitter potion in one gulp. I waited in horrible expectation. What would it do to me? Would it bring on the warrior fury the men all spoke of? My palms began to itch, and I breathed deeply to calm myself, uninterested in losing my senses to either the *haoma* or the gods. But now, my head swam, my heart raced, and I felt strangely detached from myself, as if my mind floated high above my body.

I glanced toward Aric, searching for an anchor to pull me back to earth. He seemed to be peering over the edge of a vast, black chasm—his eye fixed yet fixed on nothing. His jaw rigid, his breath hard through flared nostrils. But his hands trembled, even as he clenched his fists to steady them, and a rage swelled in him.

The other men looked much the same. They began to knock the shafts of their spears against their shields in a steady rhythm. In time to this, they stamped their feet in a circular march, like a dance, around the fire. Step, step, step, leap. They'd brandish their spears high in the air each time they landed—step, step, step, leap.

A chant rose into the night, their voices rising and falling in a jubilant song, chanted in time with their steps. Though I didn't understand their garbled words, I mumbled along as best I could. Bornon's bulky form swept past me, his long brown hair shaken loose, and he pulled me into the line. I followed along, thumping my shield, stomping my feet, and shaking my spear at the sky. One by one, the men began to howl as their chanting morphed into a chorus of hungry wolves. Thumping and clashing their spear shafts, stamping their feet, they circled the fire in a heaving mob of harsh cries and eerie wails.

Then suddenly, the dance broke up, the men howled in unison, and their glistening faces beamed in ecstasy. They hugged one another as though drunk—exuberantly and affectionately. I watched as they gave their rough embraces, sinewy and strong, and wondered what it felt like to receive men's brutal, brotherly affections. How they differed from the tepid, birdlike clasps shared between ladies, stingy and unsatisfying. But men, it seemed, plied the full force of their bodies in almost painful locking of grips and slapping of hides, their boisterous affections more like wrestling than comfort. I envied it. I despised my gentle life and the delicate care of those around me.

We scattered to mount our horses.

The horses seemed to dance in anticipation of the battle as the riders took their places according to rank, spears held high. More chanting followed, as the warriors raised their voices in cheerful calls that soon gave way to wilder baying. Spirits flew high, thanks in no small part to the haoma, the cloak of darkness, and the crisp nip in the night air. But most of all, we were giddy with the unknown.

The night was brighter than I imagined it would be. I thought we'd have more cover. The sky was dark without the moon, but the Shining Road gave enough light to guide our way and show the riders near us. Being tall, from a distance, none would assume I was a woman, for which I was grateful. I wore a pointed cap with long flaps like the men, and, again, I pulled a scarf over my nose and mouth to hide my lack of beard. My loose tunic mostly concealed my form. We wore no armor, though my light shield of wicker and leather was strapped to my back. I wore a thick vest of quilted hemp cloth under my caftan, which could turn indirect arrows and sword cuts. But death would not be the worst fate here. I couldn't imagine capture in a Hellenic colony. Or rather, I didn't want to try.

A modest ditch surrounded the village, and from its fill was mounded an even more modest bank. Atop the bank stood the beginnings of a rough wall of dry stone, only about knee-high, the steppe being bare of timber for palisades except what the Skythai consented to supply. The plan was to disperse the villagers, burn the settlement, pull down the structures, and destroy the crops. Ensure there was nothing left for them to return to. Aric ordered us to leave the horses, oxen, and wagons intact and fight only those who attacked. Those who wished to retreat could do so unharmed. Our purpose was only to drive them out. But if they resisted . . . well, hopefully, they wouldn't be that foolish.

A HORN SOUNDED IN THE DISTANCE. The settlers had scouted our arrival and were mustering a response. Hopefully they were covering their retreat, and it wouldn't be a long and bloody battle.

We rode hard toward the river amid howls and shouts in a dizzying frenzy. On the horizon, a cloud of dust rose into the night air and billowed ominously toward us. They were coming.

Once within range of the dust cloud, we would shoot our bows, raining a hail of arrows down on them before we ever saw the enemy. I braced my spear under my thigh, took a fistful of arrows in my bow hand, an arrow in my rein hand, and kicked Aruna forward into the pack of riders around me.

Aric reached into his goryt and withdrew a handful of arrows. Then he gave the command to loose our missiles. In what seemed a single, fluent motion, he set the first of his arrows upon his bow-string and, with supernatural ease, stretched back and released the graceful limbs of his mighty bow, all in the blink of an eye. Then, another arrow. And another, until they were spent, and he delved into his quiver for another handful. With an effortless strength and grace of movement, he braced briefly in the saddle, nocked his arrow, drew back his arm, and let each fly, the next ready on the string with a swiftness I could scarcely comprehend.

Entranced, I realized I was not shooting my arrows. Fitting the nock to the string, I angled my bow above the horizon and began to shoot, letting loose bolt after bolt with the others as we galloped toward the sound of the approaching thunder.

Soon, arrows began to rain upon us, their tips flashing silver in the faint starlight. Aruna had thick pads of quilted hemp draped over his back and shoulders, much like the vest I wore. The kara wore wolfskin capes like my own, and the vazarka wore their distinctive caps with pointed crowns also lined in wolfskin. More potent than armor of iron or bronze, these would turn any weapon if the gods so chose. Nevertheless, some of the points got through. A handful of horses and riders dropped back as we rode on.

At the far edges of the field, the dark shapes of horses appeared from the dust—shadows of hooves and legs. Muzzles and ears dipped in and out of the silver cloud, advancing and retreating from view.

And then they emerged—a wall of men, old and young, twenty across and three deep, shoulder to shoulder. The front row bore spears and roughly made round shields, while those behind them carried scythes, pitchforks, and sharpened stakes. They marched slowly, steadily, into the charge of our horses. A little over a fur-long away, they were within sight range of our bows. Fitting the nock to the string, I chose a target, a man at the edge of the pack. Aiming for his thigh, exposed beneath his shield, I drew back and let my arrow fly.

The moment it struck, my breath caught in my throat, and all the men upon the field seemed to hesitate and stay their fighting, their moving, their very breathing. I looked in wonder as the clash froze before my eyes. Though I had never been in battle, a charged, uncanny simultaneity overcame me. The coincidence of *this* field, on *this* day, at *this* moment, *this* fight. The face of every warrior. Somehow, it was all familiar. Could I have lived this moment twice? Could I have seen all this before in a vision? How could I have forgotten? There must be something momentous I should remember! I scrambled to collect my thoughts and recall the outcome, so I might warn the others.

But no. No. *Of course.* There was the smell. The fetid odor of foreboding. Of panic. Of fear. I knew what it meant and what was coming. Inside my mind, I begged, *Not now; not here.* I could feel the rhythmic jarring of my horse's hooves beneath me, but they no longer made any sound. And as the world around me flashed into black oblivion, the belly of my bow, braced in my left hand, became more solid and real than anything in the universe. I tried to hold it—to anchor myself to the world with it. To feel the earth beneath me through Aruna's hooves. But that fist, clinging to my drawn bow, was the last sensation I remember before I disappeared from the battlefield.

I STOOD SHROUDED IN DARKNESS, my feet resting on the dewy ground. Aruna was gone. Strong, constraining arms wrapped around me, crushing me. My arms lay pinned at my sides, and I thrashed against my captor with all my strength, but he gripped me harder and held me fast. Quitting my futile struggle—for now—I could feel the dagger hidden in my undervest, squeezed against my ribcage in the vise made by our bodies. The hunter learns to wait. Sooner or later, he had to let go.

I could not see him, but a thick pelt around his shoulders pressed softly against my cheek. It rose and fell with his breathing, which grew harsh and labored. He was somehow familiar, as bed is at the end of an arduous day, and I suddenly longed to close my eyes and sleep.

"You are returned?" he asked with a ragged voice, abruptly releasing his grip and stepping back, his face mostly in darkness. But I knew it as intimately as I knew the moon, even when shadows obscured its face.

"I'm here," I answered uncertainly.

"Only just," he said. It was then I saw the dark stain spreading across the side of his thick leather caftan. I felt its clamminess on my own hand. Had I been shot? Though I searched, I felt no wound. I looked at him in confusion. Blood dripped to the ground from beneath his caftan. An arrow shaft stuck out from his flank.

I gulped.

He said nothing but placed a horse's reins in my hand—my horse—looking unhurt, if a little spooked.

A gush of panic surged through my body. "Is it bad?"

"I've had worse," he said through his teeth. "Help me with it, will you?"

Aric. His name was Aric. Slowly, the disparate elements of my mind chose to make their way home again. But the remembrance was like the sun dawning, burning away a dense fog of doubt.

"Of course," I said, "but not here."

"There is nowhere else. I will not retreat from the field."

"All right. But lay down low in the grass. We're targets just standing here." Even in the dark, I felt exposed. All around us, the sounds of the battle still stirred. The whir of arrows. Grunts of men grappling. Shrieks of downed horses in pain. The chink of iron on iron. Here and there, silver and gold flashed in the pale light of the Shining Road.

Most Skythai warriors wore iron scale armor and bronze or iron helmets, making them nearly invulnerable in battle. However, like any karik of the sacred warband, Aric wore no armor, trusting only in his courage, prowess, and patron gods to face what threats lay before him. His only defense was his shield, which remained slung over his back as he rode should he need it for a close fight. After all, friend and foe alike agreed it was craven and shameful to shoot a man in the back—only, now, someone had done just that.

I looped my reins over my elbow and crouched low over him, cutting through his caftan, padded vest, and tunic, which had helped curb the shot. I examined the wound. The arrowhead was small, not deep, and clear of the kidneys and any vital veins. But the muscles had wrapped firmly around it. And it was probably barbed. It would tear a lot of flesh if I just yanked it out.

"I can't see."

"Just do it," he hissed.

"All right. Try to relax." I placed my knees on either side of the arrow, drew and held a deep breath, gripped the shaft near the wound with both hands, and, with all the force I could muster, gave the arrow a slow, forceful yank. He growled briefly, then looked at me and frowned. I looked at the arrow and frowned, too. The arrowhead was not on the shaft.

"Oh, shit. I don't know what—"

"We'll get it later." He grunted as he heaved himself back on his feet with a painful grimace. He snatched the arrow shaft from my hands and snapped it in two. "Mount up."

AS ARIC PROMISED, the fighting was over in minutes. But in moments, it was a lifetime. Dawn seemed an empty promise. With bleary eyes, I watched the east, expectant and apprehensive. I listened with my whole body for that terrible thunder to return—marching feet hammering as upon a drum, resounding through the earth beneath me, echoing through my bones.

How many hours could be in a night? I had lost all sense of time; it seemed neither to pass nor even exist. Momentarily, I'd been freed of its bond in my frenzy, exultation, and exhaustion. From above, I watched my form as one looks down into the reflective water of a flowing river, helpless to retrieve it.

In the last desperate hours of night—in the muck, listening to the moans of the dying, the wretched screams of wounded horses, the inescapable stench of spoiled blood, fermenting sweat, wet animals, and dung—the world crept back in. All the horrors, the physical pains—and worst, all the body's demands—were returning. My flesh was torn and needed tending; it was cold and needed shelter; it was hungry and thirsty. And what of Aric and his arrow? What of fallen companions and horses?

In the murky darkness, it was hard to see. Was that a hound carrying a severed hand in its jaws? Had the hand held the sword of an enemy or an ally? The ravens and crows had already arrived, their harsh caws biting into the predawn to finish what we'd begun.

Besides brief flashes, I remembered almost nothing of the battle itself after the spell came over me. But now it was over, a belated terror crept in. The inescapable thread of fear began to needle itself into the fabric of my mind. I cast my eyes anxiously east and waited.

Finally, a faint glimmer over the crest of the hill as the stars slowly disintegrated into the light. The entire world seemed to breathe a sigh of relief. In the still, cold rays of the sun's first light, I blinked and blinked and closed my heavy lids for just a moment, heedless of the destruction around me. Not caring what came next.

CHAPTER 24

SCALP

Aric stood and turned to me, holding up the
man's head by his hair, eyes still open,
mouth gaping.

How selfish to sleep when so much was still to be done. *Where had Aruna run off to again? What of Aric's wound? And the injured horses?*

The vultures and crows were already picking, feasting on horse and man. Behind them, the remains of the village were engulfed in flame, smoke from the timbers and thatched roofs wafting over me in a sudden gust, stinging my eyes and throat. As always after a spell, I was nauseated. I stood and staggered through the crowds of weary men, searching for Aric or Antisthenes.

"Thank the gods!" Aric shouted, and I spun around to see him standing behind me. "Where the fuck did you go? I've been looking everywhere." His anger seemed to abate as he spoke. "Say something."

Aric was beside the settlers' defensive ditch, standing over a corpse with an arrow stuck in its ribs.

Looking around, I whispered to him, "Aric, is this . . . *real?*"

He hesitated a moment, confusion written on his wrinkled

brow. "Real enough." Then he inhaled deeply, and his manner turned grave. "You are finally a warrior this day."

I swooned a bit, turned aside, and vomited into the ditch. Wiping my mouth on my sleeve, I looked at him apologetically. He pressed his lips together, nodding. Then, he reached for the dagger in his belt and, nursing his wounded side, crouched over the body. I could not see him working, only hearing a sound like wet cloth ripping.

"Your horse is safe. He's with mine."

He knew my mind well. "I hope I didn't disappoint too much?"

"You did well for your first real fight."

"I regret my *absence*." Missing the battle because of my spells lacked even the dignity of being thrown from my horse. "You know I can't control—"

"Don't worry. You persisted despite it," he looked over his shoulder with a raised eyebrow, apparently as shocked as I was. I wasn't sure I wanted to know more.

"Well, I regret the arrow. Thank you. Truly."

"I owed you," he smiled.

He worked quickly with his blade, and I peeked over his shoulder to see what so occupied him. Was he stripping the man's armor and clothing to collect the valuable bits? I glanced toward the arrow sticking out from the man's ribs. It bore a curious forked marking on the shaft—*the antlers*. It was one of mine.

Aric stood and turned to me, holding the man's severed head by his hair, eyes still open, mouth gaping.

"Congratulations," he said dryly. He thrust it toward me, slick and dripping. I'd made my tally.

Fuck. This can't be happening. I shook my head.

He frowned, and the confusion spread across his face. "Go on. You've earned this." He dangled the bloody mass before me like a bauble.

I only stared at him. I wanted nothing of it. Not the scalp, not the skull, not what followed. I hadn't meant to kill anyone. Indeed, I tried my best not to. Some intuition assured me I wasn't yet finished here. I couldn't go back—not to the life that awaited me at court.

His arm fell limp to his side. In his hand, the earthy hair still clasped in his fingers, blood hanging from its strands in clots.

"*Take it*," his frustration mounted, and he shoved the head within a hair's breadth of my face.

"*Not yet*," I pleaded. I didn't flinch, but I didn't yield either. "You owe me another life." I rummaged through the pouch at my waist for the two gold rings and offered them to him. "Take them back; we're even now."

He regarded me for a long moment, his brow wrinkling in bemusement, consternation. "All right," he finally said, his expression softening as understanding dawned and his choice was made. But he waved his hand dismissively at the rings.

"What now?" I asked tentatively.

He crouched over the head, working with his blade, and lifted it before me. Rivulets of blood ran down the face from long gashes across the forehead and around the ears. With a quick snap of his arm, he shook the head, and the skull slipped free from the cap of flesh that had once been the man's scalp. It fell to the ground, rolling into place at my feet, the eyes staring up at me, jaw slack.

Aric looked around us, and his voice softened to almost a whisper. "I'll keep it for you until you want it." With a flick of his wrist, he gave the scalp a snap to loosen the clots of blood the way a dog shakes water from its fur. Spatters of blood struck the ground, and he held it before his eye to inspect his handiwork. Satisfied with the result, he wrapped the scalp in a chamois and stuffed it into his belt.

"I'll make three kills like a real Skythai does," I stated as if I now had the power to change the terms of the arrangement.

I dipped my fingers into the pooling blood spilling from the decapitated body, still warm, and touched it to my tongue.

His lips thinned, but he gave a curt nod. "That's one."

OF WIND AND WOLVES

He yanked the arrow from the man's ribs and handed it to me. Wiping the blood from it in the grass, I slid it back into my quiver.

THE WARBAND SET ABOUT THE GRUESOME TASK of dispatching those who would not survive their wounds. I was neither prepared to handle such a job nor a warrior of high enough status to deserve the right, for the Skythai deemed it necessary for the hand wielding the blade to be of equal or greater honor than the victim—a dignity offered to friend and enemy alike.

Instead, I saw to the horses, which seemed the least of anyone's priorities but had nonetheless received wounds as horrific as any man. They thrashed helplessly on the ground, hamstrung or dying, or gimped about the field, lamed from their injuries, or ran themselves ragged in a frenzied panic. Someone had to quiet them and pull the arrows from their wounds, too. With a kindly young karik named Artavardiya to assist, we quickly assessed those who could be healed and those who would not recover. For the latter, the spike end of my sagaris to the place beneath the forelock took away their pain forever.

Frantic shouts from farther afield drew my attention—the vazarka called Aric's name with urgency. Though wounded, Aric sprang onto his horse and galloped toward their cries. I leapt onto Aruna and followed. A group of men huddled around something on the ground, and when they saw Aric, the crowd parted, revealing a man lying with his head in the lap of another.

Their vazarka brother, Tokhak, had his horse speared from under him, and he was crushed beneath it. They'd rolled the horse away, but now he could not rise or move his legs. He was asking for his dagger so he could put an end to himself, and the men called for Aric.

I turned to Gohar, standing beside me. "Can't he live out his days at court? Take up the mantle of the anarei?" The men nearby all gaped at me like I'd just uttered a curse over him.

"And live like a woman?" Gohar asked incredulously.

"He will never ride again," Olgas said. "To sit in the wagons," he spat on the ground, "what kind of life is that?"

"But he can be with kin, drink wine, and still be useful somehow. Share his wisdom, learn divination . . ." I grasped desperately for something that might sway them. "Has he not earned that?"

The man on the ground spoke up, and the gathering hushed itself.

"To be as a woman is worse than death," Tokhak sputtered, mustering the breath to speak for himself as his chest deflated and heaved with the effort. "Look at the life I've been honored to live. How can I live any other way than this? I don't grieve, so don't grieve for me."

He bid his comrades farewell and asked to be buried with the brave horse that fell in battle with him as he wheezed and closed his eyes. Then Aric unwound the bast girdle from the man's waist, and I knew what was to follow. Maybe I even agreed in my heart, but I didn't want to watch. I gathered my reins and led brave Aruna away.

CHAPTER 25

ARROW

My mind turned inward. And all that waited
there was doubt.

Aric thrust a cup of wine into my hands. "Drink," he commanded, his voice hushed and harried though we were safely inside our tent. Now, the mask of fortitude had fallen away, and he grimaced in agony as he downed his cup and poured another.

Those first few sips of wine always did something strange to me, like a shiver emanating down my throat and into all my limbs. My pulse throbbed, and a light dew sprinkled my body as it was warmed by the liquid fire in my cup. All the hairs on my scalp tingled, and I felt as if I would melt into the earth like spring snow.

Aric wanted me—not Galati, the camp's healer—to remove the arrowhead. I should have been flattered by his trust, but his request rattled me. As I considered the best course, I ground a paste of Apia's tears and honey to apply to the wound. He'd left it too long, and the muscle was raw, inflamed, and beginning to bruise. It would be hard to extract the arrowhead now and doubly hard to heal. I was loath to cut more flesh, but I hoped that if I could grasp it with the arrow-pullers I'd been using on the horses, perhaps I wouldn't need to.

Before he allowed me to begin, Aric seemed desperate that I cut his hair as though there were no more urgent matters at hand.

"You refuse to cut your hair or trim your beard before a fight?" I asked as I weighed his shears in my hand, testing their bite in my grip. "Yet now, after the battle is over . . . ?"

"A bull has his horns, a stag his antlers."

"So?"

"So, too, a man in readiness for battle brings forth his attribute, drawing his strength from all creation. The great stag bears Arta's gifts until after the season for fighting is passed, when he returns them to their origin. I swore to eradicate the Hellenic threat from the steppe. When a man makes a vow, he shall not cut his hair until it is fulfilled. It is consecrated in this way. And when his vow is finally achieved, he delivers his gifts to their source in gratitude, as the deer sheds his antlers back into the earth. We sustain the Arta as it sustains us."

"So, it is your horn?" Men's minds really did work in strange ways.

"Why else does nature mark men thus?"

It was a fair enough question, and I could offer no reasonable explanation. I gently grasped a lock of his hair and drew a deep breath. He should not have asked something so onerous of me. There was no time for such things with his wound yet to heal. And what if I should deface him? Make him a laughingstock? I'd only ever cropped the manes of horses. I had no expertise in the grooming of men.

But I could not afford to delay. Gripping the hair between my fingers, I held my breath, clenched my teeth, and snipped. Silky and fine, his wheaten hair smelled of dried sweat and leather as I combed my fingers through it and cut again and again until it bore some uniformity. Though I'd touched it only briefly, his fox-colored beard was as I remembered from the day we first fought—thick and unexpectedly soft. For the first time, I noticed several strands of grey hair coursing through it, which surprised me for one so young. This I cropped evenly to a finger's breadth, working as swiftly as I dared, conscious ever of the arrow still festering in his wound. I believe I did a satisfactory job for my first try, and with his scruffy hairs neatened, he looked quite regal, though I tried to restrain the proud smile that sprang to my lips as I surveyed my handiwork. When I was through, he only ran his hands over all and nodded, never reaching for his mirror.

I gathered the clippings into a pile, which he snatched up and folded inside a scrap of hemp cloth. "They must be returned to the earth," he said, "where they will once again become the grasses of the plain." He looked meaningfully at me for a long while, and I realized finally that, without asking, he wished this favor of me.

"Of course, I . . . will bury them for you?" I said, still uncertain of what he asked. My people buried our nail clippings, though so seldom did we cut our hair that I'd never had the need, but mostly this was so they did not fall into the hands of sorcerers and those who wished us ill. Powerful dark magic could be performed with a scrap of hair or fingernail from an unwitting victim. But his face lightened and he smiled gently in thanks, nodding and handing me the sack of clippings.

"Turn around so I can apply this paste to your wound."

He lifted his tunic and lay face-down on his bed while I daubed the wound with the paste of dried poppy sap, reserving the rest to feed him after the surgery.

"So, before a battle, you grow your beards," I asked as I prepared the rest of the things I'd need: arrow-pullers, water, bandages. "Afterward, are you not weakened by the cutting?"

"It is how we renew our strength. We draw our vitality from the elements. But this diminishes our world little by little. After the battle, we must sacrifice and replenish the great reservoir. To restore the world and renew its vitality. A man can only take so much without also giving."

"Brace yourself. This is going to hurt."

With a clean fingertip, I probed the wound until I felt the ferrule of the arrowhead. He held his breath. The muscle had wrapped tightly around the arrow. I slid the slender blade of a sharp dagger alongside my finger to open the wound, then inserted the tip of the arrow-pullers, which were as narrow blacksmiths tongs with spoonlike shields over the jaws to aid in extracting barbed arrowheads. Getting a firm grip with both hands, I squeezed the arms as hard as I could. I'd not let the arrowhead slip away a second time. I braced both my knees against his flank. Aric, for his part, lay deathly still. His body was tensed, and he inhaled slowly and steadily despite what had to be terrible pain.

Gripping with all my might, I heaved, and the arrowhead slipped free with the sickening moist sound of raw meat being sliced.

"I have it!" I washed it in the bloody basin of water I had used to wash the wound and examined it. The barb was bent but intact; the wound was clean. "Are you all right?"

"Better now," he said with a groan and several deep breaths.

I placed the arrowhead in his palm. "You should heal now. It will likely abscess and ooze with foulness for many days. I will anoint and bandage but not stitch it."

"Do what you must," he said, "but my blood is upon this; I must first salve it." He held forth the arrowhead in his open palm.

That an object might become so intimately entwined with a man's being as to continue affecting him even at a distance seemed odd and obvious. "Of course," I said, passing him the ointment.

Working the grease into the three faces of the bronze, he tucked the arrowhead carefully into a leather pouch and paused to look up at me. "Thank you."

"It's I who must thank you." Once again, I removed the gold rings from my pouch and held them forth.

"Keep them. It's my honor."

"Please, I will not take without also giving."

"Let us not keep tallies between us, you and I?"

After I tied the last bandage, he eased himself gently down onto his pallet, relief chasing the pained expression from his face as he wrapped his arm around the fleece he used as a pillow. "Now that you've fought your first real battle, I think it's time you had a stronger bow. I have just the one," he mumbled as his eyelid drooped and, with a sigh, drifted off to sleep.

SLEEP SHOULD HAVE COME EASILY. We were exhausted beyond the limits of the flesh. But the silence of the tent was cruel. With nothing to divert my attention, my mind turned inward. And all that waited there was doubt. Over and over in my thoughts, I lived each conscious moment again, re-ran each step, re-aimed each arrow. What little I was lucid for was enough for a lifetime—each stride, each draw, each scream, each wound. I fought it over anew a thousand times.

Mostly, it was the screams of the horses that plagued me now. There is no more heartrending sound on earth than the cry of a horse in anguish. It haunted me far more than the cries of the settlers. As did the panicked expression of fear and betrayal in their eyes when they realized they'd been led to slaughter—the immediacy of dispatching them with my own hand. In the clamor after the battle, the kindest thing was to end their suffering quickly, but now, in the quiet of the tent, their distress was constantly in my thoughts, played out vividly before my mind's eye.

Men know what battle is and who it serves. They understand what weapons are and what they do to flesh. But horses do not fight for gods, kings, or glory. They care nothing about our boundaries nor our honor. They go to battle because we ask them to. But that's a lie. We don't ask. They want no part in our wars; they share none of our enmities beyond the loyalty a friend shows another in his time of need. Too often, we sacrifice these, our loyal friends, without even a passing thought. They were left on the field where they fell—or the fresh ones were butchered for meat. I refused to eat it.

If only I had the power to keep my wits instead of drifting off when they needed me most. When they *all* needed me. Returning to court with the funerary wagons laden with the bodies of the dead—four of the novices and the old vazarka Tokhak—I would soon face those questioning eyes. Why you? Why has my son not returned, but *you* are still here? Aric would also be dead now if the wretched settler had been a better bowman. *Why not me?*

The men drenched themselves in wine and retreated to the cannabis tents to be cleansed of their cares and fears. I didn't blame them. But I didn't join them either. Too much was beyond my control; I wanted to keep my wits about me. I lay uncomfortably on a lumpy pallet, staring into the dark, unable to rein in my mind and sleep. Antisthenes snored deeply—likely still drunk—but, though he was still, I knew Aric was not asleep either. Was even a warrior like him plagued by such thoughts?

After rousing himself for the evening meal, he'd shambled through the tent flap just as the fire died out, and I prepared for bed. His clothes and hair smelled of cannabis smoke, and his eye was red. But his expression was serene as he kicked off his boots and dropped gingerly onto his bed without undressing, laying on his uninjured side. We lay in solemn silence, willing sleep to arrive, like hosts who sit in expectation of a late guest making a long, arduous journey. Across the sword between us, he reached and placed his hand on my forearm.

"I know," he said in a tight rasp.

With that, the dam weakened against the flood of emotions. My whole form began to shake as I stifled my sobs, warmed by his solace, braced by the strength in his fingers.

What did he know? Did he know how the horrors I'd seen still flashed before my eyes no matter how many times I blinked them away? How the screams of the suffering horses still raked through my skull? That I didn't even know the names of the four young novices who died? That, though I tried to summon pity, I felt nothing for the man who strayed into the path of my arrow—except perhaps resentment that his foolishness nearly caused my leaving. I couldn't tell these things to Aric. These were not things people said aloud. What if, like all the rest, he should consider me a monster? Was there pain or anguish in him as well? I longed to ask. To nestle close and comfort—be comforted by—him. But how many rules could I break in a day? I searched instead across the impenetrable black for a glimpse of his face and found nothing.

"Does it ever end?" I asked timidly of the darkness, afraid of the answer.

"There's only time," he whispered bitterly.

It wasn't an answer. *Time.* Did that mean never? Was that the source of the turmoil that roiled beneath his still surface? Why he kept to himself and drowned himself in drink sometimes? After all he had seen and done and suffered, he possessed a knowledge beyond ordinary human endurance. And there could be no way to gaze upon it—stare it in the face—and remain human. How did he endure?

At that moment, I wanted nothing more than to hold him—and to be held. He had to want that, too. And the distance imposed by our oaths only added to the ache because we lay so close, yet across an unnavigable sea where there could be no passage.

"What am I to do?" I asked. "Make my heart a stone, cold and hard?"

"Some do." He paused a moment. "Others forge their hearts in iron."

"Iron is just as cold and hard as stone."

"It might seem so. But think of a sword and how it's made. Stone is strong, but it can weather, crack, or be chipped away. Iron is bled from the ore by fire. Fire makes the iron change form and become something new. As we may, by the grace of Tabiti. We burn, we are hammered, we bend, we change. It hurts, but finally, we're tempered and take our form, stronger, sharper, more enduring than before. A warrior's iron is made to be resilient, not rigid. So long as it doesn't fear the fire and the forge."

CHAPTER 26

PRIESTESS

What do you even say to the dead?

IN THE AFTERMATH of the battle, the camp took on a melancholy mood like I had never seen. There should have been celebration after such a sound victory. But the men must have sensed, as I did, that there was no glory in this fight. It may have been justified, it may even have been necessary, but it was not noble. There were no great spoils to be won or long-standing rivals to be routed, merely a tract of land and the upper hand to reclaim—and not without considerable risk. We had not heard the last from the Hellenes on this account. Having swatted a single wasp, sooner or later, the nest would rouse itself in fury.

The injured men remained indoors for the most part, and their brothers stayed to care for them. Others ventured only far enough to fulfill the duties of hunting and riding patrols. Aric's wound was still mending, so I remained close to camp, looking after the horses and performing chores with Stormai. He'd pulled his shoulder out of joint falling from his stumbling horse and carried his arm in a sling. While he couldn't draw a bow, he was stuck doing the undignified jobs of a novice with me, gathering cow pats to make bricks for the fire and checking the fish traps and snares.

We brought our waterskins down to the river while we checked the last of the traps and sat to take a bite to eat in the dreary midday light. The day wouldn't brighten, no matter how hard I willed the sun to shine. But the cold water was clear again, and it felt good on my stiff hands. The scent of fire still hung in the air. After the remaining settlers had fled in their carts, we'd burned everything but the stock and the hay. Unlike horses, sheep and cattle hadn't the sense to dig beneath the snow to find food for themselves, and even the Skythai had to make hay for them when they grazed far from the reedy riverbanks in winter. We took everything we could carry and burned the rest.

Amid the ashes where the village had stood, Aric took clay and water from the river to build an altar and sang verses over it while he lit a fire. All through these last days and nights, the men kept the fire burning to reclaim the territory for their people. Yet, I'd seen these waters run red with blood, and ash, and other things less noble, and I wondered how much had to wash through this place before it would be clean again. Perhaps that was the beauty of the river. It was never the same from one moment to the next. So much water had flowed from yesterday to today.

Stormai leapt to his feet, and I turned to see what had roused him. Behind us, a band of some twenty of our men marched toward where we sat by the riverside. I'd never spoken to any of them and didn't know one by name. If I screamed for help, no one would arrive in time—if they came at all. I wasn't sure Stormai would fight for me, even if he could with his poor arm. And against a mob like this, I wouldn't ask him to. We were outnumbered.

I stood up straight and forced myself to meet the eyes of the pack leader. I recognized his scarred face. I think I'd heard the others call him Hvaspa around the camp. He was a fine horseman and a veteran karik. Old enough to have a few seasons of such battles behind him but young enough to still harbor passion behind his shining chestnut eyes.

"Blessings, my lady." His voice was soft but tremulous.

"And to you, Sura," I answered guardedly.

"May we speak alone?"

We walked a short distance from the crowd. I was anxious about a trap, but the presence of Stormai gave me a certain solace. He watched us closely.

"As well as warriors, it's said the hamazan are also priestesses? I've heard it said that even Aric seeks your mediation. That you travel among the dead and can speak with spirits."

I held up my hand, about to protest. My other hand hovered near the handle of my dagger, which was concealed in the undervest beneath my caftan.

He shook his head. "I'd not like to see such a place—not for many years," he insisted, looking at his boots as if to hide from the thought. Through his disheveled hair, he peered up at me. "But if you should go there, maybe you'd bring a good word to my blood-brother, Tokhak. Tell him—I don't know," he shook his head and looked at me desperately, his brow furrowed. "What do you even say to the dead? Tell him we'll look after his kin and see him soon. Tell all our brothers when you meet them there?"

He stood in silence, staring at me in utter earnestness. The crowd, just feet away, held themselves in silent anticipation. Their forlorn faces, long and pale, looked at me across a distance I recognized in myself. It was the horizon that stretched between me and sleep when the fires had long gone out, and nothing but quiet and stark memories filled the night. I hadn't the heart to tell them the truth. I had no such gift. The dead hid from me as they hid from all the living. Yet, it seemed a harmless enough untruth, small if it brought solace to the grieving.

"The ways and paths of that world are difficult." My voice splintered as I spoke. "But I will search for your companions. Should I see them in the place beyond, I will bring them your good words."

It was not untrue. If I could, I surely would. And I wished, then, with all my heart, I had within my power to perform the feat they asked.

"Bless you, *satanaya*," Hvaspa sobbed, with tears welling in his crinkled eyes, and clasped my hands tightly in his like we were old friends.

CHAPTER 27

FLESH

I was never convinced there was anything
sacred in mankind.

WITH THE CHILLY AUTUMN weather come early, there were
no more fish traps to set. The fish had moved to deeper waters,
as we would soon move deeper into the steppe. This morning, I
came to collect the last of them and found Aric standing naked
on the shore.

I froze in my tracks and quickly averted my gaze. "Oh! I didn't
see you there; I'll return later," I stammered and spun around to
leave. His wound was mostly healed now, but he hadn't fully resumed hunting or watches yet, and I didn't expect to find him this
far from camp so early.

"Anaiti, wait," he called, "I was only about to bathe."

I'd probably never get used to seeing the many scars and tattoos
inscribed across his skin. The Skythai did not often show their
flesh to the world. Not only was the climate too harsh for bare skin
in both summer and winter, but undress was something private,
sacred, held between themselves and the gods. This was because
they covered their skins with images unsuitable for uninitiated
eyes—holy signs charged with mythic meaning only their own

knew how to read. Many were singular images spawned by dreams or mystic rites. Most of the marks remained a mystery, and it was not my place to look on them.

Erman told me that men in the earth's walled cities prepared animals' skins—sheep and the like—to be painted with wise sayings. They called these inscribed hides books. Others pressed and dried the leaves of plants or planks of linden wood to scribble on. Or scratched into slabs of clay or wax. With these texts, they recorded the sayings of their people and the laws of their gods. And they collected these scrolls and tablets in great repositories and temples. But the Skythai had no storehouse but the people. So, they carried their scriptures in their flesh—in their memories and on their skin. Each man and woman was a leaf in the great Skythian book. Each kept his portion of the story. Over a lifetime, some grew to be epic works of art, and after their owners were carefully embalmed, they were buried like treasure in the earth. Others were flayed and prepared like those scrolls—illuminating for all the people the wisdom gathered in the ancients' wanderings and the knowledge of the long journey ahead.

"Why don't you join me?"

"At this hour?" I asked, still averting my eyes. "The water's freezing."

"You're not scared of a little cold water?"

All my embarrassment receded with his well-aimed jab at my pride. Indignant, I stripped to my underclothes and stepped, haltingly, just into the stream. Every muscle in me contracted. I bit my lip and held myself still as gooseflesh erupted across my bare skin.

He unbound his hair and shook out his arms. Then he strode straight into the depths and disappeared beneath the surface. My flesh crawled just watching. He reemerged, pulled in a deep breath, beamed, and splashed the frigid water at me. I flinched as if dodging an arrow.

"You'll never get wet standing there," he said, swiping the water back from his face and hair with both hands.

"I'm coming."

I wasn't. My feet rooted themselves to the shore.

"You must go all at once. To do it by degrees is torture."

He was right. And I was a coward. Closing my eyes, I plunged myself into the frosty current. The water closed around me like an iron vise, and I went rigid in its grip, sinking to the bottom. My heart may have stopped. Then I remembered the air and light above me. Pushing to the surface, I gasped more from shock than breathlessness.

"Oh shit! I've done it!" It was like swimming through a sea of swords, but I was fully immersed in the frigid water.

He laughed his hearty, mellow laugh. "You could do it with less shrieking."

"I'm not sure that I could!" I giggled. "I don't understand. How do you bear it with such ease?"

"I don't mind it. It's only flesh."

"Tell that to *my* flesh."

"You must tell it to your own," he said as he waded toward the shore. "You dwell too much in your flesh."

"Where else should I be?" I asked with perhaps more sarcasm than necessary as we climbed ashore again.

Aric, dripping before me, handed me his cloth to dry myself. "The priests say there is something in man that is sacred; that is not destroyed by death. I remember this when my flesh complains or cries out in pain, and I want nothing more than to submit to it." He scrubbed himself with the cloth when I was through.

"You make me feel ashamed," I said as I slipped on my linen tunic and wrapped myself snug in my fur-lined caftan, my underclothes still damp.

"That's never my intention." He pulled on his trousers and tied them. "You've no reason to be ashamed. But know that one must train the inner beings of mind and will as much—or more even—than this outward form."

He stood with his hands on his hips, watching me dress.

Embarrassed, I stopped, holding my caftan close about me. "We can train the spirit?"

"The body is weak. It bleeds. It dies. You needn't let this pain taint your spirit. I ply my form with hardship each day, not to fortify my flesh, but my spirit."

I was never convinced there was anything sacred in mankind. But for the first time in my life, I hoped it might be true. "I wish I could do it over: go back into that icy water again."

"Don't worry. Each time is like the first."

CHAPTER 28

BLOOD

Will my bones lie silent in a field,
forgotten like these?

THE DAYS GREW SHORTER as Holy Month drew to a close. We slowly made our way north now that the pastures had time to recover. Aric and Antisthenes spoke of moving the camp to a buna farther west, on the banks of the Tura, for the winter. But for now, on a crisp morning with frost in the grass, we rode up the Madhu Water and camped. We'd found signs of bandits, so we mounted a patrol to scout the area before making camp.

We waited for the signal from the east under the breast of Eagle Rock, an outcrop of cold, grey granite in the shape of a magnificent raptor with wings outstretched. We sat in its shade, beneath the spread of its wings, beyond all warmth and light. The wet soaked through even my waxed cloak. I was miserable, and the flash of light from Stormai's mirror came like a sign from the heavens. Aric flashed a signal back, and by midmorning, we were on the move again to our next lookout point on Thorn Hill and back in the warmth of the sun.

My clothes dried quickly against the heat of Sakha's sides and with the sun and wind at my back. Before long, we were on a high bramble-covered knoll overlooking a creek at the head of a shallow valley. We splashed our faces and necks with the icy water and refilled our flasks. The grass was beginning to fade at the end of summer. But late blackberries rallied in some of the brambles cascading down to the stream. Ripe berries hung heavy on the lithe canes. We picked handfuls, our skin bitten by the thorns, and lay in swaying feathergrass, letting the waning summer soak into our greedy flesh. The horses dozed in the afternoon sun, their lids heavy, muzzles drooping, their ears twitching, and their tails swishing idly at the season's last flies.

Aric rose in search of more berries, leaving his bow in the dry grass. My eye traced the graceful, sweeping curves of it where it lay. It was a stout, powerfully built weapon with thick layers of wood and tough sinew, gracefully curved and well-worn. Aric had gifted me a beautiful new bow, as promised. It was twice as powerful as my old bow, and I surprised myself when I could draw it with ease, stronger now than I had been when I arrived. But I was curious about the draw weight of Aric's warbow.

I glanced at him as he wandered further around the hill, distracted with his foraging. Cautiously, reverently, I took the weapon into my hands, caressing its bold, sweeping lines. Its grip polished with use. I fitted my palm to it and touched the string, testing it. It was heavy, and stiff in my hands. I could bend it, but not fully. I stood, widened my stance, braced myself, and tried again in earnest. With all my strength, I barely nudged the bow past a three-quarter draw. My muscles began to shake, and I had to ease the arrowless string back, careful not to release too quickly and risk shattering the bow. I marveled at the beauty and power of the thing in my hands a moment before setting it back as I had found it.

He soon returned with a double handful of berries, which he offered to share. A cemetery of small, unremarkable barrows overlooked the creek at the end of the valley. Everywhere we rode in this country, we encountered earthen mounds. So well did they merge with the landscape that it was often difficult to tell which were natural features and which were man-made. Others were ringed with stones, some bore stone idols or trees atop them, and others were so vast, tall, and round that they stood out upon the flat plain as something utterly foreign. High as mountains they seemed, and more magnificent than any barrow built in my homeland. I couldn't imagine how many men it must have taken to construct such things. Surely, kings slept beneath such mountains.

"Do you know whose tombs these are?" I asked Aric.

He wrinkled his brow. "They're ancient. Not barrows of Sky-thai. Kimmeroi, I think. They were here before our people came."

"Where did they go?"

"Most who remained went south, I think," he said, popping a blackberry into his mouth. "To the Kimmerian Peninsula, Tauris, and the Bosporus. Some went far west, they say, in search of the Summer Isle and were never heard from again. These tombs were all they left behind."

"That's sad. I hope they found it."

"There is no greater misfortune than abandoning the graves of one's ancestors. I can think of few things worse than for a people to concede the ground where their forefathers are laid to rest."

"But it was your people who took their land?"

"They *lost* this land. No people, no pack, is owed the patch on which it feeds, the ground on which it walks. They must hold and defend or cede it to those who are cleverer or stronger than themselves. This is nature's law."

"Will you say the same when the Hellenes come and take this land from the Skythai?"

"If we should be so heedless and weak as to lose this land to them, what else is there to say? These are the richest pastures in the world, and all creatures—men and beasts alike—lust after them. A man, a tribe, is owed nothing—not territory or existence. We must defend what we wish to keep."

"I was wrong to have suggested it. That will never happen to you—to the Skythai," I tried to reassure him, perhaps in vain. Who could honestly say what the future held for any of us?

He regarded me earnestly. "Won't it? I watch my people grow weaker each day. They forget. They begin to disdain this life for one of indulgence—for indolence. For rows of stone houses and markets; for Greek wine and easy bread. And this is the most coveted land for the herdsmen of the earth. The eastern tribes, hungry for our lush grazing, will continue to press us as we pressed the Kimmeroi. Next will come the farmers to put it under the plow. Our time will pass like these clouds. And me? Will my bones lie silent in a field, forgotten like these? My name and works lost forever?"

It grieved me to hear him speak this way. "I'm surprised then that you don't wed."

"You mean make sons to carry my memory? Recite my genealogy? Recount my deeds?" I detected more than a hint of sarcasm as he spread his arms wide in mock pomposity.

"Something like that. I thought that was what all men wanted?"

"Most men, I think," he plucked absently at the grass beside his boot.

"I suppose you've got a hundred sons already. They are loyal to you like kin."

"The warband? Truly, they are three hundred motherless bastards, but they do me proud. I suppose they're the closest thing I'll ever have." He lay back on the ground, his hands tucked behind his head, his tawny hair spilling around him into the crisp, sunburnt grass.

"I heard you had a wife once?"

He remained silent, staring up at the sky.

Regretting my question, I attempted a retreat. "I shouldn't have asked. There's no shame in sorrow," I offered.

"You mistake me, Ana," he said, inclining his head toward me and shielding his eye from the sun with his hand. "Many believe

I keep this life out of grieving. Let them believe as they like. But you should know the truth."

I nearly stopped him. I wasn't sure I wanted to hear what came next.

"I don't grieve." Averting his gaze, he cleared his throat and continued in a hushed tone. "I didn't wish her ill. Not really. But the king arranged it. I never wanted her."

"I didn't even know kara were permitted to take wives."

"A karadar is. His wife has a special, sacred purpose. She is the satanaya—Mother of the Hundred."

"And she was. . . ?"

"Unfit. She'd have brought misery and misfortune upon us."

"Not every tree will root in every soil."

"You don't understand. I was glad when she was gone. My heart was full of secret joy—and guilt. I am not proud, but it's the truth."

"Why guilt?" I pressed gently, recalling the sinister whispers Antisthenes spoke of.

He combed his beard with his fingers as he seemed to search for an answer. "Because maybe I willed it. Maybe the gods granted me my heart's wish."

"Oh, Aric, that's nonsense."

Crowned in tufts of brittle meadow grass, he drew a deep breath and clasped his hands over his chest. "Now the gods play games with me."

"How so?"

He sighed and worried his brows. "My father still tries to make matches for me from time to time. It's funny. When the subject of your father's pact first came to our court, the king proposed you for me. I refused." He shook his head and let out a defeated chuckle. "I didn't know then. How could I have known?"

Stunned, I fell still. Motionless and mute, my mind groped for words but found none worthy of saying aloud. In a daze, I sat, palms pressed into the grass, blades grazing my fingers, as the flies buzzed around us. I stared at him blankly, the sun shining adoringly on his face, turning his hair and beard to gold. I had a vision of reaching out and touching him, laying my hand over his, running my fingertips across the gilded contours of his cheekbone.

Instead, I tried to break the spell. I withdrew my gaze and envisioned fading away from this place where the sun shone and the bees hummed—disappearing from the world.

"The gods play with us both," I said before the silence could stretch too long between us, "but whatever grim fate they may have planned for us, I will never forget you, not in this life or the next." My eyes and voice filled with tears, and I suddenly felt imprudent.

He was quiet for a long time, lying in the grass. I thought perhaps he had drifted off to sleep. Then he began softly to speak, his voice tremulous and deep:

"Let me be forgotten. I care nothing for these bones. Let the wolves gnaw them. May they crumble to dust. Let this blood pour out and wash into the sea. My name—let it vanish like smoke into the air. But, when this body has gone to its grave, my mind, I think, will never leave this plain. It will roar like the tempest or the howling of wolves. Or whisper, maybe, like the breezes that rustle the grass—that play with your hair just now. Let whatever I possess of luck or skill go to my people. I do not desire another life, the halls of Gœtosura, or the meadows stretching beyond the Iron Gates of Yama. My will, my thoughts, my memories—let these never leave this place, but return to the wind that flies over this boundless steppe."

"Let my thoughts join them," I whispered to myself.

He pushed himself upright and looked me in the face, frowning, a fistful of grass clenched between his fingers. "You say you can't see the future. Nor can I. But I see this moment. Our tribe has a noble practice that unites two people in sacred fellowship, body and spirit. There is nothing the Skythai pride themselves on more than sharing the hardships and hazards of their friends. When I look upon the warband, I have many loyal comrades but no friends. Would you join me in the sacred blood-bond?"

"I don't understand."

"This form is a poor container," he said, laying a hand over his heart. "But it is all I have. To keep the peace among the men and not favor any above the others as blood-brothers, I have sworn to make no such oath to any man. To you alone, I would be bound—and you to me—in noblest friendship, in this life and the next. This flesh, these bones, this blood, they are yours."

"But you have sworn not to?"

He shook his head and grinned impetuously. "You are no man."

I held his gaze for a long moment, trying to make sense of his words. *Blood. Friendship. Bound.* They filled me with a cold foreboding. But the keenness in his voice and the honor of his offer thrilled me and filled me with desire.

"Our lives have never been our own," I mused aloud. "It would be an honor to be bound to you, and you to me . . . as equals. What must I do?" I asked, stifling the giddiness that sped my breathing and made my palms sweat.

He beamed broadly and quickly set to work. "I've only ever seen this done by others. Do as I do."

He rose to his knees, withdrew his dagger, and pricked his finger. Into his drinking horn, he let the drops of blood spill. Kneeling beside him, I drew my dagger and cut my finger, squeezing the wound to wring out every drop into the horn until the flow ceased.

Our blood mingled in the cup as it trickled down the translucent sides of the ivory horn. He then mixed some wine from his wineskin. Then, we dipped the tips of our blades into the cup.

"Repeat these words," he said, holding the horn before us. "I swear by Vayu and Ari—Wind and Sword—to live together and, if need be, to die for one another."

With both arms clasped around one another's backs and our hands around the drinking horn, I repeated the words and placed our lips to its rim, cheek to cheek, and drank in unison. His beard coarse on my cheek, I swallowed the potion, spilling some down my chin. Tipping the horn, our lips met on the rim of the cup, but I did not pull away. When we had drained the drink, I looked at him and smiled to see his copper beard glistening with wine. With my sleeve, I sopped the wine from my lips and, guardedly, from his. He ran his thumb along my throat and wiped a stray drop that had trickled down my chin.

"What comes now?" I asked, shyly meeting his eye.

"Now we drink some more," he chuckled as he moved to fill the horn again.

"Wait." I lay the horn aside for a moment and turned to face him, clasping his right hand between my palms. "*Hamazor beem,*" I said, full of hope.

"What does it mean?"

"It means: 'Let us be one—of equal strength.'"

With his left hand, he warmly pressed my hands between his as I pressed his between mine. "*Hamazor beem,*" he repeated solemnly, holding my gaze.

We knelt, sweating hands clasped, restlessly staring into one another's eyes. I knew I should move or speak, but I could not. I sat on my heels, his hands trembling in my grasp—or was it my hands that shook? A thrill not unlike panic washed over me, and I could hardly catch my breath.

Aric suddenly turned away. A rider—one of our Ravens—approached from the north through the pass between the hills above us, hooves drumming the hard ground.

"Say nothing of this," he whispered, though there was no one around us to hear.

CHAPTER 29

SACRILEGE

We would never birth such strife—not if I could
strangle it now.

SILENTLY, THE SCOUT LED the way back through the pass to
a field of more barrows—another forgotten cemetery. Gohar,
Stormai, and Bornon were there, waiting. By them on the ground,
bloody and bound, lay two filthy strangers dressed head to toe in
black. Scattered around them, hemp cloths lay arrayed with gold
and silver trinkets, masses of jewelry, a sword, arrowheads, horse
tack and ornaments, heaps of clothing, drinking vessels and plates
of silver, carpets, tapestries, and even a pile of bronze nails.

Behind the men, a wagon and two horses stood hitched and
ready, but I doubted they were going anywhere soon. A subtle trail
of trampled hillside grass had been worn in the side of the nearest
barrow leading to the summit. There, lone and gallant, grew an
ancient warden tree bent low and gnarled by the incessant winds.
Whatever watchful daimon dwelt within it had made good its
promise of protection today.

Gohar strode forward and spoke, pointing to the second largest
of the hills. "We caught them emptying this barrow."

Aric paced beside the cloths spread on the ground, surveying the loot from the tomb. He marched up and back, studying but not touching any of the goods.

"These are Skythai you've robbed—my ancestors you've desecrated," he said to the prostrate thieves.

"We've got mouths to feed," the bolder of the bound men spat. "Any man'd do the same."

They looked well-fed to me. The man wore better boots than I did. His companion's akinaka had a golden sheath.

"I know your kind," Aric said. "*Parasites.* The Skythai are generous to the needy. You are simply greedy and favor feasting upon those who can't fight."

The man struggled to his feet in empty answer to the challenge, but Aric raised his hand, and Stormai locked a massive forearm across his throat.

"We should replace these things," I said to Aric. "They belong down there." I glanced toward the barrow. I could see the way even kara eyes widened at the treasure. It would be easy enough for them to divide what was before them. The sooner it was gone from sight, the better.

"I agree," Aric said, "but it's not right for us to enter the tomb."

"We could just, you know, throw it down the hole and seal it up," Gohar suggested. They all nodded in agreement.

"I'll go. Pass a rope down and lower the items to me. I'll see all is made right."

They glanced uneasily at one another, but no one moved. So, I went and fetched a rope from the robbers' gear.

"Absolutely not," Aric insisted as he stood blocking my path up to the summit.

I shoved past him and tied the rope to the warden tree as he threw up his hands in exasperation. Rolling the most valuable jewelry into a hemp cloth, I prepared to descend into the shaft cut in the barrow's roof by the grave robbers.

With his flint, dagger, and a twist of dry thatch, Aric lit one of the robbers' tallow pots for me. "I don't like this," he said, placing it grudgingly in my hands.

"I'm not afraid. Besides, who better to send into the realm of the dead?" I asked, smiling wryly.

"Be careful. We'll be near. Shout if you need anything. Tie the rope around your waist . . . *in case*. I'll pull you up when you're ready."

Aric took hold of the rope, and Bornon lent his calloused hands to help lower me through the narrow hole. Descending the shaft through the mound's heaped turf, I was soon below ground level in a spacious chamber dug into the earth beneath.

Musty and thick with the scent of decay, the dark, log-built chamber was larger than I expected and cool like a cellar. I could stand easily without ducking my head. Above me was a timber ceiling of thick logs sturdy enough to support the earthen mound above. Whole trees propped the walls and doorways over passages, all now sealed. The homes of living Skythai were nowhere near this substantial. Yet, the white felt that lay crumpled on the floor must have once lined the wooden walls, as did the looted tapestries above, making it bright like a felt-house when arrayed. Beneath my feet, over the clay floor, stretched layers of reed mats. The carpets lay neatly rolled on the grass above my head as well. A couch stood to one side in the chamber and, in the center, a bed, probably too large to remove. But everything was remarkably well-preserved. Through the passage, I could see the shadow of a wagon wheel and smell the unmistakable odor of horses buried in the next chamber—sacrificed to accompany their dead owners. The far corner was filled with cauldrons, pots, huge kraters of wine, and masses of spoiled food.

As I moved my circle of light to search the other corner of the chamber, I encountered the tomb's occupants. A sudden, inexplicable pang of guilt washed over me. It was a couple—a man and a woman. Torn from their resting place, they were stripped of their clothes for the gold sewn to them. Both bodies had been decapitated to remove their necklaces more efficiently. The lady of the tomb also had her hands and feet hacked off. All her jewelry was gone.

I had no sense of how long ago they'd been laid to rest there. They'd been embalmed, both corpses hollowed out and filled with herbs and peat, then sewn up again and covered with wax. They were in otherwise fine condition. The man seemed to be middle-aged and was probably a warrior in his lifetime. Likely a chief. The woman was of a similar age, with greying hair and a humble, kind face. I laid the light, dry bodies side by side upon the bed and set their jewelry around them.

As the men above lowered more items to me, I replaced them where they seemed most fitting. These beloved things would not be as they had been but would remain where they belonged. I covered the naked bodies with one of the tapestries, laid the carpets on the floor, and set the dishes at their bedside.

The silhouette of a head appeared across the tomb's opening, eclipsing the small circle of daylight. "You must hurry, Ana," Aric's voice rang down the shaft. "The day closes. We shouldn't remain here after dark."

"You're blocking my light," I shouted up to him. He worried too much. The dark silhouette slipped away, and the circle of deep blue sky reappeared.

Another shadow passed in front of the aperture. A darkened face peered down at me. "The sword," Bornon's booming voice echoed through the chamber with an unfamiliar urgency. "Above all, you must replace the sword."

"I'll see to it," I reassured him.

"Bless you," he said, slowly withdrawing from the opening.

No others appeared, though I saw now how the sky darkened overhead. Part of me longed for someone to show himself again, speak, or make a sound to remind me that I was not alone. My lamp burned down almost to nothing. I rummaged through the various packs until I found the one bearing the sword. It couldn't have been worth much to the robbers, rusted out as it was in its crumbling scabbard. But it must have been worth something to the dead man in his life. I laid it carefully at the warrior's side.

The tapestries still lay in a heap on the floor. I wanted to hang them again, but my candle was nearly out, so I lay them flat, filling the empty vessels with the last arrowheads and nails. And as the flame sputtered and died, I said a small prayer for the couple. From the total darkness of the tomb, I breathed deeply and called up to the men to pull me back to the surface. A small eternity passed between that call and the first tug I felt upon the rope. In the small window of the thieves' tunnel, a silhouette appeared against the darkening sky, blotting it from view. I held fast to the rope and watched that shadow draw nearer until it became a face, then several, at the end of the short shaft. I closed my eyes against the loose soil and stones as they grasped my hands and pulled me back up into the last remaining light of day.

We sealed it as best we could with floor planks from the wagon and earth, then rode our horses over it to conceal the entrance.

The tomb robbers were strangled by garrote and beheaded. I thought they would perhaps be burned or drowned, their crimes being mainly ones of greed, but the warband explained that in their transgression against the dead, their greater sin was spiritual, hence the noose. Stormai was charged with fixing their heads on stakes amid the cemetery as a warning to would-be robbers, the bodies flung at their base.

"You just leave the bodies in the open? Without burial?" I asked him as we turned away.

"They've not earned our help finding the next life," Stormai informed me. "Let the gods be their final judges. On the steppe, it takes only days for the wolves and carrion birds to take a body to its bones."

DESPITE THE COLD, I needed to wash in the creek before return-ing home. I asked the men to wait for me while I went down to the water.

"Wash with this," Aric said, lifting a clay beaker from the grass and extending it to me. I peered inside, catching a whiff of urine, and recoiled.

"Is this a joke? Fuck off."

"It should be bull's urine, but we made do with what we had," he said.

"I'm not bathing in your piss! Which one of you did this?" I demanded, scanning their faces. "Or was it all of you?"

"We waited for one of the horses, my lady," Bornon said, and I glared at him for taking part in such sport.

"You must purify yourself after contact with the dead," Aric said, proffering the beaker once more. "It is no joke. The *athravan*—keepers of the dead—all do the same." His expression was earnest, his tone grave—desperate even. He was not asking.

I eyed the foul beaker in revulsion. They were serious. "What must I do?" I asked skeptically.

"You must bathe the skin and hair with it after handling the dead. Then rub the skin with fine earth and wash with pure water."

"I am not putting urine, sacred or otherwise, in my hair. Only my hands touched the dead, so only my hands need to be purified." I raised my brows at him, daring him to challenge me.

Aric's face relaxed into relief as he nodded his agreement, and I removed my caftan, rolled up my tunic sleeves, and let Aric de-contaminate my hands with cold, cloudy horse piss, making a show of rubbing them together well for the men. He poured a double handful of fine silt over them, which I rubbed in well, producing a filthy brown sludge. Then at his nod, I got on my knees upon the creek bank and immersed them in the running waters, glad to be cleansed of all of it.

I was still covered head to toe in dust and grime from the tomb.

The men were eager to get home, but Aric and Stormai agreed to stay behind with me while I bathed. I believe they both wanted to wash the day from their faces and hands as well. Aric said we should be all right if we crossed the creek before sunset.

As the sky darkened, we took up separate posts along the banks of the creek, close enough for safety as evening fell but far enough for discretion. We undressed and waded into the calm flow of the stream. I gave myself a hard scrub in the bracing current. Before the men finished bathing, I rushed to the bank, dried myself, and hurried into my clothes just as they climbed ashore.

Stormai dressed with his back to me, but as he pulled his tunic over his head, I noticed the strange tattoos on his arms—rows of thick blue-black bands. Although he was Aric's cousin, his tattoos were utterly unlike the twisting mythical beasts and symbols the other Skythai wore. I knew I'd seen bands like his before but couldn't place them.

His caftan on and sleeves pulled down to his wrists, Stormai went to gather his horse. "I'm ready for my dinner and a good drink," he said, smiling broadly.

"I'm with you," Aric said, joining us. "This day has dragged on long enough. Are you ready, Ana?"

"For a drink? Always." As the sun prepared to set, we mounted and crossed the creek toward camp. Stormai, eager to be home, rode on ahead.

"I've been wondering something, though . . . ," I said to Aric.

"Hmm?"

"Of all the gods by whom to swear, why Vayu and Ari—Wind and Sword. Why not Gœtosura or Eraman or Thagimazda even?"

"Ah, the Skythai would tell you that, among the elements, fire is the most sacred, as it consumes our sacrifices. Water is purest. Earth richest. But wind is the noblest. The hidden world within a man is no different from the hidden world within the earth, the sea, and the sky. What is a man but damp earth, quickened from within by some feeble fire? If my flame flickers out, I waste away; if the water seeps from these veins, I return to clay. And what would it matter to see so cheap an earthen vessel smashed? But the same spirit that churns the waves of the sea, and herds the clouds across the sky, and howls from the caverns of the earth to shake the grasses of the plains—this also swells within man. Without the breath of wind in this body, I sing no verses, speak no truths, swear no oaths. I am nothing. Make dust of these bones and ash of this flesh should Vayu ever leave me."

"And the Sword?"

"Ari, the Great Sword, was formed from the ores of the earth by Papahio to serve gods and men in the upholding of justice. To swear by him is to invoke his wrath should the oath-taker fail his pledge. The oath-taker petitions his sword to turn against him—to dull its blade, fall from his hands, and pierce the very one who wields it—should he ever break his sworn word." He glanced my way as if to gauge my comprehension: had I wavered in the face of such dire repercussions? I met his gaze steadily and without reservation.

"The sword—not the man—has this power?"

"Who, when they behold a sword, does not perceive that it is suffused with a divine spirit? Nothing so wrought is an accident of men's designs alone. Each noble warrior binds his own spirit to this when gifted a mighty sword—to do the work of the gods. The hands of men are tender things, barely capable of bruising a ripe fruit. Put a sword into them, and that man becomes like a god, with the power to punish the unjust and mete out life and death. To take up this instrument and assume this charge is the greatest gift and the cruelest curse that can be bestowed upon a man. Any hunter can make himself a spear. A better man can make a bow and learn to aim it. Fewer will possess and learn the swordsman's skills—possess the temper to bear this duty. And the sword judges his every deed. Not all warriors will be granted the gift of a sword to wield in this life. And the gods will direct his hand and his blade against him should he fall short of his purpose—a blade, like a horse, will play a man false should he abuse its sacred trust."

I hoped what he said was true, but I had my doubts, knowing dispirited horses to obey both fools and bullies and blades to blaze in the hands of outlaws. Perhaps even the wisest of horses and swords were fooled—or cowed—by tyrants. It wasn't a kind thought. I preferred to believe that a sharp eye and a steady hand guided my arrows rather than the whims of the gods. But if the gods chose to make my eye sharp and my hand steady, I was grateful. If it was a just order they sought, I'd do my part in its keeping.

I thought about the weapon at my own side: all the arts that had been consolidated in its making. Was it for some greater purpose? If what he said was true, its creation had imbued it with a spirit of righteous power—and infused some of Aric's youthful temper in its atoms. All these combined to make something maybe I was not equipped to handle. Was anybody?

An archer loves his bow. It makes him equal to all the beasts of nature, both predator and prey. Whether a bird in the sky or a swift animal of the plain, it cannot outrun an archer's arrow. And no man stands before him taller, faster, or stronger than a well-aimed dart. To the Skythai, the bow betokens one's merit and mettle; the sinews of its bowstring are as the sinews of his body. He might achieve all life's necessities through its use—hunt game, hold land, keep stock. Thereby, honor comes to him before the members of his tribe, and he carries on their tradition so long as he has the strength to draw its string.

A duel of swords is something very different. Two men faced equally with only their blades and skills have nothing but themselves and perhaps the gods' favor to answer for them. An intimate dread manifests in this liability to one's limbs. The contest of swords is the contest of raw fates, and some dim recess of men's souls craves it, stripped of all the trappings of law, daring themselves like beasts in the wild to know the truth of their final worth upon this earth. It is nature's most potent urge, its most integral impulse, preceding all others.

"Bornon," I said, "was very eager that the dead chief should have his sword back."

"Rightly so. Some men gift their swords—along with their luck—to their progeny, some take them to their graves, and others—others sacrifice them. But let no man take it from him by force. Such swords are cursed."

"I imagine so."

"Should I fall, I bid you cast my sword into the sea."

"Me?" It seemed impossible he should ever fall. And if he did, I would surely not be far behind. But what was one more promise between us today?

"I entrust this task to you. The sea, or into the shining waters of a river that flows to the sea."

"Why the sea?"

"I have no one to bequeath my sword to. And I would not have the kara fight over its possession. Or see my tomb plundered and have it fall into the hands of the undeserving, used in the service of evil deeds. Give it to the gods. Return it to its source. And may it never be taken up by my enemies and used against my people."

"There will never be a need," I said hollowly. But then Aric fixed me in one of his humorless looks that told me he was not making idle chatter or flattering me with false confidences. He was resolute on the matter. I swallowed and nodded to him in earnest. "I swear it. Yet this," I said, curling my fingers around the gold pommel at my side, "has fallen into undeserving hands. What would you have me do with it when I must depart this place? Will you receive it back from me?"

"It belongs now in your keeping. Do with it what you will. May you continue its story in fair-handedness—do it justice, and may it lend you fortune and speak of you in honor."

We rode in silence the rest of the way home now that night

had fallen, slowly catching up to Stormai's lead. And it was then I remembered where I saw the strange tattoos like his: on the arms of Agathyrsi warriors captured in battle against my people.

———◆◆———

MY EYES FLICKERED OPEN in the near dark of the tent. Something was wrong. Heart thumping, ears straining, I realized Aric was struggling.

Someone whispered, *shhh*.

I turned to find Antisthenes sitting up beside me, his finger pressed to his lips.

"We should wake him," I whispered.

"Too dangerous."

"How so?"

"You want to startle him?"

He had a point. I'd not like to be anywhere near Aric when he was alarmed or frightened, especially not as he emerged from whatever nightmare haunted him just now. But it seemed worse to do nothing. "What have you done in the past?"

"This has never happened before."

Suddenly, harsh and loud, Aric screamed, and the shock seemed to rouse him. He lurched upright and searched the dim tent, bewildered.

"Are you all right?" I asked, resting a hand on his arm and examining his face in the dark for the cause of his terror, finding no clues.

"You were *gone*," he gasped between panting breaths. Before he could finish, hurried footsteps approached, and voices outside called to ask what was wrong.

"Everything's fine," I called out. I wadded up my hemp blanket and poked my head through the door flap. If Aric wanted to share his dreams with the camp, he could do it by the light of day, in his own time. Now, we all just needed some peace.

Their tent nearest, Olgas and Bornon stood outside, half-dressed, disheveled, and bleary-eyed, clutching their scabbards, hands on their sword-hilts.

"It's my fault." I flashed a sheepish grin. "I stupidly left my blanket too close to the hearth, and it caught fire. No one hurt. But," I smirked, "I'm sure I won't hear the end of it. I regret the disturbance. Please, go back to sleep."

After some grumbles, laughs, and sighs of relief, they dispersed, and Antisthenes scrambled back onto his pallet without another word. I lay down in the dark tent and spread my blanket over myself. Aric still breathed shallowly and fast. He offered no explanation, and we asked for none. His dreams were his province, and I'd not trespass there. But my assurance was quietly shaken. He lay back, and I stared at the grey, smoke-stained ceiling of the tent, mute. By the way his arms remained stiffly at his sides, I knew he was not asleep. Slowly, I turned my face toward him, unsure if I would try to speak.

He spoke first.

"I don't want you to lie for me," he whispered without shifting his stare from the ceiling.

"You lie for me," I whispered back.

He squeezed his eye shut and exhaled slowly.

A knowing silence stretched between us. The kind of silence where resentments were born, enmities were nursed, hatreds were reared. But we would never birth such strife—not if I could strangle it now. What would we gain by dwelling on the wrongs we'd done, or might yet do, while our words were lofty, but our world remained base?

I slid my hand under the blanket, pausing at the sword, lay my hand over his and held my breath. He twined his fingers up through mine, locking them tight to his sweating hand. He sighed and soon drifted off again to an uneventful sleep. I held to wakefulness as long as I could, standing a futile watch against an unknown threat.

CHAPTER 30

GUTLESS

*If I dueled every man who thought or spoke ill of
me, I'd do nothing else in this life.*

THE DAYS SHORTENED, and the green things faded toward their
long hibernation. The solemn feast of Yamadin approached,
beginning Slaughter Month in the camps. We called it Harvest
Month back home, though they were essentially the same thing.
Nothing delighted the weary farmer like the sight of ripe grain
waving softly over the fields in the waning sun of autumn. We'd
sharpen our scythes and, day and night, go reaping in the fields
while the weather was fine. The weary stockman must feel something akin to that now, seeing his herds fit and healthy at the end
of the season as he also sharpened his blade for the stock he'd be
unable to feed through the night season. A long term of eating salted, smoked, and dried meats was upon us after a season of bounty,
and grim as that prospect always seemed, the coming winter was
also the time for rest.

With the raiding season soon ending, all but the kara would be
leaving the marches to return to their families as the young novices
took up their lessons, and those who'd both made their tallies and
reached their twenty-first winter would be leaving for good.

We forded the upper reaches of the Pantikap River on the way to meet up with the court above the cataracts of the Volosdanu before it began its forty-mile descent down the Nine Steps, which some said one could descend to the underworld.

We rode through farm country, finding the recently harvested fields and pastures revived by the grudging rains of late summer. Those few Skythai permitted by King Ariapaithi to settle and farm made fair use of this fertile strip of land nestled between the Volos and Pantikap rivers. Now, it seemed the whole kingdom descended upon it for the festival. With the animals at their fittest, it was time to collect taxes.

It was also an occasion for gift-giving. Chiefs brought gold and silver on behalf of their clans while warriors paraded horses captured in raids. Herdsmen brought hides, cheese, and fine cloth, and the farmers presented the fruits of their fields. Gifts were also exchanged between friends, and for bereaved clans and those who suffered hardship, the more fortunate showed their generosity with donations of food and clothing.

Nonetheless, the festival's peak was the ceremony celebrating the achievement of this year's crop of novices who had survived their ordeals, reached their manhood, and were finally fledged. They could now resign their warband duties and take up their rights as members of the tribe. After Yamadin, our numbers would be reduced, but the burden was also lighter as these young men prepared to leave for the lands and herds of their fathers' clans and defend their—and Skythia's—holdings in earnest.

The long-awaited moment had arrived when they could bring their war trophies—heads and scalps—to the head of the tribe and be granted the privilege of drinking from his golden bowl, gaining full rights of citizenship. They stood on the platform above the crowd, offering up the scalps they'd taken from the field. No longer servants of Gœtosura, Aric stood before each, ready to remove their iron torcs, burn their bast girdles, and thrust their heads into a massive cauldron of holy water to quench the warrior fury within.

I stood on my toes and lifted my chin, searching above the crowd for Antisthenes, hoping I might lend him some comfort, but in vain. He had his reasons for being elsewhere today.

Flanked by the tribe's elder officiants and several anarei—for the Skythai lacked any formal priesthood—they came before Ariapaithi to be permitted, finally, to dip their cups into the king's wine and forevermore drink alongside the other men of the tribe. This was the moment they'd waited for all their young lives—the moment they confirmed their worth and received their rights as Paralatai, as Skythai.

I should have stood among them.

With my scalp secreted away, I suffered a pang of conscience as I watched. I studied Aric for some sign that he felt it, too. If it caused him grief, he didn't let it show. He seldom let unquiet spirits rise and ripple his still surface, but I knew they must boil there sometimes. Was this such a time? I had no method to read his mind, divine his fears, or learn his plans despite how I tried when the spells came over me or when we lay silently in the dark awaiting sleep. I would pore over the day's conversations, gestures, and looks, trying to piece together some significance from them in the way the seers found meaning in the spatters of blood from a sacrifice or the death throes of the victim.

Was I exposed? No, I trusted him with my life. But should I trust him also with my secrets? It might have been foolish to give him—or anyone—such jurisdiction. In doing so, I'd given him something more valuable—more powerful—than my life, which suddenly terrified me. The price paid for a deception this consequential would be steep. Not just to me, but to my people. Father did not have the forces to fight both the Agathyrsi and the Paralatai. Aric understood this better than anyone. He was still Ariapaithi's son. It was a lot of faith to place in one man. Too much, perhaps.

KNOWING THE OTHERS would be at the ceremony a while longer, I slipped away from the rite and went back to our campsite. I avoided our tent for fear of encountering Antisthenes. Instead, I rummaged through the wagon where our spare things were stowed. Extra clothes and blankets, leather for repairs, hides to trade, my old bow. It had to be here somewhere. I knew Aric would have stowed the scalp in a safe place. I just had to think where. For a man who traveled light as he did, he had a surprising array of trinkets and knickknacks stashed away. The gold, jewels, and rare foreign goods I understood. The perilous Mard-Khwaar dagger was also carefully wrapped and stowed for safekeeping. Those had clear value. Of less obvious worth was a carved wooden horse, well-burnished with age. A small clay model of a wagon with a broken wheel. A perfectly smooth and white but otherwise ordinary river pebble the size of a walnut. And a painted and glazed potsherd from a red and black Greek-style vase bearing the broken image of a woman's face in profile and a disembodied hand clutching the shaft of a spear.

My vexation had reached its end as I surveyed the destruction I'd wrought inside the wagon I'd now have to set right.

"Looking for something?" Aric's phantom voice froze me like a dog caught digging in the garden. He mounted the stairs and ducked into the wagon.

"I'm putting it all back." I was still on my knees amid the pile of scattered things as he stood over me.

"Found it, then?" His tone was patient, but it was restrained patience.

I didn't look at him but chose my words carefully. "I should have been up there today. With them."

"So, that's it."

Was he angry or hurt? It was almost impossible to tell the difference with him. "You do realize," he continued, "this goes badly for us both if you reveal what we've done."

"I hadn't considered that." In my eagerness, I forgot that there would also be consequences for my accomplice.

"You truly wish to go?" he asked, more accusation than inquiry.

"Of course not." I could no more bear the thought of relinquishing my arms than bedding the aged king. He could keep his golden bowl and bitter wine. I'd found a life far fuller and nobler than any king could offer me at any court. But I still couldn't face Aric. I stared at the reed mats covering the planks of the wagon's floor, unweaving them with my gaze. "But it weighs on me."

He grabbed a bundle of hides and shoved them aside to kneel before me. "It weighs on me, too." He exhaled sharply and took my hands. "You're free. But Anaiti, the road is treacherous, and I have need of you. I hope you will stay."

I forced myself to meet his gaze. "I don't want to leave, but someday I may have to. I cannot do that unless I have it in my possession."

"Of course," he said, his words tinged with gloom.

He moved aside a few packs near the front of the wagon, pulled back the reed mat, and, withdrawing his dagger, pried up a short plank that was not nailed down. Beneath was a small, hidden compartment containing various pouches of waxed cloth. He extracted and passed me one of these. It appeared to be filled with dark hair and white leather. I breathed deeply, uncertain what I would even do with it, if anything, but oddly lighter than I'd been in weeks.

"Thank you," I said, setting the pouch back into the false compartment before replacing the board and the packs.

I LEARNED THAT HORSE RACING, held in the eastern pastures on the second day, was a festival tradition. The races promised to display horseflesh unrivaled anywhere in the world. The Skythian horses, having spent all season grazing on lush meadows and traversing great distances in pursuit of cattle and commerce, were in peak condition and would be racing fit. Some had even brought specially trained racing steeds for the main events later in the day.

A few of the men had badgered me to enter Vatra in one of the smaller, informal races. It would be fun, they assured me. Olgas, Bornon, and Gohar goaded me relentlessly, yet when it came time for the race, I noticed none were riding. But Vatra was a competitive horse, always resentful of the protocols of rank, which usually held us to the rear of the field. I'd longed to see what he could do if given free rein. With some anxiety, I relented and rode to the post to join a half dozen of the other karik in a friendly match.

After all, who didn't love a horse race? Few sights in this world were as perfect as a horse in motion. Nothing could quite equal the power and grace of a horse in full flight. Its coat shimmering, its muscles rippling like water over a stone. The joy it exhibits with every beat drummed, every hoofprint stamped into the earth, each footfall proclaiming a fierce but unpretentious pride.

We lined up and waited for the count. Peraka, Azarion, Mourdag, Galati, Bradak, Rathagos, Artavardiya, and myself. Then the starter waved a flag, and we were off, galloping hard across the rough pasture toward the finish post, about eight or nine furlongs away. While I kept some tension on the reins, Vatra had no trouble keeping pace with the others. The race would be over quickly.

Peraka's calm and steady horse fell behind immediately. He had no chance of catching any of us. Bradak rode a beautiful bay with a ground-devouring stride, but he drove him too hard at the start, and I knew the big horse would soon fade. Azarion's horse did nothing but fight, tiring himself out against the bit. Mourdag kept his rangy grey at an even pace, but he seemed to lack the fire to pull to the front of the pack. But Rathagos's horse was quick. He'd be the one to watch. An eager, aggressive chestnut, I'd seen him in the field many times before, angrily chomping his bit and flaring his nostrils any time he was made to stand and wait instead of thrashing his hooves across the plain. He leaned into his bridle as Rathagos whipped him on. I eased off Vatra's reins, and we made to pass them. Rathagos pulled the chestnut hard right and bumped us, crushing my leg between the horses and launching Vatra into an incensed bucking fit, his head between his knees, his back up like a feline pouncing upon invisible prey. Somehow, he galloped on. I sat down deep and rode it out, but it set us back a few paces.

After Vatra had settled again, we stared at the haunches of Bradak's sleek bay, who had slipped past us. Beside him, Azarion's leggy liver chestnut was inching forward and closing my path between them, clods of turf flinging up in our faces. I leaned forward, fed Vatra more rein, and nudged him with my heels. He flattened his ears and dug in hard. A surge of muscle and fury pulled us forward as if by a thousand hands heaving a great rope, and we passed them both with ease.

The post approached. A small crowd of onlookers, including Olgas, Bornon, Gohar, and Aric, stood beside it. We were about to pass Rathagos again. Vatra's previous bucking fit got me thinking. He was a sensitive, opinionated horse. If I pressed my heels hard to him, he bucked. He struck with his foreleg when I touched my whip to his shoulder. And if I tapped his flank with my whip, he kicked out. So, I steered near Rathagos's horse, ready this time, and tapped Vatra behind my leg with my whip. His hind leg shot like lightning bolt toward Rathagos's fiery chestnut, catching him hard in the ribs and stunning him for a stride. It was all Vatra needed to gain the ground he lost, passing him and the post by at least a stride's length. Shouts and a single cheer rose and fell as we galloped past, and I struggled to rein Vatra in, circling in the pasture beyond the course. I rubbed Vatra's mane and threw my arms around his neck.

Bradak, Azarion, Mourdag, Peraka, Galati, and Artavardiya pulled their horses up alongside me in the field, and we congratulated one another on a good race. I was wrong to have doubted the men. Glad for their badgering, we trotted back to the group, triumphant, and a shameless grin overcame my face. Aric nodded approvingly.

"I'd have won if she didn't cheat," Rathagos announced as the others caught up. "You all saw her bump me."

My smile died. He couldn't be serious. Olgas and Bornon looked at one another and shrugged, and Gohar gave me a sympathetic half-smile.

"Excellent race, Rathagos," I said with a pleasant smile. "That's a fine horse you have there."

Stepping forward, the master of ceremonies came with my prize, which they saw fit to award me this time. He wished me awkward congratulations as he handed me a circlet of plaited wheat from the harvest.

I placed the crown on Vatra's head, where it truly belonged. The crowd dispersed, and I dismounted and loosened his girth before walking back to camp.

"I bet on you to win," Aric grinned triumphantly.

AFTER THE DAY'S CEREMONIES, we barely had time to tidy ourselves up and change clothes before the feast began at sundown. With only half of our things unpacked, I couldn't find my clean woolen caftan and trousers with the lovely, embossed gold plaques. Consequently, I was, as usual, running late. I promised Aric and Antisthenes I'd catch up as soon as possible and sent them on ahead.

Cursing myself for not doing a shrewder job of packing, I finally found my dress clothes, not too severely scrunched and wrinkled, rolled up with the extra blankets I was sure I'd need but hadn't unpacked yet in the warm weather. By the time I'd finished dressing and emerged from the tent, everyone else was gone except for Gohar, who also rushed out of his tent, his long brown hair streaming behind him, still fastening his warbelt around his caftan. A horn sounded in the distance, summoning us to the feast.

I hailed him and asked if he'd walk with me to the feasting grounds, as I didn't like wandering about the sprawling camp alone. Twice as large as I'd ever seen it, this festival drew members from all the affiliated tribes and clans of Skythia to court to pay their taxes and welcome the novices home. There were more people and animals than I'd ever seen in one place.

As we walked, the shouts of men and bellows of stock mingled with the scents of manure and cooking fires in the crisp evening air. The sun had already set, and the light faded quickly. We followed a torch-lined track worn by many boots toward the voices in the distant pasture. Some cattle-herders passed us along the path, cupped their hands to their mouths, and shouted "Gohar the Gutless," then laughed among themselves and strolled away. I scowled at them as they passed, and if it wasn't beneath my honor, I'd have fought them then and there. But Gohar's graven features were unmoved. His narrowed eyes focused only on the path as if he had never heard or seen them.

"Does some law forbid you to defend yourself?" I asked him, apparently more offended than he was. "Those men are beneath you." He was one of the finest men I'd ever met—certainly one of the bravest. I'd heard the nickname uttered behind his back many times in the marches, and I'd assumed it was spoken in irony or jest. But to encounter it here, at court, spoken so boldly from the mouths of far lesser men, seemed wholly unacceptable.

"I do nothing *because* they are beneath me. Because if I dueled every man who thought or spoke ill of me, I'd do nothing else in this life. And I have much to do." We walked silently for a few more paces, and he turned his head toward me. "But, if you wish to know . . . ," he shrugged, holding his palms up to the starlit sky, "you might as well hear the truth. I once hung my goryt outside a woman's wagon." He drew a long slow breath and sighed. "I was young then. The court had gathered at Gerrhi for Merhedin; she was the most beautiful woman I'd ever seen. Maybe the most beautiful woman in all of Skythia. I was bold enough to tell her so." He smiled to himself as if at a private joke.

"What happened?"

"She invited me in. Her husband was away in the fields tending his cattle. When he heard, he came home to challenge me."

"She had a husband?"

"She did. Any free man in good standing may make such a claim. And any woman is free to refuse or accept. But he may have to answer for it: her man came for his answer. But he was just a herdsman, and I am a vazarka. There was no honor for me in dueling him. It was not cowardice that stayed my hand, but this ring around my neck. I've gladly taken away the lives of many challengers in battle. But I'd not deprive that fine woman of a husband when I could not replace him. I walked away."

"This they call gutless?"

"The herdsman himself gave me this name. It has stuck with me ever since."

"They only prove their dishonor by repeating it."

"You're kind to say so. But he was right. If I could not make her my own, I didn't deserve the right to hang my goryt there, no matter my rank. Perhaps I deceived her. Perhaps myself. But I'd no claim to her. He didn't make me pay with blood. But I have paid."

JOINING THE FEAST, I ate hungrily and laughed heartily with the kara over the funniest ways we'd all fallen off our horses. We poked good-natured fun at one another as the drink flowed and ate ourselves sick on the bounteous fare. The mood was light around the table for a change. I sensed that the novices were grateful to return safely to their families, and the warband was glad to be rid of them.

As we finished our meal and prepared to retire to a warm hearth, a dour man in Hellenic dress approached Ariapaithi and the princes from where the Hellenic governors and wealthy merchants had been dining. Skyles arose to meet him, and they spoke at length before the two approached the head of the king's table.

Skyles addressed his father: "Demetrios, the governor of Kremnos, has just told me the most shocking thing!" he exclaimed with affected outrage. The king and all his guests now turned to fix their attention on the pseudo-Hellenic prince. "He tells me that Aric's kara have ravaged a Greek village on the Lykus River. Not a man has survived the raid. They destroyed crops and buildings and made off with goods and livestock." His dark eyes scanned the silent space as the eyes of the guests shifted between Ariapaithi and Aric for answers. I chewed casually while I furtively watched Aric, anxious about what he would do.

It was Aric who spoke first. "This good man must be mistaken, for that is impossible," he said. "There are no Greek settlements north of the place where the Lykus and Hygris rivers meet. As the good governor is surely aware, these are the terms of our covenant with the Hellenes. There has never been, nor shall there ever be, a Greek settlement beyond this meeting of the waters."

The man looked confused, his face reddened, and a snarl contorted his thin lips. "You deny slaughtering these people?"

"You stand before King Ariapaithi and confess to settling and farming lands outside your already generous endowment without the king's consent?" Aric countered.

The governor glanced nervously at Skyles, who showed no concern or even notice of him. "I should know when my own people have been slaughtered!" he barked, seemingly more out of desperation than wisdom.

"If your people have come to harm, you should tell them not to wander where they don't belong."

Demetrios looked reproachfully at Skyles. "We had a deal!" he said in Greek.

Aric rose from his cushion to face the man, who barely reached his elbow. Towering over the now meek governor, his tone became more stern. "*I* am Warden of the East March," Aric answered him in Greek. "There are no covenants, no grazing rights, no settlements, no trade, no passage there *but through me*." He stared hard at Demetrios until the man shrank with terror and—casting a last fretful look toward Skyles—scurried back to his seat among his fellows, no doubt to commiserate about the savagery of the barbarians.

"How dare you?" Skyles scolded Aric once the man had left.

"You blame me?" Aric raised his eyebrow. "Perhaps if you spent less time consorting with them and more time governing them. . . ."

Skyles finally met Aric's steady gaze. "Consort?" he asked, leaning in close. "I negotiate. A foreign concept to you, apparently."

"That's an odd term for it."

"I, too, am a warden of this kingdom," Skyles said, locking Aric in a fiery stare. "And I must be diplomatic with my wards, or my connections won't be open to making trade with me."

"Bullshit," Aric said coolly. "I bargain and treat with man-eaters and goatfuckers every day. Never once have I eaten a man or fucked a goat. Yet somehow, we have prosperity." He sipped his wine. "Tell them what you like, but you do it because it pleases you. And that's fine. Do as you wish. But don't bullshit me about your reasons."

"They come here," Skyles waved his hand over the banquet before them, "and participate in our festivals. Why shouldn't we participate in theirs?"

"Because they're *our* tenants, we are not theirs. In need, they came to us. They must earn our trust in our land by honoring our ways in good faith. Instead, they scorn and disparage us here in our own home. They make outrageous demands. Bring decadent practices to our shores. You are a prince of *this* kingdom. Act like it!" Aric lowered his voice to a whisper so only those few at the head of the table could hear. "Soon, the cattle-herders will learn what you do—what is done *to* you—during these perverse rites. What will they think?"

Skyles's face reddened to match his tunic color, and his beard, less black than I recalled, reflected his ruddy glow. But he restrained his anger. "I care nothing for what cattle-herders think. Besides, what's so decadent about worshiping the gods? You like Greek wine well enough. Why disparage the one from whom it flows?"

"I like *plentiful* wine; the Hellenes do not disappoint on that score. But we were making wine in Skythia long before they and their mad god arrived. Do not try to supplant our ways. Break the pillar that props the roof, and the tent collapses."

"So what if it does? If something better is built in its place?"

"Tell me, what is better than being free and unconquerable? What do you imagine will replace all this—our noble way of life?"

"The Hellenes are a great people. They are ancient, wise, and powerful."

The guests, no longer whispering, fell silent. I held my breath as Aric stepped closer to Skyles, confronting him face-to-face.

"Truly, they are. I bear them no ill will. I even respect them. But what do they know about life on the steppe? About breeding hardy horses and herding mobs of cattle among reaving clans? And living in wagons? Continually finding fresh water and grazing for a whole camp and its stock? Fighting enemies who swarm in on horseback? Outwitting armies who come for our lands? Have they seen our winters? For fuck's sake, they don't even have the sense to put on a pair of trousers when the snow is up to their balls. They can't feed themselves in their own land, so they spill onto our shores and beg for our goods. They know only cities and towns. How will they survive out here in the open? Where the rivers flood the plains in spring, and the soil is hard as stone in summer so no seed will sprout? The turf is so dense a common plow will not cut it. What will they eat then? When the rivers and seas freeze so solid we can drive our wagons clear across? And the wine freezes so hard we must chew it! Where there is no wood for fuel or building because no tree will take root? Over the ages, we have forged a life—an empire—upon the steppe the hard way, through heat and cold and more blows of the hammer than numbers can count. We, too, are ancient, wise, and powerful—or have you forgotten that?"

Skyles was speechless, and it seemed he had no answer, his face overtaken with a strange, painful emptiness.

"*I forget nothing*," he said at last, shoving his way past the servers and out of the feasting grounds, leaving his meal unfinished and the guests murmuring in his absence.

CHAPTER 31

VAZARKA

The wolves are being wolves, and the deer are
being deer. But, when the hunt is over,
each will tell very different stories about
who is good and evil.

Since we arrived, I had been eager to speak with Erman again. His wagon-tent sat on the outskirts of the camp, and I climbed the stairs to knock on his doorframe.

"Anaiti, come in," he called from behind the closed door.

"How did you know it was me?" I asked, peeking inside.

He just smiled. His hair was pulled back into a knot with no tie, and he wore his usual white linen skirt and a tunic of felted wool. "Have you come for your tattoo?"

I'd forgotten. The last time we spoke, he mentioned having a vision of an image meant for me.

"Please," I said, entering and walking straight into the dried horse phallus again. As I removed my dusty shoes beside the door, I thought how much less the shriveled cock made me feel lucky and how much more it reminded me of the unfortunate horse.

"I will paint it now if you wish." He gestured to a place on the tufted carpet.

"What have you chosen?"

"Ah. Well, you are a huntress. And what creature is more sacred to Artimpasa herself than the Golden Hind, bright as the sun and swifter than arrows?"

"A *hind*?"

"Are you not pleased?"

There was no hiding my disappointment. It broke my heart to learn that even he saw me as nothing more than the timid, skittish companion to the great king of the wilds, the hart.

"The noblest creature of the wild is the shape-shifting deer— overleaping every boundary, traversing all the realms; antlers which grow and recede miraculously, branching into the sky like the Great Tree."

"But the hind has no antlers. She is docile, defenseless."

"Why do you imagine she is called the Golden Hind if not to honor her golden antlers? This is what makes her revered."

"Can this be true?"

"It is only the rarest who possesses antlers, but it is so. And in the northern lands of the Budini, there is a species whose does all bear horns like the bucks."

How had I never heard of such a thing in all my years? I suddenly felt deprived of a vast wealth of knowledge, having grown up shielded within the confines of Bastarnia's forts. "I should like to see such a deer."

"Let me draw one for you."

I found it difficult to hide my anticipation.

"Her head rests on your breast," he began to trace the image as he spoke, "then comes around your shoulder and back."

I trembled with excitement. The tattoos I glimpsed engraved upon the men filled me with envy, and I felt almost naked without more of my own.

"Good, then let's begin."

I tied back my hair and dressed in the white robe he provided.

He told me that parts would be excruciating, like over my collarbone, and it might not be finished until I could return at the next festival. But it would be worth whatever pain I must endure.

"So, you've fought your first true battle since we spoke last," he said as he rifled through his things, looking for his tools and dyes. "That changes things."

"I suppose it does. And it doesn't."

"How do you mean?" He spread his kit upon the carpet.

"Well, I know what to expect now. How I will react. I will be ready next time."

"Then, it was a victory." Standing over me, he held a small bundle of dried steppe sage, which he ignited in the fire. Wafting the smoke over and around me, he chanted verses in an ancient tongue that I scarcely understood. He drew an image on my bared skin with paint, outlining where he would prick the design. Sitting close beside me, ever so gently, he lifted my chin and turned my face away. Then he stretched the skin just beneath my collarbone between his thumb and forefinger and gripped the needle. I held my breath, and he began stabbing out an image.

"I don't know," I said tentatively. I wished I could tell him about the scalp. "The worst part is what happened after."

He stopped working and frowned. "What happened after?"

"Some of the men asked me to speak to the dead on their behalf."

"Did you?" he wiped clean his needle and set it on the inkwell.

"Well, not really. I guess I offered—to try, anyway. Obviously, I cannot. I should have simply told them that, but I didn't want to disappoint them. To break their hearts."

"Why is it obvious you can't?"

"Because I don't even know if such a thing is possible."

"And yet, they believe you do this?" he raised his eyebrows and then shrugged. "Aric believes you are twice-born—a traveler to the other realms, able to leave your flesh and walk among the shades—though I can see you doubt this. Perhaps they have spoken to you, and you mistook the signs? How do the dead speak to the living? They don't have mouths. And if corpses ever speak, run for your life!" He tittered to himself at the thought. "Yet many voices compete for attention in our thoughts, our dreams. Do you know where they originate?"

He resumed working on the tattoo, dipping his finger in the inkwell, smudging the powdered dye into the wounds he had made, wiping them clean, and starting anew.

"But if I don't know, how can I answer? Does this not make me a liar? A fraud?"

He wiped blood and ink away from my chest, the white cloth stained black and red. "Ah, so it's not the dead but your conscience that haunts you."

I exhaled a deep breath it seemed I'd been holding for months. "Aric is so certain of everything. Of the two sights, the gods, the just outcomes of battle. I'm not sure of anything—except that I don't know what's real or what's true."

"Do you believe Aric is wrong because of this?"

"He is the cleverest man I know. But that doesn't mean he's always right."

He smiled. "Good judgement must fill gaps in our knowledge."

"But I want to do right—for myself, my warband, my tribe. How do I choose a course? Is there a way to divine the right action?"

"You must do as your nature dictates."

"That's no help."

"You wish me to tell you what is good and evil. But there is no such thing."

"Are you saying our right conduct and character mean nothing?"

"Quite the opposite. I'm saying the wolves are being wolves, and the deer are being deer. But, when the hunt is over, each will tell very different stories about who is good and evil. Which is true?" He sat back and fixed me in his uncanny blue gaze.

"I see. But, man is not so simple. How do *we* know what's right?"

295

"All the cosmos moves in accord with Arta, including beasts and men. Do the beasts ask what is right? The bravest of beings are the wild beasts, for they alone die willingly for their liberty. They are also the most just, for they live according to nature's law and no other. Nature sometimes fails to attain its end: obstacles hinder her workings, and monsters are her failures. But laws are the bindings of men upon one another for *our* failures. Nature contains the means for restoring balance. We aim to understand this order and place ourselves in accord with it. Man cannot correct what is already perfect. And even laws cannot make us gods. Be a human being—no more or less. The wise do not seek to break the world to their will, for the world cannot break those who seek harmony with it."

THE FESTIVAL WAS NEAR ITS END, and no one seemed certain whether I would remain behind at court with the other novices or return to the Wild Fields with the warband. Erman had said I would not be joining the novices for their lessons in lore and verse, so there seemed little to gain in remaining behind. Still, when I asked Aric at the next feast, he leaned over and whispered in my ear, admonishing me to be patient, saying we would speak in private after the guests had left the table.

Such talk from him always left my nerves frayed. I had also wanted to speak with him ever since that governor, Demetrios, accosted him days earlier. The whole affair had been weighing on my mind. I spent the rest of the meal poking at the food on my plate, wondering when the axe would swing. But as the guests departed the table, he grabbed our cups and a pitcher of wine, and I followed him to one of the bonfires out in the field, where we sat in the cold, damp grass, and he poured me a cup.

"Why such secrecy?" I asked with apprehension. "Is something wrong?"

"On the contrary," he said, his eye flashing in the firelight as he poured a cup for himself and downed it. "Drink," he said as he refilled his cup.

I took a tentative sip.

"Is something troubling you?" he asked.

Where would I even begin? "I'm all right," I told him, "just very tired."

"Well, I have a gift for you," he said with a wide grin I'd not seen in weeks.

"But I have nothing to give you," I all but pleaded.

He extracted a heavy, cloth-wrapped lump from the breast of his fur-lined caftan. Slowly, I peeled back the folds to reveal a bronze mirror and held it beside the fire, the warm glow revealing an intricate spiraling pattern on its back and an ornately cast handle in the form of a woman whose legs gracefully tapered into twining serpents. Her hands, held elegantly above her head, supported the rim of the golden mirror.

Was this his idea of a gift? I didn't care much for what I looked like these days, and I was afraid to look in it just now.

He frowned. "You don't like it."

"No, I do, thank you," I said, swallowing my bitterness as I carefully wrapped the cloth over its face. "I suppose I should have one of these."

"That's what I thought," he smiled again, his cheeks dimpling.

"I sometimes forget I'm a lady." I combed my fingers through my hair. "It gets away from me out there with the wind."

"Hmm? Oh, no, it's not for that," he said. "No, it's for your divining. Seers use them, do they not?" he asked tentatively, and I found his deference to my authority so charming I completely forgot my embarrassment. "The otherworld, they say, lies behind the reflective surfaces of still waters, mirrors, and the like."

"Oh, of course," I said, having no idea whether seers used mirrors. When I saw Erman next, I would ask him about it.

"Well, I saw you didn't have one, so . . ."

"It was very good of you. Again, thanks. Perhaps you could teach me to signal with it as well?"

"I will. But first, there is another matter."

Ah, of course there was. No gift was truly free.

"Since the death of Tarana, I have not had twelve loyal warriors to fill the ranks of the vazarka."

"Why have you not yet promoted a man?"

"Because it is not suitable for just any warrior. Only those with something rare to offer the warband are chosen. And it is an unyielding commitment—never to leave the battlefield without the kara-daranaka. A lifelong duty, unless released by me or by death."

"There are many karik who'd gladly take that place."

"I've considered many, but I had not found one I deemed worthy of the honor. Until now."

"Who is he?"

He began to snort and chuckle to himself, and his face flushed in the bonfire's ruddy glow.

"No. You can't mean. . . ?" *No.*

"Why not?"

"There must be someone better. I know there is. Many others. What have I done to deserve it?"

"You've proven yourself worthy time and again. Your counsel has been sound, your instincts noble. You've saved this miserable hide more than once. You're my only blood-sworn friend. And, of course, you have the two sights; Erman believes a powerful daimon attends you. Who among the kara can claim all that?"

"But, the king, my father . . . how can I commit for life and also uphold their agreement?"

"Have no fear. If—when—the time comes that you must leave this place, you shall be released from your oaths to me."

"I haven't even made my tally—not officially. There are men here who have killed . . . I don't know how many enemies. Who have been here for years. They surely deserve it more than I do.

And they'll resent us both if you prefer me with not even a scalp to show for my time here."

"Being a vazarka is not about how many enemies one kills, but how many of *us* one saves. You protect us and make us thrive. That is why I want you with us. You are the rarest of creatures—our satanaya in all but name. We need your counsel."

"Well, if I can offer you counsel now, don't do this. Many men think themselves more worthy of the post than I, and many others will resent me just because I'm new and inexperienced. Or because I'm a woman. Why provoke them? Why test their loyalty?" I rambled, troubled thoughts coming more rapidly than I could speak them.

His expression darkened. "Because the composition of the vazarka is *my* choice. Not theirs."

"And if I say no?"

He drew his head back in surprise and gawked at me for a moment, wide-eyed and mouth gaping, bewildered. I don't think he even considered it a possibility. "You wouldn't refuse?" he asked, more hurt than hostile.

"What has Antisthenes said about all of this?"

"What business is it of his?"

"He was your confidant before I arrived, and I'd not like to usurp him. He is a great friend to you and a man of great value to this warband. It wouldn't be right to place me before him or make such a choice without his opinion."

He chewed his lip and nodded. "I see your point. I'll await his judgement. But he will agree."

I wasn't so sure. Maybe Antisthenes could talk some sense into him. "Ask the Hellene and the other vazarka. Put it to a vote like any other matter that affects them."

"Do you care so much what others think?"

"No," I said defiantly. "Not for myself."

He gripped my arm and grinned. "Then you're ready."

"But I must care for your sake. I will not agree unless they do. Speak to them first?"

He nodded slowly. "Tomorrow, then."

OUR HUNTING PARTY had followed the hounds up the valley and into the hills above the rapids. They'd been on the scent of a stag since before dawn, and we rode close behind, hoping to glimpse their quarry across the dewy fields before it could take flight. Then, we could decide if it would be worth the chase.

Aric had called this hunt to inaugurate me as a vazarka. On the festival's final day, we met the other eleven an hour before sunrise at the northern edge of camp. Aric had put the question of my membership to the others as I'd asked, and most had agreed, he said. Not all. He'd not mentioned who the dissenters had been, but I was surprised any at all had agreed. I spent the better part of the ride trying secretly to root out the objectors. By dawn, I had assembled a gang of suspects.

Far ahead, in the dimness of predawn, I spotted a mass of moving shadows beside the river. Aric raised his hand to signal us to stop and whistled to the hounds to bring them to heel.

Horses ground-tied behind us, Aric summoned Stormai and me to creep closer through the tall grass with him for a better view of our quarry. A young stag strutted along the riverbank, bellowing to a small herd of hinds downriver. The hillside, sweeping low to the river, was all black, thick with ripened fruits and pods of woad plants as far as the eye could see.

"He's a fine stag," Stormai said. "The ground is good. We should be able to get him."

"Indeed," Aric said and waved his hand to the men behind us. Everyone knew his duty and made for his post. Rathagos and Siran, Bradak and Azarion, Galati and Mourdag all quietly rode away, circling wide around the field in an easy canter. Crouched in this cover, we that remained prepared to take up our positions. With our hands, we gathered the dew from the morning grass and washed our faces so that we might be pure before asking leave to take a beast in Artimpasa's charge. My new tattoo still stung beneath my caftan, and I said a little prayer to the Mistress, hoping she'd smile upon our hunt on this day especially.

Olgas and Bornon, Gohar and Peraka, Aric, Stormai, and I were to spread across the field, descend into the valley like a living net, and ensnare the creature as it fled. But the stag below spun around and roared. We all froze in our tracks and crouched down.

From out of a covert, a great hart trotted down the hillside north of us and entered the valley floor. He bellowed mightily before the hinds and the young stag, and I thrilled to see the magnificent beast. Crawling through the grass, I propped myself on my elbows and watched. Aric inched up close beside me.

The two deer met and began to walk side by side, sizing each other up. The hart must have had over ten winters and was in fine health. The younger stag couldn't have had more than three or four winters. If he had any sense, he would have fled. But he was in rut and wasn't giving up on those hinds so easily. What a strange thing it was, a spectacle such as this. Neither threatened to devour the other. There was neither a portion of earth nor life-sustaining resources to battle over. Both risked their lives for the pleasure, the privilege, of a brief mating. It hardly seemed worth the hazard, yet this young stag had decided to test his mettle against the seasoned warrior of the steppe.

The venerable hart reared back and clashed horns with the younger stag. The fight was on. Scrambling in the dirt, the clashing and clacking of antlers as they bent low, locked heads twisting, bodies grappling, the hart threw the younger to the ground, but he scrambled to his feet. They locked horns again, each losing ground and regaining it.

Thrashing with their forelegs, they ranged to and fro over the field. Their great horns clashed across the plain like claps of thunder. The hinds, barely interested, circled the ground, sometimes looking up from their grazing to watch the battle, sometimes inching closer, sometimes fleeing from its path.

The hart leapt forward and smashed his great horns once more into his opponent, driving his head down and into the dirt, and the young stag pulled back just as the hart twisted his head free of the locked horns and caught him in the throat. The tine of his antler punctured the young stag's neck. The stag pulled away and fled but quickly stumbled, crumpled, then fell. He struggled to rise and fell again, gasping on his side in the grass beside the river. Then the rise and fall of ribs slowed, sputtered, and ceased.

The hart stood panting, his head hung low. Exhausted and confused by what had just happened, he neither fled from nor approached his fallen opponent.

Aric and I were still as well. We were so close that the hairs on my arms stood on end, touching the hairs of his arm. Though our skin never met, it sent a shiver through me. The wounds Erman made over my breast and shoulder burned now after laying propped on my elbow in the grass for so long. The others were waiting out in the field for a signal from Aric.

"Ready?" Aric asked.

"I say we leave him be."

He stared at me, puzzled.

"Why do men always conspire to destroy the best of things? For their pride? Fuck their pride. Should we not winnow the weak and foolish and leave the best to thrive? That hart was the winner of this and every prior contest. He fought bravely and deserves to live. We should gather the fallen stag and be content."

He frowned and scratched his beard as he studied the hart. "You're right."

"You agree?" I had readied myself for another fight.

"There are many deer on the steppe. But few kings like him."

We stood to collect our horses. Bornon, Gohar, and Peraka gathered nearby.

"How do we approach?" Stormai asked, confused.

"We do not," Aric said firmly. "It's over."

"Bullshit," Olgas protested. "There's no finer prize than him. And what could be more fitting for a royal feast?"

"Aric is right," Stormai said. "He fought bravely. Leave him to his hinds. He's earned them."

The other men voiced their assent.

"Well," Olgas waved his hand in acquiescence, "when you put it that way . . ."

"Good," Aric said. "The choice is made. We go to collect the young stag."

The light was yet too dim to signal with the mirror. But he waved a signal with his arms to Rathagos, Bradak, Siran, Azarion, Galati, and Mourdag, who had positioned themselves farther up the field, and whistled for them to return. The hunt was off. Those down on the valley floor were already making their way back up the hill to join us.

"Where is Rathagos?" I asked, searching the hillside below.

He wasn't among the group of men returning up the hill. Aric turned to scan the field. And as my eyes swept down along the riverbank, I saw the herd of hinds scatter as a horseman crept up to the herd and approached the battle-weary hart.

"Rathagos, stop!" Aric bellowed and held up his hand in warning just before Rathagos drew his bow and shot an arrow into the side of the exhausted beast. After it had fallen, he leapt from his horse and stood over the body, placed his foot upon its neck, drew his sword, and stabbed it through the heart.

No one spoke. We waited in tense silence, watching for a sign from Aric as Rathagos rode back triumphantly, either oblivious or entirely indifferent to the scorn he'd just earned himself. But Aric was eerily calm, so none of us dared move or speak.

"Now we've got two fine beasts for the king's feast," Rathagos announced as he approached. "Let's get the cart down there and pick them up before the crows come."

Kicking his horse forward, Aric met him halfway. "What the fuck was that?" he growled at Rathagos. "He wasn't yours to take."

"No, then whose was he?" Rathagos barked back, reining in his horse before reaching the place Aric stood.

"You forget yourself. Every creature of this steppe belongs to the king, and I am his voice here. I gave a command, which you refused to heed. There will be a reckoning for this. From me, and maybe yet from the king. You'll be lucky if he doesn't have your hand—or worse."

Rathagos seethed with anger, but he seemed to think better of openly defying Aric further. His hot temper burned in his reddened face and neck. His fists, clenched on the reins, wrenched savagely at his horse's bit as he rode away, leaving us to clean up his mess. We collected both kills and rode home in silence. I was afraid of what reckoning would come but pleased as well; Rathagos was a constant thorn in my heel. But the death of the hart troubled me more than it should have.

THAT NIGHT, Aric pulled Ariapaithi aside and spoke with him, telling him what had transpired with killing the two noble deer. And the king, feeling generous—or perhaps cautious—because we were at the close of the holy festival, decided not to punish Rathagos. However, unwilling to serve poached meat at his table, Ariapaithi ordered that the venison be brought to the pastures as a gift to the cattle-herders. Rathagos's face twisted as he bit back his indignation while watching his prize being hauled away in the back of an oxcart to be consumed by a nameless multitude.

CHAPTER 32

RATHAGOS

*Without its head, a snake eventually
loosens its grip.*

O UR NEW BUNA lay in a deep valley in a bend on the dawnward bank of the winding Gerrhos River. The Wild Fields lay
beyond its boundary, and fording the river again felt like coming
home. We would follow it south for several miles, then make our
way across the tablelands southeast and seek camp in one of the
many small, mostly unoccupied valleys along tributaries of the Poritas, just a few leagues above the Swamp of Maeotis. Most of the
kara rode ahead to begin unpacking our gear. Aric said it would
only be temporary until the pasture was gone, which shouldn't be
long with winter approaching, even with our numbers and stock so
reduced. The south would be warmer this late in the year and easier
to restock our supplies, though, eventually, we'd head back north.
But this valley seemed perfect, with its soft pastures nestled between
low, fading hills and a bright, shallow river quietly rambling by. We
hadn't seen another soul for days, and I'd happily stay here forever.

"You warned there would be a reckoning," I said to Aric as we
waded into the river to wash our laundry before the water froze.
"What did that mean?"

"I can't allow Rathagos to challenge me so openly," he said, dumping an armful of underclothes into the water. "But I don't wish to punish the men. There's been too much dissent among them already."

"Because of me."

"Because of many things."

He went to work on his clothes with a lump of soap while I draped my items over the smooth boulders. Aric didn't want to blame me for the discord, but I wasn't blind. He rode more watches with me now than the other men, and that alone was beginning to cause a stir. He told them it was to further my training and honor his oath to protect me, but they must have noticed how he often pulled me aside to speak his thoughts aloud and seek my mind, something he rarely did with them. I saw the way they looked. Now, for some mad reason, he'd set me among the vazarka, which would never sit well with many of them. And I was the one who'd pushed him to ravage the Greek settlement—a rash affair, the bastard spawn of which was only just being born. A fellowship like this could not hold without trust, but Aric could not command without respect. Now, he tested both.

"I told you from the beginning that I didn't want to cause you any harm."

He handed me the wedge of soap. "And I told you I'd never let that happen."

"I'm not sure it's within your control," I said, scrubbing a stubborn spot on my trousers, my hands full of suds. I couldn't tell if it was a grass stain or horse slobber, though I suppose they were the same. "Some of the men are jealous of your attention. They seek fault in me to oust me from your good favor." I tossed the soap onto the flat boulder near the bank and rinsed my spare trousers in the current, waiting until his back was turned to scrub my undergarments. "They don't have to look hard."

"There is no fault to find."

I raised my brows at him. "Isn't there? What of the raid on
those Hellenes? You thanked me for encouraging this course. But,
listening to that friend of Skyles, Demetrios, I'm no longer certain.
Sure, he's an arrogant ass, but *he didn't know* he was breaking your
covenant. Maybe those farmers weren't being defiant; they were
just being duped. What if they never knew they broke the law?
Skyles offered them that land to settle, and they defended what
they believed was rightfully theirs."

"And what would you have done differently with this knowledge?"

"We could have tried to reason with them."

"Maybe, but do you think those people would have abandoned
all they'd built because we asked them nicely? Explained the situ-
ation? They had the promises of Prince Skyles and their governor.
They had an investment in the soil. That's not so easily abandoned."

"Skyles sacrificed them." I did not yet understand the meaning
of this revelation, but I knew it to be true. "His allies, his own.
What could be his purpose?"

Aric only shook his head in bewilderment, unwilling as I was
to proffer answers to the inconceivable.

"So many deceptions, so many schemes. I failed to see any of it."

"You see more than I. It took seeing through your eyes for my
vision to clear. I viewed those closest to me through a veil, which
has finally been lifted. It is time I take this troop—this country—
in hand before I lose my grip entirely. Beginning with Rathagos."

"Rathagos is just the head of the snake. Mourdag joins him.
Siran. Galati. Azarion. Bradak, I think."

"No, not Bradak," he mused, "he's solid. Just a bit odd and hard
to read. Don't assume he and Azarion are joined in this. He and his
brother are rivals more than partners in most things." He pulled
his tunic from the cold water and twisted it into a rope, wringing it
so tightly it looked like it would burst. "They are all my brothers. I
need them, but I'll not let them rule. They have a duty as well as I."
I averted my gaze as he casually shook out a breechcloth before me.

"I know what kind of men Rathagos and Azarion are." He hung his underwear on a nearby branch to wave like a banner in the breeze.

"Then, I don't understand why you trust them." With my back to him, I wrung out my linen undervest and breechcloth.

"I've seen them before."

"Men like Rathagos?"

"Your underwear."

Turning around, I attempted to scold him but choked, my face burning with embarrassment. When words didn't come, exasperation did, and I flung the sopping garments at his face. He caught them handily and snorted to himself in his amusement. Then methodically shook them out, one by one, and hung them on the branch beside his flapping breechcloth. There, they waved in the breeze like a captured standard, mocking me.

"You are angry," Aric said, "but you view mankind from the wrong place. And so, you will always be disappointed. You want to believe people are honorable and good, so you give them the benefit of the doubt. This makes you feel good. Then, when they prove dishonorable and bad, you're discouraged."

I ignored him, continuing to give my trousers another good scrub against the boulder.

"I see people for what they are: animals. I expect them to behave like animals, and when I encounter one who behaves otherwise—who reasons, speaks the truth, or acts justly—I'm pleasantly surprised. But I'm never caught off my guard by the misdeeds of animals masquerading as men. Their wickedness and debauchery never dishearten me. I wait and allow people to earn my respect: I don't first give it in hope and later rescind it in regret."

I wrung out my trousers and spread them over a patch of dry grass. "Oh? Why, then, does Rathagos hold the title of vazarka? I can't think of a man less worthy of respect."

"I don't respect him. But Rathagos is among the men I rely on the most."

"How? He's clearly envious of you and does nothing but try to undermine you."

"I rely on him *because* he despises me. He despises you and everyone else. I can trust in that like the sun rising each morning."

"What the fuck does that mean?"

"The other men are loyal. I consider them brothers. They want my favor. I want theirs. A man like Rathagos doesn't care about any of that. He understands that his malice toward mankind is entirely mutual."

It took a moment to swallow that. "That doesn't mean he's not dangerous."

"No, quite the opposite. But he also does the work I can't do."

"Such as?"

"Every camp needs an attack dog. He makes accusations I could never make and tests the loyalties of friends and guests I can't afford to challenge beside my fire. I tolerate his bark because it serves me; he tolerates mine because it serves him."

I stared at him in disgust, trying to grasp how he could will-ingly allow a creature like Rathagos to ply his craft so openly. But when the fog began to lift, I saw he might be right. And I wondered why Aric believed he needed my counsel at all. When I looked at a man like Rathagos, I saw only liability; Aric saw opportunity. To Aric, he was the fire that warms homes, cooks meals, torches villages, and roasts enemies. To me, Rathagos was the poison fungi on the fallen tree, only able to feed on what was rotten. Men like him stalked the courts across the country. I'd seen glimpses of them all my life at my father's court, visiting with kings and chiefs of tribes great and small, pouring poison into the ears of all they encountered, using their office and skill at arms to unseat weaker men for profit. I feared Rathagos's end was to unseat Aric. An inept, craven man, he couldn't usurp his karadar in open combat, so he would have to defeat him with cunning.

I didn't know if it was better to keep a man like that close or as far away as possible. Better yet, I wished he would disappear from the world entirely.

"It worries me," I said. "But you know him best. Keep him if you think you need him," I said, unconvinced of the wisdom in my own words.

"I can't keep him now," he shook his head absently. "I've never had any of the vazarka openly rebel against me. Argue with and challenge, of course. But openly defy me?"

"If he doesn't beg your pardon publicly, then I think you must send him away, not just from the vazarka, but from the kara. What happens when your attack dog finally turns and bites you?"

His brow furrowed deeply. "You believe he will?"

I nodded. "But I also worry what will happen if he believes we have conspired against him. Take care with this. Because Rathagos speaks so freely, many will assume he is honest, guileless, and brave. Undoubtedly, he will exploit this belief against the prejudices already harbored by our enemies. No matter what lies or slanders they contain, his words will carry weight."

"Then, I can neither keep him nor send him away." He shrugged hopelessly and shook his head.

His words thrilled me more than I dared admit, and I tempered my reaction so he would not guess how much I longed for him to act swiftly and finally.

"I fear we've waited too long," I said solemnly. "Your moment to deal painlessly with him may have passed." I drew a slow breath before turning to see his reaction.

He glanced sidelong at me, refusing to meet my eye. "I take your meaning, but I will not resort to duplicity and backstabbing either. His penalty must be forthright and fair, regardless of the consequences. Any injustice by us will only vindicate his desire for a feud—and gain him allies."

"I agree," I said grudgingly, knowing as a practical matter that he was right, but longing deep in my marrow to scourge Rathagos—if not in body, then in spirit—though I knew not how. "But you're wrong about one thing."

"What's that?" he said, climbing ashore and unrolling his trousers.

"Men are far worse than animals," I said. "Beasts simply obey their nature. We must *choose* to lie, cheat, and betray. I wish the king *had* cut off Rathagos's troth-hand. Then he'd leave this place and never trouble us—or anyone else—again. Maybe then the men he incites would forget their animosities as well. Without its head, a snake eventually loosens its grip."

"After Tarana, I hoped it would not come to such things again," he said as he sat on the bank and pulled on his boots.

"I'm not saying it's come to that . . . yet." I dropped down beside him on the bank, unrolling my own trousers. I saw the cause for his reluctance, and I didn't blame him. "I'm only saying if you can't keep your hounds well-fed, watch your back. They will turn and feed on you when they're hungry."

Resting his lean forearms on his knees, he looked at me skeptically. "It's good for a man to be a little hungry, no?"

Avoiding his look, I pulled on my wool stockings one by one. "Real hunger has never inspired anyone to noble deeds. You once told me all war was about hunger. About the survival of one's own tribe." I turned to fix him with a pointed look. "Rathagos may live in our camp, but he is of a very different tribe."

CHAPTER 33

REAVERS

Maybe these fragments were not revelations,
but stolen glimpses of some forbidden kingdom
we were never meant to see.

T HERE IS AN IMPERCEPTIBLE, secret world around us to which
we are blind and deaf, yet we know it exists because the beasts
perceive it. They see and hear and smell what we cannot, alerting
us to a world just beyond our reach. What lies beyond *their* reach?
What other senses must we lack, and what other realms must exist
beyond it all? There are some among us who, like the beasts, are
permitted to glimpse this hidden world, the way horses sense an
approaching storm, or take flight at hidden dangers, or a dog hears
creatures a man cannot, or follows the trail of things long vanished
in the wind. I could feel the vibrations coming up through the earth,
along my nerves, through my bones, inside my skull. The ground
shook. My whole body quivered with tremors as the burnt smell
of fear rose into my awareness. This was no ordinary spell.

"Something draws near," I said to Aric, who stood guard over
me as always when the spells came.

He peered through the flap of the cannabis tent where we were
concealed and scanned the moonless night, straining in the silence

of the sleeping camp. Then he paused, holding his breath. For that moment, all was stillness. I stared, the outline of his face blurred in the faint glow of the brazier and the veil of incense. Then he turned to me and whispered, "I think I hear it, too."

Sheathing his dagger and handing me mine, he tucked his amulet back into his belt, drew his cloak around his shoulders, and thrust a hand toward me, which I grasped as he yanked me through the tent flap and to my feet. Giving a slight nod, he drew a sharp breath and turned to run, shouting an alarm.

The men staggered from their tents beneath a clear, star-filled sky, strapping on weapons. Ducking inside our tent, I gathered our spears and tack.

I emerged just as a rider approached the camp, his horse in a lather and panting hard. He rushed past me, pulled up before Aric's upraised hand, and dismounted to stand at the fore of a gathering crowd. The rider spoke heatedly, gesturing wildly with his arms, pointing northwest.

From a distance, I watched Aric turn to the men behind him. Suddenly, they scattered like a flock of birds taking flight, all rushing for their bridles. I ran to him.

"A raiding party. About three hundred strong. Coming for the horses and gear."

"Three hundred? The fuck?"

"Exactly. Get . . . *everything*."

"Should I pony my spare horses so they can't be driven off?" Perhaps if we led them by their halters from horseback instead of driving them before us, there would be less chance of losing them to rustlers in the confusion.

He thought for a moment. "It could work. Can't hurt to try."

THE RAVEN WASN'T LYING. When the reavers came into view, they descended the valley like a swarm of flies, black and angry. We assembled nearly all one hundred of the remaining karik from our camp, though some of our scouts remained in the fields. Aric ordered each rider to do as I suggested and lead his remounts from horseback so they couldn't be swept up in the chaos. It would make it harder to fire a bow but make the easily panicked beasts more manageable in the dark.

The raiders swarmed over the valley's rim toward us. We remained on course and rode straight on to meet them. Suddenly, they changed direction, circled around, and rode back over the hill just as quickly as they came. We all eyed one another and shrugged. Then, we pulled up and waited. Perhaps it was a trick? Maybe they had reinforcements. We waited some more. Then another Raven, dressed in grey, galloped up and said they had retreated and were riding straight for home. Baffled, we slowly dismounted and untacked our horses, still leery of deception, waiting for the second wave to hit us. Something had to be wrong. I was anxious about releasing my horses. What would make a band of reavers do something so mad?

"You know what I think?" said Bornon, pulling off his wolfskin cap. "From a distance, it looked like we had double or triple the riders. They thought they were defeated before they fired a shot."

"You may be right," Olgas agreed, throwing his greaves onto a pile with his saddle blanket. "Or perhaps when they saw the horses all bound up in our possession, they realized it would be a much more difficult fight to get them and gave up."

"In any case," said Stormai, carefully resting his long spear against the side of the nearest felt-house, "it was quick thinking on Aric's part. Now we can go enjoy some wine."

"Thank Anaiti," Aric said. "It was her idea."

Everyone turned to face me. I smiled humbly, uncomfortable with their eyes upon me. Then the dreaded rush of panic swept over me, and everything went black.

I OPENED MY EYES to see a ring of men standing over me where

I lay, my head throbbing where I struck it on the hard earth. Aric and Olgas half-grappled to my left, falling to the ground in one another's grip.

"Are you mad?" Aric roared, gripping Olgas by the front of his caftan and shaking him like a wet rag. "You never speak the names of seers when they're in the trance! Her spirit could be wandering far from here. If you wake her, it might never return!"

"How the fuck should I know that?" Olgas barked at him.

I called Aric's name, and he froze and looked back.

"She returns." Antisthenes stood beside me, stone-faced, raising his hand to signal the others to stop their quarrel.

Aric released poor Olgas, and they both, bloody and dirty, fell to their knees at my side.

"Are you all right?" Aric asked, leaning over me.

"What's happening?" I asked. I lay on my back under a clear night sky, the dry autumn grass tickling my ears.

"He said your name while you were . . . I feared you'd die."

"But what *happened?*" I strained to lift my head.

"You gave us a good scare," said Stormai. He held a wineskin out to me as I gingerly propped myself on my elbows. "One minute you were standing there, and the next, well, you weren't."

I looked past Aric and Stormai, and nearly all the camp was gathered around. Over his shoulder, Mourdag scowled down at me, arms crossed tight over his chest. Rathagos stood beside him, whispering something in his ear. Bradak had a bewildered look on his face. Galati, the warband's healer, stepped back and slipped away from the crowd—to where I didn't wish to know.

I sat up, aching all over, and took the wineskin.

"You just fell limp to the ground," Aric said, his face scrunched with unease. "Has this ever happened before?"

"I don't think so."

"We should get her inside," Gohar said, eyeing the crowd. "She probably wants some rest."

INSIDE THE TENT, Aric stood, shaking his head with his hands on his hips. If they had suspected or heard rumors before, now the whole camp knew about the spells—saw with their own eyes. And of all the attacks to witness, they had to see the worst.

"Where did you go?" Aric asked quietly once we were safely inside.

"Just now, I briefly saw the empty streets of a great city like Bastarnia. But there are no cities here." I puzzled over this, wondering if perhaps some part of my spirit was homesick. But Aric slowly nodded as if in recognition.

"*Why now?*" he whispered to himself.

"What about *them?* Maybe I can explain," I said.

"This is a blow. Many will not accept it," he muttered, unfamiliar distress distorting his features.

"It takes more than that to shake me loose," Gohar said, and Olgas and Bornon nodded their assent. "You said yourself; her advice spared us today. Besides, she sits a horse better than any man, and she bends a bow well as most," he jutted his strong chin in my general direction.

"You know I think you're a brave fighter and an honorable woman," Stormai said. "But, if I'm honest, I don't approve of sorcery." He glanced nervously at Aric, like he was waiting to be scolded.

I understood their fears. I was like them before I began speaking with Erman about the nature of my spells and the secrets of divination. Now, I became defensive, not only of my own skin but also of the sacred knowledge I had been entrusted with.

"It is not sorcery," I said. "You practice little divinations every day when reading the weather or judging the ripening of fruit on the tree. When watching the skies for storms. For the turn of seasons. When to harvest or make hay. When the mares are in season, or the calving begins. Nature shows us signs of what is to come. Some can see them more clearly than others. That's all."

"That's all?" Stormai frowned, disappointed.

"To some, spirits might reveal other signs—of the past, the dead, distant places, the causes of sickness. The real danger is not their existence, but that they're never enough."

Antisthenes had moved to stand beside Aric, whose eye had begun to swell from his scuffle with Olgas, and glanced worriedly at him now. "In my homeland, they have another name for it," Antisthenes said stiffly. "They call it 'the sacred disease.' Many say that the father of King Kurush the Great, called Kambujiya by the Skythai but Cambyses by the Hellenes, also had since his birth this sacred affliction, and yet he was a great king and the ruler of a great empire."

Aric gripped Antisthenes warmly by the shoulder and nodded solemnly. "Thank you, my friend. I will go and try to reassure them," he said, slipping through the door.

"It's not your conjuring that worries me," Olgas leaned in and said quietly to me, his lip cut and swollen. "It's what the men think it does to Aric."

"Oh? And what do they think it does to him?"

"They think it makes him soft."

STORMAI WAS LEFT BEHIND with me while the others resumed watches in case the reavers returned. I studied his face in the warm hearthlight as we sat in silence, wondering how two cousins who looked so similar could be so different. I would never have spotted their kinship, but once Antisthenes had mentioned it, his resemblance to Aric couldn't be unseen.

"You're very quiet," I prodded Stormai. "You don't have to be afraid of me. The hamazan don't eat men—only little boys," I joked. He didn't even crack a smile. Either my jokes were worse than I thought, or something was troubling him. Likely both. "Come on, what's wrong with you?" I asked bluntly. I wasn't prepared for a night of sitting with a sullen lump.

He made a nervous pretense of retying the thongs on his boots.

"What do the men say?" I tried again.

Olgas's revelation confused me. Sorcery and divination were effeminate arts, but why should they think *my* use of them unmanned Aric? He looked away into the shadows of approaching evening. Even as my frustration with him grew, his obvious discomfort and pathetic attempts at avoidance amused me. I was sure he would burst the thongs on his boots from so much twisting.

"It's that bad?"

Knotting and twining his fingers before him, he drew a deep breath. "You would not like it."

"The men want rid of me," I said. "I know. But I'll hear it from Aric. If he wants me gone, he'll have to tell me so himself."

He shook his head slowly and spoke to his boots. "You know he won't. He swore an oath."

"That's what the men fear? That his obligation to me endangers him?"

"Something like that."

"But I've safeguarded him how many times? What more must I prove?"

"It's not your skill with arms or cures the men worry about."

"Then what?"

He gave a half-smirk and shrugged.

"It's not like that, and you know it."

"I didn't say I believed it. But some think it's why we don't raid as we should. Why he keeps you close and away from fights. To protect you—and himself from failing his oath. And because—"

"Enough. Perhaps you're right. I won't be the reason Aric's men turn on him." Had the men seen it, too? Of course they had. They couldn't fail to take notice. Aric seldom took a piss these days without first asking me to divine which direction the wind blew.

"Pardon, my lady. Truly. But you spoke of divination? Well, most men fear a white crow as an ill omen. I believe it's the right thing for you to go now."

"You're Aric's cousin?" I prodded, the curiosity gnawing at me for too long. I tried not to stare.

"Wh—who told you that?" he stuttered, scrunching his face like I'd just scolded him.

"People talk. I've noticed you cover your tattoos around the men. Why?" I asked gently, "you've nothing to be ashamed of."

"Why do you cover *yourself*?"

I nodded. *Fair enough.* "You're a long way from home, though. What strange fortune brought you here?"

"I ask myself that all the time." He chuckled half-heartedly. "I was just a boy when I joined with Aric," he sighed and lay back, propped against the blankets tucked along the walls. "The day my father took Aric's eye, I was there. We'd never met, but I knew he was my kin. And I—I was so ashamed of what he did. It offended honor. Offended the gods. It was cowardly and cruel. And there was this boy not much older than me, behaving the way the *brazman* had taught me I should. He was my true blood that day. And I thought, *I want to go to a place that makes men like that.* Where people live how they speak. Where I didn't have to be ashamed. So, I followed Aric home. And here I am."

"I understand more than you know. You miss it—your home?"

He leaned forward, propping his elbows on his knees. "Of course. Sometimes. The food was better." He smiled. "And I miss my mother." He suddenly seemed to regret saying so, as if I might think him unmanly. "I—I just mean she didn't understand. I think it must have broken her heart." His voice tightened and became tremulous with the memory. "I wish I could have told her that I . . . ," he pulled at his beard with his fingers and shook his head.

"She's your mother. She knows." I squeezed his hand, and he smiled. "Mothers love their sons no matter what."

He swallowed hard, and tears simmered in his eyes. "It's been hard." He wiped his nose.

"I know. But look at all you've achieved."

"The others didn't trust me at first. Some still don't." He met my gaze for the first time all night.

"Why do you stay? You're kind and, if I may say so, quite handsome. You'd have no trouble finding a good wife for yourself. You could ask Aric to release you from your bond."

His cheeks reddened boyishly at my compliment, but I suspected it was nothing he didn't already know. He would have been popular among the women back at court who clawed for a chance to bed a member of the sacred warband—and a vazarka was a prize of the highest status. They no doubt slavered over a clean, fit young man with all his teeth. I could easily see him making his way on some choice range of steppeland like one of the householders with a nice well-born girl, a train of wagons, and some good stock. His burden of gifts and share of the spoils must have been substantial by now.

He looked wistful for a moment, then shook his head. "Even if Aric would release me, what honorable girl's father would have the son of Spargapaithi?" he asked dolefully.

"If I, of all people, can wed the great Ariapaithi, you can have anyone your heart desires."

"Begging your pardon, my lady, but you haven't wed him yet."

"Well, you have a point there." It had crossed my mind that there was another reason he had sent me out here. What better place to dispose of an unwanted obligation than a lawless wilderness like this?

"I don't mind," he assured me. "This is my home now. We're karik—brothers and bastards alike," he said with the dash of defiant pride I'd often heard from the others.

"So be it, then," I said. "But don't let them get to you," I pulled up his sleeve to peek at the bands on his skin. "Some men are witless enough to care more about the vessel than its contents. I know something about that, too."

"It is so. They slander you same as me," Stormai said, seeming

320

embarrassed to have even heard such things, though I knew someone in his tenuous position would never speak up for me. I understood. And I forgave him.

"But Aric trusts you," I reminded him.

"And I him."

"You've been a good friend to me, Stormai. I'm glad to have known you."

"Likewise, Lady Anaiti." He sniffled and wiped his cheeks. "You know something?" he said with renewed vigor, his blue eyes pulsing with feral intensity as he met my gaze again. "*Fuck them.* I take it all back. You can't go. Let them talk. Aric trusts you, and so do I. Your place is here, with us. If they don't like it, fuck them."

THE REAVERS DID NOT RETURN, and eventually, the routine around camp resumed its usual pattern, though a tense calm had settled over the band. As we prepared a porridge in our tent for dinner, I related Stormai's warning to Aric and Antisthenes. Aric waved it off as nonsense and seemed unconcerned, saying passions always ran high after raids, and in a day or two, it would all be forgotten. Stormai was right; I should ignore it. I nodded in relief, unsurprised by Aric's disdain for mob rule.

"It is Rathagos who instigates it," Antisthenes said as he busied himself, placing handfuls of ground wheat into the warm cauldron. It would be difficult to ruin a porridge, but I was confident he could find a way.

"Why is Rathagos so filled with this spite?" I asked. He had been my sternest critic since the day I'd arrived in Skythia, though I'd done nothing to provoke him. "Is it the product of a deformed spirit, or has some grave injury been done to him to make him act this way?"

"Rathagos didn't want this life," Aric answered. "His father, Akasas, was a chief, but he lost his wits one day and slew a more powerful chief. To avoid a deadly feud, he gave up everything he owned, but it covered only a portion of the blood-fees. His clan is in debt. In such contracts, an equal pledge is wagered until the debt is fulfilled. A father may elect his son to serve as debt-slave in his stead; Akasas pledged Rathagos to serve as his surety. Rathagos joined the kara instead, leaving his younger brother to bondage, where he remains. Without sons, the household was left destitute and disbanded until the remaining debt is repaid—its honor restored. And Rathagos remains unable to inherit his title."

"He must have gotten many fortunes in cattle and gold by now. Why has he not made his clan whole again?" I asked.

"Who can say?" Antisthenes replied. "Whatever he gets, he spends on women and weapons."

"Even while his kin count on him?" I asked. Then I remembered my own reluctance to leave the kara. Perhaps I had judged Rathagos too harshly. "He must love this life dearly to shirk his other duties."

"Oh, no," Antisthenes said, smirking as he stirred his pot. "He finds the kara beneath him."

"When Akasas lost his fortune," Aric said, "he dedicated himself to the service of Mother Apia. I'm not sure what Rathagos found more shameful: slavery or his father's submission to the goddess."

"Where's the shame in that? Don't all Skythai revere Apia?"

"The rites—or should I say vices—of fertility and abundance belong to the cattle-breeders and plowmen, not warriors and chiefs. Rathagos is proud; he could never forgive his father."

"Can you not force him to retire, then?" I asked. "If you pay the bond, he will be indebted to you—as will his young brother. Let him return to his clan but let him—and all of Skythia—never forget his debt to you. Let it hang forever over his head like a thundercloud."

"I will lose the allegiance of Rathagos if I humiliate him publicly," Aric said.

As if you ever had it. "That horse has bolted," I said. "You can try to win back his loyalty like a man wooing a woman who has cuckolded you. But how much is that kind of fidelity worth? He cannot be reined in gently. So, hobble him and cut him loose; see how far he gets then."

Antisthenes stopped his cooking and looked up at Aric, who pulled his fingers through his copper beard in silence. "Might it not be best to spare his pride? Quietly pay the outstanding debts in his name. Allow him to claim publicly that he has earned enough to settle his family obligations and—with your generous permission—wishes to do the honorable thing for his clan. Everyone saves face; meanwhile, you are rid of him."

"Antisthenes is not wrong. But Rathagos has gone unfettered too long. Turn him loose without restraints, and there is no telling what mischief he might make. I say present him publicly with this generous gift. In refusing, he loses face. In his inability to reciprocate, he concedes his inferiority. In accepting, he'll have no choice but to honor Aric and place himself under a new debt. Force his voice in either challenge or praise of you, and then we will see where his heart lies. Every gift is a test."

Antisthenes gave a slight, curt nod. "It might work. He will rage—but in silence."

Aric stared into the cauldron, which was beginning to boil. He hadn't rejected either idea outright, which meant he was already working out the details in his thoughts.

I nodded. *Good. Let Rathagos rage. Just let it be far away from us.*

Antisthenes spooned in some butter and a pinch of salt, and we ate our porridge, which was surprisingly tasty. Covered and hoisted up on the cauldron chain high above the hearth's flames, there was enough left for the morning. With the lowest rank, washing up duties usually fell to me, and I took the dishes to the river to scrub while the men prepared for bed and likely continued to mull over the Rathagos problem.

With my belly full and my mood improved, I took back all the unkind things I'd ever thought about Antisthenes as a cook. By the time I returned, the steward was already asleep, and Aric had nearly finished undressing for bed.

"Tell me: what is it like?" Aric whispered as I removed my goryt and hung it on the peg beside his.

"I don't want to talk about it just now," I answered. "Ask me another time." Things were too uncertain around the camp just now. If even some of Stormai's fears were justified, some things might best be left unsaid, even between friends.

"You said that the last time I asked," he reminded. "I wish to protect you."

His insistence on looking after me was honorable and usually heartening. But in this matter, he had no authority. It irked me that he thought he had jurisdiction here. That his strength and command—virtually unchallenged in this world—extended to whatever realm I fought in. That he could come to grips with forces I'd been battling my whole life unsuccessfully and somehow prevail. I didn't know what upset me more: his presumption or his weakness.

"How can you protect me when I don't even know what threatens me? When what I fear is a shadow, formless and nameless. Can you protect me from that?" I asked, my distress breaking through.

"I can try," he said achingly, his brows knit together, his lips pressed tight.

I threw more fuel bricks on the fire and sat before him—I on my bed and he on his. Antisthenes was already snoring away on his pallet. The man could sleep through a battle and wake refreshed in the morning.

Maybe Aric couldn't help me any more tangibly than I could divine the future or speak with the dead. But he wanted to try. Sitting cross-legged before him on my pallet, my back to the warmth of the fire, I was at a loss for a beginning.

"Tell me first how you send your spirit forth from your flesh."

"I've told you; I don't think I send it forth. I have no control over it. It leaves me of its own will. Or else, as I fear most, perhaps something comes and takes it."

"*Something?*" His eye grew wide, and his brow furrowed deeply as he reached into the pouch at his belt for his amulet and wrapped it snug in his fingers. "But . . . *what?*"

"If only I knew. First, I feel ill in my stomach. I feel like I am spun in a whirlwind made of sparks, though my feet are rooted to the earth. I feel fright, though nothing is near me. I smell a peculiar scent, which is always the same—like burning but kindled on no substance of this earth. Then, I sense a presence. Just behind me. Hushed and unseen. Its approach—or my approach to it—is always familiar. It is always filled with dread."

"Can you summon it?" He seemed to restrain an urgency as he spoke.

"It usually comes in time with the new moon, as you know. Or with great stress. And if I choose, I can bring it on if I abstain from food and drink or sleep."

He nodded, and his eye shone fiercely in the firelight as he leaned closer. "And what do you see?"

"Well, before it comes, there's a great confusion; not a sense of traveling to past or future, but of being in two places at once—of two simultaneous lives. The world before me is fractured, divided in two, and I see . . . I see the world concealed inside this one. Something pulls back the doorflap between our realm and a secret other, which is not in the skies or the caverns below. It is spread over this earth, and men do not see it."

He smiled tenderly at this and took my hands in his. "*Men do not see it,*" he echoed, his giddiness bubbling up slowly. "Is the past or future also revealed to you then?"

"It is. And is not. I can't truly say. Sometimes, I think it's more like a memory I haven't made yet comes too soon—rises to the surface before its time. It's as if all the memories and thoughts I will ever have are present at once, past and future, but they are a tempest, and I can bring no order to them. I sense that I already know what will happen soon, but it is memory, not prophecy."

"But this *is* prophecy. You already *know* the future and are but *remembering* it," he whispered more urgently.

"Possibly."

"Do you send free your spirit to travel then?" he asked. "Across the world? Or ascend to the heavens? Descend beneath the earth?"

"I couldn't say where. It becomes like a dark sea, and, as I stand on the shore, a great wave sweeps in and washes over me. When the wave comes and swallows me up, I'm dragged out to sea. All my solid footing is pulled from beneath me, and the shore disappears. And then . . . I'm gone, beneath the waves, far from sun and moon. I can't see, or hear, or breathe. I feel nothing. I float in a darkness like the space between the stars. Then I become darkness, and I am no more."

"That can't be all there is," he said.

"But it is. I have no recollection once the darkness comes. I know nothing of what happens between the vanishing and my return. It's an ambush. But it's not like being taken captive, where, though your body is bound, your thoughts and will are still your own. It's something else entirely to have your mind seized and carried off by . . . who knows what? Returned to a form you don't even recognize. It's a terror you can't understand."

He leaned in close, resting his forearms across his knees, and absently turned the amulet in his hands. His eye caught the glare of the fire. "But I want to understand it," he whispered earnestly. "I want you to take me with you."

I hadn't made myself plain enough. "That's not possible. Besides, I would never inflict that upon you. You have no idea what you ask."

"I have some idea."

"How? Because you play at it with your potions, your incense?

That's all a game. It will subside, and you have the choice never to revisit it. *You can't know.*"

He held the amulet in his palm, tracing the lines cut into the worn face of the stone. "I had a deadly fever when I was a child. That is how the gods test their servants—with sickness, pain, or travail. It has always been a wonder to me that the so-called sages of the Hellenes are pampered men who have lived lives of ease and never dirtied their hands. They put their faith in those who claim the mantle of light but have never endured the shadows.

"When my fever broke, it was much as you describe. The anarei and Master Artabanu believed I had been gifted the two sights— that the gods showed me secret things. Sacred things. I shall never forget the things I saw. With the blissful visions, my heart flooded with unbearable joy. I would trade all my days for another such moment. But after I had fully healed, the visions ceased entirely. They disdain me now. I still offer sacrifice. I fast for days when I am able. And sometimes, I think I catch a brief glimpse. Wine, the cannabis tents, tears of Arti offer only dim shadows in comparison. I gave up all hope. But when I watch over you in the spell, I recall some of what is lost to me. The gods have seen fit to withhold the visions from me. But they have also sent you here, and I have to believe this is no accident. You possess a rare gift, not to be disparaged."

Had he really heard the call of the Nameless and stood entranced at the altar where it speaks? More, if what he said was true—and why would he lie—it had released him from its bonds of service. Such a thing was possible after all.

"Tell me what *you* recall?" I asked, eager to learn his secrets, should they contain some clue to the end of his torment—and mine.

"It was so long ago. It's more the small things that I recall best. I disregarded my own name, even as people spoke it to me. It was like a word in a foreign tongue, totally meaningless to me. I was freed of myself as a mist evaporates into day; I vanished into nothing. My limbs were not mine, yet I was calm, as though my spirit laughed at the absurdity of flesh. I saw how glorious were the underpinnings of nature and my place amid it. Then the vision ended, and I was nauseated at seeing this shadow-world devoid of all I had witnessed. When the visions withdrew, I tried daily to recreate them in my memory, though they grew faint with time."

He stared at me so intently that I had to look away. He *had* seen. He knew. Nothing I said now could shock or frighten him. Nothing I said could deter him either. Some force *did* protect and watch over him; that was clear to me now. It had released him from the torment imposed by the spells when his sickness passed. Yet he refused to see this for the blessing it was.

"I know you don't believe it," I said, "but you are blessed. Your visions were kind and gentle, perhaps because you were just a boy. But not all revelations are so beautiful, so blissful. Many are horrific. They are a terrible burden, full of fear, not something to be craved."

"Whatever comes to us from the gods—"

"Who says they're from the gods?" I snapped. "Do the gods also send the thief in the night? *This* thief steals name, will, and honor. It finds its victims unawares and ravishes their spirits. I have prayed, and the gods ignore my pleas. If the gods even exist, they play a petty game with our souls."

"Don't say such things. Don't even think them."

"If the gods torment and twist us for their sport, then they are vicious—or corrupt."

He shook his head in seeming dismay. "I think we glimpse only distortions and fragments, like trying to see a reflection in rippling water or reassembling shards of a painted vase with only a handful of pieces. The images may never make complete sense to us, but it doesn't mean they're incomplete. Perhaps we cannot see all things as the gods do?"

"Perhaps," I conceded, though I remained skeptical. I'd not yet found anything to convince me of the existence—let alone benevolence—of the gods. I'd seen plenty to indicate the opposite.

Then again, maybe these fragments were not revelations, but stolen glimpses of some forbidden kingdom we were never meant to see. "Maybe it's all a mishap," I mused, "and we are trespassers in the gods' realms."

He bit his lip and took my hands in his, squeezing them tightly. "Is that what worries you so?" he whispered.

I shook my head and breathed a moment, ordering my scattered thoughts. He might think me mad, but where else had I to turn? "I am afraid that one day, when I return to this form, something will have taken my place."

He frowned in consternation. "How?"

"Before I go, even strange people and places seem familiar—like some part of me knows them already. When I return, I'm lost." I swallowed hard. It was more challenging to speak of than I thought. "As you said, I recognize nothing, not even my own flesh. What if my thoughts, my will, my senses, my skills, my memories, when they leave me, should be scattered and lost? What if they cannot return to reclaim my form?" I could no longer hold back the tears. "I feel whole, but can I be sure? Each time is a little death, and I'm a little different. How do I know it is all of me that returns?" I sobbed and looked away, embarrassed to have revealed so much.

With coarse fingers, he gently wiped the tears from my face. "Spirit or flesh, I would recognize you." He clasped my face warmly in his hands and pressed his brow to mine. "If you were anyone but Anaiti, I would be the first to know."

How many years had I lived in secrecy, hiding my darkest fears from all those I knew, kin and outsiders alike? Imagining what they might do to me and what this thing might do to them turned my heart to lead. Speaking that dread aloud would have meant destruction. Yet now, I had done just that. And the nagging voice inside, the gnawing in the guts that usually warned of danger, was quiet and still, replaced by the warmth of something unfamiliar— something like trust. The Skythai had a particular understanding of freedom. It was not, for them, the same as liberty. A free person had a hearth to sit beside, and faithful companions to share in bearing life's burdens. In speaking those words to Aric, I was free.

"From this day forward," I said, my voice still choked with tears, "I promise to hold nothing back. I will tell you all I see and share all that is revealed to me. Every feature, however small. You shall know all that I do if that is your wish."

With his rough hands resting softly on my cheeks, he kissed my brow. "I could not ask more of the gods."

"But you must promise me something," I said, tightening my fingers around his wrists.

"What is your wish?"

"If ever what returns is not all of me, you mustn't let it have this form."

He scowled, then nodded.

"Say it. Swear you will do it."

He hesitated and swallowed hard. "I swear it."

CHAPTER 34

RUTHLESS

*Out here, men and beasts will stalk you. You
will stalk them.*

E VENING CAME EARLY NOW as winter approached. A thick
snow fell overnight, followed by a warming sun and a balmy
southern wind. From it, a heavy mist rose from the melting pack,
which had thickened the air with a dense, unyielding fog. Many
feet wore many tracks, and I followed a muddy path beside the
river, which joined the heart of camp. I groped my way home in
the hazy light of a waning moon ahead of Aric, feeling sleepy after
a long day of riding and a hearty meal of venison beside the hearth.

From the mist and rushes, the hulking shadow of the plowman,
Siran, leapt out in his bulky coat crying "Ho!" and swinging his
sword. All I could think was that it must be a bad joke. I was too
tired for games. But with the blade raised over his auburn head, he
slashed downward, aiming for my face. I had no time to draw my
own weapon. Sidestepping the mad blow, I slipped in the muck,
and the cut glanced off my iron torc.

As I spun away into the firmer footing of the deep snow, I'd
just enough time to come around with my sagaris and plant the
spike end deep in his left thigh. He howled like a hungry dog and

fell to his hands and knees. I had to brace my foot against his leg to yank loose the spike. I kicked hard at the old coat's slack folds, drove my toe hard into his guts, and watched him curl up in the mud. When I was sure he couldn't follow, I ran the rest of the way home along the riverbank, my axe dripping blood upon the snow.

"NAMING ME A VAZARKA HAS PROVOKED THEM!" I shouted at Aric in our tent, still raging from the fight. "I warned you this would happen. Even with Rathagos gone, they will never accept it."

"I will not accept blame for another man's dishonorable deeds when we have done nothing improper."

"They have been waiting for a reason," Antisthenes said, standing beside Aric. "It was only a matter of time before they found one. If Rathagos were still here, they would have found something else."

I nodded as his words burrowed into my mind. Daily, I rehearsed the secret names I gave my detractors—Rathagos the Accuser, Azarion the Rogue, Galati the Ghost, Mourdag the Doubter, and Siran the Plowman—nearly half the vazarka; not to mention anyone else among the kara they could appeal to. Rathagos and his comrades had tried to push me out and failed. Rathagos was gone, yet I remained. Three days ago, he had been released from his vazarka oaths and stealthily exiled from camp. Aric had chosen Antisthenes's more subtle plan of allowing Rathagos to leave with his honor intact, and he'd made a peaceful exit—too quiet for my liking. Aynar, the blacksmith, a jovial mountain of a man who smelled of charcoal and cheese, was elevated to his position. It all happened so quickly. I had no sense of life before I arrived, but it could not have been this chaotic. *Could it?*

"You were right that they wouldn't sit idly by," Aric conceded, "but you are a vazarka. Don't you understand? You are their equal!" I believe he was angrier with me than with Siran.

"I didn't ask for this."

"Who ever has? But if you wish to remain, these trials will be part of your life. Deal with them or go back to court." He waited as I considered his words.

I turned to Antisthenes, who stood beside the hearth. "Tarana, Rathagos, Siran. What have these men to fear from me? It's absurd."

"Is it?" Antisthenes asked. "The hamazan are man-haters and man-killers, are they not? They, too, should be feared."

"Ha! As if men have not killed more of their own—and women besides—than all the hamazan could ever hope to slay. These are Greek slanders; Skythai should know better!" My voice rose. "*You know me.* Do I not live among you men in friendship? Do I ever lust for men's blood?" The idiocy of it was amusing in its own sad way. "If anything, I despise women for how they degrade and whore themselves for their keep. It's *their* company I shun, which isn't hard since they don't even show their faces to the light of day."

Antisthenes opened his mouth to speak, then held up his hand as if to concede.

"No, speak freely," I said. "There are no secrets between the three of us."

He glanced uncertainly at Aric and cleared his throat before proceeding. He did not look at me when he spoke. "I do not say these things for myself. But many fear the hamazan are shapeshifters," Antisthenes said quietly. "That they get their strength from sorcery like the anarei do. A woman is a passive, gentle creature, bringing forth and nurturing life—not destroying it. To do otherwise is unnatural—an abomination. Only deranged women behave this way. They are no better than the women of Lacedaemon— worse even. Like impure souls afflicted by madness or possessed by malevolent spirits." He spoke plainly and without passion, as he always did, but I couldn't shake the feeling that Antisthenes did not just relate the sentiments of ordinary men, but of his own heart. He seldom spoke his true thoughts, and it was dismaying to hear him—a man I knew and esteemed—justify the condemnation of the hamazan in such stark and personal terms.

"A hamazan doesn't kill for glory or sport," I challenged him, "but to protect the things she loves from harm. To defend herself. This is the way among every free beast that roams the earth. Only among men is it deemed unnatural."

He shrugged apathetically. "For a man, losing his pride or position to another man is grim enough. But losing his place to a woman—how does he reckon with that?"

"You say 'his place' as if it were granted by the gods. A man is owed only what he earns or wins in a fair fight. Same as I."

"If you dare."

"Is that a threat?"

"No," Aric finally looked up and spoke, answering in his steward's stead. "Not from us. Just know that even those you call allies may conceal their true feelings. Take nothing for granted."

I'd always known I would face doubters, but I suppose I let myself forget Antisthenes might be among them. Or was I being too suspicious? He was protective of his companions and doubly so of Aric. But did he view me as a threat? How could I ever prove that I was neither a fragile woman they must coddle, nor a soulless man-hater determined to make geldings of them all?

"I could challenge Siran to single combat for my honor. Show him—and the others—that I will not be intimidated."

"A duel?" Antisthenes asked dubiously.

Aric clenched his jaw. "Only duel if you absolutely must. When all other options are spent."

"You don't think I can win?"

"You might. He's stronger, but you're quicker. And he's not very clever, as you've seen yourself. But he has experience and callousness on his side. And losing comes with a heavy cost."

"I thought a duel was only fought until someone yields?"

"It is. Then, when the loser yields, his troth-hand and the greater portion of his honor are forfeit. Is this a price you're prepared to pay in pursuit of vengeance? Is it a price you're willing to extract?"

I hung my head, chastened. It was not. Even the likes of Siran deserved better than that.

"You got the better of him. He'll think twice before he tries again, so leave it for now. And should he or any other threaten your life again, don't just wound him."

"You mean . . . ?" Against my sworn oath, was he urging me to kill a brother karik—a vazarka even?

"*Finish it,*" he said the words for me. "Out here, men and beasts will stalk you. You will hunt them. Never become sport or the hounds will keep chasing you."

CHAPTER 35

STORM

*Where water ought to have flowed, I could only
conjure a course of fleeting shadows.*

OUR NEW BUNA lay further north. We made our camp beside
a frozen tributary of the Poritas called the Shadow River
on account of its many shoals and mudbanks, which in warmer
months made it challenging to navigate. Where water ought to have
flowed, I could only conjure a course of fleeting shadows slipping
between its frosty banks, and the vision sent a shiver through me.
I'd never known cold like that which stole in with the Burning
Month. Bundled with scarves over our faces, tears froze in the
corners of my eyes, and ice crystals formed inside my nose. Prepping our mounts for the field, we groomed a place on our horses'
woolly backs for saddle cloths and mounted up.

We had often ridden the watch in the wind, the rain, and the
dark of night to patrol for reavers. This morning, we stood in a
silent snowfall, our fur-lined coats bound tight around us, the flaps
of our pointed caps snug over our ears. There was nothing to see
but falling white and only the dampening silence of the light but
steady snowfall. Even the next rider's approach was masked by the
flurry and muffled by the soft down underfoot.

I distrusted the hush. Camp was unsettled enough. Siran's thigh wound had festered since the night he attacked me, and he'd fallen into a heavy fever, unable to ride. Despite the scratch I still bore from his blade, more than a few spoke of dark forces at work, and fingers pointed my way.

As we pushed through dense drifts, the steam from the horses' bodies and breath crusted to the surface of their thick winter coats, forming an armor of ice over their bodies. Our clothes, too, became masked in this way. We shivered and froze at first in the frigid morning, but as the ice began to encase us, we soon settled into the chill and warmed inside our ice armor. Otherworldly creatures, we became a crystal army on the march through a frozen world of white, caught in the light of the low sun rolling across the horizon, scattering its gold over the snow before us.

Ahead on the steppe, a solitary wolf darted across the bare white expanse, rushing to I knew not where, and my breath caught in my throat as I halted my horse and raised my arm to point, ice shattering from my encrusted sleeve. I turned to glance at Aric. Had he seen? His eye was now fixed on the grey shadow as it disappeared over the horizon. The men had reined their horses in beside us.

"In my homeland," I said, "a wolf running through the fields warns of a coming storm."

"It is the same with us," Bornon, standing beside me, said.

"Perhaps we should head back," Stormai looked to his brothers, "and warn the others?"

Aric squinted at the gently falling sky, then at the empty horizon where the grey shadow had vanished. He nodded. "The wolf never lies."

AT NIGHT, our clothes dripped over the hearth. Though our beds were only inches from the frozen ground, a few layers of reeds, dry grass, and good, thick felt kept us warm and dry.

All night the storm buffeted the tent. I was sure it could never hold. No house of wood or stone—much less a tent of lattice and felt—could withstand an assault of such winds, ice, and snow as was hurled by the tempest. Most of all, I feared for the horses. How would they fare with no shelter, and would they flee in the fury of the storm? Hunkered beside the hearth, I didn't sleep but only listened and imagined the worst.

"My people are the children of this plain," Aric said, "made of its earth and stone, its wind and water. We know all its tricks. It gave us birth; we were made to endure its storms."

I wasn't sure what good that did me. But Aric said his people had built tents like these since the beginning of time. Or, if not that long, for long enough to have survived worse storms than this. And the horses, too, had endured the open plain long before the first man arrived. One blizzard would not be their end.

The tent somehow passed the night intact, though we had to dig ourselves free. It was midday before the snows subsided, and we could venture out, only to discover that the herd had been spooked by the violence of the storm and run off seeking shelter. I went in search of them, following the river through an eerie landscape of mist, ice, and the refracted light of the noon sun. Branches, twigs, and winter berries were all encased in a sheath of ice. A towering, centuries-old tree had snapped in two under the weight of the shimmering ice, the ground littered with its crystallized limbs.

All around this wasteland at the forest's southern edge, limbs lay strewn beneath the scattered trees. The destruction was immense, more like a battlefield than a woodland, more like a war than a storm. I worried, inexplicably, for the trees that remained. They bore the weight of all that ice in silence, and none could tell the point at which they might crack. That their brittle branches could bend so far and not break seemed miraculous. But the horses were happy for something new to gnaw at, stripping bark from the toppled trees.

I found them at the edge of the wood, nibbling on fallen branches. They'd fled here for what little shelter they could find. The grease in their thick winter coats could repel the rain and snow, but it provided a scant barrier against the hard-biting wind. There was no shelter from it but to huddle near the edge of the sparse wood and turn their tails. With little natural defense against the wind, horses in the open take turns using their bodies to shelter one another throughout the day and night.

As I checked the herd, the horses nuzzled me, rubbing their faces on my thick coat. I found Sakha, Aruna, and Vatra among them. Tying the ropes I'd slung over my shoulder into a makeshift bridle for Sakha and halters for the others, I swung aboard and turned for home.

Dark falling now, the wind had caused the snow to drift. I was uncertain of the path I had taken but tried to retrace my footsteps back over the nearest rise to camp. We walked among the other horses, parting the herd as we passed. A few followed, and some ran ahead, eager to return to camp.

The moon froze to the face of the snow, icy and indifferent. The loose horses trudged through the drifts around me, following and leading me home. From the rise, I could see a depression spreading over the valley floor at its base. The horses broke into a trot, racing down the slope toward the bottom, and my stomach fell, a wave of sickness spreading over me. I remembered this place before the storm and knew where they were running. The frozen river at the valley floor lay blanketed in snow, invisible now in the aftermath of the storm. I didn't trust that the ice would hold under their weight. If we ran after them, we'd only push them there faster. But perhaps we could outrun them and head them off before they reached the bottom. Dropping my other leads, I put my heels to trusty Sakha's ribs and galloped ahead, riding wide of the herd, trying to cut them off. Some began to rush alongside us as we raced along the valley floor, but we'd nearly passed the lead horse.

I prepared to rein Sakha around in front of the rushing herd and turn them back before reaching the depression. Then I heard it. The terrible, unmistakable sound of cracking ice.

I LAY GASPING AND SHIVERING on the snowy riverbank. How I managed to pull myself out, I didn't know. I remembered the crackling of the ice. Then watching helplessly as the horses plunged one by one into the waters. The frozen river, concealed under the snow, gave way under their weight. Unable to reach them, unable to move, I shrieked until I thought I'd burst my lungs. Then, the ground broke beneath Sakha, and the icy waters closed in. Now, my body writhed and shook on the snowy bank, numb and confounded with cold.

Where was Sakha? Had he managed to climb ashore as well? We'd turned away some of the charging horses before the ice gave way. But all was silent now. Gaping black holes stared up from the snow-covered ice. No horses were in sight, only deep tracks in the snow down the riverbank. My heavy, sodden coat, warbelt, and weapons lay on the snow beside me, though I didn't recall removing them. My skin burned, and my muscles cramped. Another spell threatened. I lay there huddled on the riverbank, with the wind howling and the faint stars winking overhead, and closed my eyes.

Shouts, torchlight, and the crunch of snow under a small army of hooves and boots filtered into my awareness.

"Have you gone mad!" Aric roared as he sprang to my side, pulling me to my feet. He tore his fur-lined coat from his back and wrapped it around my shoulders, almost knocking me over again in his haste to cover me, holding its folds tight in his grip. He stood close, staring into my face as I looked away, my teeth chattering uncontrollably, and tried to forget the numbness in my hands and the half dozen men sitting before us on their horses, gaping faces aglow in the torchlight. I could barely raise my head to look him in the eye. He took me by the arms and shook me. Then slapped me across my face. My senses roused briefly, but then I dropped to the ground, my form twisting involuntarily into a knot.

He dragged me to my feet again and sternly spoke my name. I tried to ask about the horses, but the words came out all wrong. His expression morphed from one of authority to one of alarm. Then, his face blurred before my eyes. He scooped me up and carried me to his horse.

"Can you ride?" he shouted into my ear.

I nodded, though I had no idea if I could. My limbs quaked, and I could barely stand without support. Aric slung me up onto his horse and vaulted up behind me. We set off for camp at a brisk canter, his arms around me.

The moon rose above us and turned the snow an eerie blue, though I noticed little but icy wind clawing at my face, warm horse-flesh beneath me, and Aric holding me tight to him so I would not fall.

CHAPTER 36

WARM

These bodies may bear us, but
we are not our bodies.

IN THE TENT'S SHELTER, Aric laid me down on my pallet, pulling off my wet boots and trousers as Antisthenes rushed to gather extra blankets. The scents of dung fire, oakbark-tanned leather, and woolen carpets brought comfort, if not warmth, in the mellow glow of the fire.

"How bad?" Antisthenes whispered as he stood over me, scrunching his brows.

"I don't know how long she was in the open," Aric answered, "but in this cold, I fear frostbite; they're not yet black, but she could lose fingers and toes. Maybe her ears. It's too early to say."

"But she'll survive?" He raised his wide eyes to Aric.

Survive. What kind of survival was that? If I lost my fingers and toes, I'd never ride or draw a bow again.

"I believe so," Aric said, his voice full of doubt. "But we should cut them off," he said, pointing ominously toward me. Antisthenes nodded solemnly, and together, they reached into their belts for their daggers.

Cut them off?

I tried to open my throat and make words. But the cold water I'd swallowed, the frigid air I'd breathed, and the frantic screaming I'd done all conspired against my voice.

"*No!*" I wheezed uselessly. Quaking with the cold, I thrashed my arms and legs as I struggled to fend them off. But as I fumbled, Antisthenes rudely pulled off my tunic and pinned my feeble arms to the floor while Aric slid the blade of his dagger under the laces of my undervest, slicing through them.

"*Be still,*" Aric whispered. "We must get all these wet clothes off!" He moved to cut away my other wet garments—my stockings, my breechcloth—slashing at the cloth as the weakness in my limbs left me helpless to fight and desperate to cover myself.

They quickly heaped a mound of blankets over me—every rug in the tent, including the reeking bearskin from the wall. It was the first thing Aric hung each time the tent was erected somewhere new, and if it cured me tonight, he'd probably never pack it away despite how gamey it was.

Antisthenes busied himself, setting a cauldron to boil and piling up more dried dung bricks until the fire roared. It helped little. The shivering had ceased, but my limbs remained contorted, my muscles rigid. Possessed by an inner chill like that from a terrible fever, I was both hot and cold at once. I closed my eyes and let myself drift.

"What do you think?" Aric whispered, uncertainty in his voice.

"How should I know? This is *your* miserable country."

"Her skin is so cold."

"We are doing all we can," Antisthenes reassured. "It is for the gods now."

More urgent words were exchanged, but I couldn't make sense of them. They blurred in my ears like the lowing of anxious cattle.

"—another way to quickly warm a frozen form," Aric said tentatively.

"I am listening. . . ?"

"You must undress; lie flesh to flesh and warm her with the heat of your body."

Silence.

My eyes flickered open to see the two men across the fire, staring at each other. My thoughts roared like the winds, and I clamped my eyes shut, pretending to be unconscious.

"*I* must do this?" Antisthenes asked.

"It is so. I command it," the tension strained Aric's voice to a new pitch, and I peeked as he folded his arms across his chest.

"Command me? In all these years, you have never *commanded* me to do anything. You are her sworn protector. Do it yourself!"

Aric shook his head violently. "I cannot."

A glaring silence stretched between them.

"Well, neither can I," Antisthenes grew adamant, and I didn't know whether to be relieved or insulted.

"You don't even like women," Aric's hushed voice hissed.

"I am still a man. And I have no kin, no clan. She is a king's daughter and another king's betrothed!" I'd never heard Antisthenes so excitable. "Both would make sport with my head. How would we explain this to your father—or hers—if she complains?"

"I swore to—it wouldn't be *proper*," Aric stammered. "Besides, she's delirious. What if she comes to her senses while I'm lying, you know, naked upon her?"

"Now you see my problem. But she is a clever woman; she will understand. But wait any longer, and you need not worry because she will never wake again."

Aric groaned. "I don't like it."

"I do not see you as having much choice."

A sudden, loud thump and rattling through the tent's poles and lattices made my eyes snap open. Aric had punched the wall.

"*Fuck.* You'll pay me for this one day, brother." He paced the carpets up and back, clenching and unclenching his fists until he seemed to calm himself. Then he stood, drew a deep breath, and let his hands go limp at his sides. "There's no other way." Aric said the words almost to himself. As a man waking from a daydream, he roused as he stood over me and began to undress. His steward moved to leave the tent. "No, stay," Aric said, "nothing improper is going to take place."

"I know, my lord," Antisthenes replied with an abrupt formality. "So, I need not remain; I will fetch some men to collect and tend the horses. They will be frozen as well."

Maybe it was a gesture of faith. More likely, it was a small mercy to spare us all the embarrassment of what was about to happen. And I had to admit my relief. But most of all, I was grateful to learn the horses had survived and would be cared for.

"If you can hear my voice," Antisthenes said, "be well, my lady. I will return after with hot broth and more fuel for the fire."

I tried to speak, but my voice was still raw and hoarse from shouting in the cold, so I only nodded as he turned to duck through the doorflap into the night.

HIS BACK TO ME, Aric was nearly naked. I'd seen his bare form before, but only ever at some distance. Its approach now unnerved me. He wore only his linen tunic and a tattered, threadbare breechcloth, which amused me even in my sad state. The poor thing was worse off than I was and should have been put out of its misery long ago.

Pulling the tunic over his head revealed his tattoos of strange symbols and fearsome creatures. Across his whole body, they writhed furiously, animated by the stirring of hardened muscles beneath. Terrific battles and horrific contests played out forever between predators and prey. Until now, I had never allowed myself to really look. I'd only ever seen glimpses, like disjointed and strange images that flash through dreams. But the whole was a wild landscape of mythical beasts and mystical symbols, which in the flickering of the firelight now turned toward me and crouched to envelop my helpless form.

I'd seen travelers' maps of the world painted on leather or carved in wood. But this was a map of a secret realm written in living flesh itself. Few but the gods themselves would ever see it entire.

Of course, Aric had just undressed me, but as he pulled back my blankets, my instinct was to cover myself. Mostly, I tried to hide my right breast, hoping he'd have the decency just to look away.

He knelt above me, and my eyes fixed upon the hundreds of notches he'd nicked up and down his arms each night, all in varying states of healing. Frowning, he asked nonsensically, "You all right?"

I shuddered violently and turned my face away. With gentle fingertips, he brushed my cheek, where I could still feel the sting left by his palm.

"Just try to be calm," he whispered. It seemed he said the words for his benefit as much as mine. But still, he hesitated, the bulk of his form hovering above me, glowing in the light of the fire.

I closed my eyes and tried to find the calm he spoke of. I thought of his words that day when we bathed in the cold river. I must not allow myself to dwell too much in—

"*No, Anaiti, don't leave me.*"

All at once, he pressed himself close. His sudden heat was overwhelming, his trembling unnerving. I drew a deep breath to steady myself and tossed my limp arms around him. He smelled of leather and sweat, pine tar and campfire. My thoughts blurred.

All was somber and quiet except for the sound of our shallow breathing. It should not have been so discomforting. We often grappled in training and healed one another's wounds. Now, there was no place to lay a sword between us. But as his warmth soaked into me, I could feel life and blood returning once more. He pulled the bearskin up over us.

How long we lay that way, I couldn't say. Beneath the bearskin, my limbs slowly regained their strength. Borne on the hypnotic ebb and flow of his breathing, like the waves of the sea, I soon found my own breast rising and falling in time with his. In my chest, I could feel the potent drumming of his heart. The cold faded, and with it came the excruciating tingle, which heat kindled in my fingertips and toes as the blood revived them and feeling slowly returned.

Beneath my hands, I could not help but feel the multitude of scars that etched his flesh. Absently, my fingers wandered along their course, and I struggled to imagine all he had suffered in acquiring—and surviving—them. I brushed across the wound that I watched nearly kill him. I touched the place in his side where he had used his body to stop the arrow meant for me.

"I—I don't know how you've endured so much," I croaked, finally finding my voice.

I felt him shrug, his arms still wrapped around me. "It's only flesh." His resonant voice vibrated through my chest.

"But some wounds leave scars deep beyond the flesh."

"And what of yours?" he said, pulling away and propping himself on his elbow.

I covered my scarred breast. Gently, he took hold of my hand and moved it aside. I did not stop him, but I had to turn my head away.

"Why so shy?"

"Doesn't it bother you?" I asked, both fearing and craving the truth. When he didn't answer, my heart caved. Then I felt his fingertips trace along the scars. Tears welled in my eyes.

"Do mine bother you?" he asked humbly.

"Of course not. They're a map of your life. Where you've been; the man you are."

"And yours are different?"

"Aren't they?"

He scrunched his brows and scowled. "Fate has made these inscriptions. They tell of your strength to those who can read the signs." He wiped away a tear from my cheek. "Why then do you weep?"

"Because I know men's minds. What others see when they look at me," my voice strangled in my throat.

"This world will put its marks on us. Proof of our resilience, our honor, our quality. Perhaps that's all flesh is worth—proof that we fought and endured the torments of life. An unmarked body is nothing to boast about. All flesh will succumb, but the spirit isn't so bound. These bodies may bear us, but we are not our bodies."

We are not our bodies. In another life and place, these words might have sounded like heresy. "I hope we are more," I said with conviction, but I still looked away, unable to face him, but then his lips pressed warmly upon my scarred breast. All at once, the storm clouds in my eyes let loose.

"Oh, Ana, I am disgraced," he gasped, turning his face away from mine.

"No, not at all," I reassured gently, combing his hair with my fingers.

He shook his head and refused to meet my eye. Suddenly, he'd become the shy one. With shock, I felt why. A sudden panic like shyness quickened my pulse and shortened my breath. My thoughts receded into a shimmering haze, like the distortion of the air over a flame. A searing heat flushed my skin.

With my hand on his bearded cheek, I turned his face toward mine and let my thumb graze his lower lip. He froze, wide-eyed. I took his lips in mine and kissed him slowly, the scruff of his beard pleasantly rough on my skin. In the red glow and faltering shadows of the fire, we caressed one another with rough hands and soft mouths, the weight of his body pressing perilously against mine.

Since the day I first met this ragged nomad, I'd done nothing but strain against some invisible tether I sensed bound me to tribe and duty. As I strained this time, I felt that tether snap. The intensity in his eye unsettled me, yet I couldn't look away. My fingers tore at the last shreds of linen cloth between us.

"AWAKE," HE WHISPERED urgently in a singsong voice, "awake."

"I'm here," I sighed hoarsely, opening my eyes to find his.

"I thought you were possessed by one of your spells," his frown softened to gently raised brows.

I brushed aside a strand of hair from his forehead and smiled at him. "Not this time."

With his eye clamped shut, he held my face in his hands, pressed his brow to mine, and began to tremble. I wanted to hold onto him with all the force in my limbs, but my strength had ebbed. Instead, I wove my fingers through his damp, tangled hair and closed my eyes. The solemn peace of sleep was taking hold of me, lulled by the quiet ebb and flow of his breathing.

Then, his breath came more rapidly. Suddenly, he thrashed the floor beside my head, then, with a growl, he pushed himself away. On the blanketed floor beside me, he sat with his back to me, drew up his knees, and covered his head with his hands. Frightened and dumbfounded, I clenched the edge of the bearskin in my fingers and stared at his tattooed back, my eye captured by a gryphon preying upon a deer.

Hidden from view, in a whisper, he asked of the flickering shadows, "What have I done?"

"What terrible thing do you imagine you've done?" I asked as I sat up beside him, bewildered.

There was silence as he slowly shook his head. "I am a thief."

"You've taken nothing I didn't give freely," I whispered reassuringly. *If anything, it was I who did the taking.*

"You don't belong to me."

"I belong to no man," I shot back. "Not yet. Perhaps not ever. If I'm lucky, I'll die first."

He turned to glare at me. "Don't ever speak of that."

"Of what? Dying or being your father's whore?" I taunted.

He clenched his fists beside his head and turned away. "He's my king. And I'm oath-bound to protect you—*even from myself.*"

His words, too, were ice. I reached for his shoulder, but he flinched away. "If you're my enemy," I said gently, "I surrender." He may have sworn to the king, but he also swore in blood to me.

"This was a crime," he insisted. "A most serious one. We must forget it and never speak or think on it again."

A crime? Could that even be true? "Loyalty to our comrades comes first, even before king and kin. You told me this yourself—made me swear to it before the gods."

"This isn't what I meant."

"No? Men have forsworn their kin and lords for you—to stand or fall beside you and their brothers. Is that also a crime?"

"Damn it, Ana! We can't."

A wave of nausea swept over me as it dawned on me how very foolish I'd just been. How naive, believing the noble Aric could ever stray from duty, no matter how unjust. "I see," I said sheepishly, pulling the blanket up to cover myself. "Then it's time. I'll take my scalp and go."

With the palm of his hand, he smeared his tears across his face and turned to look back at me. He shook his head violently as his eye flooded anew. "No, Anaiti," he begged, his voice quavering, "don't leave me. Not now."

He wasn't making sense. And I was too tired to think—we both were. We could sort it out in the morning. So, we spoke no more that night as we lay on my pallet, clinging to one another with our heads beneath the blankets.

Soon after, Antisthenes returned. We feigned sleep so he would not see the tears and confusion on our faces. I listened as he fed and stoked the fire and stirred the cauldron. I was finally warmed but wholly spent. Longing to savor this moment—the warmth of his skin against mine, his soft breath in my hair, the strength of his arms around me, and the secret knowledge we shared—I fought hard against my heavy lids. Still, I proved powerless against the insatiable sleep that quickly overtook me.

UNDER THE OPPRESSIVE WEIGHT of many blankets, the previous night's events slowly trickled into my groggy mind. An involuntary smile stretched my lips as I recalled Aric's arms around me, pulling me close. The feel of his bare skin. My fingers in his hair. The scruff of his beard on my cheek. How strange it would be to face him now in the day. I was almost too shy to open my eyes and greet him in the morning light, the secret fire burning behind our eyes. But as the delirium of sleep wore off and awareness dawned, I reached out my hand and felt about beneath the blankets to find only emptiness. I had been tucked in snug and warm, but he was already gone. The bearskin, too.

"Are you well?" It was Antisthenes. I had only just opened my eyes. "Aric had to go, but he asked me to tend to anything you needed. And to give his regrets."

"Regrets for what?"

"That he could not be here himself. To ask after your wellbeing."

Sure.

"You slept all morning," he continued, stirring something in the cauldron. "I will let you wash and dress. Then you should really eat something."

"Thank you, I'm not hungry." I just wanted to pull the blanket back over my head and be left alone. "How are the horses?"

"They are fine. Better than you, it seems," he tried to smile, but he always looked uncomfortable feigning pleasantries. Soberness suited him far better. "Fortunately, it was not too deep downriver where the other horses broke through, and they could scramble back to shore. You need your strength. Put these on." He deposited woolen trousers and a fresh tunic beside my pallet. "I will return and fix you some food and drink." He ceremoniously placed a basin for washing on the table behind the hearth and smiled kindly. "I am glad to see you looking so well. You gave us a good scare last night."

"Thank you, Antisthenes. You've always been a good friend to me. If I may call you that?"

"And you to me."

Too weary to resist, I gave my aching body a quick wash, lingering momentarily as my hands grazed over those places so recently warmed by another. Angered by this pathetic tenderness, I thought instead of my sore cheek. I was lucky to have escaped frostbite, and all my extremities had survived intact. With a clean linen, I scrubbed myself dry and struggled into some fresh, warm clothes, as even beside the fire, the chill from outside began to creep into my tired bones. I stared at the door and shivered. There were not enough garments to make the world beyond these walls bearable now.

CHAPTER 37

WISH

Maybe oracles are not allowed to see
their own road?

NIGHT HAD FALLEN, and Aric hadn't returned. I had reason to believe he might not, and both longed and feared to see him, wondering if he would steal in like a thief as we slept. Before preparing for sleep, I ventured out to make a check on the horses. My strength had returned, and I needed to see them with my own eyes. They appeared sound and healthy, and Sakha came and rubbed his face affectionately on the front of my coat, covering it with white hair. I wrapped my arms around his neck and buried my face in his mane, relieved to have my oldest friend safe and near.

From the pasture, I saw a small fire burning on the rise north of camp. In the light of the fire, a man's silhouette sat hunched, draped in a thick hide.

SNOW FELL THROUGH THE NIGHT and into the morning. The recluse remained at his vigil while I stayed safely indoors, and Antisthenes fetched more fuel for the fire. He greeted me briefly and set about his work.

"Do you have news?" I asked, wondering if he had seen Aric.

He set down his basket of dung bricks and looked at me gravely. My heart seized. "Perhaps you should sit."

"Just tell me!"

He nodded and seemed to gather his thoughts. "Siran has died in the night of his fever."

"Siran?" *Fuck.* My momentary relief gave way to a fresh flood of panic. In the tumult of the last days, I'd forgotten about Siran. Galati had been treating his thigh wound with his best spells and tonics to no avail. And now the fool had gone and died, and for what? To be buried too soon in a ridiculous coat. "I suppose they will blame me."

"Many will."

"What was a plowman even doing in the Wild Fields? He was not meant to be a warrior."

"Nor was I when I arrived. Who among us really is? True, Siran might have tilled a field somewhere in the west. But he asked to join the kara so he might become a warrior and one day avenge his father killed in an Agathyrsi raid. He wore his slain father's bloodstained coat as a daily reminder of his vow. You cannot begrudge him this."

"We'd all be better off if he'd lived to satisfy his vow." Angry as I was with him, I wished Aric was here now. "What's to be done?"

"I do not know there is anything to do. I just thought you should know. And be ready."

"I'm no good to anyone, am I? Why am I even here?" I mused aloud. I could find nothing hopeful about this morning. "Would it be best for Aric if I just left?"

"Well, of course, you mustn't leave until you take a scalp," he said with a knowing twitch of his eyebrow. "As for what is best, are you not supposed to be an oracle?"

"That's what they keep telling me. But I can't see what road I'm meant to be on."

"Maybe oracles are not allowed to see their own road? But I believe signs point to such things if one is willing to see them.

Where I come from, we have a story about a sea captain and his crew who find themselves lost for many hard years when returning home from a long war. Much of their trouble comes because they ignore the portents out of foolishness and arrogance. Some believe they can outwit the gods."

"Does he ever find his way?"

He scraped the bottom of the cauldron and handed me a bowl of lentil, onion, and mutton stew that had lain simmering in the bottom all night. When one was hungry, nothing tasted better than a well-simmered stew.

"It's a long story."

"I've got all day."

With a bowl in his lap, he sat to tell me stories from his homeland all morning as we ate. We spoke of the sea, his family, his childhood in Athenai, and finally, how he came to be in Skythia.

"When I was a boy of about eight or nine winters, my father, an educated man but not a citizen of Athenai, decided he would move our family to the colonies. They offer great opportunities for people like my parents. I had a wealthy uncle who had made his fortune in Nikonion, and he persuaded my parents they should venture there and do the same. He offered to foster me, and with what little money they had saved, my parents sent me on ahead to stay with him until they could follow. I was in my uncle's household for less than a year when my parents set sail for the port of Nikonion. But the Skythian Sea is known for its storms. Their ship was lost at sea."

He said it in the same manner as one who'd accidentally dropped a coin in the river, watched it disappear beyond reach, shrugged, and thought on it no more.

"That's awful. What did you do?"

"I was a child. What could I do? My uncle, realizing there'd be no further payment coming his way and not wishing to be stuck with me, sold me as a slave."

He related this, too, simply and without sentiment, as if he were reporting the weather outside. He tossed a frozen fuel brick on the fire, and it crackled and hissed for a moment before beginning to burn.

"But you're a free man? Did you escape or slay your master?"

"Slay him? No. My master paid honestly for me. He provided me a warm place to sleep and fed me well. He had a shipping company, and because I had some schooling, I came to manage his warehouses and the loading and unloading of his ships. It was respectable work. I harbored him no ill will. And I found *other* ways to earn. When I had saved enough, I bought my freedom. Once free, I went in search of my faithless uncle. Now," he shrugged, "I have no kin. And I cannot return to that world. So, I sought the court of Ariapaithi to see if he had use of me. I can read and spell Greek words. I know their ways and laws. But, as fate determined, Aric saw a different purpose for me. The gods led me here, and here I have been ever since. Likewise, they will reveal their purpose for you when the moment is right."

ARIC DID NOT CEASE his vigil for three days, and no one approached or disturbed him while he sat beside his fire. I resumed my duties slowly, sometimes looking to the rise where he sat huddled and hungry in the cold. At night, it glowed like a beacon above the camp as we dined and went to our beds. The men were strangely silent about the absence of their karadar, but they cast anxious glances toward the north, as did I. What he did there, I didn't know. But why he did it, I could guess. I alone, perhaps.

It was long after dark on the third day when Aric finally returned. Crusted with snow, he smelled of campfire, artemisia, and the cannabis tent. Antisthenes and I were already in our beds. With my face turned toward the fire, soaking every bit of its warmth, I pretended to sleep as he stripped off his wet clothes and lay down without a word. But my mind flooded with questions, worries, designs. For days, the words had dammed up in me.

I lay still a long while, watching the bricks of the fire burn. When I closed my eyes, the ghosts of the flames remained behind my eyelids, seared into my vision. I turned onto my back and stared at the empty shadows on the ceiling to try to wash them away in darkness, but the flames still shimmered in front of my eyes. When I closed my lids, all I heard was his soft breathing beside me. Beneath the blankets, I slid my hand toward his. Between our beds, my fingertips found not warm flesh but cold iron. The sword lay between us once more.

THE FOLLOWING DAY, the sun was a shadow in the sky as the air filled with fleecy snow, cloaking the whole of the earth in thick, barren white. The streams had frozen, leaving us to hack at the ice with our axes to make spaces for the horses to drink. We spent the morning fighting the ice as it rushed to freeze again over the surface. The horses licked and pawed relentlessly at the snow, trying to find a stingy blade of grass to nibble. We packed the snow into the cauldrons to save us from carrying water from the river for ourselves.

Watches resumed after the storm broke, our eyes always sharp for quarry to fill our cauldrons. Standing on a knoll above a creek that fed the river, I searched the shadows of a covert, looking for tracks in the snow. A small stand of wood grew at the juncture of creek and river, and around its edges formed a tangle of bramble and a long expanse of brittle, thigh-high grass, dun-colored and coarse. A small trail of trampled grass pushed into a break in the underbrush. It was the perfect place for animals to seek shelter, for deer to bed down in the day, unseen.

Into my mind, unbidden, crept the image of the two of *us* hidden there crouched upon our knees. His weight pressed against me—his ragged breath in my ear. My skin warmed beneath my heavy coat as the icy wind tore at my face.

"Everything all right?" Aric broke my ignoble reverie.

357

Hearing his voice for the first time stung me like the bitter wind.

"I was taken with a vision," I said, keeping my eyes forward so as not to meet his.

"Of the future?" He asked warily.

"The past. We should keep riding." I kicked on past the covert and past him. I couldn't allow myself to become distracted. There was still work to be done.

Rumors had already begun to fly, though not the ones I feared. These were perhaps worse. Why, some wondered, was I not dead? What kind of woman drowns in a freezing river and returns to life? Word had spread through the camp that Aric had pulled my frozen corpse from the ice. And somehow, the hamazan witch had risen from the dead—just as poor Siran had expired from the cruel wound she dealt him. Aric did nothing to allay their suspicions with his strange behavior on the hill by his fire. Following Antisthenes's lead, I tried to resume my duties and avoid joining the ranks of madness.

I AWOKE TO A FULL MOON on the western horizon, still visible at dawn. It hung above the ridge like a giant's silver coin tossed into the air and frozen in the blue haze of early morning. The daybreak was crisp and the sky clear, but the gloom didn't seem to lift.

Whenever I needed a confidant's trusted ear, I sought out the only friends who never betrayed, judged, or chastised. I tacked Sakha and headed to the edge of the forest, where I had found the herd that night. Much of the storm's destruction lay under new snowfall, but the fallen and cracked trees were stark reminders of its fury. I thought I'd begun to know this place but could still lose my way and stumble into harm.

In spring, there was commotion in the fields, the grass aflutter with the mating dance of insects and the love songs of birds. A riot of innocence and joy all beneath my feet. I bent my ear to listen, envious of its ease. Why was our life not like this? Why was everything so fraught? I wanted to be like the insects humming in the sward, unaware of the boot descending. But this was winter. Life in the meadow was in arrest. If there were signs, I was blind to them. I would have to choose.

I'd fulfilled my duty. Now I'd become a burden—a liability. That was the last thing I ever wanted. I knew I'd make enemies here, but he must never become one of them. It was finally time to take my scalp and go. I would tell him in the morning.

I'd turned toward home when I noticed a black speck moving on the horizon. A lone rider on a dark horse approached from the west. The sun's glare on the snow made it impossible to identify him from this distance. I withdrew my bow, uncertain whether I should fly for home, wait for a glimpse of the approaching rider, or something more direct. He nudged his horse into a canter and rode straight for me. I might not outrun an arrow even if I turned and ran.

Shit. I withdrew a handful of arrows from my quiver and fitted one to my string but did not draw. As the hooded rider came closer into view, his hands appeared empty. He let his hood fall back, unshading his face from the noon sun and revealing a worn fox-skin cap with long earflaps and, jutting from beneath it, sun-colored hair and flame-colored beard. A dark shadow filled his left eye. Breathing deeply, I lowered my bow and stuffed my arrows into their quiver. Footsteps crunched through the newly fallen snow as his horse drew closer, and he broke to a trot. He dismounted his horse before me. Maybe I wouldn't have to wait to tell him.

"You've traveled far to find me here."

"You shouldn't be out here alone. The ice is still thin." He smiled but did not look me in the eye. His cheeks were red with the cold, which turned his eye a brilliant crystal blue.

I dismounted, too, and stood with my back against Sakha's shoulder, not wanting to speak.

In an eager rush, he stepped closer, clasping my face in his hands before pressing his lips to mine in a feverish kiss. And then, he bent his brow to mine, his eye closed, and whispered, "I've been waiting so long to do that, now nobody's watching." Pulling away, he brushed my hair from my forehead while I stood dumbfounded. His face darkened. "Is something wrong?"

"No, I—I'm only surprised."

"Why?" he frowned.

"I guess I just thought you were—" A lump welled in my throat.

"Being overly cautious? Maybe I am."

"I was going to say 'ashamed.'" I couldn't look him in the face.

He took my face in his hands again and raised it so I would have to look him in the eye. "*Never*," he said with such vehemence I almost believed him. His tone softened, and he looked down at his boots and spoke into my cloak. "It may not have been right," he said, "but I don't regret it," though his voice trembled.

"But what about your father?"

He drew back, hooking his thumbs in his warbelt. "What about him?" he said flippantly, his jaw set defiantly as he spoke. "Does he ever think of us? We live our lives for him. We serve, we sacrifice. What do we get in return?"

I shook my head. It disturbed me to hear him speak this way, even as I struggled to imagine what benefit any of us gained from blindly doing the king's bidding—especially Aric.

"What are you saying?"

"I'm saying you were right: our first loyalty is to one another and the kara. If you wish it, I will speak to my father—speak to yours. I would take your hand in good faith. You would be our satanaya."

I found myself with fists full of his coat as I pulled him close again. Was such a thing even possible? My barren winter began to thaw, and the sun broke through my grey sky.

"Do you really think we can?" My heart raced. "Should I bring my scalp?" My thoughts came faster than my mouth could form questions, and none of them made much sense. But real hope had dared to awaken in me for the first time in a long while. I didn't even try to conceal my excitement.

"Then you would?" He sounded more shocked than I.

"*I would.*" My words sounded distant and strange, as if someone else was speaking them. "Of course I would."

"I won't be a king," he warned, raising his brows, his voice grave. "You won't be a queen."

"I never wanted that anyway. I want this," I raised my eyes to the clear sky over our heads.

A wide grin broke across his face, dimpling his cheeks and wrinkling his eyes. He grew so giddy he looked like he might burst out with laughter. "Then I'll petition the king at Rathadin," his eye ignited. "We'll speak more when we can be alone. Until then." Furtively, he glanced about and stole another kiss before pulling away and swinging up onto his horse.

A bitter wind tore at me, but it was like the sun on my flushed face as I watched him go.

CHAPTER 38

WHEEL

*It's said that a bird's territory reaches only
as far as his song.*

"Does it look like snow?" Aric asked, shielding his eye from the silver glare of the overcast sky.

"If it snows," I said, "it should not be much." The air was crisp and dry, but the brisk wind made me think the clouds would blow over.

"We should have left two days ago," Aric said, unusually fretful. Perhaps he was just anxious, as I was. It would take at least a fortnight to reach the feasting grounds at Gerrhi, where the Rathadin festival took place each Midwinter.

"You said the festival lasts two weeks. We can surely miss a day here or there."

"We mustn't be late." He swiveled around in his saddle, looked back at the slow-moving procession and frowned. The vazarka rode at the head of a long train of wagons, cattle, and warriors. "Once Rathadin begins, no wheels may turn. Not a millstone, nor potter's wheel, nor spindle."

I turned to survey the line of wagons as well. Unlike the court's wagons, we kept no runners to replace our wheels when the snow became deep, wanting no excess bulk to carry through three seasons. With Aric preparing to petition the king on our behalf, I'd never been so eager to reach court. The thought of waiting another fortnight before learning our fate seemed almost unbearable.

Rathadin was the year's longest festival. As the Midwinter solstice drew near, it marked the turning year in the Skythian calendar, though I was warned it was a fraught time. Since the night season began, the men spoke excitedly about a ritual nighttime ride. I never heeded ghost stories, but it was easy, on long nights when the wind howled, to believe spirits might be prowling about the places untouched by light.

"Tell me about it—the Hunt," I said to Aric, hugging myself close against the sharpening winds.

"Ah, this will be your first," he said. "Well, Rathadin is like two sides of a coin. The sun has two faces, one light and one dark. The sun's dark face turns toward us more in this portion of the year than the bright. When he reaches the farthest end of the earth, he turns his face and travels back over the earth, casting his glow elsewhere and leaving us in darkness for a time. These journeys vary in span as the sun traverses his realms, and we must await his return to ours when he will let fall his light upon us and bring life back to the land."

"They say it is the most sacred season of the Skythai."

"I think of Rathadin as a dream. Time passes differently for the gods, the way the lifespan of a man is greater than that of a butterfly. So it is with Gœtosura. A day of ours is a single blink of his mighty eye. And our year is but his day. At the end of that great day, he veils his tired eyes and sleeps. We are suspended for a time in his dream."

"How can that be?" I asked. "The sun still rises each day, even at Midwinter. And the Moon still follows its regular courses."

"We live inside two years—one of sun and one of moon—like the two axles of a wagon—one wheel large and the other smaller—turning individually, but over the same ground. The wheels mark slightly different tracks. And as the year prepares to turn over, between them lies a valley—a dream. And in this valley lies twelve days of chaos. A nightmare, perhaps. With no one to keep watch, the shades of that other realm rise and cross the Volos River into our land. And there is nothing to stop them—no light to make them shy away, no order to rein back the hosts from beyond. The wheel of time stops, and, for those few days, we dwell inside the dreams of Gœtosura. And the spirits, at times, may dwell inside us."

"And what's that to do with the Hunt?"

Aric tugged the long flaps of his cap down snug around his ears. "In some ways," he said, "it's the reason the kara exist. The Fathers return to the world they helped create to take stock of our steward-ship. To see how we have honored all they've bequeathed to us. For it is through us they are made immortal. Have they been honored by our remembrances? Are they proud of our achievements? It falls to the kara to safeguard and sustain what they have begun. And it is through us that they receive sacrifices. They who dwell in the earth decide whether we are worthy to receive its bounty."

FLURRIES FELL throughout our two-week trek, but the snow Aric feared never came to hinder our journey. The court was still being assembled when we arrived at the fort, and Aric went in search of Ariapaithi to make our plea. To keep my nerves from fraying as I waited for his answer, I sought Erman, hoping perhaps to steal a few moments of his time. Maybe I could *tell* him? Like a cow waiting to be milked, I wanted to unburden myself of all my latest hopes and worries.

Reaching out in the frosty wind just after noon, my hand to-ward his door, I listened in the solemn stillness for the distinct sound of his irregular movement, for the whisper of life. I knocked. Nothing. I took a deep breath and pushed the door aside to peer in.

Erman sat in meditation. His eyes were closed, but the lids, like his lips, were slightly parted. I studied him in wonder. What did he see in this half-dreaming state?

"Anaiti," he spoke, motionless, "come sit with me."

Stepping out of my boots beside the door, I tiptoed over. He fluttered his eyes open and smiled gently. "It's good to see you. Are you looking forward to the celebrations tonight?"

"I suppose," I said, sitting cross-legged before him on the carpet, the gaming board between us as always.

"That doesn't sound like a festive attitude," he sniggered.

"You know how I hate smiling for the courtiers."

"Well, I'll be singing tonight. Hopefully, you won't have to pretend."

Strange, come to think of it, that I'd seen the lyres and fiddle hung on his wall but never heard him so much as hum a tune. "What will you be singing?"

"It's a waking song for the dead—to call the sun from the dark realm."

"Oh, is that all?" I asked with a smirk.

His deepened voice resounded as he lowered his chin and fixed me with a stern stare. "You'll have to wait and see." Tucking his hands into the sleeves of his caftan, he grinned cryptically. "But now I've been waiting to hear about your adventures since I last saw you. You have much to tell."

I decided not to read too much into that. "Have *you* had any adventures since I left you?"

"*Me?* Ha! No, this," he raised his palms to the ceiling of the felt-house, "is the extent of my world."

"There must be more to your days than sitting here in your tent. You are the seer to the king."

"I hear the odd story now and then . . . ," he trailed off. "There are rumors that Aric consults you now as his seeress. That you're a real soothsayer, and he scarcely makes a move without asking for your divination first."

I stared into his black, cavernous pupils, wondering what they saw when they looked at me. "You certainly hear a lot of gossip."

"Gossip is often true," he smirked playfully.

"And more often, it's horseshit."

Clapping his hands together, he snickered. "So true. But does he not place quite a bit of faith in you?"

"Is he wrong to do so? Is his faith in me misplaced?"

He shook his head. "My apologies."

"No, you're right. He places too much trust in me."

"Aric may often be unbridled, but he is seldom careless. Have faith in his faith. Be humble but proud. Against many odds, you've earned the trust of worthy men. I know something of this."

Erman's life fascinated me, but I never dared to ask him how he ended up here, as an anarei of all things. It always seemed he did the asking. "How, if I may, did you come to be Chief Diviner to the High King of the Skythai?"

"The Skythai are generally not fond of priests and shun castes of men who would exert their influence through access to sacred rites. You may have noticed there is no formal priesthood in this country. Learned men may ply their skill as lawspeakers, healers, and sacrificers, but their kind holds no special sway in court. More often, common seers give answers to vexing questions and heal men's spirits when they wander or are attacked by sorcery. I am of the Agari, famous for our soothsayers. Though we're best known for our knowledge of poisons and their antidotes," again he chuckled to himself as if the novelty of the fact had just struck him for the first time. "My family were mere shepherds in a smallholding north of the Swamp of Maeotis. It's an unlikely road I have traveled to find myself here."

"You seem young for one so accomplished and . . . influential."

"I'm often surprised myself. When I had about nine winters, I helped to tend the sheep. A storm blew up from nowhere, and before I could flee to shelter, I was struck by one of Papahio's bolts.

I should have died, I suppose. When the heavenly fire smote me, the entire camp danced around me in a circle where they found me, singing as I lay upon the ground, roasted like a lamb on a spit. I can still see them in my mind, hovering like vultures. Being soothsayers, my tribesmen were keen watchers for portents. Any man, beast, or tree so struck was forever deemed sacred—too sacred for contact with the camp's profane affairs. Those left alive were sent into the wilds to dwell with Artimpasa, far from the taint of daily life."

"That sounds more like exile than consecration," I said.

"Oh, indeed, I was so bloody sacred I was untouchable. No one would look at me, much less speak to me, for fear of incurring some moral curse. It is a plague worse than leprosy to be held so sacrosanct. No one wants the burden of something so precious, so inviolable within their midst. So, they set me on the road into the wilds with our flock, which I had been tending. These were also marked so that no one would harm them. With our stock barred from slaughter, milking, or shearing, my family was left destitute. We had no choice but to sell the sheep in the colonies—for a tenth of their worth—and go to the city in search of work. A traveling sage, Master Artabanu, met us on the road."

"I know that name. Aric speaks of him sometimes."

"He was Aric's master as well. All the young karik must study with the masters during the night season.

"My mother offered Artabanu what little she had left of her dowry and begged him to take me in fosterage. He refused payment, and we left that morning for the sanctuary here in Gerrhos. He called me Erman after the one whose pillar draws the heavenly fire."

"So, Erman is not your given name?"

"It's the only name I want," he pressed his lips together and wiped his nose on his sleeve.

"You might have done anything. What led you to this manner of devotion?"

"It is through Artimpasa that gods and men learned to divine.

But I will tell you something I have never told another. I also chose this path because I saw a way to become both of great good to many and indispensable to a great family. Many masters come from learned families. They have great wealth, power, and influence. Like all men, they seek more. They seek to secure influence and wealth for their heirs. I have no heirs. And therefore, the king places his trust in me above all. For myself, I have no earthly ambitions or desires. I am a man yet may inhabit a woman's domain. And I live beyond the laws of both. I have nothing chaining me to this world and nothing but wisdom and faith guiding my hand. I have the absolute trust of the king and the freedom to travel this entire kingly realm—and beyond, gods permitting. Small sacrifices, great gains. Do you see?"

"When you speak that way, it makes perfect sense."

I stared at the gaming board between us, its colored squares empty and meaningless to me. I'd looked at the board so many times, and it only now occurred to me that I didn't know what the game was or how to play it.

"How did you come to be at the court of Ariapaithi?"

"You wonder why the king chose me from among all the sacrificers, lawspeakers, and seers? The answer is simple. All the other priests prophesied that Spargapaithi would be the next king. Spargapaithi was a brutal warlord with many victories, but a coldblooded leader with no foresight. His own men despised him. But many anareis feared his power. Ariapaithi, however, was judicious and had the love of his followers. I foretold that he would not only become king but that he would unite the tribes west of the Volosdanu. I was little more than a child then, but I was the only one who spoke in support of Ariapaithi—who saw what he'd become and what could be. With help, the king's brother was soon driven out, Ariapaithi was victorious, and what I foretold has come to pass. After that, he trusted only me to prophecy for him."

"Does what you foretell always come to pass?"

"It does. As you will learn, good prophecy is less about what is ordained by the gods and more about what is manifest in men. If you watch closely, speak prudently, and keep the company of predictable men, your prophecies will also come to pass. Tell me, Anaiti, about your visions. What do you see when you look beyond sight?"

"Nothing. I see nothing. It is like trying to catch a fish with my bare hands. It always slips through my fingers before I can take hold of it."

He wrapped my hands in his long, white fingers—rough and calloused for one who did no heavy labor. "And what do you *feel*?"

"I feel . . . I've been molded in too-soft clay and can't hold my form. Like the world around me is new and unfamiliar; even my flesh is loose and strange on me," I wanted to wipe my eyes, but he would not release my hands. "But soon, it subsides. For days after, I still feel strange, as if a darkness hangs over me or a shadow follows. Do you think it is a malicious daimon?"

"Not at all," he assured me. "No, Anaiti, quite the opposite. What you feel is quite natural among true seers. You are blessed with a gift. Most must fast, drink potions, inhale vapors, dance for hours without rest, or perform painful rites to experience what you do. Now, it must be harnessed and trained."

"So Aric tells me. But to what end? What purpose does it serve?"

"None can tell you that. It's your sign to interpret. It may serve no purpose than to test you, strengthen your will, or pose questions you might never ask. Be wary of those who claim to know what cannot be known. And, no more than you'd show strangers where you hide your gold, never speak the names of your fears to others."

"Aric knows."

"He's different."

"Different how?"

He shrugged and released my hands. "For good or ill, he doesn't fear what most men fear. I suspect he's seen with other eyes himself."

Erman invited me to share his bread, cooling beside the fire, and mead from the jars on his many shelves. That afternoon, my education in divination began in earnest.

WE WOULD FEAST after sunset in Ariapaithi's Great Hall, under the massive pavilion I'd entered when I arrived here half a year ago. Erected on the high ground between the two smaller rivers, it sat beneath the king's stronghold, secluded from the bustle of the fort. Its walls were lined with plush cushions, the great hearth roared between the four pillars that held up the roof, and honored guests of the king bowed themselves as they ducked through the doorflap and entered. As we waited for festivities to begin, I wandered inside the crowded tent and found Olgas near the jugs of wine, looking unusually sharp in his new red woolen caftan and trousers. A tall, lanky man, his clothes usually hung awkwardly off his thin frame, but this suit was perfectly tailored. Even his shaggy black hair was tied neatly back for the occasion, and his thin, black beard had been well-combed.

"Olgas, I nearly mistook you for a king! Look at you," I smiled and gently shoved him.

His face turned red as he suppressed a grin and offered to refill my drinking horn. "We'd better just bring the whole thing," he said, grabbing a handled bucket and ladle as he led me toward the hearth. Around it on leather-slung benches sat Stormai, Gohar, Antisthenes, and Bornon, washed, combed, and dressed in all their best attire and adornments of gold. Aric had not yet arrived.

"Look who I found," Olgas said as we joined the others.

"Don't let me interrupt you." I sat with Gohar and Antisthenes.

"We were just discussing news of the colonies," Gohar said, flashing his luminous green eyes upon me as I sat beside him. "It seems war will likely break out between Athenai and Lacedaemon."

"Most Hellenic colonies have ties to Athenai, do they not? What are their motherland's prospects?" I asked.

"Thanks to us," Bornon said, "and the grain and timbers from tribes like yours, and the iron, meat, cheese, and leather we provide, they should be well supplied to fight a war. But hopefully, it won't come to that."

"Do they rely so much on Skythia?" I asked of Antisthenes, who'd spent his youth, at least, in Athenai and even longer in the colonies.

"The country is not a vast land like this," Antisthenes said, his dry tone more somber than usual. "There are countless islands and long coasts. Summers are hot and dry. Many are sea people, as, beyond the city, much of the land is mountainous, rocky, and arid, unsuitable for plowing or grazing. Worse, it is overrun with people who spill out onto these shores. There will always be these petty wars—or threats of them, at least. Perhaps this one will come to nothing." As he spoke, he cast his eyes toward the luxurious carpets, spinning his cup in his hands. "Much of their grain is imported from us—slaves as well. There are more slaves in Athenai than citizens, many of whom are captives of Skythai wars—too many to feed from the land and sea alone. I don't know what will happen to them if food can no longer reach the city."

"Well, I am sad for them all," I said, "Athenai and Lacedaemon. And I hope, if they must fight, the war ends quickly." I didn't know the causes or the politics, who was right or wrong—if anyone. I just knew a lot of people would suffer, including the Skythai. Should we support the colonies? Perhaps for no other reason than our interest. It was not our fight, yet it seemed inevitable that we, too, would pay a price—for choosing sides, remaining neutral, or profiting from it. There was seldom a right course, only a less wrong one.

"All this talk of war is depressing," Olgas said, throwing more fuel bricks into the fire. In agreement, we all drank in unison.

BEFORE THE FEASTING could commence, Erman, the other anareis, and the court bards gathered before the great hearth to perform music and sing. I'd never had occasion to hear Erman sing. Now, he stood at the center of the circle formed by other priests and priestesses. Small oil lamps suspended from the high roof lit the dim, smoky tent. His clean-shaven face was painted with glistening white lead, and his long, dark hair hung loosely about his shoulders. He wore a white dress, the heavy skirt deeply pleated and stitched with swirls of gold threads. Instead of his simple staff, he carried a pole topped with a bronze figure of a raven, its wings outstretched and tiny bells dangling from it. The flames twisted behind him as he slowly began to move, thumping a steady rhythm with his staff, the bells jingling faintly. Softly, Erman murmured a wordless melody to himself.

Another anarei took hold of Erman's staff and picked up the beat, striking the bronze-capped butt on the hard-packed earth beneath the carpets. Several men stood to clap or slap their thighs in time to the drummer. I caught Aric's eye as he stood beside Ariapaithi, who clapped his hands in time with the beat. Erman cradled a simple wooden lyre, his fingers resting softly against the horsehair strings. He closed his eyes and rocked his head from side to side as he swayed to the rhythm of unheard music in his head. His feet began to stamp out a beat. He first strummed the four strings lightly, moving his fingers up and down along their length to change their notes. A hum rose from his throat, which morphed into words, and soon poetry formed on his lips as his whole form shook and swayed with the chanting of verses—both a song and a kind of incantation—in a language so archaic I couldn't understand. His clear, crisp voice was the swirling of pure water in a silver bowl, bright and clean. It rang through the room as he turned in his slow dance, spinning its light into every shadow.

Erman shuddered through a twisting dance like a flame blown by an unseen breath, like a fire stoked by unseen bellows, like a curl of smoke rising on a still day, unhurried and formless. Delicate notes dropped slowly at first, then built to a shower, pattering down.

Over a subtle pulse, like a heartbeat, steady and strong, the melody danced all around it. Then, the heartbeat stopped. It skipped a beat in anticipation. It fluttered, then stopped. The thrum of strings hummed on.

Misty and raw, the melody wore away an edge of me, and I began to erode, dissolve into the night. From the void into which the drumming beat, an echo began to answer. It picked up another beat as if joined by another heart and louder than before, steady as ever. It beat on—a flutter, a skip, then steadily on again. Over and over the cycle repeat, until finally spent, the pulse gave out. It came gently to rest as the melody died down to a single note, hanging expectantly in the air, then faded into the night like a final breath in our ears. I longed for it to go on and on, but there was only silence.

There Erman stood, thin and pale. His gently parted lips were like the rim of an earthen jar, and the mead of his words poured out. I was intoxicated, yet I wanted more. Belief had entered my ears, and the reverence these people showed him was genuine. Like the simple lyre in his hand, Erman was a humble instrument whose intrinsic beauty was only revealed when made to sing.

With his painted face ghostlike in the hearth light, his dew glistening on pale skin, he was not what I could see, touch, nor even comprehend in words—he stood for something utterly arcane and immanently present. Something Nameless. As the last remaining echo faded, there was a silence like none I had ever heard in a crowd. A mob of drunken, rowdy warriors one moment became transfixed and mute supplicants the next. Some shook with sobbing and wept silent tears.

Then, all at once, they broke loose. A roar shook the timbers of the tent and filled the room with more sound than its felt walls could contain. A shy, strange smile crossed the anarei's lips as the gathering erupted in cheers and howls.

He scratched his neck absentmindedly and lifted his eyes to

mine for just a flicker, then lowered his head again and wiped his nose on his sleeve.

It is said that a bird's territory reaches only as far as his song. I was convinced at that moment that Erman's song penetrated all the realms, living and dead.

CHAPTER 39

BRIDE

*Good, let them fear me. Let them finally have a
reason to despise me.*

I FELT DRUNK ALREADY and giddy, and I wanted only to feel the
warmth of a fire and sit beside friends. But the feast wouldn't
begin until the dancers did whatever dancers do. I tried to feign
a polite measure of interest as a giggling bunch of young, unspo-
ken-for girls were herded around in a circle, like cattle in a pen,
and made to prance, flailing their arms absurdly as they went.
Girls had no shame. Obnoxiously cheerful music played, in harsh
contrast to the solemn beauty of what had just passed, and they
made their sunwise procession as the people, especially the men,
gathered round to watch. I should probably pity them, except
that they hadn't the sense to know they were being appraised as
livestock. Or worse, they did, and they enjoyed it. They seemed
happy, the fools, and I thanked whatever thread of fate had let me
escape their ranks as I hurried past.

My stomach grumbled. Searching the crowd for Aric, I spotted him beside his father on the dais where the king and queen
oversaw festivities. Standing on my toes, I tried to catch his eye
in vain. Ariapaithi was pointing to one of the girls in the dance,

though what the use was, I couldn't imagine—they all looked the same. Nevertheless, Aric's eye followed. He nodded.

The music loudly rose and fell, and the dance was complete. As the squawking dancers scattered like geese before hounds, I fought through the crowd toward the dais to greet the king and speak with Aric. As I neared, I could hear them arguing, and immediately, I knew I had made a mistake in approaching. They ceased when they saw me, and it was too late to turn and make my escape. I proceeded forward toward the dais and offered a polite curtsey before the king. About to offer a greeting, I was interrupted when another man, with a young woman beside him, stepped forward onto the platform and addressed Ariapaithi first.

The man, clearly someone of status and self-importance, eyed me up and down and smirked. "Ha!" he said to Ariapaithi, "you keep an oiorpata at court! What next? Man-Eaters to dispatch your enemies and gryphons to guard your gold!"

I opened my mouth to speak but was interrupted by Ariapaithi. "This, my friend, is the daughter of King Arianta of the Bastarnai and Princess Mahasara of the Rokhalani. She is my honored guest. Also, my betrothed. Anaiti," he turned to me apologetically, "this is Spadak, King of the Borætai."

"My humble apologies, my lady," Spadak said theatrically. "It seems you and I are soon to be family," he said as he leered and raised a sarcastic eyebrow. "The royal prince will soon take my daughter's hand," he said, nodding toward Aric.

I tried to choke down my shock as I glanced at Aric. With his arms folded across his chest and his jaw set, he breathed like a bull through his nostrils, but he never raised his eye to mine. My eyes fell anew on the girl beside Spadak. She was a dark-haired beauty with the sly, mischievous look that all men were unaccountably drawn to. It must have taken three handmaidens to dress her for the evening and hoist her preposterous headdress into place. Even over the three men standing beside me, I could smell her pungent perfume. But this one was no faint foreigner. The Boraetai were powerful. They were said to be rich in cattle and had long ago seized control of the southwest's best grazing lands. Why should he refuse?

But sly and knowing though she may be, I caught the look on her face. The quiet terror behind her eyes. I knew that fear: it wasn't unfounded. When I first met Aric, I thought him a heartless savage. I soon learned the truth. There was no denying that, at times, he was more beast than man, more wolf than dog. The marches wrung the tameness from us all, leaving nature to work her sacred arts. Such instincts could be unnerving to behold, especially when I began to hear their voice within myself. Guile would not spare her nor prepare her for what followed.

"I wish you both good fortune," I lied dutifully and, before the primal fire in me could rise, turned to fight my way back through the crowd.

I COULD SAY I AVOIDED ARIC for the rest of the feast. That was my intention. However, it wasn't much of a feat, as he was nowhere to be found. The kara had feared I would weaken Aric, and perhaps they were right. If he lacked the guts to stand up to his father and reject this offer, could he ever fulfill his promises to me? Whatever hold Ariapaithi had over him was far more potent than any bond we two might share; that much was clear.

Good. Let the Boraetai bitch follow him into the marches to risk her hide, give him counsel, and salve his wounds. Let us see if the men would call her satanaya. I was done with it all.

Now that the Hunt was upon us, I went in search of the vazarka. I had no real sense of what was to come, but I was eager for it, whatever it may be. Ready to throw myself into service, or ritual, or battle, I needed a task—a purpose to set myself to.

I located them by their raucous laughter. I could always listen for the sounds of mirth, ribaldry, and song and find them engaged in some kind of mischief. Nestled in a covert just below the rapids, the vazarka and some older kara gathered around a stout campfire. From there came the sound of the rushing waters defying the freeze. I came bearing a jug of wine and some cheese I'd liberated from a feast table, and Bornon and Olgas invited me to join them by the fire while they planned their ride for the Hunt.

"What are you playing at?" I asked.

The men had spread a leather mat on the ground. On it was painted what looked like a four-spoked wheel, and they were casting knucklebones onto it.

"This is no game," said Bradak. "We're casting lots to determine our stations in the Hunt." Bradak clattered the bones inside his closed fists and rolled them onto the mat. He studied the scattered lots and nodded approvingly over the outcome.

"Should I wager, too?"

"The White Crow wishes to take a turn?" his brother Azarion asked eagerly. "To know what role the gods have in store for her?"

"Give me the bones."

I knelt with the others around the leather mat. I had no idea what I was rolling for, but I cupped the knucklebones in my hands and rolled them across my palms. As the men's voices grew louder, encouraging me with their cheers, I shook my hands harder. Then, I raised my arms with a flourish and dropped the bones onto the wheel.

The crowd went deathly silent. The cheers all stopped. I looked at the bones staring up from the mat. A sheep's knuckle is different and distinct on its four faces, and each face holds its value. The small, curved sides all faced up from the mat, each the same as the next. I'd rolled "ones."

"Is that good?" I asked, searching the crowd's silent faces. "What does it mean?"

"*The Dog*," said Bradak.

"We should let her roll again," Olgas murmured, glancing

nervously at Bornon, whose broad, scarred face darkened as he silently folded his arms. "It's her first time. No one rolls a dog on their first."

"Certainly not," Azarion said indignantly. "Men have wagered and lost their freedom—their lives even—on their first roll. It stands. She's gone to the dogs."

"Gone?" I began to worry now. "Gone where? What dogs?"

"I suppose it makes sense," Stormai said grudgingly. "She's a woman, after all."

"The Mistress has chosen her. It's fate," Mourdag added as if settling the matter.

"*No!*" a voice roared from above our seated circle, and I looked up to see Aric standing over the gathering, his face contorted in rage. Panic spread across the faces of the men like a bloodstain spreads on snow. "What have you done? How could you trick her into this?"

"We didn't trick her," Azarion leapt up to defend himself. "She took her turn, same as we all."

"She doesn't understand the laws," Aric barked at him, "or the consequences."

"What's happened?" I asked again, more forcefully now. I was no less confused, and my chest began to tighten.

"You rolled a *spaka*," Aric answered for them. "A bitch. You lost. Now, you must embody the Huntress."

"The Mistress herself? How is this a loss?"

"Think on it. Every misfortune of the coming year will be yours to own."

"And every blessing," I said.

"Trust me, they never remember you for the good you bring them," he scoffed. "But sure enough, they'll blame you for every ill. The Huntress chooses the living *and slain* in the coming year. And tomorrow night, she will wear *your* face."

He stared pointedly at me as if to frighten me, but the dread he hoped to instill in me never formed. *Good, let them fear me. Let them finally have a reason to despise me.*

Glowering, his eye swept slowly across the faces of the men, menacing each in turn. "These men know better. They should never have allowed this." He exhaled and shook his head. "But it's in the hands of the gods. Even I may be powerless to stop it now."

"I don't *want* you to stop it," I snapped.

Placing his hand on my arm, he leaned closer to lower his voice to my ear. "I need to speak with you . . . alone."

I flinched away from his grasp. "I have to make ready for the Hunt."

He frowned. "Let me help you prepare."

Prepare for what? A little ride around camp? His urgency was meant to frighten me—straight back into his arms. But I didn't need or want a protector any longer. Not at that price. "Like you said, it's in the hands of the gods now."

I HURRIED BACK to the wagons while the court prepared for more feasting. Night's shadows came quickly, and the warband's camp was silent and empty. The wagon where my secret scalp was stashed stood nearby. If I chose, I could announce myself after the Hunt and not return to the marches. I had a duty to become Ariapaithi's one day if Aric wouldn't fight for me. Was this that dreaded day? Would Aric release me from my oaths now if I chose to stay? I was at his mercy, and I hated him for it—hated myself for falling into such a trap.

While the feast began, I collected the scalp and rummaged through my packs in the wagon for the few items I'd cached. Carefully, I packed a leather satchel, telling myself I would be all right. This was not as bad as it seemed. But despite the stiffness in my spine and the hardness in my hands, I began to sob. I'd been a fool. Though I'd only been a child, my mother cautioned me not to let my heart run ahead blindly and choose my path—that it was like an eager but ill-trained dog, likely to trip its owner in its excitement. Shuddering with grief and rage, I rained blows upon the satchel and hurled it across the wagon.

Gathering up my scattered possessions one by one, I stuffed them in the pack and set it back in the corner, throwing a saddle blanket over it to hide its fullness. With my dagger, I pried up a deck plank at the front of the wagon, returned the scalp, and gently tapped it back in place. *Not yet. I have unfinished business still.* I wiped my eyes and prepared to join the ceremonies.

CHAPTER 40

HUNT

Amid the clamor of hungry fiends and the jaws of savage beasts, I saw a man among the monsters.

ASTING ITS LAST FULVOUS LIGHT up to the belly of the clouds, I watched the sun slowly sink toward the bleak horizon. The first night of the sacred festival would soon begin. The king strode out from his hall to meet the athravan who would perform the sacrifice. Oustana was an aged man, tall and solidly built for an elder, with precisely parted grey hair and a neatly clipped beard. He might have been mistaken for a spectator except that, like all holy men, he wore no ties in his long hair, and his undyed felt trousers and caftan were free of ornament, closed only with a simple leather belt and slide buckle of gold. His sheepskin boots also bore no knots or ties.

They stood near the makings of a massive fire. Over the stacks of fuel hung an enormous iron cauldron, big enough for four men to bathe comfortably inside. A bowshot from the cauldron, priestly attendants held a wide-eyed bull by his halter. His breath steamed forth in the night, and he bellowed as the sacrificer approached. The beast couldn't have known what awaited him, but by the look in his eye and the set in his shoulders, he suspected ill tidings. I didn't want to watch it. I'd seen my share of sacrifices, and they were none of them pleasant. I searched for an escape. But being with the warband had granted me the honor of being closest to the rite. If I fled, everyone would witness my leaving, and I could not afford to dishonor the sacred traditions of my hosts.

Another man in similar dress, the *zhotr* who presided over the rites, chanted holy words before the beast as Oustana placed a loop of rope around the bull's neck. The sacrificer looped another length of rope around the bull's pasterns, close to its hooves. Standing behind the bull, gripping the rope, he raised his left arm above his head. With his left leg bent, his foot no longer touched the earth. He shut his left eye tightly. In this strange manner—on one foot, arm raised, eye closed—the grey-haired athravan stood before all and waited. It was the king himself who spoke.

"Three hundred and sixty spokes there are," said Ariapaithi, speaking not to the crowd but addressing himself to the heavens, "all fixed to the nave of this everlasting wheel:

The Great Wheel has turned; the world has passed.
O Eternal One, immortal and unyielding,
By the Wheel's turning, the world is renewed.
By its passage, days rise and fall,
Seasons wax and wane, yet thy light endures.
We invoke thee, immortal Lord, bearer of wisdom, inspiration, and truth.
Even as the days have waned, never did we forget thee,
O Mighty One, as we began, so now we end. Do not forget us.
Bring us your light and ward off the darkness.
Bring us strength and ward off fear.
Bring us bounty and ward off hunger.
In awe, we tremble before your glory, O Lord,
And walk beneath thy watchful gaze.

With that, the sacrificer Oustana let his upraised hand fall like the downward stroke of an axe, and with it came the rope fixed to the forelegs of the bull. A hard tug pulled the loop tight so that the bull's legs were swiftly knocked from under it, throwing its shoulder down to the frozen ground. As the bull fell, Oustana shouted the name of Gœtosura and pounced upon the helpless animal, thrusting a stick under the loop of rope already about its neck. This the spry elder quickly began to twist, tightening the rope and strangling the startled animal within minutes. There was no blood, and the poor beast choked once but then went still and did not struggle. It was over quickly. Once dead, the bull was skinned, butchered, and its flesh placed in the cauldron to boil. Its meat would be distributed equally among the gathered tribes and clans.

As the sacrifice stewed, the novice sword dancers took their positions. In the marches, I learned that warriors' dancing is nothing like that of stockmen and farmers. For ordinary people, dancing was meant to impress, entice, or seduce. But our dance was free of conceit. It was not presentation; it was transformation. I recalled the endless hours of training in steps and flourishes of spears and swords to foster our swiftness in battle and delight the gods with our excellence. I fondly remembered the many drunken nights we linked arms, spun ourselves around the hearth, and sang just because it made our spirits light. And the time before the battle when we stamped our feet and clashed our spears on our shields, chanting ancient words to summon the burning chaos as we relinquished our names, our wills, our very selves to some unspeakable rapture. Tonight, the dance felt similar but not the same, maybe because I was just a spectator now.

"Where have you been?" Aric surprised me. I'd become so preoccupied with the sacrifice and the dancers I forgot to keep an eye out for him. "I've looked everywhere for you." He phrased it like an accusation. "Please," he softened his voice as he leaned closer, "may we speak before the Hunt tomorrow?"

"There's no need for you to concern yourself."

"There is. You've no idea what you've gotten yourself into."

I turned away from him, staring at the young sword dancers performing before the king and his queens. "I don't care." The dance paused as a roar rippled through those gathered in the field, flashing swords brandished high. The sun slipped below the horizon.

"Ana, don't be foolish. Allow me to do my duty by you."

With nightfall, the new day had begun. A chant arose from the celebrants as the mass joined the dance.

"Those words from you mean nothing now."

"Is that meant to hurt me?"

"Ha! Nothing hurts you, does it? And I suppose I should congratulate you. She's beautiful."

"I will not take her for a wife." He said it with such conviction I nearly believed it.

"Oh? And does Ariapaithi know this? What did he say when you declined? I'll bet he was disappointed. After all, this one's so perfect. Everything a man desires: petite, pretty . . . *pliant*."

He bit his lips and shook his head. "Wife or no, nothing changes between us."

"It's amusing that you should think so."

The dance concluded just as quickly as it had begun. All went silent as Oustana took the first offering of the flesh and liver of the bull, which had been carefully laid before him on a bed of dried grass and clover, and, while chanting a verse, consigned them to the holy fire. This signaled the commencement of the feast.

Aric moved to speak, but I shoved past him. "Go! Dine with your betrothed. I can find my own place."

AFTER THE LONG FEAST, the camp slept most of the short day in anticipation of the night's festivities. As the sun sank into the horizon, an order passed from the athravan through the camp that all fires must be extinguished and not relit again until the king's great fire was rekindled; from its flame, they would draw their first fire of the dawning year. The constellation of the Huntress rose in the southern sky to bless our rites.

A cold wind blew from the north as the warband massed in the pasture south of camp for the lighting of the king's fire, signifying the start of the ritual. Their bare skin had been painted like the dead, with ash or soot mixed with water. And they wore costumes of animal hides, evergreen boughs, and thatch, with masks representing all manner of underworld beasts, real and monstrous—wolves, stags, bears, goats, horses, and bulls prowled the grounds in wondrous and terrible hybrid forms.

My own costume was no less strange. Dressed in a gown of white felt lined in rabbit fur, the priests gave me a paste of gypsum to whiten my face and hands. Over my shoulders, I wore a short cape of carefully sewn falcon feathers secured with a golden eagle's talon. The dress had been made to fit a man but had laces to pull it snug and a sash of goatskin to cinch it about the waist. I wore a veil of long, silky white horsehair over my head and shoulders like a mane. Atop all this sat a circlet of ivy.

In a dress again, I had no weapons but the dagger I concealed in my linen undervest. A skirt always made me feel useless and vulnerable. How does one ride, run, or fend off an attack so encumbered?

A hand grabbed my arm from behind. I spun around, my hand going instinctively to my vest. It was Aric, though his face and hands were obscured in the darkness. Pulling free of his grip, I could feel the blade beneath my dress and pressed it close to my skin.

"I didn't mean to frighten you."

"You didn't." He shocked me, though. He stood dressed all in black—a belt, greaves, and boots all of black leather, a coat and trousers of shaggy black goatskin. He draped his grey-black wolf-skin around his shoulders. Soot blackened his hands, face, hair, and beard. Dark as dusk, he was barely visible as he moved among the shadows. Only the girdle of faded golden bast tied about his waist let any color escape. Beneath his arm, he held a mask. A helmet fitted with an animal skull and six-point antlers protruding from the top. In his other hand, he carried a stout staff. His goryt was absent from his side.

A horn sounded, and the doors of Ariapaithi's great felt-house were thrown open before the gathering. With a fire drill of wood, the High King of the Skythai lit the massive hearth between the four mighty pillars propping the hall's roof. In the dim light, a curl of smoke rose, and the king cupped the source of the smoke in his hands and fed it with his breath until it began to glow. To this, he added incense from a golden bowl—twigs of myrtle and herbs—and blew on it again until a flame sprang up. Sustainer of life, yet insatiable itself, fire lived unsparingly—terrible and benevolent, wild and tame, lethal and needful. No creature to conjure carelessly. All those who bore witness cheered. The festival had begun. From this fire, all the torches, bonfires, and cooking pits in the camps were rekindled.

Under the stars, a golden bowl glowed in the torchlight on an altar before the king. A horse's skull fixed to a staff moved through the crowd before me, borne by an unseen man bent beneath a white cloth. Ariapaithi wore full, bright armor—its polished bronze scales gleamed like golden dragon-hide in the light of the flames. He stretched himself tall, surveying those gathered around a now-blazing bonfire that stood in the center of the enclosure, with a trident clutched in his hand, its massive shaft braced on the frosty ground. Beside her husband, Queen Opœa sat bundled against the cold in a heavy cloak and crimson gown lined in grey wolf fur. Both sovereigns seemed weary.

The kara—also dressed in black, with wolfskin capes, wolf-skull headdresses, and ash-painted faces—took out their gilded cups and clamored to be near the bowl. The haomapaithi of the Paralatai, whose duty was to prepare, pour, and sing the praises of the haoma libation for gods and men, stood before the bowl, ready to dispense the pearly liquid.

The secret elixir—a union of vegetable and animal—was pressed from the stalks of ephedra plants and mixed with the sacred cow's milk. Haoma allowed warriors to soar like eagles above their bodies, made them move quick as lightning, and on a night such as this, it was said, could even let them gaze with the eyes of the Fathers upon the sacred realms.

Upon his big black gelding, Aric rode silently to the fore of the crowd in his coat of black goatskin, the horned mask under his arm. Isiras, too, wore a fantastic costume. A leather mask covered his face and head, and from it extended branching forms like antlers covered in white hide. From the tips of each tine sprang tufts of red hair that floated in the breeze like flames. The face of the mask was dyed blood red and embellished with ornaments of gold. Above the ears, on either side of the head, spread outstretched raven's wings. Isiras resembled the creature tattooed on Aric's right forearm and on nearly all the other men, along with much of the art that adorned objects in this place. When I'd asked him what the strange creature was, he called it Sreita, "Slider," the mount of Gœtosura as he ranges between worlds, granting his rider passage through the three realms. Many of the riders had dressed their horses in like fashion for this night.

Aric filled his cup and drank.

"We have the Master of the Hunt. Where is the Huntress?" Oustana called across the gathering of men. His well-organized rite would not be delayed.

Through the crush of fur- and leather-clad men, masked faces turned to watch me as I walked forward in my gown and cloak. These were all men I should know, yet I could recognize almost none with their faces painted and masked.

"A woman?" Oustana furrowed his brow and pouted as he turned to Aric. "An *actual* woman?"

"I also disapprove," he answered. "An unfortunate mishap. We'll choose another quickly and begin."

"This is indeed strange," the priest nodded slowly as he spoke. "This is the hamazan? Consecrated on Eramandin?" He pulled at his grey beard.

"She is," Aric answered grudgingly.

"Hmm." He fixed me in his gaze and blinked once. "Proceed."

Aric gritted his teeth and refused to look at me. He snatched Sakha's reins from my hands and reined back his antlered mount. The masked warriors stood silently, waiting as the crowd drew around in a circle. The haomapaithi presented me with a small cup filled with pale liquid. I was reluctant to take it, recalling how it had hastened the flight of my spirit from my body during the battle by the river. I glanced around me. Perhaps if I held it in my mouth, I could spit it out when I was out of sight. I took in the oddly smooth and sweet drink but did not swallow, repressing a gag as it sat on my tongue. There would be dire punishment for spewing the holy elixir onto the ground.

"Repeat after me, Lady Huntress," Oustana said:

The fathers are gathered around the golden chalice,
    granting strength;
Our sanctuary in times of trial,
    vast and bottomless.
A terrible Host with force of arms enduring,
    invincible and mighty,
They arise unflinching to fall upon the enemies of our people.

Shit. With a gulp, I swallowed the potion and repeated the words. Oustana followed the haomapaithi as he carried the golden bowl to the other warriors, who took their draughts in turn.

The sacrificed bull, which the party and gods had feasted upon last night, had been reassembled, bones and all, stuffed with straw, and sewn back into its hide. It stood before the king's hall, and as the last rays of the sunlight withdrew, Oustana handed me a golden spindle and ushered me forward to stand before it. He spread his arms wide and spoke an incantation over the bull, then he gestured to me to touch the beast with the wand.

The troupe of warriors gathered around me in a circle ten men deep. Nearly three hundred masked karik were joined by the novices for the night—and all had drunk their cups. They drew their swords. I glanced toward Aric, sitting on his horse and holding the reins of mine, yet a thousand miles away. Oustana spoke again.

> The elders say this about the Mistress:
> She is the chooser of the living and slain, both man and beast.
> Three times fifty riders shall come, but one leads them all:
> A Huntress, white-skinned and golden-haired beneath her helm,
> Her eyes burning like suns. Her horses shake their manes;
> Dew falls from them over the pastures to flood her sweet rivers.
> Hail to the Mistress, bestowing bounty upon the land.

A goatskin drum began slowly beating outside the men's circle. In time to the drumbeat, the masked warriors stamped their feet. A skin-and-reed pipe played a stern tune. Within the great throng of hides, horns, and painted skin, the small circle began to turn like the wheel of a chariot, with me as its hub. I could see each man as he stepped and leapt, cutting with his sword, playing with the last of the day's light on the edge of his blade. An army of shadows all thrusting and slashing at the night.

The rhythm of the song marched ever faster as the circle spun nearer. The dance grew more frantic, brushing closer and closer. Thrusts of swords gave way to shouts as the mass of warriors spiraled toward me at its center. The tempo turned to a gallop, and the dancers were no longer leaping so much as colliding, no longer stepping so much as stampeding. And in the riot of the music, they drifted to and fro, sometimes knocking into me, sometimes catching me with an elbow or shoulder, sometimes stepping on the hem of my dress or foot. I could do nothing but clutch the golden spindle to my breast and stand fast. The swaying crowd began to dislodge me and turn me around, and for a moment, I lost sight of where Aric stood, holding Sakha. Not that I could have escaped if I tried.

I planted my feet against the writhing mob, looking for a landmark to steer by, seeking out Aric on the whirling horizon. A horn blew, and the wheel slowly came to rest. All eyes trained on Aric enthroned upon his masked black steed. While we had been dancing, he had donned his mask. A wolf's skull was set upon his forehead and partially covered his face, its black pelt intact and draped down his back, its fangs stark and gleaming white in the moonlight. Two round, polished stones of red amber were set in the sockets of the eyes. Two gleaming antlers rose from either side of the skull, three points each and white like barren trees. He blew the horn again, and the men scattered like a flight of birds. Glancing down, I saw that the skirt of my white dress was now filthy and in tatters.

SAKHA, WHOSE NECK and quarters had been draped in pale doeskin, stood patiently. Where most horses would spook at the sight of a man with antlers, a dog's head, or his face peering out from between the jaws of a wolf, he was calm. He barely batted an eye, and I adored him for it.

With an ox horn on his belt and a staff in his hand, Aric reined his black gelding around to address the restless crowd, which cried out in a tremendous roar. He waited for the sound to subside before continuing.

The Wheel has turned; the world has passed.
The fathers who walked before us,
Who bequeathed wisdom and laws,
Who carved the land and bound it with oaths,

Return in this sacred season, unseen but ever-present.
By their hands, the order was set;
In the stones and soil, their legacy endures.
Be generous to them, and their favor shall abide.
Remember their names, and they shall not forget our deeds.
Let us honor them in word and in act.
In the pattern of their lives, let ours be shaped.
As we remember, so shall we be remembered.
As we give, so shall we receive.
None who have lived can truly die,
For the dead live again in us.

From behind their masks, the field let up a deep and savage roar, eerie and bestial like the cracking of a great mass of ice over water. The horses were ready to bolt with the excitement, and the men could not hold themselves in check much longer.

Aric raised the snout of the skull, resting the mask on his forehead, and peered out from beneath as he rode beside me. He thrust a blowing horn into my hand. "Take this and keep it close. As master, I ride at the fore, sounding a horn to lead the riders on and warn others that our Host is approaching. Ride slow and steady and keep to the road. Once we leave the camp, we follow the funeral road through the burial grounds. Do not stray from the road. And do not turn back until you reach the river. Follow the sound of my horn. If you are in danger, sound your horn three times."

"What danger?"

He stared at me blankly, which shook me more than any threat he could name.

"I will do my best to lead them on," he said, "but there is little you or I can do to control them. Do not get between the hunters and their quarry. And take this." He untied a leather pouch from his belt and placed it in my hand. It was heavy. "Give one at every home. For goodwill."

Inside, the purse was filled with tiny silver coins.

"You'll see. Once taken, there is no telling what the hunters might do."

"Taken by what?"

"Those you knew yesterday are not themselves tonight. We are all soon possessed. Remember this, if you can."

I hung the horn around my neck. "Three times?"

He nodded, the antlers upon his head swooping forward and back again. "Don't stray from the road. May the Mistress bless and keep you," he said anxiously and tugged at his rein to go.

A HORN SOUNDED in the distance, and the whole thing began to move. Like a pack of hounds at full cry, the troop traveled from east to west, making a terrible tumult as they rode forward, howling and shouting along the road from the sanctuary toward the barrows where the dead dwelt. Despite the cold, I felt a tingling in my blood, and dew formed across my skin. The moon arose, full and clear, and my vision of the riders grew starker in the crisp light. Yet, as my thoughts flew, I trusted nothing before my eyes. I saw horses upon three legs, wolves upon two, bears with men's faces between their jaws, and creatures wholly unknown to me but in dreams. I saw the army of wraiths writhing like a great black snake along the road before me. I heard a tremendous ringing of bells and clanging of pots, warning the living to clear the way for the dead, the profane for the sacred. I heard a terrible roar of voices shouting in babble, bestial howls, a throng of hooves, and a clanking of bones. The stench of decay and musk arose from the shaggy, ragged, and black hides. Antlers and horns of every shape cast shadows upon the ground like a naked forest on a winter's night. At intervals, the bellowing of a horn shattered the din, its trumpeting like the roar of a waking dragon lurking ahead in the darkness. I saw a seething river of souls, hordes of monstrosities born of fever and shadows, blood on the snow beside shattered spear shafts, and rusted swords lying in the mud; I saw the bones of heroes crumbling alone in a tomb. I saw twilight and dawn together and whispered irrational prayers as I trailed the unearthly procession.

Amid the clamor of hungry fiends and the jaws of savage beasts, I saw a man among the monsters. Tossed upon that sea, rising and falling on the black waves, I saw Aric's face. His eye was like the head of an arrow in flight, sharp and bright, pointed straight at my heart. Then he was gone—if he'd ever been there at all.

I held my breath as we approached the first house. A simple wagon, its occupants had left modest offerings hung from the hitching post outside while they wisely hid indoors—cheese, kumis, mead, and a small portion of beef. Azarion, his mask little more than a grey wolf-hide strapped to his back and ash smeared over his face and hands, was the first to arrive and claim these spoils, which he dispensed equally to his brother Bradak, dressed in a deerskin and stag mask. The rest of the Hunt moved on to the next house, and I readied a coin for the family. But Azarion pounded on the door demanding entrance.

Timidly, a gentle, sturdy-looking herdsman opened the door. Peering past the man, I listened as Azarion interrogated the weathered herdsman's restless wife and their three terrified young children about their chores and whether they kept up with their felt-making and milking, his voice booming through the night. A young boy of about six winters began to cry.

Azarion pointed his finger at me and told them, "You see her? If you do not do your milking and dung-gathering, she will come and drag you off among the dead. She will slit you open, pull out your guts, stuff you full of straw, and seal you up in a log forever!"

As he stomped from the wagon with a smirk, a young girl began to pray through her tears. "Mara of the Night, protect us. Do not harm me, nor carry me off, nor cut out my heart and stuff straw in its stead. By water and fire, Mother, I beg you and your companions to bless and protect us."

"You're a rotten shit, you know that?" I said to Azarion. "Why would you say such a thing to them?" Now, these good people would spend the year believing they'd been condemned.

He chuckled as he mounted his horse and rode past me toward the clamor ahead. I dismounted and walked to the door. Inside, the children all cowered behind their parents.

"Have no fear," I said. "I give you the Mistress's blessing," and laid three silver coins upon the doorsill.

Most of the others were more interested in collecting their spoils than harassing anyone and happily went on their way when they'd taken their fill. The masses of riders spread out over the camp, each to collect his own bounty, and I kept back a fair distance, let them finish their work, and left a coin where the goods were taken. Most households left modest offerings, as one would expect of people with simple means: some mead or wine, a dish of meat or cheese, some kumis or butter. Those who were generous found themselves unharmed. Those who'd been stingy might have had their stores raided or their property defaced. For those who were clearly poor, I offered an extra coin to supplement their winter stores, and for those who genuinely seemed miserly, well, the Host dealt with them as they saw fit.

The hunters didn't bother distributing the sacrifices equally, as they'd be glutted with food and drink by the night's end. Each grabbed what he could get his hands on, and the surplus would be shared out afterward. But some men are greedier, and some houses left better sacrifices than others. When it was discovered that one householder left a pitcher of fine Greek wine, three loaves of fresh bread, a jar of olive oil, and smoked fish, everyone had somehow seen it first, and the men began to brawl. The next house offered nothing so grand as this. A generous plate of beef, a wedge of cheese, and a bowl of kumis. Good Skythian fare, but lowly relative to that exotic feast the men had just come to blows over. Feeling slighted, they set about tearing down the second house.

After an hour or two, the riders had exhausted their offerings, and most were gathering far ahead in the cemetery. The remaining riders were mainly the youths who were left to clean up the remaining sacrifices from modest households around the camp's periphery. I was depositing coins at the last few houses when I heard screams and shouts from a tent. I put my heels to Sakha and galloped toward the sound. Before me, six hunters in their black masks and hides were growling as they tore the felt from the tent's frame. The biggest, boldest of them, wearing a boar's head and hide, leapt from his horse and, with a running start, threw himself against the lattice frame of the walls. He was no karik, dressed as he was, and neither were his companions. None wore the bast girdle we all did, even this night. With the beginnings of beards, they were at the age where boys began to believe they were men. Where they had come from, I couldn't say—sons of cattle-herders or farmers, perhaps—but it seemed they had come to take advantage of the festivities to engage in some mayhem of their own. When it rattled but didn't fall, their leader tried again. And again. It finally collapsed under the force of his blows, trapping the family inside against the opposite wall. Two others rushed to join in.

Pulling Sakha up before the felt-house, I shouted to them in my most commanding voice to cease and leave the tent be. I remembered the golden spindle the priest had given me and held it aloft like a scepter and commanded them to stand back and desist. At the order of the boar-headed boy, three others dismounted their horses, pulled the felt from the roof, and held fast, looking from me to their comrades nervously, awaiting a sign. Through the opening in the roof, I saw the elderly man hunkered down beneath the table bearing the altar, sheltering his frail wife beneath his arm.

The boar-headed boy who had broken down the wall struck the old man with his whip and laughed. Pulling the couple's coats from a peg on the wall, he dropped them into the fire. Then he untied his trousers and pissed on their hearth.

"Enough! Cease this destruction!" I foolishly leapt from Sakha's back and strode through the broken wall into the home.

The boar-headed boy laughed louder and more deliberately. Then he rushed at me, and the next thing I knew, all six were upon me, and I was on the ground. The stench of wine enveloped me as their bare hands clawed my every inch. Face-down on the cowhide carpets, I tucked my limbs close, knowing I could not fight all of them as they dragged me from the tent. I caught the old man's horrified eye and tossed the bag with the remaining coins to him as they hauled me out the door. Then I felt inside my undervest for the dagger, pressing its handle against my ribs for solace.

They dragged me to where they'd left their horses and cast me down on the frozen ground. They'd stopped to argue over where to take me and how to share me. I studied the youths' faces and listened to their voices, but I didn't recognize them from the marches. While they argued, I slithered toward the nearest horse and readied myself to grab the reins and leap onto its back. I tried to tuck up and hold my skirt so it wouldn't hinder me as I mounted. With a last glance to be sure none of them were looking, I made my move for the horse, sliding awkwardly into place with the skirt wrapped around my knees.

One of the boys shouted, and the boar-headed boy lunged for me again, trying to grasp my arm and pull me from the horse. This time, I was ready. The dagger in my hand, I plunged it down into his neck, his bright blood spraying onto my white dress, then drove my foot into his chest and shoved him to the ground. Tugging at the reins, I pushed the horse through the nearby herd, scattering them, then set off galloping and quickly made for the river, the other riderless horses following our lead. Once at the banks and far from the crazed Host, I put the horn to my lips and blew three loud, clear blasts.

CHAPTER 41

MARSH

The night echoed with the howls of men.

FROM THE BANKS OF THE RIVER, a multitude of tiny islands was visible out in the marsh. I could ride the horse to the closest of them, but I would leave tracks. Instead, I dismounted and, with a slap to his rump, chased the horse and his frightened companions into the night to throw the boys off my trail. Removing the cloak and holding it above my head, I pulled the fur-lined dress as high above the current as I could manage and quickly waded into the icy waters, crossing to a tiny island.

Hidden in the reeds, I closed my eyes and listened to the sounds of the hunt fading. Across the distance, the faint thrum of the churning rapids reached my ears. Random shrieks, howls, and wild laughter punctuated the lull. Now, every rustle in the leaves made my heart shudder, and I trained my thoughts on the soft murmur of the river.

The dagger still in my hand, I pushed through the underbrush and hunkered down at the base of an old willow tree whose bare branches offered no shelter but whose trunk—the largest thing on the tiny island—provided a buffer from the winds. I hoped the haoma's effects were slowly fading, as the powers it imparted—the keenness in my vision, the strength in my limbs—seeped away. My heart resumed a more measured pace, though my eyelids became a conscious chore. But I felt stranger and more delirious than ever. I had to remain alert and not let myself drift.

I wrapped the short cloak close around me. Shivering, heavy-lidded, I saw the world beyond in only bits and pieces, flickers of a heatless flame commingled with the droning roar of the burning pain as the familiar cold gnawed at my wet limbs. I feared one of my spells might intrude at any moment, and I tried to herd my thoughts and hold it at bay. Nothing here seemed real. Time seemed to blur as I struggled to capture images too slippery to hold. I drowsed and woke suddenly, like I'd nodded off beside a cozy fire, only to find myself in icy darkness, my limbs numb, my heart racing.

Then, I heard a rustling in the brush.

Crouching behind the tree trunk, I squeezed the dagger's handle. I wasn't afraid. I was ready to answer for it all.

But when I saw it, I did not fear it, the beast that came ashore. A wolf's face with gleaming red eyes, riding a horse with flaming horns. Fur matted with burdock and tangled with thorns. Horns casting branching shadows in the moonlight. Skin like the silver-grey bark of a beech.

Dismounting, it approached the tree and named me. *Anaiti.* A shrill scream in the distance shattered the brief silence, echoed, and faded in the mists of the marsh. Torchlights flickered past as gruff voices roared incomprehensible words beyond the edge of the waters. The snap of a branch nearby froze us both. It searched and smelled the night air but soon took the dagger from my hand and let it fall to the ground. I drifted away like an ember on a breeze.

Rotting leaves, brittle twigs, and vines armed with thorns spoke of things past, things unsalvageable. My thoughts groped for signs of greener things to come. And then the moon overhead ducked behind a dense cloud, and he was gone.

Only its breathing in the night air remained. I bent my ear

closer and reached out my hand. We moved together in a kind of dance. Lulled by the music in the vines. The marsh, the brambles, the beast, and I. Beneath starless skies and flitting wings, the night echoed with the howls of men. With the silent, inner wailing of something voiceless, ageless. And the untamed god of the marsh seethed around us, within us.

The cloud withdrew, and, by the moonlight, a shimmering frost clung to the leaves, the bark, the thorns. It clung to us.

IT WAS NOT YET DAWN when I opened my eyes again to see Aric's familiar face, smeared with wood ash and soot, next to me beneath an ancient willow tree. My head throbbed, and I blinked, hoping my blurred vision would clear. The night Erman had sung his waking song, I was sure I knew the melody, but I couldn't recall where I had heard it before. I'd hummed the tune to myself a hundred times. I didn't understand the words, but the melody haunted me for months. Now I remembered. Aric had sung that same song to me to wake me from my spells. He sang it now.

"It's not yet morning," I said groggily. "We don't have to be going so soon, do we?" The sky was brightening in the east but still dark, and my buzzing head had finally cleared of the wretched haoma. An antlered wolf mask lay at the base of the old willow, and the white cloak hung on a branch above it. But my skin still bore traces of white paint. "Or are you afraid of angry spirits prowling the dark?" I snickered, only half-joking.

"Not when I have you to protect me," he said, grinning.

I stood, brushing the dried leaves from my torn skirt, which fluttered a ghostly white in the grim cast of predawn. "Are you making fun of me?"

"Don't be silly. Why are you acting so strangely?" he asked.

I turned away, searching the darkness across the marsh, but saw and heard nothing. I told him what had happened with the boar-headed boy.

"What now?" I asked.

He rose to his feet and paced quietly, methodically, as he often did, like a wild beast who'd been confined. "That's two kills," he mused absently, his voice raspy with sleep. "But have no fear; you have not yet made your tally."

"But will I face punishment?" I asked, remembering Tarana.

He stood before me, and most of the soot had fallen away. Brushing his fingers softly over my hair, he let them rest warmly on my flushed cheeks. "Mayhem always breaks out during the Hunt. All who ride know the dangers. And those farm boys will not dare tell their story in the light of day." And then he pressed me close to his chest, my face buried in the shaggy black fur of his goatskin coat. "I'm only glad you're safe."

I released the breath I'd been holding as he spoke and pulled back just enough to look into his eye. "I wish we'd never returned to court. We've been cursed since the moment we arrived."

"Now you understand why I had to confess to the king—to temper the judgement of Thagimazda, who punishes oathbreakers."

"Confess!" I felt the heat of anger and panic rise in my chest. "Are you deranged? That's not what we agreed!"

"I swore before the king's hearth. What was I to do?"

"You will ruin us both with this." He thought he could please his father, and somehow, everything would be all right. But the king would never forgive either of us.

"You don't trust me?"

"Aric, I don't want to be angry anymore. But I grow weary of this. If the king will not concede, and you will not challenge him, then let it be over."

He frowned as if my words surprised him. "Is that really what you want?" He leaned back against the tree as he watched me.

I walked across the little plot of land between the brambles, turning away so he would not see me bite my lip and blink away the tears welling in my eyes.

"You were right last night," I said. "I shouldn't be here. Look at me, here in hiding. I've failed."

"You—*we* are here because some things are beyond our control. You did nothing wrong."

I stopped and turned, staring at him with my eyes stinging. "I ran."

"You *survived*. The wise warrior knows which fights are winnable." There was an unfamiliar resignation in his voice. "I am the fool. Thinking, after all I've sacrificed for him, that I'd earned some grace with my father. I should've known. He will never yield, not even for me. He's a stubborn, overbearing old man used to getting his way. And once Ariapaithi has entered into a covenant, he'll never be the one to renege on it. This is what comes of trying to do the honorable thing. He used it against me, saying if I was now willing to wed, there was no reason I shouldn't accept his choice." He slid down the tree trunk until he sat cross-legged at its roots, resting his elbows on his knees and his forehead on his palms. "Why must things be so complicated? Surely there was a time when life was simpler than this?"

"This longing for simplicity is the curse of our nature. The Rokhalani believe that at the beginning of time, before the world took shape, heaven and earth were formless, swirling as in a vast cauldron where everything originated and where everything will end." I began again to pace. "All were one being then. And this form slept in bliss beneath the waters, dreaming. Then, it stirred from its peaceful slumber. When it awoke, it emerged from the deep and realized it was alone in the chaos. It cried out in longing with such force that it split itself in two: one male, one female, each forming the dome of the sky and the body of the earth." I stood again before him, and he finally raised his eye to mine. "The sky sent storms—winds and lightning and rain to embrace his mistress, the earth, and through their coupling, they brought forth all the plants and creatures, giving birth to the abundance of nature. But since then, they and all the wondrous things they've made have been diminished—only half-formed follies, longing to recreate the first—to be whole again, to be one."

"You torment me," he said, a deep frown distorting his eye.

"I don't mean to," I said, suppressing a smile.

Seizing hold of my hands in his sweating palms, he whispered, "Don't stop," as he pulled me down onto his knees.

WE LAY TOGETHER beneath our cloaks on the hidden island until dawn. Aric's horse stood tied on the other side of the island, waiting. The sounds of the night had quieted now, and the fires had all gone out. A thin crust of ice had formed over the water, which was readily broken. As I washed the flaking gypsum paint from my face and hands, my thoughts went to Sakha.

"I need to find my horse," I said. "He fled amid the chaos. Now he is out there, loose in this strange place. I'm worried for him."

"I'll help you look," Aric said as he splashed water from the icy river on his face, scrubbing away the grey soot. "Then we'll return, and I'll speak again to the king and tell him there will be no union. If I can't change his mind, I can at least loosen his grip. Don't despair; I'll think of something." He smiled hopefully, his face red with the cold of the water, his eye shining clear blue in the morning light.

WE FOUND SAKHA wandering the marshes. Or rather, trying to escape them. Sunk deep in the thick, half-frozen mud, his tendon was bowed again. When he saw me, he whinnied and tried to approach, but he was too lame to walk, and even from a distance, I could see how swollen the leg was. When we caught him, my heart broke to see it. Aric looked at me and shook his head.

"It's too late," I said in disbelief. It was all my fault. I'd let Sakha go in the tumult of the Hunt. When he needed my protection and guidance, I failed him, and now here he was. Nearly split in two, his tendon was beyond healing. Hot and swollen, it was too painful to even touch. He could bear no weight on it, and I'd be unable to cool or bandage it. Back home, in my father's stables, I might be able to rest and heal him with enough time and let him live out his days in a sheltered paddock within the fort. Out here, there could be no shelter, no rest. He'd never be able to withstand the demands of a dry summer in long search of pasture, the deep mud of spring, the hardships of winter's snow and ice, or keeping up with the herd in flight. It was this or leave him to the wolves. In that light, this was a mercy. But for the first time since I'd arrived here, I ached for the comforts of my old home.

We stood him in the marsh. The ground was too frozen to dig a grave for him now, but I'd not leave him for the scavengers.

Aric drew his axe from his belt. "Let me."

"No. He's mine. It should be me."

He nodded. "Be swift and true. As he was."

I took the sagaris from Aric's hand and readied myself.

Sakha had been my most faithful friend since I was a girl. He was gentle and kind, honest and loyal, resilient and trustworthy. Whatever I asked of him, he did his best to oblige. Once, out hunting, I fell from his back, and instead of following the field, he waited by my side. And I tried to return his loyalty with my own. But looking at him here, I knew that I'd failed. Once I placed the bridle over his head, my duty was to protect him. And I had not been there. Despite Aric's generous attempts to bolster my courage, I had proved inadequate and forsaken my duty. I must live with the knowledge of that negligence for the rest of my days. Seldom have we done right by the noble beasts who we make our companions. Few appreciate them as well as they deserve, including me. I could not have survived the steppe without Sakha; indeed, none could survive long in this place without a good horse.

It was time to say farewell. And offer thanks. Sakha sweated and shook with the pain, and though I longed to embrace him one last time, he wanted no comfort from me. I understood, and I did not weep for him. I had to put down so many horses over the years that, though it seemed harsh, it didn't upset me. The first one hurt terribly. I cried for hours, then again for days. But I eventually learned that sentiment didn't lighten the burden. Other responsibilities remained, regardless of my grief, and I could not honor both. I still missed them but couldn't let myself become a wretch. There would be time for tears later.

Aric held Sakha's head; I steadied my hand, swung the axe, and watched him crumple. It was over in the space of a breath. He buckled, and his powerful form sank quietly under the water's dark surface, sending a sharp surge to lap at our legs and the shore. Just deep enough to keep the animals away. Just enough for a bit of dignity. Aric pierced his side to keep him from swelling and floating to the surface. I watched until the face of the water became still again, dark with the clouds moving overhead, and I gazed a long while into their reflection, remembering. Then, I hung his studded bridle and bronze bit in the branches of a tree near the shore.

CHAPTER 42

HIDING

I'd seen something dire, but it wasn't a vision.

AFTER THE HUNT, the Fathers were invited to return home with firm but gentle spells; the warband had been entreated to do the same. I was more than happy to oblige. The court would have usually moved farther south to warmer climates after Rathadin. With the prolonged drought, the grazing was decimated, and they were forced to remain in the colder northern reaches where more pasture remained, and they might yet hunt and trade to supplement their stores.

While the court headed from the Volosdanu into the bend of the Pantikap River, we hunkered down for the coldest days of winter along the upper reaches of the Hypakris River near the edge of the forest-steppe, where hunting and trade were good. We lay low through the storms and snows of Winter Month, deep in the Wild Fields, tending the herds and riding the watches and roads.

For the most part, the karevans ceased trading while the roads and rivers were often impassible, though the Skythai rarely settled for long. Runners replaced the wheels on the wagons, and where the rivers were frozen solidly enough, horses and oxen were driven straight across. Even the sea could ice thickly enough to cross in winter, Aric said, though I couldn't imagine such a sight.

Though our stores dwindled, between our herds and hunting, we seldom struggled to eat. When passing into new territory to camp, each clan's chief took his turn in preparing a bull from his herd. After midnight, when the moon was full, he would lead it to a place north of his camp and sacrifice it, after which the warband would come and receive it on behalf of Gœtosura. This ensured his goodwill toward the clans in the coming year—and ours. Those who could not afford cattle left offerings of milk, yogurt, butter, or cheese. With the hungry young novices back at court for the night season, the offerings stretched further and were a welcome relief from our grey, salt-cured rations.

Not long before ewes began dropping their lambs and milk began to flow, farmers began preparing their fields for sowing seed. Winter was not yet over, but the days were lengthening, frost receding, and here and there, spring's first heralds—blackthorn, snowdrops, and other small shoots—defied the cold and broke the snow and frost. Though the days were overcast and ice crackled on the river, greener days ahead brought some consolation.

The horses, too, began to shed their winter coats. The court camp was too far to make the long trek for the Ushas festival, celebrating the dawning of spring. I was grateful. The harsh final words Aric had exchanged with the king before leaving likely fed his desire to stay away. When I pressed him about the outcome of his last confrontation, he promised me they had come to an understanding, but something else about the exchange weighed upon him, and he would say no more than this.

The muddy tracks and dreary days left me wanting only a warm fire and the company of friends. Aric stuck close by my side and pressed me continually about the future. Though I had nothing to offer him, I was troubled, too. The exercise of divination was more fruitless now than ever because my spells never appeared.

Aric sat his regular vigil with me in the new moon's darkness, but nothing came.

"It's just the winter," I assured him as he looked at me with skepticism inscribed across his wrinkled brow, trying to keep my mood light. Despite the cold, he wanted to feed me half his rations so I would not weaken in the harsh climate. Women, he said, were not made to endure the cold. Good intentions and misguided notions aside, the next moon came, and still nothing.

"Is it to do with my fate?" he demanded in a sharp whisper as we sat hidden under the cannabis tent. "What are you concealing from me?" In the light of the small brazier, consternation overtook his face as he leaned in and stared intently at me, waiting for an answer I didn't have.

"I know nothing of your fate—nor mine. There's been no spell; you're with me night and day. I would tell you if I knew."

"Have you stopped them? Was it something dire?" He shot his questions at me.

I had seen something dire, but it wasn't a vision. "I think it's just the harshness of the season." I'd been telling myself so, willing it to be true. "Don't worry."

I hadn't had a spell in two months. But my courses had dried up, too. It might have just been the bitter cold, the rough work, and the scarcity of ripe food. The long hours of hunting and riding in the blasting wind and wet took their toll, that was for sure. And we'd not drunk wine or eaten bread or butter in days. We'd run through our stores and were kept from the nearest trading outpost a day's ride northeast of camp by heavy snowstorms, only melting away now. I prayed it was just a dry season brought by exhaustion, but I feared something far worse. Despite the care he had taken to spill his seed on the ground that night in the marsh, perhaps something had taken root.

I left Aric and the cannabis tent and found myself alone in our felt-house, warming a small jar of frozen liquid between my hands. After the encounter with Tarana, I'd stowed away Erman's potion in secret, but I hoped I'd never need it. Since I was young, I knew I'd been made without the parts that cause most women to crave and adore children. I looked on them with abhorrence—the cruelest burden ever put on womankind, designed to shackle and make us incidental for all our lives. To keep us from the world and its trove of knowledge. If the gods had indeed granted me a gift, it was awareness of this. This trespasser threatened to destroy everything I'd ever hoped and fought for. It would ruin him as well.

I told myself this was for the best. I did it as much for his welfare as mine. But as I prepared to break the seal on the bottle and down the potion inside, I paused. I closed my fingers around the vial. For myself, I had no doubts. It was the wise and sensible thing to do. And Aric, much as I trusted his wisdom, had not been acting sensibly of late. I must decide—for the good of us both and the kara. For the covenants between our fathers, our kingdoms. That is what I would counsel now if he asked. But could I deceive him, even to protect him? How would I ever look him in the eye, bearing such a betrayal within me, even knowing it was for the best?

I tucked it safely away again. There was time. I must tell him and pray he saw sense.

THE SUN HAD NOT YET RISEN, and a cloud hung low in the field over the river. I descended into the mist to the alder tree where Aric waited. Once alone, I had promised to tell him the truth about the spells. We met beneath the ancient tree, its naked branches disappearing into the haze above our heads like a whisk into a great bowl of frothy kumis.

"Perhaps the gods have heard your pleas and finally released you from the visions," he offered, sounding disappointed.

"Perhaps." But I lacked his faith in the gods.

"Are you still trying to punish me?"

"You think I'd be that petty?"

He folded his arms and fixed me in his gaze. "I think you're still angry."

"My anger lies elsewhere. And I've always spoken truth to you." *In my fashion.*

"It is so, you have." Relaxing his arms, he let his gaze fall to the ground.

"I will speak more truth to you now, though it frightens me to do so. It is not only the spells that have abandoned me. My courses have also ceased," my hands went instinctively, unconsciously to my belly.

His usually stony expression became oddly distorted. Was it surprise or panic that widened his nostrils and arched his brows? He looked away into the steppe and frowned.

"There's a potion," I rushed to add. "I have a potion for it." I studied him for a response. Still as stone, he gave none. "No one need ever know."

I watched him in silence, uncertain if I should keep speaking. Expecting him to turn around any moment and say, *Of course, that would be best.* But he never moved or shifted his gaze from the horizon. The silence grew intolerable. So, I continued, stammering whatever would fill the strained void between us. "Or else, my time here will have to end sooner or later. We both know this. Perhaps I should take my scalp and go now. Before it's too late."

His head snapped around, his nostrils flaring like a bull's. "What's that supposed to mean?"

I should have remained silent. "I know what my future holds. One day, I must leave these Wild Fields behind for the life of a broodmare. If I go now, at least what I must bear is ours and no other's." That was some consolation.

He clenched his jaw and looked away, breathing hard through his nose. "No," he said flatly. "You dishonor me—and yourself— with this talk. I'll have no heir of mine born a bastard—of deception and lies."

"I wasn't suggesting a lie," I said defensively. "I was only thinking of protecting you."

"I don't need your protection!" he barked.

"Oh, is that so?" I snapped. "These gold rings I bear say otherwise. Perhaps I should return them to you as well!"

Without warning, he growled as he drove his fist into the tree trunk. Then, just as quickly as this storm blew in, it died down, and he fell still. I stood blinking, my heart racing, and stared at his bloodied knuckles in silence.

"I need no one's protection," he said flatly, the calm returning to his features. "But I am grateful for yours. I have broken my oath regardless. Tell me, what is it you wish?"

"I wish never to see that look on your face again."

"It's not for you." He wiped the blood from his hand and stared at his boots.

"You know I'd never leave your side if I could choose."

"Then choose."

"Ha," I huffed, "it's just that simple?"

"What if it was?"

I gawked at him, incredulous. He was upset and not thinking clearly. "What are you saying?" I asked gently, as I would settle a horse in high spirits.

He took my hands in his, warm and rough, and squeezed them softly.

"I'm saying we could go," he spoke quickly, his voice ringing with zeal. "Take these horses and ride off. They'd never find us."

He couldn't be serious? I pushed away, needing space to breathe. Abandon kara, kin, duty? Cast our tribes' pacts to the wind? He may have been impulsive, but he was far from stupid. He stared at me eagerly while I struggled to herd my thoughts. "You know *why* they'd never find us. There's nothing but a hundred lawless bands of reavers to prey upon us. Even you would be no match for them out there alone."

"We could join them." He grinned, but he almost sounded serious.

"They're outlaws and exiles."

"I envy them," he said. "They answer to no one; they take what they want and make no apology for it."

"But that's why we hunt them. Isn't that what you told me?"

"I know what I said. But out here, the only real law is survival. The king's laws couldn't touch us. We'd truly be free. Not dictated to, not owned, not ruled."

"Won't our fathers hunt us?"

"Let them try."

I'd never heard him speak like this; he was scaring me. Maybe he was going mad. But did I not owe him the chance? After all he'd sacrificed and risked for me. All he'd given. Foolish, terrifying, treacherous as it was, I knew I would agree, even before I'd heard his plan.

"How would we live? Where would we go?"

"Anywhere you wish."

"I don't know of anywhere else."

"We could live like this, hiding in the steppe. Or I know a half dozen tribes we could join. Or we could buy passage on a ship—go to Nymphaion or Symbolon where none will know us."

"So, it's really possible?"

He only nodded, his bright face blushing in the cold.

"The spells . . . what if they don't return?" I asked, anxious about his answer.

"Hmm," he mumbled as his momentary joy gave way to a frown. Then his brow softened. "Perhaps you will give me the son you spoke of?" He tried a smile, his cheeks dimpling in their irresistible way.

"Maybe a daughter." I searched his expression for disappointment.

"One of each," he joked, his grin broadening, grabbing me by the hips and pulling me close.

I took hold of the front of his caftan. "In the east, a daughter is as good as a son. And there are queens as powerful as kings."

He nodded and smiled. "Then we'll go east. And I'll be glad for anything and everything you give me. I am bound to you and you to me, forever."

"I regret all the trouble I cause you," I said, staring into the folds of his caftan, unable to look him in the face.

Pressing me against the tree, he lifted my chin and sought my gaze, grinning mischievously. "I love the trouble you cause me."

CHAPTER 43

SHEPHERDS

*You are not Skythian until you know what it
means to burn everything you have to keep
everything you love.*

I T HAD BEEN NEARLY A WEEK since I spoke with Aric alone.
With grain stores and other necessities running low, he and I now
embarked on an expedition into the northwest along a tributary to
the Varga River to negotiate an exchange of goods. Trading bases
stretched east and west along the forest's edge. We hadn't come
this far north again since our mishap with the Mard-Khwaar, but
the camp desperately needed supplies. According to our scouts,
the court camp drew nearer with each successive move, though
we had not encountered them since Midwinter, and Aric hoped
to keep it that way.

Being such lonely country, we were unlikely to meet much
trouble this season now that the Man-Eaters had been ousted
from the territory. But though the tribes that now dwelt here were
friendly, we were just as likely to encounter wolves as bandits on
the road. We could have used some more men. But Aric insisted
the others could better serve the band by guarding the stock and
hunting than by touring the local villages with us.

Despite the snowstorm that blew in midmorning, we rode on. I could see a small fort of earthworks and palisades in the distance. It looked like the other trading outposts we'd visited, but we rode by it. We rode through scattered flocks of sheep poking aimlessly at the snow or curled up in their fleecy coats, their legs tucked beneath them. Sheep did poorly in high snow, and some poor shepherd would likely have to come to dig them free if the storm got much worse. The country was otherwise empty of settlements, which must have been hidden away in the forest.

We rode this way well into the evening, over rolling hills peppered with trees and brush, before finally breaking to rest in front of the charred gates of an abandoned fort rising stark and black against the snow as the last light of day faded behind them. At this hour, I was uneasy at the edge of the forest. Dusk was when the wolves prowled.

"What is this place?" I asked.

"This was the hub of a great wheel of trade whose spokes extended over all the steppe—and beyond. Goods that fed the great empires in every direction of the wind passed first through these gates."

"A city? Here?"

"A fortified city called Gelonus. There are a few like it along the tribal borders. But this was the greatest. Destroyed many years ago."

"Was it besieged?"

"It was burned before it could be. Darayavaush, the Dragon, was eager to capture it to satisfy his insatiable greed. To hold the Skythai hostage and take possession of the trade routes across the steppe. If he had possessed this place, he might have possessed Skythia.

"The three Skythai kings argued over strategy. My great-grandfather, Idanthyrs, wanted to fight the Persai in the open, while the other kings wished to gather their possessions and hide behind these walls, awaiting the armies of the Dragon. So, Idanthyrs burned it to the ground, denying them all. Leading a coalition of the three Skythai kingdoms before the invader's path, Idanthyrs spoiled the wells and burned everything that might have been of use to the enemy's forces—including the city. The Dragon's armies couldn't survive on the steppe without water and pasture for their stock, much less force the Skythai to fight, so he gave up and went home in shame and defeat."

"Was it worth it?"

"We are still free."

"Such sacrifice. I don't know if I will ever understand the Skythai."

"You are not Skythian until you know what it means to burn everything you have to keep everything you love."

The fort was in the rough shape of an arrowhead, shot into the junction of two rivers, and we stood at its southern tip where the rivers met. Before us stretched massive bank-and-ditch walls towering nearly forty feet high. The remains of burned wooden palisades stood against the sky in the fading light. My father's fort was the most impressive thing I could imagine. Its banks and walls were half as big and encompassed one hundred fifty acres. Even in ruins, this made that feel quaint. Three massive keeps, now destroyed, stood stark and imposing over the empty country, filled with overgrown fields, encroaching forest, and forgotten barrows.

"Why was it never rebuilt?"

"From time to time, the Geloni still try. Their ancestors are a mix of Budini, Skythai, and Hellenes who came north from the colonies long ago to get rich off the spoils of trade. They built temples alongside their workshops and worshiped the same mad god they do in Olbia. It is said every third year, they held a festival in his honor, and I'd not be surprised if somewhere out there, the lot of them aren't raving naked in the woods. They would have this place again if they could. But you saw the grand barrows that

surround this fortress. And the Mard-Khwaar controlled access to
the Volosdanu along the northern rivers after Gelonus fell, keeping the Geloni from growing too powerful. This stronghold and
its trade made its masters rich. Any tribe who held it would be
almost untouchable."

"Where are the Geloni now?"

"They farm the riverside and herd their sheep. Their villages
are scattered through the forest, but we come and clear them from
the fort from time to time. The Budini are a separate people with
a language and ways all their own. They're nomads and keep to
themselves, living by their tame reindeer herds; they've also gone
north into the wood."

My eye swept the dusky treeline, fading into shadow. There was
no sign of a trail in the freshly fallen snow. No trace of a village or
any human habitation. The ruins gave no sense that anyone called
this forsaken place home.

"Are they so dangerous? Deer herders and trinket merchants?"

"It is a fragile thing, the covenant that binds this kingdom's
many tribes and clans. One gift the destruction of this fort gave
the Paralatai is that it unified our people and brought all the tribes
of Skythia under the command of a single High King. But should
our kingdom fall, it would shatter like a clay pitcher, and all these
small pieces would lie scattered about, jagged and dangerous. Any
one of them might move to seize control. Or all of them will. There
would be many kings and many wars, as in the past. Such chaos
makes us ripe for invasion."

"And Ariapaithi doesn't want this place for himself? All this
effort to build it . . . seems a waste allowing it to languish when
there is so much trade to be had."

"Our trade flourishes without it." He turned and allowed his
eye to scan the charred walls. "Like all settlements, the war proved
it was a target—and a last retreat. Our strength is our mobili-
ty." Then he lowered his gaze and continued to speak in a hushed,

almost apologetic tone. "Its time has passed. Fate takes the dead for a reason—it is not for us to resurrect them."

"Then why have you brought *me* here?" This was not what we planned. He'd deceived me.

"Because I feel an odd kinship with this place," he said with a sigh. "And I wanted for us to be alone."

At the edge of the forest, at this late hour, shadows stretched stark and solemn over the snow, and the air hung damp and dank with the rotting wood of the fallen walls. And all of it lay in uncanny silence. Even the stray sheep that pawed and grazed about the fortress walls were voiceless. And the faithful voice within Aric I longed to hear was most silent of all.

"We can be alone anytime," I joked, trying to banish my nerves, "just volunteer us to set the rabbit snares in the snow."

His eye locked on mine as he grabbed hold of my arms. Then he looked away but did not release his grip. "I've been losing sleep. But I've come to a choice—a hard choice. But the right one. I'm sure now." He swallowed and moistened his lips, tightening his grip on my arms. "I can't let you return to Skythia. For honor's sake."

A wave of panic flooded me. The wilderness. The ruin. The storm. There would be no trail, no trace. *No return.* What had I done? Blood rushed in my ears, and the fire of panic burned through my veins as I tried to steady my breathing. I had nowhere to run. I was faster, but he was stronger. I could ride, but I wore no armor against his mighty bow. The iron throbbing of my heart, trilling blood through the vessel in my throat, heat in my cheeks, trembling in my hands, and lightness in my legs all conspired against me. How could this come to pass? Above the crashing surf that thundered in my ears, I could hear only my father's voice berating me: *Trust no one.* The only lesson he cared to teach me in my life was the one I'd failed to learn, and like some foolish girl, I'd let myself be led here. I knew better and had still been blind.

I flexed my arms and squared my shoulders, resisting his grip and drawing myself up before him. I raised my eyes to his. "I'm no match for you," I said, my voice quavering despite my defiance. "But at least let me go with a weapon in my hand. Let me die fighting. You speak of honor; you owe me that."

Shaking his head, he released my arms and stepped back, searching my face. "Good gods, Ana, what the fuck are you talking about?"

"What are *you* talking about?"

"I promised I'd leave with you. That's what I'm doing. I can't let you wed my—" he swallowed again, "the king. What in the name of Gœto did you think I meant?"

"You want to go *now*?"

"If you still do?"

I breathed deep to steady my hammering heart. "But why here, like this?"

"The Budini. They keep to themselves and owe their allegiance to no one. If we wish to pass this way, they won't betray us. We can shelter here."

"And you didn't trust me enough to tell me this before we traveled all this way?"

"The others couldn't suspect anything."

I lunged at him, driving both hands into his chest, shoving him with such force he fell back two steps before recovering himself. "Don't *ever* deceive me again," I said coldly, then looked away and drew a long breath, exhaling slowly.

He nodded, still looking confused.

"*Swear it.*"

He frowned. "I swear. By all the gods." His face softened into pleading. "We keep going?"

I nodded, my throat too tight to speak.

He lowered his head and glanced sidelong at me. "Did you really think I was capable of—*of that?*"

"I regret that I even thought it."

"You know me, Anaiti. I am capable of many things, but hurting you is not one of them."

I did know him. Whether he admitted it or not, he was perfectly capable of hurting me. As I was of hurting him.

He held me to his chest. "We're safe now."

It was far from true. Yet, our words and arms made it briefly so.

WE STABLED SÆNA and Aruna in a shop overtaken with weeds and found refuge in the shelter of a burned-out house. Little was left of it but the square angles of broken walls amid the charred wood and ash of a falling roof. Some broken pots lined the wall where a pantry must have stood. Aric warned me not to wander about the fort but to stay on the paths we'd already walked. Concealed beneath the snow lay a network of pits, snares, and traps the warband had laid to punish trespassers.

We hunkered down in the far corner where the fierce wind did not reach the dusty pallets. We covered one with dry grass and a blanket of waxed hemp. The cold might have been unbearable since the ground was too frozen to dig pits for a smokeless fire, but we spread Aric's bearskin over us and huddled close. Of all the different silences, none is so eerily sublime as the still eye of a storm. Here was a lull, and we basked in the peace, knowing what must follow.

"It's too dark in here," he said, rubbing his eye with the heel of his palm and fumbling to light a wick in a small pot of deer fat with his flint.

"Here, let me," I said, taking the flint and striker from him and lighting a tiny wisp of tinder grass. The lamp made a gentle glow in the cold, dark space, flickering wildly in the confused winds rattling through the broken walls.

"Your hands are cold," he said as I reached for him in the dark. "Let me warm them." Clasping my hands to his breast, he pulled me close, and the nearness of our bodies made a warmth of their own.

"Think of it," I said, "soon we may also spend our summers just like this but in some quiet valley by the side of a creek. You will tell me stories of the steppe, and I will tell you of the forest. And we'll lay under the shade of a tree, laugh together, and forget these troubles."

He drew a shuddering breath and spoke, his voice quavering, "Even the richest king could not buy that."

I COULD FEEL THE WARMTH of the dawning sun through my eyelids. Without opening my eyes, I drew the golden light deep into my lungs and held my breath. As I opened my eyes, Aric combed his fingers through my tangled hair. "You'll never be a queen now."

"I told you, I never wished to be a queen."

"And I don't know what happens with your father's treaty."

My father. "I hope our fathers can still mend things if they discover what we've done. But you've also sacrificed your claim to the throne." In the excitement, all he'd sacrificed was quickly forgotten.

"I'm a karik. I need no other crown."

"I've taken that from you as well."

"I have all I want." He smiled reassuringly and pressed me closer.

"Then we shall be the lord and lady of this place. Let us have our kingdom here, free from the eyes of the world."

"Mmm, you and I shall be the King and Queen of Gelonus." He grinned impishly. "I like the sound of that."

"And what a formidable king you'd be. That first night in the marches . . . how did you know I hid my dagger under my pillow?"

He looked at me quizzically. "It wasn't in your belt after you made your bed. Lucky guess." He beamed, his eyes crinkling.

When he smiled like that, his eye became a crescent moon suspended in a shining sky. I took his face in my hands and kissed him.

"You've been wondering about that all this time?" he asked.

"I have," I chuckled. "You should've let me believe you were all-knowing."

He raised his eyebrows with mock wariness. "I'd be afraid to know your thoughts," he said with a stilted laugh.

"They'd turn you into a monster, swelling you up with pride," I teased. "No man needs that." I wrapped my arms more tightly and nestled into him.

"Even if you can't hear my thoughts," he mused, "I trust you already know them well."

If only that were true. How well could one ever know the thoughts of another? That with all our tools of language and art, we forever strove to apprehend the inner worlds of others—and to make our innermost hearts plain to them—and fell woefully short on both accounts. Mere blunders through a cave without a torch. But I trusted in him—in the notion of him I held—and had to hope that the woman he saw in that dim light was some semblance of myself and not a shadow I had artfully cast.

"What will become of the warband when we don't return?" I asked. "Won't they be searching for us now?"

"Antisthenes is my steward. He takes temporary command in my absence. He has instructions that if anything should happen to me, he must assume my place after a week's time. After a period, the men will call a gathering and choose a new leader. I hope it will be him—no man has a better grasp of the duties demanded of the warband both in times of bounty and hardship."

"Would they choose a Hellene?"

"The Skythai do not ask after the tribe or kin of noble spirits. We listen without resentment to the glories of both friends and enemies. My tutor, Ispakaja, was an Issedoni warrior. He served as karadar and I as his steward for many years until he fell in battle against the Massagetai."

"Are the Issedoni not also man-eaters?"

"It is so. Yet I've never known a man of greater virtue or courage. He was Skythai in all but birth. Antisthenes is as well."

"Then, I hope they see the worth in Antisthenes."

"We should set out within the hour. The sun will soon rise."

The thought of prying myself away from this shelter of comfort and warmth filled me with anguish. I was likely a coward, but I was beginning to regret our leaving. I would miss Antisthenes and many of the kara. And once we were gone, there'd be no coming back.

"Where are we headed?"

"We can't just ride across the plain. We could take refuge with the Navari or the Fenni until spring. Or I know a few places in the Wild Fields where we could hide. Places abandoned this season. Or we could go downriver to Symbolon and find a ship east."

"I've never even heard of this place."

"Taurica. The Tauri are a good people. A strong people. The last of the Kimmeroi and great raiders on land and sea. They go where they please. The world belongs to them, and no one stands in their way."

I did like the sound of that. "Then we're really going?"

He sat up and furrowed his brow. "What troubles you?"

"Well, won't they worry for us? We never even said goodbye."

I'd left Vatra behind. He would let no one ride him but me. Who'd care for him now? I thought of Antisthenes. Of Bornon, Gohar, Stormai, even Olgas—the men who had become my friends. Of all the lifelong brothers Aric was leaving without even a word. I thought of my family.

"When you run, you don't get to say goodbye."

I swallowed hard past the lump in my throat. None of this troubled him?

He took hold of my hands. "Speak now. Have you had a vision?"

"Not exactly."

But something nagged at me. Something felt off. Disjointed. Why could I not celebrate this leave-taking—this freedom—as Aric did? I closed my eyes and tried to compose my thoughts—to summon my will. We were finally free of all our obligations, all our duties. Soon Skythia and the danger would be behind us. But we were leaving work undone, promises unkept, all on a whim, for a future neither of us had designed. For things I never wanted.

"It's just, all of this fills me with dread," I confessed.

"I know. But what else is there for us?" He forced a smile, which was meant to hearten me, but only bruised my heart more.

I wanted to share his conviction. Wasn't he right? Didn't we have our own lives and hopes, too? We might have but a moment to live them. This should have been a joyous time—free as the winter birds perched on their bare branches, their songs ringing clear in the cold morning, defiant of the raptors circling somewhere in their same skies.

We began readying the horses for our departure. My hands worked numbly at the straps of Aruna's girth. I would go as I had promised. But my feeling of foreboding persisted. A shadow stretched and grew inside my mind. My guts tied into a knot as I looked around and realized why.

"Aric? The shepherds—where are they?" I exhaled in relief as I said it, even though I was sure it foretold something dire. Hoping, praying its ill portent might spare us something worse—something inspired by madness.

"Hmm?"

"There are no shepherds."

"Good. Then no one will see us," Aric smiled, cupped my face in his hands, and kissed me.

I pushed him away. "Were you listening to me? Who leaves a flock untended? Especially in a storm? You heard the wolves in the night. We rode for a day and never saw a single shepherd. Where are all the Geloni men who should be tending these flocks? Was there a plague in this country, or have they all gathered elsewhere?"

For a long moment, he looked past me, staring at nothing, then gazed back into the south, from where we came. His eye narrowed, and his jaw clenched tight.

"Indeed. There is only one purpose that gathers all a tribe's men."

CHAPTER 44

PLOT

This, the stern silence before battle, was the
peace of eternity.

THE PLACE WAS EVEN STARKER in the early morning light. We were surrounded by a snarl of trees and underbrush on the edge of a dark wood. A daughter of the forest, I'd always found trees wondrous and groves welcoming, instilled as they were with the gods of my fathers. But here, the coppice choked with brambles, and tangled treetops blotted out the sun. The damp thicket, its floor a black mass of decaying leaves, gave cover to anything that wished to hide from view. A thick mist rose off the melting ice of the rivers and snow, shrouding all in a cloak of grey. The bony fingers of leafless branches twining overhead obscured the sky. How nomad tribes dwelt here, I couldn't imagine. I peered into those woods and questioned what kind of people might make such a place their home.

"I've seen raids all my life," Aric said as he saddled Sæna. "Never has an enemy been so bold as to march on our court. All this time, the Geloni have been partners more often than rivals." A rare apprehension worried his brow as he secured his pack behind his saddle. "I don't know why this is happening or what they hope to gain."

"Nor do I." It had caught us entirely unaware, which I believe was the point. I'd already tacked Aruna and readied my things for leaving. But I was still numb with disbelief. "You're certain they're planning an attack?"

"I'm not certain of anything. But what other reason could they have for leaving flocks unguarded but to muster all their men to an army?"

"Perhaps they make war on the Budini?"

"We cannot take that chance."

"Why now?" I asked, more angry than confused. It couldn't be the drought. It was clear that they had plenty of sheep, and the woods were full of game.

"The gods punish us for our faithlessness," he said with dismay. "Our tribes will suffer for the oaths we've broken."

"Maybe the gods brought us here," I said more in hope than belief, "*to see.*"

He brightened at that and nodded slowly as if assuring himself. "Then, by the will of Gœtosura, we may yet reach the camps in time. But should I fall in the coming battle—"

"You *will not* fall," I said, grabbing handfuls of his coat. "You will die in my bed in a time and place far from this." I uttered it half as commandment, half as prophecy, willing it to be true.

He pulled away with a scowl. "You curse me three times over."

Was it such a curse to trade glory for time? "I forbid you to die," I scolded him futilely as he swung up into his saddle and gathered his reins. Court camp seemed to lie on the other side of the world.

"Take it up with the gods, then," he mocked half-heartedly.

I was in no joking mood. I could only gaze up at him astride Sæna, preparing to leave. His golden hair was covered in a soft morning mist, and he seemed wraithlike as if he might drift away or fade into the dawn. I could not hold onto him even if I tried. This was as fate decreed. I let out a resigned sigh. The future stood on a knife's edge.

"Which way should I go?" I asked, knowing I would have to find my way back alone. I was truly on my own.

"The way we came is slow but safe. Ride hard until you cross the stony creek we passed. See then if you can use your mirror to signal the scouts ahead of you. There may not be enough sunlight, but try. Stop for nothing else." Then his face darkened, and he scowled down at me. "When you arrive at the buna, stay put. You hear me? A small force remains to guard the camp. *Stay with them.*"

I grasped him by the wrist. "I'm ready. I'm not afraid."

"I know. But this is not your fight."

"Skythai fights are my fights."

He took my hand in his, and his voice went low. "Things are different now."

"How? Am I not Skythai, too?"

"I—I don't know if I can keep you safe," he stammered.

"What about you?" I asked, my throat constricting with emotion. "How can I keep *you* safe if I am so far away?"

"I'll have an entire army beside me," he said stubbornly. "I go to my duty. You mustn't worry for me. Look after yourself now. Collect your scalp and the gold rings I gave you and keep them close. You may need them. Until we see each other again—in this life or the next—do what you must to survive."

Gripping his calf, I closed my eyes and rested my head against his thigh, assuring myself he was real—this was really happening. He placed his palm atop my head. His hand's warmth, the brush of his fingers on my hair, sent a chill shimmering down my spine.

Then, the faint sound of a horn blowing far off in the distance woke me. I shook off the trance and mounted up, though I could still feel the warm imprint of his hand on my scalp. I drew a full breath as I gathered my reins and stroked Aruna's neck to calm him—and myself.

"*I forbid you,*" I said as Aric turned to go, already desolate at the thought of making this ride alone.

WE RODE OUR SEPARATE WAYS—I to muster the warband and Aric to warn the court. As I galloped Aruna across the plain, I had time to consider what the men would think on my arrival about the story I had to tell and why I was now alone. Would they believe me? They must. But their trust in me was sorely tested, and my allies in camp dwindled to only a handful of friends. Would their word be enough to counter the suspicion and slander of all those whose ire I'd provoked?

Besides the soft padding of hooves in the snow and the rhythmic snorting of Aruna with each stride, there were no sounds. No sights. No signs of life but for us, alone in the world. And only I knew why we galloped so hard across the empty plain. Aruna trusted I had my reasons. For miles we ran. The plain bleak and white. The sky grey as smoke. My thoughts empty as a shattered vase. Retracing the road that took us away.

The steppe is the loneliest place on earth, except perhaps the sea. What must a person feel in a boat on the sea far from the sight of land? It couldn't be much different from what I now felt. The earth featureless. The sky formless. The wind relentless. And the silence endless. The kind of silence that gnaws into a mind. That frays the thoughts. Begins to unravel them and wear them through. It's a different kind of loneliness than that of an unhitched wagon, an empty tent, the hush of a hunting forest. This, the stern silence before battle, was the peace of eternity—the impenetrable stillness of the tomb. I'd heard it before. I rode through that silence like riding through a cemetery, speeding like I could outrun death. The graves blurring past, opening around me. Only, I didn't run from it; I ran toward it.

I pushed Aruna harder than I should have. The horses had begun shedding their heavy winter coats, but it wasn't enough to ease the sweat that lathered his neck and flanks. With the snow still melting underfoot, going was slow. Aric had said to take an easy pace and spare the horses. The Geloni, mostly plowmen, would be on foot rather than horseback and slow to cover ground. But there was no telling how many were coming. How could I be easy?

After crossing the shallow, stony creek, I stopped to let Aruna rest and drink. I tried signaling under the grey sky toward camp with my mirror, but I couldn't catch a beam of light. In every direction, I angled the burnished bronze disk and saw nothing. Then polished its smooth face and tried again. The horizon remained silent, and no light answered mine. I could wait no longer for the grudging sun and resigned myself to press on alone.

WHEN I ARRIVED AT CAMP, I found Antisthenes, who seemed surprised to see me. He had a younger karik care for poor, spent Aruna while he invited me inside for a bowl of bone broth beside the fire. He hushed me when I tried to speak and bade me take some nourishment first. I could hear the men gathering outside the tent as I quickly slurped down the warm broth, and the heat of the fire made my bones shiver with such comfort that, had I not been so afraid, I would have been in danger of drifting off to sleep. When I had finished my bowl, Antisthenes came and sat beside me.

"Now, tell me what has happened," he said calmly, his keen eyes shining.

I told him about the Geloni shepherds' absence in the fields and how Aric and I believed the men might be gathering somewhere in preparation for war. If they were to march on the nearby Paralatai camp, the Skythai would be taken entirely by surprise, with few defenses prepared for such an assault. Aric rode ahead in hopes of warning them, and I returned to alert the warband. To his credit, ever the faithful friend and steward, he asked no questions about our absence, though I suppose he likely guessed already. "I understand," was all he said, then called the vazarka to muster.

Gathered near the hearth in the ring of wagons, I stood before the men and told a tale Aric and I had agreed upon. I had a vision that revealed a secret plot of war. Aric didn't want to alarm the camps until he'd confirmed my prophecy for himself, taking me along as his guide to help interpret the signs. When we uncovered the evidence needed to prove our fears were founded, we rode back to warn the separate camps—I to the warband and he to the court. It was not entirely untrue. And though I disliked deception, I disliked upsetting the men in this time of necessity more.

"How do we know this isn't one of her witch's tricks?" surly Mourdag said, his grey eyes shining coldly from his square face, his thick oakbark waves frizzed by the damp. He'd called me a witch when I first arrived, and I told him then to fuck himself and struck him upside the head. But now I needed him, so I said nothing. "If she divined this, why did the king's seers not do the same?"

"Right," said roguish Azarion with his habitual smirk, "or maybe this one has stuck her dagger in Aric's back somewhere out there, and we're getting led right into an ambush." Feverish assent and dissent roared between the other vazarka, and Azarion continued: "I say we ride north to search for Aric. Trust your eyes, not a woman's words."

More cries jumbled in dispute over the credibility of my word. I couldn't tell which way the men leaned, and I dared not try to sway it with more talk.

Finally, the deep, clear voice of Antisthenes boomed over the assembly: "How do I know she speaks the truth? I know because Aric warned me of the danger they tracked before he departed. You call this a trick? I call this a blessing. Anaiti risked herself to bring us this report. Will we waste time airing our grievances or make use of it? We can outwit and outflank an enemy army as it marches on our king. Those who wish to indulge in petty squabbles and outlandish intrigues can remain here. Those who would defend their king: prepare to ride with me. I shall summon the kara to arms." He didn't wait for their response but turned away from the gathering toward home.

"You should stay here with the guardsmen. Rest," Antisthenes said to me as the vazarka dispersed. He walked briskly toward our tent, and I followed.

"You didn't have to do that."

"A lie saves time. But you know this."

I nodded, unable to look at him. "Thank you."

"I did not do it for you."

"I know."

He paused before the door of our tent. "Another hard ride lies ahead. He would want you to stay behind—stay safe."

"I can't. *He's* there. My kara brothers all go to fight." I couldn't help but feel this was somehow, if not my fault, at least my responsibility. I couldn't point them to the slaughter and walk away. I'd tried walking away already, and it didn't sit well. How often had we assembled around the hearth and eaten, argued, wept, or sang? This was where I belonged if we were lucky enough to return to it. Aric belonged here as well. We were fools to ever think otherwise. "What good am I if I don't join them, to win or lose this fight by their side?"

Pursing his lips, he frowned. Then nodded. "Let us make haste then." He ducked through the doorflap.

THERE WAS NO TIME TO WASTE. The bulk of the Geloni army would be moving on foot. They would travel slowly even if they had a head start. If they'd mustered an entire army, they likely had designs on the court, not just the warband's small camp. If we left now, we could get to court first, or at the very least, meet them on the road and delay them for a while. Antisthenes dispatched our Ravens to muster the allied tribes' warbands in the event it was a long fight.

Inside, I tested the few pieces of protection I'd acquired—a thickly quilted hemp vest and a light crescent-shaped shield of wicker and leather. I crammed a few more items in my pack that I'd left behind—like the wolfskin cape Aric placed around my shoulders the night I was initiated and the lapis lazuli amulet he gave me after the Mard-Khwaar attack. The amulet was stashed in a hole I'd dug under my bed, concealed beneath the reed mats and carpets. In the same spot, I kept the little bottle of potion that Erman had given me, and I'd hidden away. Aric would be angry, but I could only hope he'd understand. What good was I if I couldn't keep my oaths—to him and the others? My vows to myself? Whether I was Bastarnai, Rokhalani, or Paralatai, hamazan, karik, vazarka, or satanaya, I couldn't say. Maybe I was none of these things. Regardless, this was where I belonged. This was my purpose. *I will not abandon my comrades at whose side I stand. I will not leave this land diminished but greater and better than when I came.* These things I swore.

I took out the bottle and thawed it between my hands as Antisthenes strapped on his shield. With my back turned to him, I broke the beeswax seal, said a little incantation, and quickly downed the bitter liquid. I removed the amulet, shining like the dome of the night sky, and stuffed it into the pouch at my waist, carefully replacing the reed mats and carpets over the hole. Then, slinging my saddle to my hip and my pack on my back, I grabbed my spear beside the door and rushed out to find Vatra. Aruna was spent, and we had a hard ride ahead to reach court before the Geloni army.

CHAPTER 45

FOES

The prospect of combat delighted
and ignited their passions.

W E WATCHED THE INVADERS from a broad hilltop overlooking a dried-up river course, churning the snow and tawny winter grass to mud as they came. In a mass of thousands, they swarmed into the valley like bees from a hive mouth. Upon seeing our forces ready and arrayed across the field, their progress halted, and a shudder pulsed through the hulking body of the army as they seemed to be considering retreat. But the brief spasm was quickly followed by a deep breath of silence. One primal roar followed another from the men. A rallying cry went up from their chiefs to be echoed across the ranks, and with renewed vigor, they pressed on. Soon, the massive force was arrayed across the field below, in lines stretching along the stony expanse of the dry riverbed, a thousand sparks floating in the dormant grass, awaiting but a nudging breeze to ignite and ravage everything in their path.

To our surprise, the Geloni did not come alone but marched with unlikely allies: the Saudaratai. Both tribes were tall and fair like the Skythai, but that is where their similarities ended. The Geloni people were unmistakable, as they mainly came on foot and dressed in woolen tunics and cloaks of fur. They carried axes of bronze and spears of sharpened bone, with long, curving bows and breastplates made of stiffened hide. Among them were hints of Greek armor and arms—a handful of bronze helmets, a few dozen iron spear points, well-bossed and strapped wooden shields, and greaves of bronze—some antiques, some bright and new. From their ancestors, they remembered how to make the things of war. We'd soon see if they had also remembered how to use them.

Flanking them on either side rode horsemen in crudely assembled iron and bronze armor, with swords at their sides and bows in their hands, dressed all in black. The Hellenes called the Saudaratai *Melanchlæni*—Black Cloaks. Their black dress and short black capes were unmistakable. Like the Mard-Khwaar, they were man-eaters, hunting men to capture their souls.

Longtime adversaries of the Skythai, there could be any number of reasons they would now seek an alliance with the Geloni, not least of all a chance to vanquish an enemy they could never defeat on their own. But it was just as likely bloodsport. The Skythai and Saudaratai had a long-standing rivalry. Raids, kidnapping, head-hunting, murder, and tomb robbing were all part of the dispute between the two tribes for as long as both could remember. Neither side had much claim to any high ground. They shared a mutual desire to control the same vast plot of land between the Sirhis and Varga Rivers. With the help of the Geloni, today, the Saudaratai might finally get the upper hand.

The Geloni army was much like the one we faced in the settlement we destroyed on the banks of the Lykus. Though greater in size, their lines were disordered, and the soldiers carried various weapons, many of which were tools: axes, billhooks, and scythes. The core of the force, perhaps a thousand men in total, were foot soldiers. The best of them stood in rows at the front of a formation some twenty men deep and maybe a hundred across, though I was never good with such large estimates. It might have been twice that number for all I knew. Against the court camp and the three hundred kara, they seemed a formidable force. All armored and armed with long bronze- and bone-tipped spears. The deeper into the pack, the cruder the weapons became. Men bore sickles, wooden pitchforks, daggers lashed to poles, and just about anything else they could think of that might put a hole in a man or horse. They carried shields of wood or wicker covered with leather. At each of the wings, there stood a pack of archers.

Several hundred mounted Saudaratai archers, their faces painted white with black rings around their eyes and mouths, flanked the Geloni army, awaiting a signal to draw and shoot.

SINCE THE WARBAND'S ARRIVAL, the Skythai princes had sat in council with the king to devise the camp's defenses, and I'd not had even a moment to speak with Aric or even to lay eyes on him. As he rode to the fore of our ranks this morning, my heart nearly burst to see him safe again and whole. With Sæna spent in the gallop here, Aric rode a chestnut gelding from the king's herds. He'd also acquired a spear and shield. Besides this, he wore only the clothes and arms he'd left with: a bronze-plated warbelt with his goryt, akinaka, and sagaris, arm guards of hardened leather, a pointed cap lined in fox fur, an iron ring, a girdle of bast, and a wolfskin cape—sparse protection for the rigors of war.

A vazarka, inspired on the battlefield, becomes impervious to all manner of hurts from blades, bites, and burns. No armor could hide him from his fate, so he faced it willingly, hoping to gain the gods' favor—or, at the very least, everlasting glory. Aric had survived venom, arrows, daggers, and more with only his skill and the luck granted him by the gods. I suppose today was no day to question that grace.

He rode past, inspecting the readiness of his eager riders and their anxious mounts, offering words of encouragement to the kara, both novices and veterans. I smiled my assurance to him. His glare, in return, left me cold as he rode by without a word. I didn't understand. What had I done?

OKTAMAZDA, COMMANDER of the Paralatai forces, led the bulk of the army. In addition to a flood of further cavalry from his substantial militia, he had mustered a considerable body of mounted archers and foot soldiers from among the nearest householders; though they were not hardened warriors, they were all capable with a bow. The mounted bowmen would do most of the work in breaking the enemy ranks, and of those, the Skythian army had more than enough, each with quivers filled with hundreds of arrows, riding tireless, fleet horses. They would descend like a windstorm, then, wave after wave, swoop in from all directions toward the enemy lines, scattering a hail of barbed arrows and retreating again before the stunned soldiers could recover, leaving chaos and disorder in their wake. Once the arrows had found flesh, dozens, hundreds of men would retreat to be healed somewhere—or die, slowly and painfully. Then we'd ride them down with spears and swords.

But the enemy was thick on the ground, well-armored, and could lock their shields together like the scales of a serpent's back. This would not be so simple as a raid. Horses were loyal but not stupid. They wouldn't charge headlong into a solid wall, much less a living, pulsing wall bristling with sharp points. If we couldn't break their lines and expose them with a barrage of arrow fire, we'd have to try to lead them to steep terrain and harry them until they panicked and ran. Here, the mounted spearmen did their work—where we three hundred kara would stand or fall. This was Aric's plan, anyway.

In the rush to prepare, we hadn't time for our usual rites and dances. No sacred haoma had been pressed, and the warriors would have to fight without its stirring sustenance. Instead, we painted our faces with water and ash, as we had done for the Hunt. And a magnificent golden bowl of wine, blessed by the king himself, had been brought before all the warriors to drink. After the necessary invocations and blessings had been performed, the warband had made its way here to the field of battle to take its place beside Oktamazda's forces. The camp roared to see the kara arrive as the defenses were prepared, and the wagons were drawn up in a circle.

As we now took up our positions, I tried to draw near Aric so that I might speak a word to him before it all began, but his face darkened when he caught sight of me. He gritted his teeth and kicked his horse, not speaking a word to me as he rode past in a tempest, shouting an order to a confused mass of novices trying to calm their panicked horses. His tawny hair trailed behind in the soft light of early morning as his gelding's hooves drummed the frozen ground. I watched his back as he faded into a swarming crowd of riders, iron-tipped spears in their hands burning like torches in the dawning light.

Even Prince Skyles had arrived on the field with his guard of some fifty well-outfitted warriors. I had imagined he'd be far to the south this time of year, in his beloved colonies. And among his guard rode one I was even more stunned to see: Rathagos. He'd not returned home to his clan after all. And his presence here, in Skyles's service, drove a chill deep into my tired bones.

I nudged Vatra with my heels and rode farther afield, searching for Bornon and my orders for battle. Aric's strategy was to place the novices—easily spooked and swift like young colts—at the fore. When the fighting pushed through that first line of defense, they were to retreat into the country quickly, luring the brash enemy into pursuit where stronger troops lay in wait. These, too, would soon take flight. Each succession would draw the enemy deeper into the territory and into contact with the next contingent of more advanced warriors, still fresh for fighting. Eventually, the enemy would find themselves tired, diminished, surrounded, and facing the best troops of the Skythai. Men in the fury of battle, lacking all restraint, fell for this every time. Pride and spite, it seemed, would not allow men to accept a straightforward victory but always drove them to take more than warranted. As the attackers' confidence rose and their stamina—and numbers—diminished, they'd allow their formations to break and be surrounded and routed, perhaps in a small valley or hollow specially selected for the job, where the practiced and heavily armed vazarka would be waiting to finish them.

According to Bornon, Aric had selected such a place beyond the rise on which we now stood. If the battle lasted that long and reached this far, we would feint a retreat over the hill and into the plain, drawing them onward, and the warband, alongside Skyles's and the king's guards, would then turn and finish them as they lay trapped in the valley behind the slope of the hill.

We had practiced such retreats a hundred times before, and I knew the signals and when to turn and shoot my bow. Vatra was as ready as he would ever be. With my quiver full and my spear in hand, I was eager for the battle to be underway—and over. The men around me crackled with glee as they waited for the fighting to begin. Something about the prospect of combat delighted and ignited their passions, but the primal ache they felt had never stirred my blood. Though, I was surprised to find that, this time, neither did fear.

CHAPTER 46

FALLEN

The blood was warm and strangely comforting.

FAR AHEAD ON THE PLAIN, the battle had begun. Oktamazda's men were doing an admirable job of introducing chaos among the Geloni ranks with their arrows, and the Saudaratai, for all their attempts to outflank the Skythian cavalry, had so far been thwarted by the sheer numbers and speed of our riders. Watching from above the valley floor, the only sounds that reached my ears above the low and ceaseless rumble of the men's war growls were the blasts of horns and the panicked cries of horses.

The fighting swept forward but had not yet reached the war-band, where we waited amassed across a hillcrest at the western edge of the valley overlooking a gentle bend in the old riverbed. Aric stood apart from his vazarka astride the leggy chestnut. With the butt of his spear anchored to the ground, its long, sharp point aimed at the sky, he assessed the carnage below. King Ariapaithi, in full battle array, surveyed the field of combat with his royal guard surrounding him from a vantage behind us. Though out of sight, Skyles and his small guard were positioned down the hill's back slope, protecting our rear.

So far, the strategy seemed to be working. The remaining

enemy troops, weary and scattering, were succumbing to the assault of the most skilled warriors. For a time, it seemed we might not even be called upon to fight, and whatever qualms consumed Aric about my presence here would prove unfounded—I would risk neither making my tally on these fields nor putting myself in harm's way. But his hounds were straining at their tethers. Used to being in the vanguard of every assault, they chafed at being called to heel. Even Aric could not hold the leash for long. I watched him for a sign. Any moment now, the vazarka would ride down that hill into the fray with their spears, ready to break the final resistance.

A SHOUT ROSE UP BEHIND US, and then the sound of iron clashing upon iron. A horse shrieked. There was a loud scuffle of hooves as horses rushed to and fro in panic. I spun around to look. A crude band of fifty or so Saudaratai riders had stealthily outflanked us and summited the hill from behind. They were likely no match for the king's royal guard, but they shouldn't be there. Had Skyles's guard been overwhelmed?

I raised my hand and shouted to Aric, but the din of hooves and screams of men and horses was too loud, and the men's eyes were all trained on the armies grappling in the field below. No one seemed to grasp the threat from behind.

With all the kara on the field, the battle between Oktamazda's forces and the remaining Geloni crawled up the slope of the hill. The vazarka, on Aric's order, charged down to meet them in hopes of ending the battle. Aric lingered atop the hill, glancing over his shoulder at me after I'd failed to follow the others into the fray. Spear in one hand, he yanked at his reins and kicked at his horse's ribs until it stood beside mine, his face warped with rage and regret. I held his livid gaze as he opened his mouth to shout something, and by the curl of his lip, it was something unkind. But I raised my hand to point up the hill toward the king's position and the invading Saudaratai. His eye followed and grew wide when he saw the black-cloaked riders. Drawing a deep breath that expanded his chest, he turned his eye to the sky. Breast heaving, panting hard, his body began to sway. He clenched his trembling fist on the reins, and the chestnut gelding began to prance frantically beneath him. Unblinking, he stared over the hilltop as if blind and released a fearsome roar from deep within his chest, spooking his mount. Brandishing his spear over his head, he drove his heels into the horse's flanks and galloped, not toward the battle, but up the hill toward the king.

I reined Vatra back a moment, unsure of what had happened. Then I put my heels to him and followed Aric, plucking arrows from my quiver as I rode, my bow in hand.

As Aric galloped alone into the tumult, I saw him in pursuit of a Saudaratai warrior riding a quick little bay. A warrior in Skythian armor approached from his right flank, and I hoped Skyles's guard had finally arrived. It looked like Rathagos's eager chestnut, angrily chomping his bit, flaring his nostrils, and thrashing his legs wildly as he galloped into the chaos. He leaned into his bridle as his rider whipped him on. As I got closer, I recognized the man, if not the new armor. Rathagos had indeed joined the fighting. But he was alone. Skyles and his men were nowhere in sight.

The royal guards had quickly surrounded the king and whisked Ariapaithi off to safety, battling the swarming Saudaratai as they galloped across the hillcrest. None of the vazarka had noticed Aric's absence from the battle and followed him here. Could Rathagos be the only one to ride with Aric to the king's defense? Was he the only one of Skyles's guards not to be overwhelmed?

Galloping hard, Aric nearly caught the Saudaratai rider. He raised his spear, ready to strike. Suddenly, another spear flew and caught not the enemy warrior but the Saudaratai rider's mount. *Rathagos's spear.* The quick little bay shrieked, then tumbled and lay in a heap, its black-cloaked rider thrown hard into the dirt beside it. Aric's chestnut hesitated, then made an awkward leap, trying to clear the writhing bulk of speared horseflesh and thrashing legs before him. But the gelding was too late; he faltered as he left the ground and got tangled in the tumbled horse's limbs as the wounded beast flailed. Aric's horse tripped in flight, flipped in mid-air, and fell with a crash onto its back.

Aric struck the frozen ground hard, his head thudding heavily amid a whirlwind of brittle chaff. It looked like the horse had crushed him in its fall. The chestnut gelding thrashed atop him as it struggled to its feet, then fled. Aric lay where he fell in the torn grass, still as death.

The battle had moved on, and all was calm. I froze, pulling Vatra to a halt fifty paces away. I had to go to him—I had to see—but I couldn't ease my grip on the reins.

Rathagos trotted to where Aric lay and pulled up his horse long enough to look down at his unmoving form. Then he turned away and kicked his horse on, riding away down the back of the hill. It was clear what he'd decided: Aric was lost.

For all the cold fire coursing in my limbs, I could not make them move. Numb, the arrows and bow I'd drawn from my goryt fell from my dead fingers. A roaring filled my ears, and a voice inside my mind chattered, begging him to rise. Endlessly repeating his name. Imploring, coaxing, commanding, in vain. My watering eyes awaited a sign, and as the voice grew more urgent, it grew fainter, as did the hope he would heed it. The moments stretched on, and he still did not stir.

I longed to ride to him, but I did not dare. I'd seen my share of horrors on the steppe—some portion of them my own doing—but I was not prepared to look on this one. Not today. So, I remained frozen, awaiting a sign that would not come. Praying for the other warriors to return.

A spear's throw away, the unhorsed Saudaratai rider slowly pushed himself to his feet and searched across the field for his comrades. Sighting them down the back of the knoll, he began to walk, unaware I was watching him. And then, halfway down the hill, he stopped. He glanced again toward Aric, unmoving where he fell, and drew his dagger from his warbelt. The most precious trophy left on the battlefield lay there for the taking.

Like in dreams, I tried to scream, but no sound came. Had I tried to run, my legs would have rebelled. My strength had fled, along with my courage. I shrank in coward's fear before a duel I could not win. What could I do? And what could it matter now? He'd told me time and again it was only hide. We were not our flesh. By the way he spoke, it seemed only natural that predators should gather around a kill and have their fill. Maybe it was so. He would forgive me.

But inside, a nagging voice cried *go, go, go*. And without a thought, I put my heels to Vatra. He, at least, was immune to whatever doubts betrayed me, and he closed the distance in only a few strides. Then, my sagaris was in my hand, and it hurtled through the air like a hawk to a hare. The spike caught the Saudaratai in the thigh, and he fell to his knee, trying to wrest the prong from his leg.

I reached for my sword. As I closed with the warrior, I leapt from Vatra in mid-stride, hacking the akinaka's blade into the back of his skull, where it cracked like a walnut shell. Blood flowed, and the man's head jerked back as I landed on him, my left arm around his shoulder, my legs wrapped around him. His chest heaved as he tried to scream but only choked, falling face-down in the dirt. I withdrew my slick sword, grabbed a fistful of hair to pull his head back, and tore the blade across his throat, severing his windpipe and veins in one swift motion, cutting so deep I could feel iron against bone. I squeezed my legs around his hips until he stopped bucking under me. A spurt of blood surged forth, and I leapt back as his limp, twitching form lay on the ground, the gore pooling at my feet.

The blood was warm and strangely comforting. As I saw the man's force and menace drain from his face, my fury flowed out with it. I breathed deeply and turned to Aric's lifeless form in the center of this chaos of fallen horses and spent arrows and knelt over him, my hands beside his face, calling out for him to wake, as he had done with me so many times.

There was breath in his body still. Faint though it was, he was not dead.

More Saudaratai riders approached in the distance, their bows drawn.

"*Awake*," I begged, shaking his stubborn bulk. "Awake!" But his eye rolled back into his head as he began to writhe and quake upon the ground. There was blood and foam on his tongue as he spoke words I could make no sense of. He was dying. Vatra was gone, and I saw no shelter, no aid. I could neither defend nor surrender him.

The second wave of enemy riders was coming upon us now, and our warriors, I knew, were all occupied with a feigned retreat further south. How had the Saudaratai broken through? Where were the other bloody vazarka, sworn to protect their daranaka unto death? I could hold off a few, perhaps, but what then? In desperation, I did the only thing I could think to do. I laid myself over him, covering him with my body.

I slid the shield still strapped to my back up over our heads as the troop thundered by, and a hail of arrows turned from the shield. Like being kicked and trampled by a hundred hooves, every bolt was a violent blow, luckily unable to pierce the quilted, waxed hemp I wore concealed beneath my caftan. But the backs of my legs were left unprotected for riding. One arrow lodged in my hip, and another grazed my calf, pinning my trousers to the ground.

A body landed hard on the ground beside me, and I turned my head to see if it was dead, my dagger in my hand. A rider pulled his horse up nearby. Then he dismounted, yanked the point of his spear from the corpse, and stood guard over us. Through the gap beneath the shield, I recognized Stormai's waxed leather boots.

A third wave of riders rushed by, but I felt no more arrows. I slowly lifted my head when I didn't hear any more hooves or voices.

The fight had moved north into the plain. Aric lay still, but he was breathing quietly.

"Awake," I pleaded again in a whisper. His eye flickered, but he didn't respond.

I reached back to release the arrow pinning my trousers to the earth so I might be free to move. The arrow in my hip I tried to pull out on my own, reaching to brace the shaft with one hand so I could draw with the other. With the slightest bit of tension, the shaft slipped free, the loose tendon bindings dangling bloody from its end. The head would have to wait. I knelt straddling Aric, speaking to him, pleading with him, and trying to summon him back from whatever dark place he had descended.

Finally, slowly, he opened his eye and blinked against the sun for a moment. Then he tried to sit up, but I gently pinned his shoulders to the earth.

"Lie still."

He grunted and fell back, his eye scanning my face. I wasn't sure he knew me. "The danger is passed, and the king is safe. But you've been thrown from your horse. Rest a moment to be sure you're not hurt."

He looked around him, frowning and confused. Stormai stood guard over us, his spear gripped tight in his fist

"Anaiti," Aric said with a soft smile. Then his brow furrowed. "Let me up!" he pushed his palms into the cold ground and struggled to sit upright.

"Please—you've already scared me half to death," I insisted, trying to hold him down.

"You should take the lady's good counsel," Stormai said from behind me.

"You mean I've missed the whole thing?" Aric groaned hoarsely. "I am disgraced." He propped himself up on his elbows as he looked around.

The other Paralatai riders were making their way back,

Rathagos riding at the fore. I flinched at the sight of him and struggled to my feet.

"Where the fuck were you," I barked at Rathagos, "when your prince needed your help? You saw Aric fall, and you just rode away."

If he could play the accuser, why couldn't I?

"And how did so many Saudaratai get past Skyles's guard?"

"We were ambushed and held at bay. I rode onward to meet my prince, Skyles, and see to the rescue of the king. Seeing Aric fall as he did, I feared him lost," Rathagos said dryly. "I celebrate this turn of good fortune."

Celebrate? I bet you did.

"It was a frightful sight," Rathagos said as he dismounted and strode up to stand over us, "seeing the prince come to grief. But there is something else to celebrate: Lady Anaiti has finally made her tally." He turned to wink at me. "So, a victory for all, wouldn't you say?"

Aric's head snapped around, his eye wide with panic.

"Congratulations are in order," Rathagos added as he reached for the dagger in his belt. He had turned his back to us and knelt over the body of the Saudaratai warrior. As Aric fought to gain his feet, I tried to help him, but he shrugged me off.

I strode forward and grabbed Rathagos by his greasy hair, yanking his head back. "Take your filthy hands off!" I shouted louder than necessary. "I'll do it myself."

He turned and, in one hand, held my bloody akinaka and, in the other, his own raised dagger. I hobbled over to him and snatched the sword from his hands. *Snake.* He would not menace me. I fell to my knees over the corpse, the stabbing pain in my hip agonizing, and withdrew my dagger. Looking at the man's ruined skull, where my blade had cracked it open, now resting in a pool of cold, congealing blood, I hardly knew where to begin. His cold, blue eyes, half-lidded, stared skyward as I pressed the point of my blade deep into the skin of his hairline until I felt the resistance of bone, and I half expected him to flinch or blink or cry out. But then I reminded myself I'd hunted and skinned creatures before. Creatures that also felt pain and feared death. Why should this be so very different? Like those, the body lay still and spoke not a whisper, made not a whimper, as I began to cut in long sweeping arcs along the contours of his face, around his ears, and behind his neck. Then, eager to have it done, I grabbed the mass of his hair in my hand, recalling the moist tearing sounds I'd heard before, and I heaved with all the strength I had left. With a brief tug of resistance, it slipped loose, and in my fist, I held up a clotted, blond scalp to the onlookers. The men of the warband let up a cheer.

I staggered to my feet as Rathagos stepped in close, raising his hand before me, and tried to force his wet fingers between my lips. "You must drink the blood of your 'first' kill," he insinuated. I shoved at him, trying to escape, but he was quick, strong, and determined, managing to slide his filthy fingers into my mouth, the tang of tepid blood and salt bitter on my tongue. I tried to spit, but it was too late.

A fierce anger ignited within me, prompting me to instinctively swing the fist clutching my dagger's handle, landing a solid hit on his nose. I felt a crunch and feared I had broken my hand with the force of the blow. But as he fell reeling back, his hands flying to his dumbfounded face, I watched with satisfaction as blood flowed freely over his lip and down his chin, soaking his scraggly beard.

"*Drink your fill of that!*" I taunted, gripping the scalp in one hand, dagger in the other, as the gathered men fell so silent I believe they had stopped breathing. Refusing to let the rage inside me die, I glared at him with all the hatred I could muster, daring him to come for me again, begging him to fight. Rathagos, still cupping his spouting nose in his hands, did not approach or even speak but, meeting my eyes briefly, flashed me an inscrutable glance, spat his own blood upon the ground, and turned to walk away. Something perverse in me longed to call out after him and name him the coward all could see he was, compounding his shame, but I restrained myself, as, when tempers rise and voices roar, the shame too often removes to the accuser before long.

Savoring this small triumph amid my greater defeat, I turned toward the men when the searing pain in my hip shot down my leg and up my back, and I nearly crumpled to the ground. As my vision wavered, I looked desperately for Aric, hoping it was only pain mixing with fury and the strain of the battle. Then the wave of darkness overtook me, and the last thing I remembered was that taste on my tongue.

CHAPTER 47

INVALID

*Even with my eyes open, I couldn't trace his
voice in the moonless sea of night.*

I CAME TO VIOLENTLY. Swinging fists and elbows, I bloodied
Aric's nose and Gohar's lip as I fought to gain my feet. Blinking
in confusion at the scalp in my hand, I instinctively wiped and
thrust the akinaka at my feet back into its scabbard on my warbelt.
My whole body was bathed in another's sticky blood. Nauseated, I
limped to find a dry burdock bush where I could empty the meager
contents of my stomach.

The wound in my hip was raw, and the pain was almost unbearable. I struggled to remain standing as Aric and Gohar propped me
up, leading me to a place behind a row of carts. The oxen bellowed
anxiously where they were tethered, tugging against their ties, and
the wood of the wheels creaked as they swayed. They lay me on the
grass and began cutting away the blood-soaked garments to get a
better look at the wound. Only the pain kept me from drifting as
I clutched the clotted scalp in my fist.

"It's barbed," I reported, and Aric grunted.

"It's in deep," Aric said, his voice cracking. He prodded gently
with his calloused fingers, and I willed myself to remain steady for

his sake despite the shocks of pain each touch shot through me. "I can feel it. Not a lot of bruising or blood. It missed the vein."

"That's good, right?"

"It's not bad." He frowned. "But it's in the bone. What do you think, Gohar?"

I knew if the Saudaratai and Geloni were anything like the Skythai, they imbued their arrows with death and rot and venom. Soon that contagion would pollute my body and probably kill me, as it nearly had Aric. It likely didn't matter now.

"I think we don't do this now," Gohar said. "This isn't the place. Leave it be until we can find a healer."

"We can't leave her like this—suffering." Aric ran his hand over his hair in frustration. "And if there is poison . . . ," he trailed off as if reading my thoughts. "We must do this now. They could be regrouping or sending their wolves to scavenge the fields, and she needs to be back on her horse or in a wagon before dark." He looked at me with anguish in his eye. I was shivering with cold and just wanted to sleep. And that couldn't happen until they pulled this hunk of bronze from my flesh. I nodded to Aric. He inclined his head toward me and, in a low voice, said, "Stormai told me what you did. It was stupid."

"A simple 'thank you' will suffice."

"You have an arrow in you," he said gruffly. "Why didn't you say anything?"

There were other men and horses wounded far worse than I who needed the healers and arrow-pullers more urgently, including Aric. Mine could wait. But he would never see it that way.

Gohar pressed his lips together as if to contain words behind them. Then he spoke softly, the way one speaks to soothe a spooky horse: "I don't like this. We should call an athravan—someone practiced in knife medicine."

"It's not too deep," I said. "I can feel the ferrule. Enlarge the wound for the arrow-puller."

Gohar shook his head. "The king won't like it."

"Enough talk," I said, losing my patience with their dithering. "Do it, or give me a knife, and I'll do it myself."

Gohar looked at me with indignation as he touched up the blade of his dagger with the whetstone on his belt and held it to the flame of a torch. Feeling down where the ferrule protruded, he cut a neat slit into the skin and prepared to extract the arrow.

"Forgive me," Aric said as he took the spoonlike tongs from Gohar. Then he carefully inserted the pullers, clamped its jaws securely on the arrowhead, braced his hand against my hip, and began to rock the head loose with a strong, steady force. After a moment and a sharp pain, the point broke loose, and my blood poured out onto his hands. But the arrow was out cleanly. I closed my eyes, exhausted.

I OPENED MY EYES TO THE STARS, cold and clear and low-hanging upon the dome of the dark sky. Since departing the battlefield, I'd slipped in and out of fitful sleep. I lay on a bed of dusty hay, my head thudding against the boards of a rumbling oxcart. Just one in a train carrying the last of our food, the wounded, dying, and dead, the war trophies. Sound, healthy captives were made to walk, bound by neck and hands, in a long procession at the back. Their brief, defiant shouts—followed by the cracking of whips and screams—punctuated the otherwise voiceless night.

I turned away from the pain in my hip as the cart jostled down the track, listening to the hypnotic jumble of cattle and horse hooves padding over the frozen ground.

"Cheer up! You're rid of her now," said a voice to the right of the cart. "By the looks of things, Father may soon be, too." In the dark, it took me a moment to place the voice as Oktamazda's.

"What are you doing here?" Aric's voice growled back bitterly.

"I swore that day, same as you. Should Arianta ask, I won't have to lie."

"Son of a bitch."

"We've fulfilled our obligation here, right?" Oktamazda chuck-led to himself. It was hard to believe I'd once found his infectious laugh charming.

"Father wants her alive and well."

"If you say so. But then you should have kept her in one piece, little brother. Holy Mother of Serpents! What a mess. But I sup-pose now is no time to test Arianta. Spargapaithi has consolidated his forces, and the Delians are nearly at war again. We probably do need her to live. At least until they're married."

Aric inhaled through his teeth with a hiss, kicked his horse into a canter, and rode away. I suffered at the sound of his horse's fading hooves. Within the range of his voice, I knew safety. But there was much ground to cover before he could rest tonight, and I'd drift far from his thoughts, perhaps for good. I suppose he had reason to be angry—more reason than even he knew. I hadn't the mind to unravel the knot of all I'd done and couldn't undo—to follow where those threads led. After hearing Oktamazda's opinion of my worth, I dared not risk opening my eyes with him nearby. I allowed myself to fade back into groggy sleep.

AWOKEN AGAIN by a nasty bump as the road jarred my bones out of joint, I risked peeking through squinted eyes but saw and heard nothing. I struggled to sit up. A warm gush of blood moistened my trousers. The wound was still open.

"Don't," a voice near me said. "Lie still. We'll be home soon." It was Oktamazda again. He still rode alongside the oxcarts instead of at the fore of the victorious war party with his army. Even with my eyes open, I couldn't trace his voice in the moonless sea of night, lit by a tiny torch at the head of the cart, burning desperately against the black. I searched for Aric, and listened for his voice nearby, but he was not there.

Oktamazda's voice both soothed and disturbed. Rest now, it

said, and I tried, drifting in and out of restless sleep until the cart's wheels stopped creaking and the road stopped lurching.

UPON THE OXCARTS' ARRIVAL, the athravan, ministers to the wounded and keepers of the dead, had been summoned. Human crows of the battlefield, they flocked to the carts. Still delirious, I raised myself from the back of my cramped cart to see Aric there with them, speaking with someone concealed in shadow. His voice mingled with Erman's soft speech.

"She needs healing," Aric was saying, "and she must have a place to stay. Now that she's made her tally, it is not proper for her to convalesce with the warriors. But the women," he mumbled and shook his head, "you know as well as I, they won't have anything to do with her."

"She can remain among the anarei," Erman offered. "We will find her a wagon and—"

"Can Ariapaithi entrust *you* with this honor?"

Erman hesitated a moment before exhaling slowly. "Of course."

I didn't care where they put me. My wound throbbed. Terrible cramps and stomach pains racked my entire body. They could leave me here by the side of the road for all I cared. I just needed to get out of this torturous cart.

I braced myself again as the cart pitched and bumped along to the edge of the settlement. A sharp pain stabbed in my guts until I doubled up with the pangs. I felt around under my clothes for wounds I'd overlooked. Perhaps in the fury of battle, I'd missed a blade or point piercing me. Then, a warm gush spread beneath me from between my thighs, and I understood the pains and what was happening. The potion had finally begun to take effect.

The cart came to rest apart from the long train of wounded and supplies. Suddenly the others were gone, and all was silent. I searched the dark again for Aric, but only an ox driver remained. We had reached a wagon with a felt-house set atop its platform. It stood on a little spit of land at a bend in the creek. We were only a few feet from other dwellings, but we had crossed into another world. No one was about. Sitting up, I struggled to my knees, thinking I'd climb down, but my injured hip gave out, and I collapsed under the strain. I closed my eyes and lay back.

Soon, a horse and voices approached. Hands reached into the darkness and lifted me up—Aric's hands, helping me to a wagon-tent with a burning fire. Oktamazda, arriving behind us, followed. Despite the cold, Oktamazda and Aric stopped outside to cast off their arms, warbelts, and their shoes. They also removed mine, leaving them hung on pegs outside the felt-house.

Once the door opened, I recognized the house immediately. The dry and shriveled horse phallus hung face-height near the doorway and caught us both as we entered. The weaving beam staff propped beside the door—the shelves of herbs and potions, the altar, the carpet and its gaming board.

More blood soaked my trousers, mingling blood from my wounds and the dried blood of the dead Saudaratai—a scarlet sea with many tributaries. Aric's brows pinched together as he pressed his hand flat beneath his bast girdle and met my eyes. I took his meaning well enough and shook my head ever so slightly. He closed his eye and let his hand fall limp. Whether it was sorrow or relief that flowed through him just now, I could not tell.

"So, you got yourself shot in the ass, did you?" Erman said as he peeled away the bandage stuffed into my wound and prepared to remove my trousers.

"Um," I hesitated. "It's more like my hip." I suddenly wondered if I wanted my wound inspected after all.

"Mmm, that's probably what I'd tell people, too," he flashed one of his cheeky grins. "Turn over," he then ordered, and I reluctantly complied so that he could examine the wound. He cut away the already shredded trousers with a pair of iron sheers and poked around the edges of the injury.

"How bad?" Aric interrupted.

Erman leaned in close, lifting the clotted bandage to his nose; he drew a long, slow whiff. "I do not smell poison." He stretched the flesh front and back, poked around the edges, and peered into the breach left by the arrow. "It's deep but clean. Her chances are good. Oktamazda, I hear you are an expert. What do you think: ass or hip?" Then, blithely waved his hand. "Never mind. No stitches necessary. I will pack it with honey, but it may yet abscess."

Erman didn't wait for responses, continually speaking—and amusing himself—as he worked. "The lady must be washed. You should go," he said to the brothers. "Rest. I'll send word to the king in the morning."

"Thank you on behalf of the king," Oktamazda said. "I will inform Ariapaithi myself and have my most trusted men ride to King Arianta tonight. Be well, lady." Then he took his leave without delay, gathering his weapons at the door.

Erman stared pointedly at Aric.

"I stay," Aric said.

"Then you can help me undress and wash her."

"I—that—I don't think that would be . . . appropriate," poor Aric stammered.

"This isn't necessary," Erman said.

"What isn't?"

"The pretense. There's no time. And I don't care."

Aric bowed his head and said nothing. I glanced up at him, but his eye only flicked over me and back to Erman, who was prepping something in a mortar.

"It would be easiest if you could carry her to the stream. Strip her clothes there and bathe her quickly." I cringed at the thought of being dipped in a frosty stream. The misery must have been evident on my face. "I'll add fuel to the fire and ready extra blankets."

"I won't," Aric said. "Hasn't she suffered enough? I'll fetch water to warm here. Where are your skins? Your cauldron?"

"You're looking at it." Erman pointed to the small vessel near the fire. "I live alone and can only carry so much. If you insist, we can wake the others."

"Don't bother," I said. "I'm not a complete invalid. Cold water hasn't killed me yet." I stretched my hand to Aric.

"You can't be serious."

"Are you going to help me or not?"

Grimacing, he grasped my hand and gently pulled me up, sliding his shoulder under my arm and propping himself under me like a crutch. Erman handed him a heavy woolen blanket of green and brown plaid, and Aric helped me gingerly down the stairs to face the frigid waters of the creek.

CLEAN NOW AND WRAPPED in the thick blanket before the fire, Erman packed the wound with a roll of fine linen soaked in honey and applied a sticky, red resin beneath the bandage.

"I trust you have retained the arrowhead?" he asked, and Aric quickly produced the missile from within his tunic. This Erman also anointed and wrapped in a piece of linen, setting it near the fire. "Keep it safe always," he said, "for it is now joined to you by blood. Its life is bound to yours."

Though slighter of build than myself, he found one of his own robes for me to wear. When I was mended and dressed, he said he needed to retrieve an ingredient for making a poultice from one of the other anarei. He slipped on his heavy felt cloak and boots and thumped down the wagon steps with his staff. I watched the door until the rapping of his staff against the frozen ground faded into the dark reaches of the night.

As I turned back to face Aric, he grasped my face with both hands and pressed his lips to mine. Its suddenness stole my breath. I pushed him away.

His eye flickered back and forth, searching. Wet with tears, his cheek glistened in the stingy glow of the hearth. The anguish in his eye stirred the sweetest grief in my heart, and my whole body began to tremble with dread.

"It's all over," I said.

"It's all right," he whispered. "*It will be all right.*" But his voice betrayed desperation, and he seemed to speak to reassure himself as much as me. His hands froze in the space between us, as if he feared touching me.

I combed my fingers over his tangled hair. "Don't be angry with me," I pleaded. "I just couldn't remain behind. Tell me you understand? *I had to fight.*"

Fixing my face before his in the gentle grip of his strong hands, he held my gaze. "I'm not angry. I am awestruck."

I cast my gaze downward, suddenly feeling too shy to meet his eye. Gingerly, I lay on the lumpy bed and pulled him down beside me and I nestled into him, with his sturdy arms wrapped gently around me and mine around him. I let myself be lulled by the steady thrum of his heart, the tidal rise and fall of his breast, and his sheltering embrace for what I knew must be the last time.

"Don't let me fall asleep," I mumbled into his chest as I dozed, warm again and safe for now, but cursing the stealthy coming of sleep for always robbing us of what precious little time we had.

CHAPTER 48

SACRIFICE

Thus, I free this being to inhabit all the realms.

In the morning, Aric was gone. I had slept deeply and didn't remember him leaving. Erman, preparing a millet, cheese, and herb porridge in the cauldron, smiled warmly at me as I struggled to sit up. The pain was surprisingly small.

"How do you feel?"

I felt refreshed but oddly numb all over.

"This all must seem strange," Erman said. "But you've nothing to fear from me."

Was my apprehension so apparent? The seer's home was a sacred space, and there were protocols to observe; I knew nothing of how to conduct myself here. I knew better than to fear his command of spirits. Priests spoke impressively and showed little for it. The real peril was that he knew too much.

"It's the rest of the world that looks strange to me," I smiled at him and regarded him a moment. He'd always been kind. His inelegance and honesty endeared him to me. He'd aided me when he had no reason to—at least, no reason I could discern.

"Indeed. *They are not like us*," he returned my smile and gave the cauldron a good stir, clanging the ladle against the rim before hanging it back on its hook. Then he looked as if he'd suddenly remembered something, shuffled across the room, and began rummaging through an earthenware jar on the floor beneath one of the tables, coming up with a double handful of walnuts for his porridge.

THE CAMP ROLLED ON shortly after our victory with the fields too torn and bloody to graze. We headed south along the course of the Volosdanu beside the rapids, which make the river impassable for many miles. Here, the waters fell in giant steps and roared so fiercely they could be heard for miles. Our own dead had been embalmed according to the Skythian custom, their bodies hollowed out and filled with herbs and chaff, then covered with wax. They were dressed in their finest and placed in funerary wagons to keep until spring when the ground would thaw enough to dig.

The remaining Geloni army was permitted to take their dead from the field and burn them on great pyres fueled by the wood of their provision wagons. Some of their best warriors were ransomed for gold, livestock, or other goods. The rest we trailed behind us, bound in chains or tied with ropes of hemp. These were healed, fed, and clothed. But the walking, the cold, and sleeping huddled together on the ground was more hardship than many could shoulder. They moaned incessantly and wept, and I began to question what sort of men they were. My meager pity soon gave way to contempt. After all, it was they who sought this war. Now they tasted the suffering they had hoped to visit upon us and found it too bitter to swallow.

When the Geloni captives were pressed for their purpose in making war upon the Skythai, they claimed to want restoration of Gelonus so they might reopen the northern karevan routes and enjoy the same trade enriching the colonies. The Greek poison had spread north. Or perhaps it had never subsided but lingered in the soil, in the people, who would never be satisfied with the simple, honest life of farming but craved the gilded lives of serpent-tongued merchants. And still, they might have simply occupied the fort, but they recruited a sworn enemy of the Paralatai and came for our king's head, bent on our destruction. One could at least admire their boldness, if not their ends.

After six slow days, we arrived at a sanctuary beside the rapids, which the Skythai called *Apatura*—swift waters—and made camp. Here was a broad, flat field, at the center of which were two structures: one a kind of earthwork platform and the other an earth-and-ditch enclosure. The fold was like the earthen banks of a ringfort on three sides, open to the dawn. The mound was not unlike the barrows that cropped up across these plains. But it was oblong rather than round, with a level top and a sloping ramp leading up its broad dawnward face. On the surface, twigs of myrtle were scattered. At the top, near its southern end, there stood a low altar of weathered granite. The hilt of an iron sword fitted into the stone, its waxed blade pointed toward the sky.

We made camp some distance away from the sacred grounds and, the days being short, held no rites upon our arrival. Fires blazed before the platform as the sun set, and the grounds were prepared for a sunrise ceremony. An invalid still, I watched all from the distance of Erman's wagon as the sun slipped behind the ancient sword in the altar, its slim silhouette stark in the sanguine glow. Nearby, the warriors drank and danced and brandished their own swords in the firelight, and I wished I could be there with them instead of languishing out here, out of mind. Behind me, I could hear the captives' lamentations in the falling darkness.

"What's happening?" I asked Erman as I peered into the dusk.

"We wait. Tomorrow at noon, we honor Ari, the Great Sword. With sacrifices, we honor its giver, Papahio, our Heavenly Father, for deciding a just outcome to the battle."

"Haven't enough men been slaughtered?"

"Sacrifice is not slaughter. It is an act of healing."

I shook my head, too weary to argue.

"In times of great devastation, it is the beginning of our restoration. The world was made through sacrifice, and thus, man and all he lives by. Manu first sacrificed and dismembered his brother, Yama, and apportioned his remains in the creation of the world:

The moon was born of his mind;
From his eye, the sun;
From his skull, the dome of heaven;
From his breath, the wind;
From his blood, the waters;
From his hair, the plants;
From his flesh, the earth;
From his bones, the stones;
Thus did Manu cause the world to be created
When he bound Yama as the sacrifice.

"With this, the proper order came to be, as the first sovereign's many powers were portioned out among his corresponding parts:

The priest was from his head and mouth;
The warrior from his heart and arms;
The farmer from his loins and feet.

"Those disparate members combine to form the body of the tribe. Some its mind and laws, some its strength and will, and some its support and abundance. By this, our order is achieved."

"But why must more men die because of it?"

"When the substance of the universe gathers into man or beast or tree, they call this season birth. When it dissolves once more, they call this season death. Each generation dips its waterskin into the great well of creation, and each birth pricks a new hole in its hide, slowly draining it. Sacrifice replenishes it before it runs dry. It restores balance, healing the injury our existence has caused and reversing the world's decay. Eventually, all things return to the source to one day be reborn. Our substance is enduring, fluid, timeless. Now and then, the majesty of nature fades, and the cosmos dims. Just as slaughter and harvest nourish the bodies of men, so too must we sustain the body of the world."

REEDS HAD BEEN SPREAD under the priests' feet, and wagons of brushwood were used to light three great sacrificial fires around the sanctuary. A zhotr called Akhtar stood before the central fire and recited the sacred litanies as the Skythai warriors gathered before the mound. He bade them withdraw their swords or, if they had none, their spears. He said that the sacrificial altar was adorned with glory this day. The foremost among the gods, invited by songs and sacrifices, took their seats where the holy myrtle branches—their leaves carefully dried for such an occasion—had been laid with care beside the altar.

All gazed reverently upon the branch-strewn mound as if expectant of some heavenly portent. Akhtar told how Papahio gave mankind the sword to vanquish the enemies of gods and men with the admonition: "The sword contains a divine spirit within, known to men as law. Protect all creatures with it, dealing justice to those seeking harm. Honor its use in accord with the dictates of just laws; do not dishonor it in use upon whims." They were nearly the same words I had often heard from Aric and Bornon as they instructed me in the use of my own sword.

After a lengthy recitation of verses, the prisoners were lined up, Geloni and Saudaratai alike. There were too many to count. A thousand perhaps. One man in every hundred was chosen to stand out from the line—the weakest and most grievously injured of the dejected mass. The first prisoner, his hands bound, was made to kneel over an empty glazed wine vat where the master of sacrifice and keeper of the sacred fires, Oustana, poured wine over his head and spoke an incantation, an invocation, aloud:

Lay his feet down to the north.
Cause his eye to go to the sun;
Send forth his breath to the wind;
Send his spirit to the sky;
Send his blood to the waters;
Send his flesh to the earth.
Thus, I free this being to inhabit all the realms.

Then, he cut the prisoner's throat over the vessel. This, he took by the red-painted handles, once filled to its brim, and carried it atop the platform. There, he poured the blood over the upturned blade of the sword. One by one, the serene priest led the chosen prisoners into the enclosure to bow with their necks over the blood-soaked vessel and be sacrificed.

After the initial ceremonies, in which all were obligated to partake, I watched from a distance, sitting in the back of a cart with Erman. I resented my injuries for keeping me confined, but I didn't need to be close. I had neither queasiness nor bloodlust, neither the desire for peace nor vengeance. But I no longer flinched when the blade opened the flesh. When the blood poured out, it was merely one more consequence in a long string of events, choices, deeds, and fates I had come to accept.

This rite was enacted for some ten men. And where each of those men's bodies lay in the earthen fold, the athravan hacked off their right hands and, carrying them up the platform also, tossed them up in the air, calling out some blessing or oath to Papahio.

The warrior is from his heart and arms.

It was not the first I had seen of such rites.

These honored a different god than my homeland's, but I supposed the purpose was much the same. When the seed pits, which lay silent all winter, were finally opened in spring, it was the most fraught moment of the year. Neither the coldest night, fiercest storm, nor even the raids of enemies could compare to the breathless, heart-pounding fear every man and woman in the fort felt upon the opening of the pits, unsure whether the seed had spoiled under the influence of some malevolent force of the earth, or insects, or unappeased dead while shut away in the dark. Only once in my youth did I see a pit spew forth seed covered in a putrid mold of decay, and the people took it for a curse. They were not wrong, for all the crops grew poorly and were afflicted with rust that year.

In the good years, and more so in the bad, the Mother was given a special gift to replenish her coffers, as she—we hoped—would fill ours. When the pits were emptied, and the furrows plowed, a youth was sown into one of the pits. Usually, a farmer's boy just coming to manhood. He was almost always sickly, slow of mind, or lame in some way. And then again, with the scything of the final sheaf of the harvest, an old man would come forth to be bound up in the sheaf and beaten upon the threshing floor. For those who could offer no labor or craft, it was a great pride for their kin to see them offer themselves on behalf of the people. They took great comfort in knowing that those who had been fruitless in life might be fruitful in death. Like the gods, the people showed them great honor for their sacrifice, so they went to it like heroes—willingly and with gladness in their hearts.

These warriors were neither willing nor glad.

"You disapprove," Erman's gentle smile faded as he turned to me above the chanting of the observers.

I stared at the gore upon the mound in numb silence. "Your ways are still strange to me," I said wearily. "I don't understand what your gods want."

"They want what we want. Even the noblest kings—and the gods themselves—must sometimes be brutal in creating and maintaining our order. But Papahio shows us how even they are not above Arta. War is among the worst things in men, but it can also be the best."

"How so?"

"When it makes us seek justice and hold ourselves to account for our sins, as we conduct ourselves under the watchful gaze of Papahio, whose great blue eye looks ever down upon us."

I turned to face him. "And these men have been judged?"

"Battle *is* judgment. Matters too great for courts and councils are taken to battlefields, and what reasonable men cannot settle, fate and the gods do."

"And what then?"

"Then the time for treaties returns."

"And this is the only way?"

"If we do not fight to preserve the good order, who will?"

I stared across the blood-reddened field. Were we—heart and arms of the earth—agents of destruction or preservation? And how had I come this far without knowing which?

The bodies and arms were left where they lay, arrayed around the blood-soaked sword as our battered warriors tended their wounds and prepared for the next battle, wherever it might be. The rest of the prisoners were gathered for the slave markets in the south, the colonies, and beyond. The Geloni, of all men, should be quite at home in the lands of the Hellenes. There was a sacrifice of beasts as well, and at night, there was feasting around the sanctuary grounds. Still recovering from my wounds, I was unable to join the celebration. I watched from the stair of Erman's wagon for as long as I could until I drifted into painful sleep, propped against the doorframe.

The following day, the warband departed again for the marches before dawn—before I could see them off—which was perhaps for the best. With my tally formally made, my time among them officially had ended. I would miss them—all of them—more than they should ever know.

As we broke camps and resumed our road, the prisoners were finally silent.

CHAPTER 49

APPRENTICE

I realized, too late, that I had not been escaping
a fate in the marches, but seeking one.

E RMAN TOLD ME that Paralatai wed at the beginning of summer, when the lambs, calves, and foals are in the fields and the trees are in bloom. Until then, I would wait. Besides, I needed time to heal, and my father could not make the long three-hundred-mile journey while snowstorms threatened.

I'd hoped to become useful to Erman by now and help with chores, but my injuries slowed me more than I expected. The wound in my hip had become inflamed and painful. It was difficult to stand, and I needed a staff to walk. He and I now clunked around the floorboards of the wagon as a pair.

Another anarei came when Erman's actual duties kept him away. A young, wide-eyed, electrum-haired apprentice named Aldis. Reserved and shy, he reminded me of my young self. The kind of boy who feeds orphaned chicks until they're fledged. Who can lose himself in a field of flowers or the way light plays on the seed heads of ripened grain. Who gets chewed up and swallowed by the world. I wondered how he would ever survive in such a place as this. I once imagined Erman was like that boy, but beside him,

Erman appeared downright rugged. Where Erman had chosen the anarei mantle, the anarei mantle had chosen Aldis. I worried for him. He'd need the thick skin Erman had earned to survive as a soothsayer. But I came to adore him, and in his innocence, he revealed that, though many of the older anarei wouldn't be willing to help me, he was proud to, because we all served the Mistress.

In their company, I became accustomed to anarei rites: daily shaving, ritual washing, prayer chanting, and meditations standing on one foot, with one arm raised and one eye closed. There was a beautiful rhythm, and there was quiet humor and camaraderie among them.

As my wounds finally healed, I began to share in their chores— fetching water, washing clothes, drying herbs, beating carpets, collecting fuel, preparing food, and always keeping the fire. The anarei ate no flesh, so we milked goats and cooked from cheese, grain, and honey stores. In the evening, Aldis had lessons. I shrank into the shadows at the back of the wagon and sat in silence, listening raptly as Erman taught verses, wisdom, law, divination, and music to his young pupil. The scent of incense and a musty carpet laden with ash filled the room. The Skythai were mostly unlettered and didn't expound their philosophies to outsiders. Their sacred wisdom and verses were forbidden to be recorded, deemed far too precious for uninitiated ears. Pride swelled in me to take part, to be granted the privilege of hearing and bearing witness to their arcane rites.

During the day, Erman taught me to spin yarn and to weave upon his loom so I would have something to keep my idle hands occupied as I convalesced. It was sedentary work, but I enjoyed having something productive to do with my hours confined indoors.

When the work was done and I closed my eyes at night, I struggled to calm my thoughts and quiet the restless voice inside my head. Sleep was an unbroken horse, skittish and unwilling to let me climb aboard without patient coaxing. From there, the journey was always unpleasant, unrestful, and short.

I AWOKE GASPING in panic, unable to breathe. A hand was clasped over my mouth, and it was too dark to see. My fingers pried at the hand as I struggled to rise against it. I swung my fist in the dark and met something spongy.

"Shhhh! You were talking in your sleep," a nasal, stuffy voice whispered in the dark.

"Erman?" I mumbled into the smothering palm. I ceased fighting as understanding replaced my panic.

"You bloodied my nose."

"You surprised me," I whispered. "What were you thinking?"

"You were calling to him." The hand fell away. Blinking away the sleep, my eyes cleared and adjusted to the faint light of the hearth, and I sat up to face Erman, cupping a hand over his battered face.

"I didn't mean to wake you," I said sheepishly.

"You must be quiet now. Careful." He stood and went to the table adjacent to the altar, his back to me.

In the aftermath of the battle, Aric had become a ghost, slipping through the camp and ducking into doorways, straying into my line of sight only to pass out of the glow of the firelight. We would catch each other's gaze, but then he would vanish like a dream upon waking—real, yet not really there. I could see but not touch him; hear but not speak with him. I longed to call out his name, but to what end? He would go while I remained, banished to our separate realms. Like all ghosts, memories would become our meat.

I waited for him, hoping for a proper farewell, for a chance to explain. But a wish was just salt for a wound. I'd given up that hope as the ceremony drew near. By now, the warband would have moved to a new buna, and Aric would have discovered the empty vial in the stash beneath my pallet.

"I don't mean to disturb you."

"You don't," Erman grinned as he hobbled back over with a cloth to his nose and a cup in his hand and knelt at my side. "Drink this," he offered a bowl of kumis with a greenish powder mixed into it and dabbed at the trickle of blood from his nose.

"Is your nose all right? Let me look."

"I'll be fine. Drink." He grinned inscrutably as he handed the bowl to me.

Holding the bowl in both hands, I stared into it. "What's in it?"

"It will help you sleep."

I drank slowly, looking up at him with curiosity—and some apprehension.

"Your dreams have been disturbed for some time. And you've been brooding about like a cow waiting to be milked. Dreams are one of the arcane languages understood by the anarei. Speak your dreams to me so that I may interpret them for you. Unburden yourself before you burst."

"I don't need to be unburdened," I said guardedly. He'd been watching me, and I suddenly felt uneasy. Perhaps I'd outgrown these close quarters.

"You do not trust me?"

"I do," I mumbled, feeling queasy. "But it's nothing you should be troubled with."

"But that's what friends are for," he said softly, giving me a big, shy grin as if he was trying on a smile—or a friendship—for the first time.

"It might oblige you to act." If he was indeed my friend, he could get hurt. And if not, he could hurt me.

"I serve the gods before serving the king." He smiled sympathetically and placed his hand upon mine. His blue eyes nearly sparkled like sunlit water.

"You hear all. What do people say?" I asked.

"The things you'd expect. But that's not what's troubling you—what's making you call out in your sleep."

No, I suppose it wasn't. I heard things, too. Rumor spread around court that Ariapaithi had divested Aric as his heir, even

after his successful command of the warband and his valor in battle, risking himself to protect the king. People said it was because
the king was ashamed that his son was rescued by a woman in the
fighting—people who weren't there. But I knew it was because he
refused to take the Borætai girl to wife. His flash of defiance had
cost him his hard-won position. Aric deserved better. We both did.

"Have I not done my duty?" I asked.

He cocked his head and frowned.

"It's like all the good I tried to do is undone. After all that has
passed, I've earned no credit here. Instead, we are both punished
for it. You put this mark on my arm, but it means nothing; they
will never see me as Skythai. After the battle, when I made my
tally, there was no ceremony, no recognition: no one dunked my
head in the cauldron, and I never drank from the king's damned
bowl."

"In the chaos, the ceremony was quietly forgotten, wasn't it?"
He grinned and took the empty cup from my hands. "Would you
have given them up so willingly? Let Aric break your torc and burn
your girdle? Would he even try?"

"What are you saying?"

"He made you a vazarka for life. Though none realize, you still
belong to Gœtosura."

"I'm still a vazarka?" I shook my head.

"You're still a karik beneath that dress if you wish it. For some,
it's not so easily undone. No more than I can be unstruck by that
bolt from heaven."

"Why would he not tell me himself?"

"Because this place has invisible bindings everywhere."

"Then I am a hostage."

"A vazarka never plays the prey."

"How can I be true to my oaths when I'm forbidden to fight?"

"What makes a warrior? Is it the weapons you wield? Your
strength or skill in combat?"

My eyes drifted down to my hands, fingers nervously tracing the woven chevron pattern on my blanket.

"We are strange creatures, we humans. I always considered this the essential difference between the beasts and us. It's not wearing clothes, crafting weapons, or building cities that makes us different. It comes down to this simple fact: beasts have instincts, and humans have choices. In time, we *become* our choices. The blessing—and burden—of humanity is that our lives can be about so much more than just sustenance and shelter, sex and procreation. The beasts are slaves to their drives for these things. But we, whether warrior or seer, have the power to choose other, greater things. I also know this is not the road for all, being solitary and stony."

"All worthy roads are."

"Indeed."

I suppose it was the nature of indifferent fate that I should not come to fully grasp the life I had chanced to live until now, at the leaving of it. I didn't appreciate men like him and those of the warband or what force drove them to choose the lives they did. I realized, too late, that I had not been escaping a fate in the marches but seeking one.

"I envy you," I said. "I, too, wanted my life to be about more," I whispered.

He placed his hand over mine. "Your life is not yet over."

CHAPTER 50

WARRIOR

But the forge of the fields had hammered out
a hardwearing heart.

"THEY SAY YOU ARE MUCH IMPROVED . . ."

Like a hind startled in the woods, I froze, nearly dropping the garments in my hand. I was folding clothes in the back of my wagon when the words caught my ear.

" . . . though you spend all your time alone."

My pulse roared so that I could barely hear the muffled footsteps drawing near. With my wounds mostly healed and my limp growing faint, I'd been moved to my own wagon and deemed fit to wed. It had been barely two weeks, and already I'd begun packing my few belongings for my departure to the king's train. Rising gently over the eager singing of lately migrated birds, his voice was the last sound I expected to ever again find its way through my open door. I hadn't even heard him mount the stairs. Now, his shadow moved across the floor as his towering form filled the doorway.

"Come—come in," I stammered, and the door swung closed behind him. I'd seen only glimpses of him since the battle, but we'd not spoken since that day. How I cursed that day.

He seldom came to court now. I heard it said he came in from the marches days before, but I did not catch a whisper of him until he chose to startle me just now. Breathing deliberately, like drawing a bellows, I closed my eyes and tested my feet before turning around slowly and running my eyes up the length of him. I was relieved to find that he was sound and fit, though he had cropped his hair and beard again. Would it be unreasonable to ask why he'd waited so long? I suppose I knew the answer already. His eye darted away as I tried to join our glances.

"It's all right. My solitude is a blessing," I said defiantly. "You know me, I enjoy the company of so few."

"Aren't you lonely?" he asked, his brows drawing together in their painful, worried way.

Men liked to think of themselves as lone wolves, independent and fierce. But in the end, none of them can truly bear isolation—neither from their pack nor the comfort of women. I missed him, and there was no cure for that. But I liked being alone. It was all I'd ever really known.

"Not lonely; solitary," I said.

"There is a difference?"

"Loneliness is when the world abandons us. Solitude is when we abandon the world. Solitude is the only liberty left to me."

He nodded but looked unconvinced. "You don't seek even the comfort of kin?"

"It's because of my kin that I'm here," I said, gesturing to the walls. Then added a little too hopefully: "But if you would stay, there is so much—"

"I—" he shook his head, and his voice fell to almost a whisper. "You know I cannot. I just came to wish you well," he mumbled, looking at his feet. "And to give you this." From deep within his caftan, he produced a fold of raw crimson silk no bigger than the palm of his hand. He passed it to me. It was weighty for its size.

I peeled away the fabric like the petals of a rose blossom opening to the gaze of day, revealing hints of gold as it unfolded. Within

473

lay a finely made golden chain, at the center of which hung a gold plaque nearly the size of my palm. Wrought of intricate openwork, it depicted a vast flowering tree that gave shelter to tiny birds. Beneath the tree were tethered two horses, and a goryt was slung in its branches. A priestess sat beneath, her towering headdress entwined in the branches of the tree, and lying before her, as if asleep, was a warrior, his head cradled in his companion's lap. I recognized it as the Tree of All Fruits. Aric often spoke of the Great Tree, its roots deep in the netherworld, its trunk in ours, and its branches rooted in heaven.

The story was one I had come to know well from many nights around the hearth when tales were told by warriors setting off to face death each day. Known to all Skythai, it had also become one of my favorites. It told of a warrior, dying of battle wounds, faithfully brought by his blood-brother to the priestess, where she restored him to life. Here, the priestess wore trousers and carried a sword. That gave me a smile.

My eyes welled up, and I could find no words. Where I had expected bitterness, he came bearing grace.

"I know you dislike gifts. Yet, I would give you everything I have, as I can no longer gauge my debts—if it were even possible to settle them. I just—I wanted to give you something," he said. Shuffling his feet, he wiped his palms on the thighs of his trousers and looked away.

"It's perfect." I also avoided his gaze. "It's glorious, truly."

"Then why do you frown?" he said with a weak attempt at a smile.

"Because I can never wear this openly."

He took the necklace from my hands and laid the cool, heavy pendant gently on my breast. "The most precious gifts are best enjoyed in secret," he whispered in my ear as he fastened the clasp behind my neck. A shiver passed through me as his fingertips brushed against my skin. I wasn't sure I could bear the weight of any more secrets. He swallowed hard as he pulled away and looked solemnly at me, taking my sweating hands in his for a moment. "If nothing else, I am a patient man." He opened his mouth as if to speak more, but his hands went limp in mine, and I couldn't hold onto him. Wooden and anxious, he turned clumsily and ducked through the wagon door into the searing daylight outside.

The door swung between us, and there was no time to catch him or to call out even if I dared. Welling up inside me, a fount of all the things I wanted to say but didn't know how. I stepped toward the door. *Don't,* a voice within spoke out. Something restrained me again. Something almost always did.

Now, his gift. Even the fold of silk it came wrapped in smelled of him, so I stashed it away in a pouch that hung from my belt. Inside, I also kept the arrowhead from that day. Pulling it from the pouch, I held the narrow bit of bronze in my open hand and stared at it for a moment, turning it over against the flat of my palm. Such a small thing. I quickly tied up the pouch and tucked it away again. Then I laid the necklace against my breast—the heavy gold cool against my skin—and covered it. With my hand over my heart, I pressed upon the pendant, feeling its imprint deep in my flesh.

◆◆◆

FATHER'S GRAND RETINUE had made the three-hundred-mile journey. The day he'd been planning for so long had finally arrived, and at least he would be pleased by today's proceedings. This was, after all, my first purpose for coming to Skythia, and I suppose it was not unfair for Father to hold to those expectations long after I had forsaken them. He'd arrived in high spirits, eager to see me, and perhaps surprised that I'd survived my ordeal. As we sat to dine together, I told him stories of the Wild Fields. The pride in his eyes was almost unbearable as he spoke of my becoming a queen. As the daughter of a royal house, he said, my purpose was vital, for I would give birth to children that would bind our two kingdoms together in peace and perhaps become the future kings of Skythia. But my heart turned leaden at the thought. Such are the consolations offered to ancillaries. So lavishly venerated for our power of generation, we gladly relinquish our claims to every other office. We serve on our backs while men serve on their feet. Perhaps I was alone in seeing mere adoration as meager compensation for no longer stretching a bowstring, sitting astride a galloping horse, or being welcomed among the council of warriors—for nevermore putting my own mind, heart, and hand to the fates of men, tribes, or kingdoms. Odious though my generative purpose now seemed, the Bastarnai needed this covenant with the Skythai to hold, and I still bore a duty to see it through.

THE PANICKED BELLOWS and bleats of animals being gathered for sacrifice reached my ears from across the camp. Their dread mingled with my own. For a year, this union had been like a sword, its cold, hard edge against my throat. Now, the day had finally come. With Eramandin, summer had begun, but the early morning was crisp, and the sun was nowhere in sight. Despite the chill, I sweated through my new dress.

Queen Opœa had insisted on sending her ladies to attend to me, as I had none yet of my own, and she must have suspected no good could come of me grooming myself for such an occasion. Royal servants came to my wagon in the grave hours before dawn and, by the light of a single tallow lamp and the weak flicker of the hearth, prepared my skin with a paste of frankincense and cedar and cypress woods, which were pounded in a mortar of rough stone and mixed with water. They rubbed my skin with the mixture and left it to dry. After an hour or so, the plaster began to crack and flake away as my new, clean self emerged like a ripe chick hatching from its egg or a tender sprout erupting from the seed. They scrubbed away the remnants of this crust with wisps of pasture sage and rough hemp cloths. Beneath, my skin looked fresh and smelled sweet. But I had never felt so used up and worn beyond my years. Listening as they ushered me into their somber sisterhood with the cold comforts of wifehood and motherhood's sacred—if limited—duty, I drifted farther from them, unable to shake the notion that I was not finally embarking on a life but ending one— the only one that had ever mattered to me.

I stared unblinking as they carefully painted my eyes and sat listlessly as they plaited my hair, winding it up in a knot as married women wore. I didn't even speak up when they cut a plaited lock from it, bound it with a single red thread, and lay it on the table for me to give to my betrothed. Instead, I marveled at how long it had grown. It had been a year since the evening Aric cut off my hair and sowed it in the earth, and yet within that year in the wilds, I'd lived a lifetime. I'd been warned, but now I understood: time truly moves differently in the realms of the gods.

When all was done, they fixed a tall headdress and veil upon my head, and I stood motionless before them as they sprinkled me with mead. After the women departed, a sickly-sweet scent of perfume lingered—some mine, some theirs—that made me queasy. It reminded me of the overbearing smell of flowers at funerals; instead of making the death more tolerable, it made the flowers more perverse.

I gazed at my image in my bronze mirror, the serpent mother's tendril limbs clasped in my bloodless fingers as she held the reflective pool in her upraised hands, daring me to look. Perhaps this squeamishness about my reflection had kept me from delving into the mirror's mantic secrets, which I had not yet learned to fathom. But in the faint light of the tallow lamp, I drew it up to my face and gazed deeply. There, I saw new fine lines around my eyes where they had painted me like a courtesan. It was perfect. I could pretend I was someone else. This other woman would carry on in my stead—the old Anaiti laid upon the altar. The flowers, perhaps, were for her.

FROM BENEATH MY PILLOW, I took up the necklace Aric had given me—the dying hero and the priestess—and wrapped it in a scrap of old felt. Without knowing when I might return to this wagon, I stashed the necklace beneath a hearthstone and smoothed the ash neatly over it. Inside the bench on which I made my bed were stowed the other precious relics of that former life. Lifting the cushion, I raised the wooden planks to uncover my riding clothes and warbelt, the deadly sagaris, the sword Aric had given me at my initiation, and two unstrung bows in a goryt full of ready arrows. An uncounted tally lay secreted at the bottom. Wrapped in a scrap of red silk lay the iron torc burnished smooth with constant wear. Neatly coiled within, my girdle of linden bast. Lifting it from the cache, I ran my fingers over its fine golden braids, thinking upon the day I first wore it and the oaths I swore to earn it. I had fallen far short of them these last days, filled with grief over my sore misfortune.

Erman had warned me that until I'd been in the Wild Fields, I didn't yet know what I was; what I truly loved or hated; what I'd kill or die for. He neglected to tell me that this knowledge made none of those things easier. But the forge of the Fields had hammered out a hardwearing heart—a vessel that could contain all the hurts and the healing, all the sorrows and the joys of this life without breaking.

Would a warrior shrink now, and weep, and fall to grief?

Perhaps I should have stayed behind the day the Geloni came, and this day would never have come to pass. But then, perhaps, the Saudaratai warrior would have taken Aric's scalp that cursed day had I not been there to take his. Despite what seers profess to know, we cannot see all ends, and I have never pretended to know where men's roads lead. I have only tried—and often failed—to steer the treacherous course between *if* and *is*. Had I succeeded then, might I still ride the marches today? Only the gods and shades now know. I am glad sometimes that I don't possess the two sights, for I should not like to know the answers to such futile questions. Above all, I am grateful that fate has allowed me to live in a world where far greater sorrows have not come to pass. Without his warm smile, sharp mind, kind eye, and brave heart, this world would be a sunless desolation.

Fate decided one year ago when two kings made a covenant, that this day must come. With the offenses of the battlefield still fresh in my thoughts, the indignities of the wifely bed could only pale in comparison. I have no right to weep. I knew what I had sworn and what the cost. Yet for a moment, wild and brief, we dared to cheat all their designs. Hope is like a draught of bitter-sweet haoma, swelling the breast with boldness and urging the flesh into battles it cannot possibly win. Even then, I think we knew, but we were already drunk.

So, I shall not protest. Only a fool grieves fate. If this union is the debt I owe for a life, so be it. I would not trade one breath of his for a thousand years under the open sky. Whether I wear the insignia of the kara or the garments of court, I am hamazan, and the sharpest blade I bear is within my will. I might no longer dwell in the wilds, but the wilds dwell forever in me. The roots of its stones temper my bones. The chill of its streams turn my blood to wine. Storms rage over the plain only to break upon my brow and fall tamed at my feet. If ever I was worthy of the name warrior, what have I to fear?

I replaced the girdle and closed the cache of arms. Lifting the lock of hair from the table, I spoke a vow over the flames and cast it into the fire. Then, steadying my headdress, I ducked through the wagon door and into the cold morning.

A Partial Glossary

ÆLDAR assembly of Skythian chiefs

AGARI Skythian tribe known for skill with poisons and cures

AGATHYRS mythical ancestor of the Agathyrsi tribe

AGATHYRSI a rival tribe to the Royal Skythians and Bastarnai

AKASAS father of Rathagos

AKHTAR zhotr; invoker, recitator

AKINAKA Skythian short sword

ALDIS anarei apprentice

ALSOS Greek colony

ANAITI hamazan warrior; betrothed to King Ariapaithi; sent to train with warband

ANAREI(S) male seers practicing ritual transvestism

ANDROKTONES Greek: "man-killer"

ANDROPHAGOI Greek: "man-eaters"

ANTISTHENES vazarka; steward of warband; of Greek descent

AORSI Sarmatian tribe

APATURA "Swift Waters;" rapids

APIA Skythian earth-mother goddess, associated with Greek Gaia

ARGOTAS father of Ariapaithi

ARI Skythian sword god, associated with Ares

ARIANTA king of the Bastarnai, father of Anaiti

ARIAPAITHI high king of Skythians; father of Skyles, Oktamasda, and Aric

ARIC leader of the Paralatai warband; Warden of East March; youngest son of King Ariapaithi; brother of Skyles and Oktamazda.

ARTA the fundamental principle of cosmic order, truth, and justice; the objective reality of natural law governing the universe and every being's obligation to live in accord with it, encompassing both moral truth and the right order of nature and the cosmos, including social conduct and the harmony between humans, nature, and the divine.

ARTABANU priest

ARTAVARDIYA novice who helps Anaiti heal or dispatch horses

ARTIMPASA Goddess of sovereignty, Mistress of Beasts, associated with Celestial Aphrodite, Artemis, Anahita.

ARUNA Anaiti's chestnut gelding

ASCHY a kind of jam or sauce made from cherries

ATHENAI the city-state of Athens and its political sphere

ATHRAVAN master of sacrifice and keeper of the sacred fire, minister to the wounded, and keeper of the dead

AYNAR warband's blacksmith

AZARION vazarka; brother of Bradak

BASTARNAI tribe allied with Skythia; Anaiti's people

BASTARNIA the Bastarnai capital

BORÆTAI a collective of Skythian tribes

BORNON vazarka; leading swordsman

BORYSTHENES Greek name for the central river of Skythia; present-day Dnieper, and its diety; aka, Volosdanu

BRADAK vazarka; brother of Azarion

BRAZMAN elder, sage

BUDINI northern tribe of reindeer herders

BUNA the "ground" or camp base

CAMBYSES Persian imperial ruler said to have suffered from the "sacred disease." *also* Kambujiya, Kurush

DAGARIC a champion of the Bastarnai whose hand was burned by Spargapaithi

DAIMON inspiring spirit, protector, fate

DARANAKA "leader"

DARAYAVAUSH Persian king Darius

DEMETRIOS governor of Greek colony Kremnos

EKA "one," individual, free from the bonds and duties of society

ERAMAN Skythian god of friendship, alliances, and the protection of social and cosmic harmony; associated with Hermes, Airyaman

ERAMANDIN Festival of Eraman, on the first day of summer

ERMAN anarei and chief seer to Ariapaithi

FATHERS ancestors

FENNI northern tribe; proto-Finns

GALATI vazarka; warband's healer

GELON mythical ancestor of Geloni tribe

GELONI mixed tribe of Skythians and Greeks based near Gelonus

GELONUS former fort and trading hub of the Geloni tribe

GERRHI the capital of Skythia

GERRHOS ancestral burial ground of Paralatai

GŒTOSURA multifaceted Skythian god of incantation, inspiration, and ecstasy, and the binding power of oaths and contracts; associated with Apollo, Mit(h)ra, Odin

GOHAR vazarka; "the gutless"

GORYT combination bowcase-quiver

HAMAZAN an equal—a female warrior

HAMAZOR BEEM "Let us be one—of equal strength"

HAOMA a sacred intoxicant drink made from crushed ephedra plants

HAOMAPAITHI master of haoma

HVASPA blood brother of Tokhak

HYLAIA The Woodland; a sacred grove

IDANTHYRS grandfather of Ariapaithi

ISIRAS Aric's black gelding

ISPAKAJA Issedoni; former karadar, and Aric's swordmaster

ISSEDONI eastern, non-Skythian tribe

ISTRIA Greek colony

ISTROS the primary river of Thrake; present-day Danube

KAMBUJIYA *see* Cambyses

KAR to fight

KARA troop, army, people

KARA-DARANAKA troop leader, commander

KARADAR one who holds/controls a troop

KAREVAN traveling troop

KARIK warrior

KASAGOS chief of Tokhari

KIMMEROI Cimmerians

KREMNOS Greek colony

KURUSH *see* Cambyses

LADY, THE *see* Apia

LAWSPEAKER one who has committed the oral traditions and codes to memory; a judge

LEIMEIA Bornon's former love; hamazan

LIGEIA Skyles's wife

MAEOTIS, SWAMP OF present-day Sea of Azov

MAHASARA princess of the Rokhalani; Anaiti's mother

MANAH wandering or free soul, mind

MARD-KHWAAR Man-Eater

MARDIA land of the Mokhsa, man-eaters

MASSAGETAI rival Sarmatian tribe

MELANCHLÆNI "Black Cloaks," aka, the Saudaratai

MERHEDIN festival

MISTRESS *see* Artimpasa

MOKHSA aka, the Mard-Kwaar or Man-Eaters

MOURDAG vazarka; son of Mordos the lawspeaker

MUDRAYAM ancient Egypt

NAVARI northern non-Skythian tribe

NIKONION Greek colony

NINE STEPS cataracts; rapids above Skythian capital on the Borysthenes River

NYMPHAION Greek colony

ODRYSAI Thracian kingdom

OIORPATA Skythian for "man-killer"

OKTAMAZDA half-Thracian prince of Skythia; son of Ariapaithi; brother of Aric and Skyles; Warden of the West March

OLBIA primary Greek colony at the mouth of the Borysthenes

OLGAS vazarka; loyal, libertine

OPŒA primary Skythian queen; Aric's mother

OUSTANA an athravan

PAPAHIO Skythian "Sky Father;" the bright, overarching daytime sky; associated with Zeus

PARALATAI "Royal" Skythian tribe ruling all others through a claim of descent from mythical founders of Skythian nation

PERAKA vazarka; known for virtue

RAIDING ROAD a common route through the steppe traveled by war parties and caravans; a proto-silk road

RATHADIN Midwinter festival

RATHAGOS vazarka; accuser

RAVENS the warband's field scouts

ROKHALANI Skytho-Sarmatian tribe, Anaiti's mother's people

SÆNA Aric's chestnut gelding

SAGARIS light battle/hunting axe with spiked reverse

SAKHA Anaiti's dapple grey gelding

SATANAYA "Mother of the Hundred," sacred role of woman among warband

SAUDARATAI aka, Melanclaeni, "Black-Cloaks"; Skythian rivals

SHINING ROAD the Milky Way

SIRAN vazarka; former farmer

SITALK king of Thrake, Oktamazda's maternal uncle

SKOLOTOI "the shooters;" Skythians generally

SKOPAS son of Kasagos; herder seeking justice

SKYLES half-Greek Skythian prince; son of Ariapaithi; brother of Aric and Oktamazda; Warden of the South March

SKYTHAI Skythians

SPADAK king of the Boretai

SPAKA dog, bitch

SPARGAPAITHI king of the Agathyrsai

SREITA "The Slider;" mount of Gœtosura, similar to Sleipnir and inspired by hybrid "unicorn" creatures in Skythian art and burials

STAURIN young warrior who has made tally and will graduate from the warband

STORMAI vazarka; Aric's cousin

SURA term of respect for superiors

SURAMATAI Sarmatians

SVADHA self-law

SWAMP OF MAEOTIS Sea of Azov

SYMBOLON Greek colony

TABITI "the burning one;" goddess of fire, the hearth; associated with Hestia, Tapati

TAKHMASPADA Median caravan leader

TAMGA(S) precursor to branding incorporating elements of heraldry

TARDIN Midsummer festival, closing

woad month when leaves were
gathered and boiled to make dye

TARGITAO hero or demigod, likely
mythical progenitor; associated
with Herakles, Taranis, and Thor

TAURI Kimmerian tribe

THAGIMAZDA Deity worshiped by
the Royal Skythians; a supreme,
all-seeing god of the night sky,
celestial ocean, horses, oaths, law
and punishment, magic, and the ec-
static fury of heavenly inspiration;
associated with Poseidon, Uranus,
Varuna, Odin

THRAKE Thrace

THRAKES Thracians

TIRANA vazarka; captures wild horse

TOKHAK vazarka; rider who falls in
battle

TOKHARI Skythian clan caught in
internal land dispute

TYRAS Greek colony

UNDERVEST a laced corset or proto-
sports bra for comfort during
riding and physical activity

USHAS festival celebrating the dawning
of spring

VATRA horse captured by Tarana and
tamed

VAYU wind, esp. in its spiritual form

VAZARKA twelve elite members of the
warband; an inner circle and guard
of sworn brothers, proto-Round
Table

VOLOS Skythian god of enclosure; a
chthonic figure; aka, Borysthenes

VOLOSDANU aka, Borysthenes river

WOODLAND, THE aka, Hylaia

YAMADIN festival beginning winter;
end of raiding season, start of
slaughter month

ZHOTR officiant, priest/invoker,
recitator

ZIRIN ransom-bearer's cry

Author's Note

IN NOVEMBER 2011, while stuck in a hospital bed for several days, I began drafting the first scenes of The Steppe Saga to pass the time. Although writing fiction had never been my ambition, my background in archaeology and experience as a horse trainer sparked my interest in the ancient nomadic horsemen of the steppe. Inspired by passages from Herodotus and a song I enjoyed, I imagined a crucial scene that evolved into a story outline. Over the following years, whenever I had the time, I researched and developed the trilogy as a single expansive narrative. Realizing it was too big for a single volume, I split it into three parts, refining along the way.

I set out to write the sort of story I've always wanted to read but have struggled to find. So much ancient fiction tends to be fantastic, orgiastic, or bombastic, usually told from the perspective of great urban civilizations whose views we often uncritically adopt while searching for insights into the past and justifications for the present. This is unsurprising, given that these civilizations were remarkable and produced a wealth of valuable documents for authors to mine. Yet, most ancient cultures had oral traditions, leaving their stories largely untold. Today's storytellers seem reluctant to consider these narratives.

But, there are two sides to every story. Herodotus tells us that, like the Scythian sage Anacharsis before him, the Scythian prince Scyles faced persecution from his savage people for embracing foreign customs—for the "sin" of abandoning his barbarian ways in favor of Greek civilization. Was he right? Or did Scyles's fate represent the predictable response to imperial Greek culture's infiltration of native Scythian society? We only have Herodotus's account. I wanted to explore this narrative from a Scythian perspective—to examine this cultural clash from the often-demonized and misunderstood barbarian viewpoint. I approached this not from any sociopolitical design or agenda but out of genuine curiosity.

AUTHOR'S NOTE

Who were the Scythians *really*? One aspect that makes them endlessly fascinating is that, although their civilized neighbors regarded them as the quintessential barbarians, they were inherently cosmopolitan, endlessly innovative, and refreshingly modern in many respects. Most notably, women wielded unprecedented power for the time, including the right to bear arms—a fact that the ancient Greeks found so transgressive that it inspired a species of mythical monster for their most important culture heroes to battle and slay: the Amazon. Archaeological excavations in the region have confirmed the burials of numerous female warriors.

Due to the sparse historical record of the Scythians and the highly subjective nature of interpreting archaeological evidence related to culture and belief, my depictions draw from various sources, including comparative studies in history, mythology, anthropology, and linguistics, always with an eye to placing the Scythians within their proper Indo-Iranian and broader Indo-European contexts. The terms I use are a mixture of Indo-Iranian words and names derived from languages ranging from Avestan to Khotan Saka. Unfortunately, Scythian cultures have received too little serious attention from researchers, and there are frequent disagreements among sources. Nevertheless, I have tried to create an authentic, naturalistic representation by not altering known facts or incorporating supernatural elements. While I adhere closely to the available evidence concerning the history, traditions, and people I depict, ultimately, these portrayals are conjectural and fictionalized. This is a work of imagination, not scholarship.

I sincerely thank editor William Boggess for his valuable feedback. I also extend my gratitude to author Daniel W. Davison for his generous help with Ancient Greek grammar. My deep appreciation goes to all the readers who have supported this book and shared their thoughts and enthusiasm along its journey. Your encouragement has truly meant a lot to me.

—JME

488

About the Author

J. M. ELLIOTT lives on a Hudson Valley farm, far from the hustle of modern life. She prefers hiking boots to heels, work gloves to manicures, and humble stories to showy prose. When she's not lost in the pages of historical fiction, you might spot her astride a horse, unearthing the mysteries of archaeological sites, or trekking into the wilds where phone signals can't reach. To learn more, visit her website at JMELLIOTT.ORG.

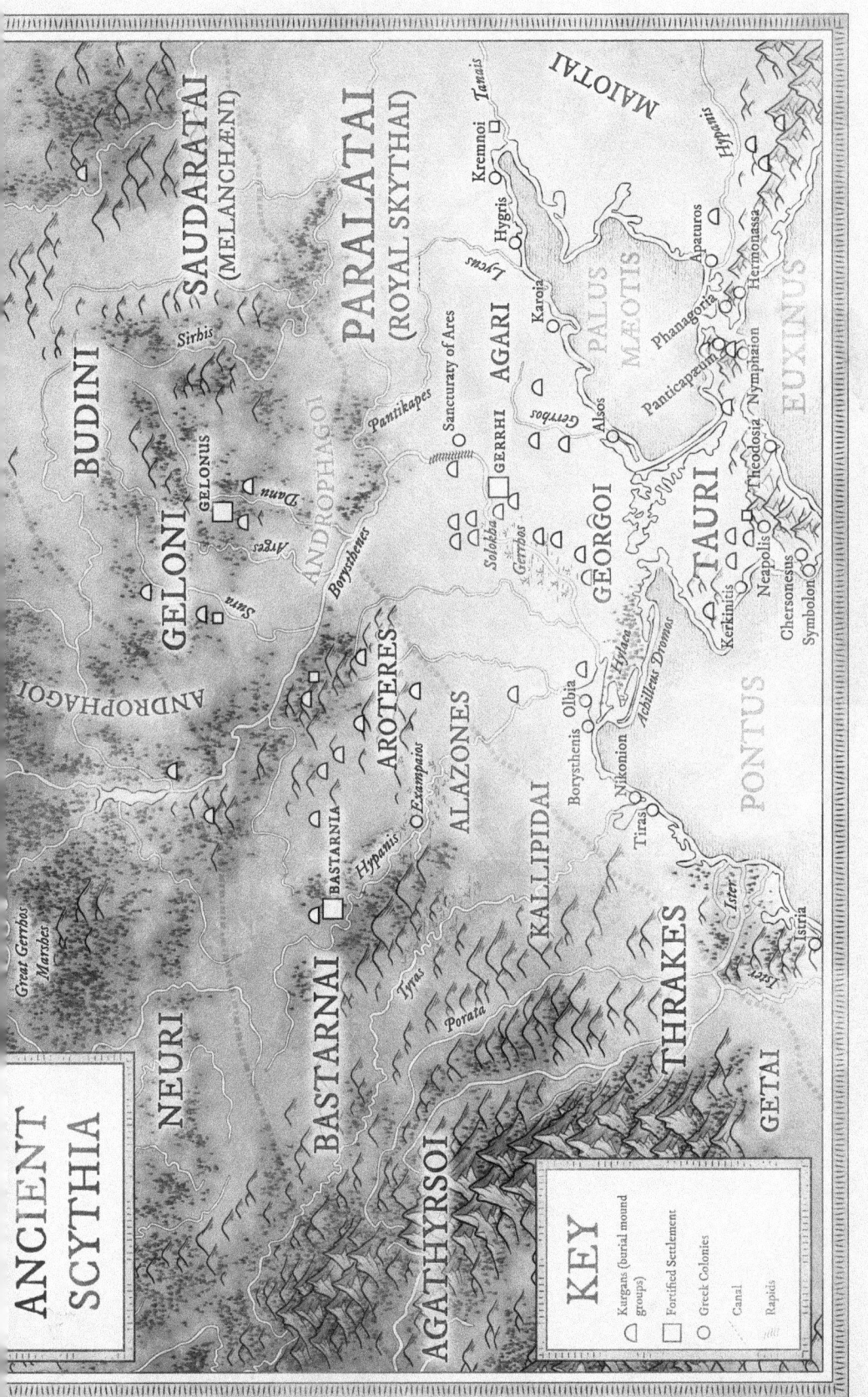

ANCIENT
SCYTHIA

KEY

◁ Kurgans (burial mound
   groups)

▢ Fortified Settlement

○ Greek Colonies

⋯ Canal

⌇ Rapids

NEURI

BUDINI

GELONI

GELONUS ▢

Sirbis

Dunn ◁

Argos

Sura ◁

SAUDARATAI
(MELANCHÆNI)

ANDROPHAGOI

ANDROPHAGOI

Panikapes

Sanctuary of Ares ○

Borysthenes

PARALATAI
(ROYAL SKYTHAI)

Lykus

Kremnoi ▢

Tanais

Hygris ○

Karoia

AGARI

GERRHI ▢

Gerrbos

Solokba ◁

Gerrbos

Alsos ◁

PALUS
MÆOTIS

MAIOTAI

Hypanis

Apaturos

Hermonassa

Phanagoria

Panticapaeum ▢

Nymphaion

Theodosia

EUXINUS

GEORGOI

Neapolis ▢

Kerkinitis ◁

TAURI

Chersonesus ○

Symbolon ○

AROTERES

BASTARNIA ▢

Exampaios ○

ALAZONES

Hypanis

Olbia ○

Hylaea

Achilleus Dromos

Borysthenis ○

Nikonion ○

Tiras ○

KALLIPIDAI

BASTARNAI

Tyras

Porata

AGATHYRSOI

THRAKES

PONTUS

Ister

Istria ○

Ister

GETAI

Great Gerrbos
Marobes

www.ingramcontent.com/pod-product-compliance
Ingram Content Group UK Ltd.
Pitfield, Milton Keynes, MK11 3LW, UK
UKHW040651240925

8053UKWH00039B/615